CYGNET OF MELMERE

Una Lamby and her family run Swansdown, a rambling hotel in Cheshire. It is 1932 and times are hard. For all of them, Swansdown has become a prison with their surly father Hubert the jailer. When Una falls in love with Robby Belmane who works at the hotel, her father objects and Robby is forced to find work overseas. Una discovers she is carrying Robby's baby and marries Cedric Pawson, Hubert's wealthy neighbour and mentor. After the birth, Una decides she must run away with her daughter. Cedric has been good and kind, but she knows she must be with Robby...

CYGNET OF MELMERE

CYGNET OF MELMERE

by

Joan Eadith

Magna Large Print Books
Long Preston, North Yorkshire,
England.

British Library Cataloguing in Publication Data.

Eadith, Joan
 Cygnet of Melmere.

 A catalogue record for this book is
 available from the British Library

 ISBN 0-7505-0870-1

First published in Great Britain by Little, Brown and
Company, 1994

Copyright © 1994 by Joan Eadith

The right of Joan Eadith to be identified as the author
of this work has been asserted in accordance with the
Copyright, Designs and Patents Act, 1988.

Published in Large Print December, 1995 by arrangement
with Little, Brown and Company (UK).

Magna Large Print is an imprint of
Library Magna Books Ltd.
Printed and bound in Great Britain by
T.J. Press (Padstow) Ltd., Cornwall, PL28 8RW.

Contents

CHAPTER 1

The Swansdown Secret
1932

Una Lamby stood there with tears of defiance on her face. Yet no one would have known it. They would have taken the tears to be raindrops from the sudden shower of a spring morning, as she stood gazing out towards the waters of Melmere. They would have seen young grey eyes and fresh pink cheeks and enough dark wavy thatch of hair to protect her from the biggest thunderstorm on earth.

'What a happy looking, bonny young girl,' the older ones would have said, 'Oh, to be that age again!'

How little *they* knew about being completely trapped. About being penned in by people who moved round her like...like... Oh, what did it matter—like! All she really cared was that today she was sixteen, and yesterday at the end of her sixteenth birthday party Robby Belmane had suggested they should run away together.

She had clung to him secretly in the

gardens of Swansdown and agreed. She would have done almost anything at that moment. His words had changed her for ever—had flooded her with joy.

But today, standing here, it was all different. She felt completely unsettled and critical. Today she was full of doubt and despair. Would she truly want to leave all this, and all her family, and her true life—no matter how much she grumbled about it? Would either of them want to go from here—for ever?

This morning she had begun to doubt it. This morning she felt older and wiser and sadder.

She had even mentioned feeling different to her eldest sister Ella in the bedroom they shared, never breathing a word about Robby and his plan.

'How on earth can you feel different, and suddenly older—so quickly?' said Ella, who was twenty-two, and completely set in her ways.

It was half past six in the morning. They were slowly starting to get dressed.

'Well I *do* feel different, Ella. Sometimes I feel I want to leave this decrepit Swansdown hotel for ever. Leave this slogging and slaving Lamby family.'

'But you are still a schoolgirl. You're talking utter nonsense.' Ella had stared at her in sudden alarm.

Una dressed hastily to avoid saying any more. Then, after gulping down a glass of cold milk from the kitchen, she had rushed outside to vast green lawns and early morning scampering rabbits. Ignoring them completely, she fled blindly along the small muddy path which led down to the edge of the mere. Here at last she could revel in her secret misery (deep down she knew she was wallowing) in the most perfect place possible in this wonderful countryside.

She tried to imagine leaving it all. Leaving her sisters to stew in the same old moaning and groaning and wearisome life for ever. Leaving them still tied to the day to day drudgery of this monster of a hotel her father had inherited from his own father and mother. (This place others saw as the most charming and picturesque place on earth.) She stretched her arms to the sky. Oh, to fly away to an even better world of proper, unhemmedin, freedom. To escape the clutches of the childhood village of Pover, where everyone bowed and scraped to those who ruled the roost. To say a silent farewell to people like the Limpets who had landed here with William the Conqueror billions of years ago, and who never let anyone forget it, and...yes...*and*... She glanced down at the loose wet pebbles as a small tide of water surrounded her rubber wellingtons. Above all forget people like Cedric Pawson, her father's friend.

It seemed to her this moment, as she stood amongst the pale green buds of untidy willow trees, with their bent branches willy-nilly in pools of dampness, that she'd been placed here by fate in a beautifully painted picture from which there was no escape.

Then, the moody flash of gloom and anger suddenly left her, as a dancing breeze arrived. She began to walk along a well-trodden, grass-bordered path dotted with blue harebells. And as she walked in the quiet fresh air of the morning, she felt slightly ashamed. Lots of people in the middle of Manchester, their nearest city, would surely regard her as a spoilt brat? To many of them Melmere was a dream world in Cheshire—completely unknown—even though it was hardly twenty miles away. A place where people, many of them careworn mothers and hordes of children, were brought to on a day's church outing in a charabanc once a year. This bright greenery and patches of water was a place to stare at for a few hours, before getting back to the grind of grim days and true poverty in the industrial chimney-stacked north, where soot floated down eternally like small black snowflakes, on to long

14

clothes-lines of steaming washing and on to prams and babies' faces.

Una began to think about her sixteenth birthday yesterday. Right now she should have been cleaning out the hotel's cocktail bar, or at least getting the eternal mountain of ironing trimmed down.

She looked across moss-strewn tree roots to where the swans could be seen. Her unruly hair rippled about in a playful flurry of air.

To her mind, her birthday party hadn't been a proper party at all. It was a quiet, family affair. Her locks had been fastened securely in plaits, away from her high creamy brow, and parted in the middle like she wore it for school. Her mother had thought it was what Father would have wanted.

There wasn't a single male in sight... except for Robby. Una had created quite a fuss with Mother to have him included. Always in the clutches of Father's opinions, Mother didn't consider it wise to invite a seventeen-year-old boy who acted as gardener and jack-of-all-trades at the hotel. 'And anyway, you can hardly have a great splash. when your father's lying there upstairs ill in bed,' she pleaded.

'Una can hardly have a big splash, because you know we can't afford it, Mother.' Una's sister Chloe had echoed

15

the sad truth of it rather dictatorially as they all washed up in the Swansdown kitchen afterwards, throwing bits of stray cake out to the birds, and wrapping the left over candles in their small, rose-shaped holders in a large damask dinner napkin for no reason other than a cautious sentimentality.

Seventeen-year-old Chloe was the only one who, up to now, had triumphantly broken through the tight family net to get herself a steady life-long job nearby away from this place. Una was a bit in awe of her. Chloe always seemed to regard Una as a child. Chloe's elderly ways belied the fact that there was only just over a year between their ages.

Una thought of her presents: a 'Boy Scout' silk scarf from Mother and Father; a small box camera from Chloe; a new Mason-Pearson hairbrush from Lindi; a bright orange umbrella from Ella, and a copy of *Hatter's Castle* from Robby. Her favourite one was the small, dark blue diary with its gold lock and small key from Granny Lamby.

Her most *hated* and most adored was the sweetest cocker spaniel puppy ever seen. At first she refused outright to accept him even though its name flooded into her mind the moment she saw him: 'Beech', with his large all-seeing eyes, his alert ears covered in floppy flaps as curly as a judge's wig—a small bundle of creamy white and shiny beech-seed brown. He was at this moment curled up in his wicker basket on a piece of woollen blanket in the warm, stone-flagged room where the fuel store was. He was her friend for life. Maybe he would still be here when she was as old as thirty? Such far away years seemed unbelievable. Cedric Pawson, her father's friend, had given her the puppy.

'No, I can't possibly accept him, Cedric. It's ever so kind of you but...' Her tone had faltered. She knew full well why.

'But what, Una?' His eyes seemed to mock her. 'Would you desert a helpless little puppy? I've no intention of taking him back.'

There was a steely streak in Cedric Pawson's modulated accentless voice. He was a large man with shrewd looks and a mouth like a rat trap.

'I scoured the place for something special for my favourite girl.' He sensed with a certain malicious enjoyment that the words would annoy her. He was intelligent enough, having known her since she was born, to realise that his ripe age of forty-six was not Una's first choice for a beau. But never mind, nothing was gained without constant perseverance. He was used to exercising patience in the wake of his own world and its financial calamities: last year's city slump, this depression, not to mention being given the cold shoulder by Tessa Truett, of the Twinkle Tea Rooms in Pover village.

Tessa Truett had been in the shadowy background for years. Starting off as his highly competent secretary, she was a widow who had always been both attractive to men and highly independent. She was a warm-hearted woman—slim, theatrical, and well able to take care of herself.

She seemed to have very little time these days for Cedric Pawson.

Sunday was quite cold and quiet. Lindi and Chloe Lamby were pacing about nervously on the threadbare carpet in the shabby, private living room. Ella, the eldest, was knitting a complicated jumper, as she sat in the corner by the window—her round, pleasant, placid face and mildly wavy brown hair disguising any real anxiety. Sometimes Ella felt like rebelling, too, but the feeling was always momentary. Generally she focused on all her blessings rather than the negative side of life. Each day she thanked God for making her a fit human being. She had trained herself to cope with what was required of her by her family.

They'd been up since six-thirty that

morning working in the hotel, in their flowered overalls. Three hours later, they'd bathed, put on their best clothes and gone to church. Then it was back again to the general grind...and the overalls, yet again.

Constance Lamby was pouring tea from the cracked spout of a deep blue, thickly glazed Royal Doulton teapot. She was a small very thin woman with hennaed hair. She looked round the room at her children.

There was hopelessness in the air; upstairs in the best hotel bedroom their father was—once again—supposed to be gasping his last breaths. His attacks came on very suddenly and entailed a great deal of drama. He would be white and sweating and the bell would be rung constantly from his room. His voice would be constantly bellowing for help as if he was totally neglected. Yet when he was himself he was quite taciturn, with long silent spells, and very rare outbreaks of sudden, over-stifled temper. He always refused to send for the doctor.

Today his friend Cedric Pawson was by his side, sitting with rather resigned dignity in a tight wicker armchair. Trays were carted up and down to the room and bottles of whisky were replenished, along with large, heavy glass soda syphons with their important looking metal squirters on

19

top. These were renewed to the sad music of Father's constant groans behind closed curtains, whilst three of his four unmarried daughters and his wife sat downstairs, chewing their knuckles in anxiety.

'He's sure to improve in a day or two,' said Chloe, trying in vain to comfort her mother with the words as they all sipped their tea.

Constance nodded with quiet resignation.

'He's just acting,' muttered twenty-year-old Lindi restlessly. 'I notice our Una's keeping out of the way.'

Like Ella, Lindi had long suffered the hotel treadmill. She had been caught by it while still at school, before she was even fourteen, and she hadn't escaped yet—mainly because of a loyalty to her over-burdened mother.

'Thank God Cedric Pawson never had designs on me, like he has on Una...' said Lindi. 'No matter how often he manages to soothe Father, or how much money he makes.' Lindi was always planning a secret getaway. She was a quiet, hardened girl: slim and positive, no groans, no regrets, no counting the costs. She was just self-centred. But she looked like an angel. Father and Mother had produced very good-looking daughters.

When the right moment came Lindi would go, but in her own time.

It was paradise looking from the hotel across Tenyard pond. Una could see a small sailing boat on the broad sweep of waters, with the ancient village of Pover reflected and lightly rippling in them.

Melmere was shaped like an hour-glass and the end where the Lambys lived at the Swansdown Hotel was known as Tenyard pond rather than its proper name of Melmere.

Una was glad she'd escaped yet another round of family tension. She was sitting against an upturned rowing boat, writing in her diary.

She looked down at the words she'd scribbled, then gazed out towards some reeds by the far shores of Melmere. *'The swans are back again,'* she wrote. She felt calmed by their presence.

Una wanted to make this diary a good one. She was looking forward to the day when she would leave school, even though there might still be years to go. She knew that to leave too soon would be a great mistake. The thought of working behind the counter in a village shop for the rest of her days or dusting picture rails here in the hotel filled her with dread. Every day in a life like that would bring her nearer and nearer to complete mummification, like a tightly bandaged sphinx in a museum. Or even worse, like ancient Miss Trill in Pover post office.

What she *really* wanted to do was be a journalist like her sister Chloe, who worked at the *Gazette* office at Shale Bridge. Shale Bridge was the nearest town before one reached Altrincham on the way to Manchester.

Chloe had landed herself a job the moment she'd left school at sixteen, twelve months ago, in spite of a horrific row with Father. Chloe was friendly with Margie Renshaw, who was years older than Chloe and who worked in the circulation department at the *Gazette*. Margie had put in a good word for her with one of the reporters, twenty-three-year-old Mac Haley. He'd allowed the news to seep through to Mr Eldew that a promising new school-leaver was available...

Una turned the pages of her diary with thoughtful longing. Darling, darling, bossy Chloe...please put in a good word for me? Then maybe we could both work under the kindly wing of Mr Eldew.

Suddenly, Una blessed her Granny Lamby for encouraging her to write, so that she might follow in Chloe's footsteps. She blessed the times she had visited her grandmother in the small red-brick cottage where she lived in Upper Pover with her two stray cats.

'I agree with you, Una,' she'd said. 'There's more to life than being tied to a hotel all one's life, unless it's what you choose. A girl these days needs to get out and about and make her own way in the world. You don't need to go to the other side of the world, but you do need to see different sides of your own little world, my darling.

'You could be a happy tadpole in the village pond, or a trout in a deep cold lake with mountains round it. You might even decide to be a starfish in the sea.' She smiled slightly. 'You might even be like me, and end up still here! We do share a name. *Una, Una, scatter-brained Una. Ran away with a piano-tuner...*'

That was how the Swansdown Hotel had started on this small peaceful lake, when Una's grandmother had married piano-tuner Toby Lamby.

'Swansdown was a broken-down old farm in those days, when I was a young bride. The rafters were rotting. The cow byres were piled high with mud and dung. Imagine a girl of today being carried over the threshold to that lot. But me and your grandad regarded it as a start. We even thought it was quite exciting! We cleared it up and soon got on to better things.

'We were so young...so enthusiastic...oh,

we had some lovely cows...' Her face shone with rapture. 'And a right scattering of hens with a cock called Nib who was so noisy and vicious that no one dared face him; except a very strange pig we once had. And I reckon our farm horses were as good as those posh 'uns of your dad's any day.

'But your grandad was a worker. He never stopped, and he wanted more from his life...and that's how the hotel came to be. With him parading around as a proper gentleman, and being on the parish council, and all. When he died it was all passed on to your father.' Grandma always stopped at this point. Her gaunt, complicated son, forty-eight-year-old Hubert Lamby, was another generation and Grandma Lamby was now merely an observer who had learned the wisdom of keeping her mouth shut much earlier in life.

Hubert's one great failing was his ability to let money trickle through his fingers... By now, in 1932, the hotel was going downhill. All of it, that is, except Father's two race horses—Final Choice and Life Blood. They were both English thoroughbred Darley Arabians.

Father's horses meant so much to him that they were treated better than any thing or any one else. And they weren't

24

his absolutely either, for they half belonged to Cedric Pawson...

'Una...? Are you there?' It was Chloe's voice, as her hurrying footsteps reached the boat.

'He's gone at last...'

The words froze Una's heart and she felt the blood leave her face. She loved her father more than any of them. She knew he wasn't just putting it on. He'd been ill for a long time.

'Poor Father...' Her eyes filled with tears. She wiped them away hastily with the back of her hand as sad and morbid thoughts flooded her head. Whatever would happen now? Would the hotel have to be sold?

Perhaps in the end it would be for the best. Mother could have a life of her own at last. Una sighed. Perhaps she wouldn't run off with Robby after all. She would hate to leave Mother *entirely*. But, oh, how she would miss Father. Never once had he said a cross word to her, even in his blackest moods...

'Not *Father*, Una!' said Chloe briskly, 'Cedric! He's gone at last, after being stuck here like a leech for nearly two weeks. No, my beloved Una, certainly not Father. Father's actually looking a bit better! He says he's getting up!'

25

CHAPTER 2

Chloe

It was early June and Mr Eldew, editor of the *Gazette* at Shale Bridge, was in a restless mood. Three times in the space of an hour that Wednesday morning, he'd been into the reporters' room. The first time, he looked round quickly at the occupants and hurried out again with the words 'Miss Lamby' hovering on his lips.

The second time, he asked Mac Haley to add an extra fifty words to a wedding write-up.

'Lady Limpet is most anxious that her daughter Celia's beaded satin and brocade wedding dress *and* quilted trayne should be mentioned in detail,' he said solemnly, 'including the fact that it is a family heirloom.' Then he added swiftly, 'Where's Miss Lamby?'

Mac Haley hardly heard him. 'Sorry, no idea.'

Mac didn't normally do wedding reports, but Lady Limpet had insisted because he'd done Celia's first wedding so well. He was already aware of her instructions from her umpteen personal visits to the offices. No one could ever ignore Lady Limpet. Oh, the fuss and palaver of it all, for a wedding that would probably fade away in a few months. Celia was entirely unpredictable. This was her second marriage. She had disappeared to Iceland only two months after the first one, and that was only eighteen months ago. Mac's write-up was still in the files. No doubt she would disappear after this one, or at least take on a lover. Mac shook his head silently. He decided to go and have a quiet cigarette.

Mr Eldew peered in once again. Chloe was there now, having a few quick words with Mrs Renshaw in Circulation. He smiled his silvery, grandfatherly smile.

'Miss Lamby, I wonder if I could have a word with you in my room?' He vanished to some far heaven like a pink, elderly gnome.

Margie Renshaw frowned. She leaned back on her chair away from her typewriter. 'What's all that in aid of then, at this time of day?' She patted her pregnant stomach with a wicked smile. 'Of course he doesn't know I'm expecting this, yet, so not a word or it might be the sack... Would you be annoyed if I called the baby after you if it's a girl, Chloe? I spend hours looking through lists of names and never seem to get anywhere. I'm certainly not going to call it Desdemona after Albert's mother! Anyway you'd better see what the old Tartar wants.'

Hastily Chloe smoothed her short straight black hair. She was curious as she walked along the dim corridor and tapped at Mr Eldew's door.

'Ah, Chloe! Take a seat.' Mr Eldew's face lit up with relief. 'It's just about this piece you did. The report of Mr Marqueson's talk in the village hall. Those excavations.'

She waited expectantly. She knew her report was a good one. She was getting better and better. She felt quite proud.

'You might be upset about what I'm going to say.' Mr Eldew's voice had cooled, in just a few seconds. 'I'm afraid I don't like it.'

There was a shocked silence and Chloe was rooted to her seat, her colour rising. She couldn't make him approve of her work. She'd reported the meeting as honestly as she could. Mr Marqueson, the speaker, was an awful fusspot, but he always made news for the local paper. No doubt next week he would be finding a full Stone Age skeleton behind his coal shed.

'Only rarely do I have to say this sort of thing to an office junior. I trust my senior staff to deal with most of the basic training. But I must be straight with you.'

28

Chloe felt her fringe sharp against her forehead with sudden sweat. Her body was like a furnace. She couldn't believe his words.

'You see, Chloe, I'm not an ogre or anything... It's just that it's my responsibility to do what I think is best for our paper.

'I have thought long and hard about your aptitude for this sort of work, and from age-long experience with other beginners I feel you would be better off in some other walk of life. It may seem very cruel at the moment, but I am sure that in years to come you will be glad of this early decision. I'm deeply sorry.'

Deeply sorry? What on earth did he mean? Chloe felt as if she was in some sort of nightmare. She was hurt to be called an office junior, too. Office juniors never did the reporting in these august premises. They emptied the wastepaper baskets, answered the telephone, sharpened pencils, and made the tea. They were very young, not seventeen like she was...

Until this second she'd always been proud to be a junior, cub reporter. She looked towards his desk and saw her work resting there. He was inspecting it again through his rimless glasses. She waited dumbly...

'For instance, what's all this about Mr

Slats "dozing off", then jumping up from his chair and saying he thought all the amazing discoveries of Mr Marqueson's were stolen property from Lady Limpet's place.'

'But that's exactly what he did say,' said Chloe, trying to conceal her mounting anger. 'He woke up very suddenly and then bawled it out.' She felt slightly sick.

Mr Eldew placed a bony, well-manicured index finger near the end of the page. 'And all this nonsense about the vicar's wife, too; burbling on about matriculation papers and ancient history, and accusing poor Mr Marqueson of not knowing the difference between a small brass poker from Woolworth's and an ancient dirk.' He gave an angry, exasperated sigh.

'I just repeated it as it was,' cried Chloe. 'It was absolute chaos. Dudley Plume was hopeless as chairman. He was the one responsible for letting it become a complete jumble.'

'Ah...' murmured Mr Eldew, sinking back in quiet triumph and surveying her. 'But you weren't sent there to report complete jumble, were you? You were reporting an orderly village gathering and a talk by our esteemed Malcolm Marqueson, a man to be honoured by all. You see, Miss Lamby, even if all these fantasies are edited out, we are still left with no proper report.'

Had he gone mad? She stared at kind Mr Eldew. Surely he wouldn't actually *sack* her?

'I'll bear your remarks in mind, Mr Eldew. Shall I take it back and rewrite it?'

'I don't see how you can, Miss Lamby.' Mr Eldew stroked his cheek with a delicate hand. 'If you did that you would be trying to alter what you now regard as the truth...it's all rather difficult, isn't it?'

Chloe was like an insect struggling for its life against a window pane, as she sat in the quiet, sparsely furnished room with its tinted sepia photographs of the *Gazette*.

Stretching slightly, Mr Eldew glanced at his gold wristlet watch. Then he stood up. 'Anyway, I hope this clearing of the air will be of some use to you in the future, whatever you decide to do.' He was like an expressionless carved saint...

She got up and tried to smile but her face quivered. He hadn't actually said, 'collect your cards as you go out.' Perhaps, after all, it wasn't as bad as she imagined.

She was so happy in the office. It was a new life away from the hotel. Everyone had welcomed her with open arms and helped her in every conceivable way. They just wouldn't believe any of this could have happened. Except for Mac, maybe; Mac had always joked and told her to beware of the editor...

'But more than that, beware of his wife,' Mac would say. 'She's the one who writes all those tub-thumping, flag-waving leaders when she's boiling spuds at home. I mean, Chloe my love, how could our mild Mr Eldew come out with it?' Mac would look at her in mock amazement.

As she gathered herself together, Mr Eldew flung his final bolt. 'Consider what I've said. Perhaps in the next few weeks you could just tail it all off. Maybe come in for a couple of hours sometimes to help with births or the obituaries.'

'Even if I did make a few mistakes, Mr Eldew,' she said quietly, as she battled with her humiliation, 'I'm sure everything will improve from now on.'

Mr Eldew didn't seem to hear her. He patted her shoulder and steered her from his room. 'Think about what I've said, my dear. There's no hurry.'

'Think about it?' gasped Lindi to Chloe, early that evening. Lindi was slicing cucumbers as thin as tissue-paper with a very sharp kitchen knife. The speed and precision with which she worked was terrifying. Her face was as smooth as a Botticelli. Her hair lay naturally in slight, fair ringlets, which shone like gold on a summer day. Lindi was the only one of the Lamby girls who had secretly lost her virginity.

She'd lost it four years ago and the experience had come as a surprise, even to her. It happened just once in a hay barn, when she was only sixteen. Lindi had been pony-riding with Celia Limpet. They had always got on well, in a good-natured off-and-on sort of way. They had met one day in the village shop when they were four years old and recognised a kindred spirit. Neither was a natural conformist, and they'd both shared a lively curiosity.

The day it happened they had been romping about with the two sixteen-year-old boys from a local farm. The girls had separated in the barn. Lindi imagined she was in love with her glowing follower, with his sunburnt, freckled face and wide, smiling mouth. She had taken on the dare of wrestling with him in the hay as a challenge of skill and agility, never thinking of it in terms of the ultimate submission. When the bout was over she realised the true extent of what they'd done and she quickly rose to find Celia. But Celia had long since vanished and only one pony was now tethered to the large iron ring in the wall outside the barn.

Her suiter had kissed her as she left.

His hands had trembled, and he'd asked to see her again, but she'd turned her head away in shame. She never acknowledged him again, and each night she prayed to God not to send her to hell. For months she imagined what would happen if she had a baby but gradually, when no signs appeared after six whole months and life plodded on as usual, she was able to pack the memory away in the far corners of her mind. In fact, she began to feel a slight superiority. She knew more about 'being done' now than any of her sisters; she knew the whole truth at last. Her eldest sister Ella had never been done. And she would certainly never have used such a vulgar phrase. Ella constantly quoted friends of hers who had been courting the same man for over five years... 'And they remained as pure as driven snow. It all depends on the girl, you know. It's up to the girls to grab their hands the moment they stray. The girls should move out of arm's reach immediately.' Then she would smile and say: 'I've always found that my knitting has been a godsend in awkward times. A set of four, thin steel needles cast on for socks or gloves are the perfect warning, and the finished gloves can make a lovely reward for good behaviour.' She would nod placidly towards her three sisters and continue knitting. It saved her from going completely mad with her unhappy state of life, in the hotel.

Lindi knew Chloe had never tried it, either. Chloe was far too dignified and sensible. And as for Una, in those days of romping in barns she had been only thirteen, and very much under the thumb of both Father and Mother. Even one piece of straw down her back from their own stables would have been queried. In the eyes of all the Lambys anyone who despoiled a girl of thirteen was a criminal.

Celia Limpet had never referred to their time in the barn after that day. They had looked into each other's eyes and said nothing. Basically, these days—four years on—they were classless independent souls, still with a secret liking for each other, but interested in their personal paths.

'As you say, Chloe,' said Lindi, snapping back to the present, 'Mr Eldew has certainly made you do that. He's forced us *all* to think about it. You've never stopped since you got in!' The girls were in the kitchen preparing the evening menus.

'The cheek of him,' said Una, back from her school at Shale Bridge. 'And to think how I've always envied you being there, Chloe. I'd never ever want to set foot in that place now, even if a job was offered on a gold plate. And anyway, Robby always says a journalist's life is more trouble than adventure.'

'Well just you tell Robby to mind his own business, Una,' said Chloe perking up a bit and still full of loyalty. 'He knows nothing about such things. Journalists don't all have to work for people like Mr Eldew. But all the same I just feel now that I never want to return. He's completely destroyed my self-confidence. I'm definitely not going in tomorrow. You see, he didn't actually *sack* me or anything. He went all round it, dropping the most awful hints—enough to make me leave of my own accord.'

She looked at them all in desperation. 'I mean, I've not done anything very wrong...' (She was in a panic of indecision.) 'All the same I'm not going in tomorrow. I just couldn't face it...but maybe after a day or two...well, you never know... It just *might* all blow over?' Her face was bright and pleading, but her heart was like marble.

Ella, who was making mayonnaise, stopped in alarm. 'You just can't not go! Whatever would Father and Mother say?'

'I'm no longer a child, Ella. It's up to me what I do,' said Chloe.

Lindi and Una gave each other a long, knowing look. Everyone was still a powerless child under Father's roof.

Lindi laughed bitterly. 'Mother and Father have got us all where they want us. You're the one who had escaped. Don't say you're going to give in...'

Chloe shrugged then gulped with despair. 'I'll go to Dr Preston and ask him to give me a note. Then I'll write out my notice and send them both in. The humiliation of it all has been too much...'

'For heaven's sake, don't be so hasty,' pleaded Ella. 'Try and get a good night's sleep and maybe by tomorrow you'll feel differently...'

'You won't be able to just walk into another job, in these hard times. And I can't see you fitting back in here again after perpetually swearing you'd sooner be dead than work here for peanuts.'

'My mind's made up.' Chloe was pale. Her pride would prevent her from ever facing Mr Eldew or the newspaper offices again. Maybe if she'd told the others what had happened straightaway, when she'd come out of his office they would have backed her up and supported her. But all the same...'I'll get another job somewhere,' she mumbled. She began to flounder: 'Maybe I *could* try coming back home? I'll just have a word with Father and volunteer to slave away for the honour of his roof staying over my head until something else crops up.'

Later that evening, just after Hubert Lamby had nodded goodbye to his pal

Cedric Pawson and was walking across to his stables in the moonlight, Chloe waylaid him.

'Father?'

He turned instantly and saw her young face caught in a sudden shaft of light. He frowned. He was always suspicious of unexpected personal contact with his daughters. He preferred to deal with them and their mother in a small group—in much the same way as one would keep a few young dogs to heel. Personal, face-to-face meetings were more difficult, more human and disturbing. And Chloe was always too much of a challenge.

He looked at her silently.

'Daddy...I just wanted to say that I shan't be going in to the *Gazette* tomorrow.' She tried to put on a cheerful face, but gradually her head drooped as she looked down at the damp, silvery, moonlit grass. 'The fact is, Father, I've left.'

It was out! There was no going back. Immediately she felt a flood of relief that the decision was finalised.

'You've *what?*' Her father seemed genuinely disturbed. 'Whatever made you do a stupid thing like that? What did Eldew say?'

'He doesn't know yet. I'm sending in my resignation tomorrow.'

'Don't you have to work your notice?'

'I shall just call my notice, holiday time owing and sickness days off.' She looked away from him.

There was silence. As they approached the stable doors he said, 'So now what do you propose to do?'

She shivered in the night air. 'Stay here and work at the Swansdown with the others, I expect...'

She waited for some reaction—surprise or even pleasure—but instead his voice was as cold as winter slate.

'You've got it well worked out then?'

'Well...I thought...'

'You've suddenly begun to think about us?' His tone was sour. 'I'm afraid it's too late for that, Chloe. You didn't give me, or your mother, or this hotel much thought when you rushed after that job in the first place, did you? If I remember correctly, it was at the height of the holiday season and your mother was worked off her feet.

'So, my girl, we managed without you, didn't we? And we can *still* manage without you.'

'But I insist on giving some help, Father. At least while I'm looking for another job.' Her voice was barely a whisper.

His eyebrows became a pained frown again and he looked so forlorn that for a few seconds she felt like flinging her arms round him and saying it wasn't true, that she hadn't left the *Gazette* after all. But his next words stifled her impulsiveness.

'I don't want your help, girl. But what I do want is to see your bedroom empty within a week. It may be just an attic to you, but to a paying guest from the city, those views across the mere to the old oak trees are worth paying for. *And* it'll be a more reliable investment...' He turned his back and went into the stables. His voice was soft and soothing now as he spoke to his horses.

Chloe watched him. Should she start to plead? To argue? She knew deep down it was hopeless. She had never been a favourite with her Father, like Una. Transparent kindness and fatherly love were only seen in occasional glimpses. But this, here in the March moonlight, was a true portrait of a man who was willing to trade an expensive, non-conforming daughter who had no interest in horse or hound for a queue of profitable, tolerant attic customers anxious to provide him with more gambling money.

She hurried back to the house, her eyes smarting with tears of temper and frustration. Then, as the chill night air assailed her and she smelled the moist tang of bracken, and saw the placidly reflecting waters she became calmer.

Chloe paused at the door of Swansdown.

Across the distance of Melmere familiar fairy lights were twinkling. They were the sort of display you'd see at Christmas, or when a small steamer was hired for a private dance or party on the mere. But she knew neither of these was the case. The lights came from Cedric Pawson's moated grange, and he switched them on whenever he felt like it.

Something must have pleased him...

Chloe thought immediately of her father. Had he been to Cedric Pawson's earlier? Was there yet another plan to recoup his losses? Cedric was always claiming that his one aim in life was to help others, and to see that all his friends were happy, but the only person who ever came out of his deals smiling was Cedric himself.

Morosely, she thought of her own awful predicament—a week's notice to leave the hotel, with nowhere to go and not a penny piece, except what she might manage to borrow from her sisters. She looked at the fairy lights again. The enemy. She had always kept clear of him. Would it be right to go over to the enemy? Would he employ her?

She hurried inside, trembling with excitement.

The last time she'd been to Grangebeck was years ago. She'd been a skinny child of ten with scabby knees, and 'Uncle Cedric' had invited her and Una to come with Mother for afternoon tea.

She remembered so clearly how it had been. He had two rather elderly bachelor cousins running his house. The place was full of Georgian silver teapots and cream jugs and small wobbly tables laden with lace cloths and giant fruitcakes. There'd been a tabby cat on a brown velvet cushion, sitting in a cane-backed chair in the conservatory.

Those days had ended when Berty, the eldest of his two cousins, took the cat with him and married Mrs Lock, a widow, who poached fresh salmon in a fish kettle. They retired happily to a cottage in Pover and began to renovate antique books.

Then Fortescue, the other cousin, joined the Pover amateur dramatic society, was spotted by a film producer and vanished to London, never to be heard of again.

Now, there was a harsher feel to everything at the Grange. No one could escape entirely the effects of the terrible hardship everywhere: the economic gloom, unemployment in every town and city, and unrest on the Continent. Yet Cedric Pawson managed to sail above it all, becoming more and more devious and increasingly wealthy with each year that passed.

With a determined sense of self-preservation she decided to ring him while Father was still in the stables. The telephone was answered almost immediately.

'Hello, is that...Cedric?'

'It is.' His voice was pleasantly smooth.

'It's Chloe. I'm wanting to ask you a favour.'

'Fire away, dear. Anything I can do.' He gave a self-satisfied chuckle.

'It's something very personal and I'd sooner you didn't tell Father I've rung you until I've been to see you...'

'Been to see me?' His voice lost its velvet tone and became more guarded. 'Surely it will wait until I come round to see your Father?'

'No. It's really quite urgent. I can call first thing tomorrow, if it's all right.'

She heard him cough a trifle irritably. 'I'm usually pretty busy. I like to get all my morning mail sorted out and read the papers... Surely it can't be as urgent as all that? Can't you tell me over the phone?' He gave a groan of frustrated boredom.

'No, I...well, you see—'

'Oh, all right then. But for God's sake make it snappy. What time will you be here?'

'Eight o'clock?'

'Eight o'clock? I thought you said *morning*?'

'I did say morning—'

'But that's the middle of the night!'

'I need to be back again to give Mother and the others a hand...before things get too busy in the kitchen—'

'Too busy? At your place? It's as slack as an old sock!' She heard him give a huge bellow of laughter. 'All right then—but don't be surprised if I'm still in pyjamas.' He rang off quickly.

Chloe gulped with relief. It was just how she wanted it. It meant she'd be able to slip out unnoticed and be back again with some sort of temporary job at his place, if she played her cards properly...

Chloe slept better than she'd expected that night, and she crept out of bed, dressed and was out of the hotel without a soul knowing. She cycled to the other side of Tenyard pond, to where Pawson's moated black and white timbered grange still slumbered.

It was eight on the dot when she rang the front doorbell.

He had a butler now called Horrocks, and a young maid who was already sloshing soapy water across the steps in front of the garden.

'Mind you doesn't slip, Miss. I've got to try and get it done extra early, see? I'm doing two jobs at once because 'e's so short of staff. Two of 'em's flitted in this past week...'

Chloe breathed with relief. There were signs that he needed help. She was willing to do anything within reason, to get some sort of a roof over her head.

'Did they live in?' she asked.

'I'll say...and too much so if you ask me. It's a wonder he didn't get splinters in his soles the way he tramped up and down to their rooms in his bare feet. Only making sure they was warm enough in that spell of freezing cold, mind, if you gets my meaning.'

The maid showed Chloe into Cedric's study. 'It's no good putting you anywhere else. It's all in a real tip. We've got sheets everywhere because of the chimney sweep coming, and 'e's sure not to be down for ages yet.'

Chloe sat alone in the large comfortable room with its thick plush curtains and huge desk. The desk was open, and the general appearance of the room was one of complete untidiness. It was obvious there had been instructions that nothing should be touched.

She peered round restlessly. She hoped he wouldn't be long or her plans of returning to the hotel without anyone having missed her would be ruined. Then, as there was still no sign of him, she began

45

to prowl slowly about, stopping finally to gaze into his desk, at a heap of letters and bits of paper in a higgledy-piggledy pile.

There was one bit of paper there she suddenly recognised. It was the sort of writing paper they used at the hotel, and it even had a few inky doodles on it like those from Father's own pen. It was folded into four, rather haphazardly. She touched it tentatively. She carefully unfolded the quarters.

Would it contain games and games of battleships? Or noughts and crosses? Or dots or hangman?

Chloe straightened out the paper and stared. Then, as the words sank in she began to tremble with shock.

It was an I.O.U. from her father to Cedric Pawson and it read quite simply:

IOU Cedric Pawson, my youngest daughter Una Christabel Lamby

It was signed unmistakably by her own father with a slightly shaky signature. *Hubert Archibald Lamby, Swansdown Hotel, 21 March 1932.*

The paper slipped from Chloe's fingers. Her own youngest sister, used as a payment to *him*. To Cedric Pawson, the man who had always haunted their lives.

There had forever been a lurking

46

suspicion about Cedric's intentions towards Una. But never, *never* would they have imagined it being carried to this kind of conclusion. Una was such a child. And even though there was little more than a year between them, Chloe as the eldest had always felt the need to protect Una.

Una loved Father more than all of them. So how could she plunge in and tell her what she had seen today? It would be brutal. Chloe dreaded to think of the consequences.

She still gazed at the crumpled slip of paper on Cedric's luxurious carpet. Then, pulling herself together, she picked it up and re-read it. If only she could send Father some sort of warning, some anonymous message to show him that someone knew what was going on and that his wicked Swansdown secret had been discovered.

Still reeling from the shock, Chloe thought fast, and shoving the IOU into her windjammer pocket, she got ready to leave the room, quivering like a leaf.

But she was seconds too late.

Cedric Pawson had risen reluctantly from his four-poster bed, when he received the news of Chloe being there.

His background had not always been

lavish. He was a son of constant hard times. All the Lamby girls knew his history inside out because their father was mesmerised by it. How poor Cedric had been born in Salford as one of ten children. How he was as sharp as a needle but had to leave school at eleven. How he trapped rabbits, bringing some home for food, and selling all the skins. By the age of eleven and a half he hung around local market stalls, waiting for damaged and rotten food which stall-holders gave him to take home to his undernourished family. It was a bleak existence, but the market people got to know him, and as his circle of acquaintances grew, the quantity of food became larger and the quality better. The family's share became less since he was able to sell the better stuff in the back streets for cash. He also became a chain smoker, preferring to eat next to nothing, picking up squashed and bent cigarette ends whenever he saw them. He scraped out the tobacco strands from thin and spit-marked cigarette ends, then put the tobacco in his own small tin cigarette roller. He was twelve by this time, and very thin with a bony, well-structured face, and a slightly hoarse voice, but he spoke carefully and well, and knew his grammar. He became a wheeler-dealer of magnificent proportions.

'When you think of his life, compared to mine as an only child,' their father would say wonderingly, 'it's almost as if there was an invisible golden spoon in his mouth.'

But the secret part of Cedric's life was never mentioned by Hubert. The war. The Royal Engineers. The Middle East. He's gone from Gallipoli to France and the Western Front where they'd met. Cedric Pawson had been twice mentioned in despatches for bravery, but it was a secret, bitter and horrible part of both their lives. Hubert never told his wife or children how it had really been...and never would anyone realise how much he'd both loved and hated Cedric Pawson.

He'd dragged Pawson from the mud of the trenches, scraped the slimy stenching filth away from his helpless, half-suffocated body and in doing so saved his life. It was a final episode of the war for both of them and never recorded in any despatches. Yet it was act of courage and brotherly love carried out by many, in the war zones amidst the killing.

Slowly Cedric left his bedroom and went downstairs to find out what all the fuss was about, and to see Chloe.

CHAPTER 3

The Easter Egg

'What an impatient girl!' His voice was irritable. 'Cycling all the way here at this hour, and then leaving before we've even spoken?' Cedric Pawson stared at her accusingly with a sleepy smile. His deep crimson and black silk dressing gown with its tailored black satin revers was crumpled and the cigarette in its long holder was down to a dimp.

He was quite handsome, with a high white forehead and dark hair that was receding towards baldness, but in the cold light from the window, Chloe saw only the pallor and lines of a raddled life. The IOU felt heavy in her pocket.

'We'll go somewhere else,' he said, glancing round. They went out through the heavy mahogany doorway and across the hall to his private sitting room. It was all velvet and mirrors, with Rowlandson's brightly coloured engravings on the walls.

'So why this sudden passion to visit Grangebeck, Chloe? Father been getting at you?' His look was full of insolent shrewdness. 'I thought you'd be busy in the newspaper world...'

She tried to be as calm as possible but her brain was racing. It was more important than ever now to get a job here, just to find out exactly what he and Father were up to.

'I've left. I'm not cut out to be a journalist. I thought I'd like to make a fresh start somewhere else.'

'It seems very sudden? Hubie said you were getting on quite well there?'

She didn't answer.

'So you've come here in secret at eight o'clock in the morning? I feel quite honoured...' His eyebrows rose a fraction.

'I'm trying you first...with your being a family friend.'

'Hasn't Hubert got owt to keep you going at Swansdown, then?' A slow coolness hung in the air.

'I'd sooner be somewhere else. After all, I am seventeen now. I'm not a schoolgirl...like Una.' She felt her face growing scarlet. Her last words had slipped out unintentionally.

'You certainly aren't that. You never have been,' he said drily. 'The only place I really need help is in the kitchen with Mrs French, or maybe as a bedroom maid for when I have visitors. I daresay I could

51

fit you in as a general help.' A glimmer of a smile crossed his stubbly face. 'It'll be a bit of a busman's holiday after your place, but at least you'll be used to that sort of work, and my kitchen's more up-to-date than yours.'

'When did you want me to start?'

'You'll live at home I expect? It won't take long for a healthy specimen like you to get here on your bike.'

'Live at home?' She out-stared him. She hadn't come over here so swiftly and secretly with the idea of still living at home in the lion's den. 'No, I certainly wouldn't want to live at home, Cedric.' She spoke hastily with a mounting fluster of nervousness: 'I'd like to live in and start straightaway. And I'd like to work in your kitchen very much.' A vision of her father telling her to pack her bags flashed before her eyes. Good riddance to him!

'Start Monday then...I'll tell Mrs French and the others. I'll be popping over to your place a bit later today so I'll let Hubie know...' Cedric looked at her hard. She was growing into quite a complicated bit of baggage. She was so different from Una...Una was going to be a woman of charm and quality. Beautiful, dreamy Una, the perfect acquisition for any man of property.

Eighteen was the right time for a girl to

be a bride. There was no greater pleasure for a man of mature years than to have a young and beautiful wife to lavish his worldly goods on. He longed to receive her favours in return. It would be a match blessed by all the heavens...

Cedric Pawson was a complex character. Romance lay in his heart but it was intertwined by the heavy blossoms of lust and the rich scents of meanness, morbidity and self-preservation. He'd observed first-hand and with cynical hardness the effects of family life on the male species—in particular on his friend Hubert Lamby—and he swore that if ever he did fall into the trap his version would be entirely different. For what was life tied to a washed-out wife and four daughters? What torture to spend one's best years tied to skriking infants and grasping children?

He nodded briefly towards Chloe, and scratched his ear.

She turned her head away and made quickly for the door.

Chloe grimly settled down to be maid-of-all-work at Cedric Pawson's, but to her surprise her grimness waned. There was no family tension like there was at the Swansdown, and life with dictator Pawson ran very smoothly indeed, as long as you did exactly as he commanded. And Chloe knew that for the time being she had no option but to obey.

Even so, the IOU still nagged at her.

It now lay tucked away secretly among her most personal possessions in a large brown envelope. She had written the word EASTER on the envelope in block capitals, for that was the time she had chosen to confront her father about his plans to sell off Una.

These days, when she slipped back home to see her sisters, whilst Father was out of the way, she tried not to mention the IOU. It was awful not having a single soul to confide in.

Then, one bright sunny Monday morning, when Mother was in the village and Father was in Knutsford, she plunged... She carried a wooden tray with small rose-coloured coffee cups through from the kitchen to the family sitting room. She put the tray on the circular coffee table, drew a deep breath and carefully began her speech.

'I've got something awful to say,' she said gloomily. 'I've been keeping it bottled up for ages... You must promise me that none of what I say must ever get back to Una.'

There was no response.

At first Lindi and Ella didn't seem to hear her. Lindi had been fixing a jazz record on the gramophone and Ella was staring at a crochet pattern, and dreaming about Malcolm Marqueson's son Monty. Rumour had it that Monty Marqueson was not getting on with his wife Moira; their roars and screeches could be heard from one end of Pover village to the other.

Ella Lamby had always admired Monty's father, and she was aware of the jealousy between amateur local historians and archaeologists. She also knew Chloe couldn't bear Malcolm Marqueson; nor, from all accounts, could he bear Chloe. Monty had told Ella one day, in strict confidence, as they stared at each other earnestly in the greengrocer's, 'My father suspects that your sister Chloe was sacked from the *Gazette* due to some scandalous remarks she wrote about a meeting in the village hall. Naturally,' he coughed apologetically, 'Mr Eldew decided not to print.'

Ella thought about the incident as she gazed at her scarlet crochet wool. It was at that moment, the way he had looked at her with his rather pale, pleading eyes, that her maternal instincts had welled up. Why hadn't she seen it before? They were made for each other. He needed a woman like her, even if he didn't know it yet. However could the poor soul exist with shrieking Moira? And the time was right for Ella; if she didn't meet her match soon she would be well into spinsterdom—for she was already twenty-two.

The knitting wool was more than ordinary red, it was as bright as a newly painted letter-box. Would she have the courage to wear it? Normally she went for oatmeal shades or browns. With sudden passion she took up her crochet hook and began busily to catch up the woollen threads. She imagined Monty's face when he saw her in church in it on Sunday and crocheted faster.

Lindi stopped winding the handle of the gramophone and lifted the needle away from the record. She frowned slightly through her fair curly hair.

She'd only half heard Chloe, but her words had finally sunk in. 'A secret? From Una? That sounds *very* unsavoury, Chloe. Don't say it's something to do with darling Cedric?'

'It is actually,' said Chloe, with some annoyance.

Ella gazed up from the white glossed page of the crochet pattern, with its picture of a woman with Marcel waves and very thinly pencilled eyebrows, wearing the beret. Yes, thought Ella dreamily, she would pluck her eyebrows too, to a very thin line indeed and pencil them in with brown eyebrow crayon, no matter how painful it was. And she would get her hair shaped shorter.

'How can we possibly keep secrets from Una? It just wouldn't be fair.'

In a sudden burst of emotion, Chloe revealed how she had come across the IOU in Cedric Pawson's desk. Lindi and Ella listened in shocked disbelief.

Chloe was moved to tears. 'It's perfectly true. I've brought it with me to show you, this morning. It's right here with me in this envelope.' She took it out to show them. 'There's no mistaking it's Father work. It's even written on our own blue hotel paper!'

They examined the IOU with mounting alarm. There seemed no doubt it was genuine.

'What are you going to do then?' said Lindi.

'Oh, thank goodness I wasn't the one to come across it,' said Ella. 'I just couldn't have lived with it. I should have had to tell poor Una straightaway. She has a right to know. That is, *if* it's true. But looking at it here, this minute, it seems undeniable.'

'We'll soon find out,' said Chloe, with a calm she did not feel. 'All I ask is that you keep quiet about it until after Easter.'

'After Easter? How *terribly* dramatic.' Lindi twisted a stranded gold ringlet of

57

hair round her slim index finger, and smiled slightly.

Chloe ignored the edge of sarcasm in her sister's voice. She was secretly hoping for a real showdown with her father. She longed to watch him collapse with guilt, ached for him to have to change his miserable plan, and destroy the IOU in front of her. Already she had a plan worked out, and it bubbled away in her mind like a spell in a witch's cauldron.

When Chloe had returned to Grangebeck, her two sisters looked at each other in silence. Lindi was the first to speak.

'I agree with you El. It's unfair to keep Una in the dark, when the whole thing revolves around her. It's not as if she's just a baby. Chloe gets too involved with trying to act the older sister with her, just because Una is still at school. Any one would think Chloe was about ninety the way she goes on sometimes. Instead of just over a year older than Una. She seems to think she's got the wisdom of Methuselah these days. I think she was an utter traitor to have gone to work at Cedric's in the first place, even if we do all hate being here at home. She didn't make any real effort to stand on her own two feet, when Father turfed her out.'

When Una returned from school later

that afternoon she was surprised to see both Ella and Lindi waiting for her in her bedroom.

'What on earth are you staring at me like that for?' said Una cheerfully. 'Don't tell me you've actually finished all your work?'

'It's nothing to do with anything here, Una. It's to do with Chloe,' said Ella slowly. 'She came round today with some very strange news. It's to do with you.'

'To do with *me?*' Una looked alarmed. What had been going on? Had they found out about Robby? Perhaps someone had seen them kissing.

'Chloe pleaded with us not to tell you but we both think it's your right to know.' Ella turned quickly to Lindi. 'Don't we, Lind?'

Lindi nodded fervently and took over. 'She has found some stupid chit of paper written by Father as an IOU, with you as the prize. A sort of slave bride for darling Cedric at some glorious future date.'

Una sat unsteadily on the edge of the bed, her eyes opened wide in disbelief. 'I don't believe it. Father would never stoop so low. And Cedric is almost an old man. I'd never dream of marrying *anyone,* never mind him!' Her words were brave but a thread of fear had spread through her and her heart was thumping.

Ella and Lindi exchanged a quick glance of satisfaction. They were cheered up by Una's cheerful reaction and comforted that she now knew what was going on.

'Quite right,' said Ella. 'That's what we thought, pure rubbish.'

'Exactly,' said Lindi quickly. 'Let's forget it entirely and get downstairs. If you ask me, Chloe's going a bit doolally working at Cedric's, but it's her own fault for ever going there at all.' Lindi smiled brightly, but really she knew she was being a hypocrite. It hadn't taken long for Chloe's tale to gather strength.

As the three sisters gazed at one another, different thoughts took sway.

Hubert Archibald Lamby felt unsettled as he tramped about the grounds of Swansdown. He was like a pining animal on a long chain, as he stared with disgruntled frustration towards the calm reaches of Melmere. It was a day for angels. Birds were busily building nests. Bright yellow jasmine glowed against the walls of Swansdown in the breezy sun. Yet he hadn't even wanted to get up this morning. He'd felt like swigging a whole bottle of brandy and taking to his bed for ever, until he heard one of his horses whinny.

As always it was the little things that

brought it all on. His wife and his daughters seemed determined to drain every penny from him. The horses weren't up to peak condition either, and although training horses and gambling on them were not good stablemates, he was an inveterate gambler. Last season had been catastrophic in the racing world. Only the firm, even-keeled, ruthless Cedric Pawson had saved him from certain ruin...

He thought about Chloe. He'd sworn to himself she would leave Grangebeck when she found she was a mere washer-up there for ever, but only this morning Cedric Pawson had doused that fond idea. Cedric had been round to talk about the racing season, and to discuss the idea of getting extra help with stable work, and riding out the horses.

'Oh by the way, and another small thing, Hubie,' Cedric had said, 'I've promoted Chloe. To be quite candid old boy, she's an awkward little thing, but I hadn't quite reckoned how smart she was with a typewriter. I never got over Tessa doing the dirty on me in that respect—with all those secretarial skills—then buggering off to those damned tea rooms.'

Hubert nodded. Tessa was a very strong-willed woman, and not one to be trifled with.

'Anyway, with your Chloe clinging to

Grangebeck as if her life depended on it, I've offered her a bit of private office work.'

Hubert gave a bleak smile, but inside he was seething. What was up with that girl, worming her way into Cedric Pawson's household? He began to hunt feverishly in his pockets for his tin of bismuth, blindly shoving two lozenges in his mouth and sucking at them feverishly.

Easter was an important time for everyone. There were three main churches in the Pover area. The tabernacle of corrugated iron, set on a small country lane was the meeting place used by the non-conformists and presided over by Parson Powell. It was the church Granny Lamby attended, and Ella went too. Many of its members were in the village choir.

There was also a large Catholic church, the Church of the Holy Martyrs, just off Pover Lane. A Gothic building, its activities were supported by Lady Limpet's sister Maria, whose naval commander husband had been killed in the War. The church was her constant solace. Constance Lamby and her childhood friend, Nelly Forthsythe, were also Catholics, but these days Constance rarely attended church.

Ruling the main roost was a rather plain Church of England edifice with a vicarage and the local village pub nearby. The church had a square tower and had been the centre of worship for over eight hundred years. Properly called St Orbell's, the church was known generally as Pover Church and supported by Lord and Lady Limpet. This was the church with which the three youngest Lamby girls had been brought up even though their father hadn't attended services in any of the places.

Easter Sunday this time was different for Chloe. She had chosen, in her two hours of free time during that day, to cycle to Shale Bridge in the hope of seeing Mac Haley somewhere about. As she cycled along in the sunny air by the side of the calm mere, with its white flower petal feathers from a myriad of roosting gulls dotted in gentle masses, she planned the surprise she had in store for her father on Easter Monday. The shock of his life was carefully hidden in a small, brightly coloured glossy papier-mâché egg, with trimmings of gold braid and its white inner frill of lacy white paper. In the egg was an almost perfect copy of the IOU Chloe had found in Pawson's desk.

On identical notepaper taken from home, she had practised forging her father's handwriting many, many times, even managing to use his own pen on visits to Swansdown when he'd left it lying about. She could imitate his drunken, shaky signature to perfection, and she'd judiciously folded the paper in haphazard quarters, finally copying the horse-head doodles.

As for the genuine IOU, it had been removed from the large brown envelope. It now rested in a black japanned deed box along with her birth certificate, her school certificate, and a small snapshot of herself with Mac Haley and others standing at the door of the *Gazette*.

'Chloe...' Margie Renshaw waved to her as she came over the small stone bridge along the almost empty main street. Chloe jumped off her bike, and they chatted casually about the weather, and Margie's forthcoming baby.

'I've left the *Gazette*, too, Chloe. He hauled me into his inner sanctum shortly after you left and said I was too much of a liability and there wasn't enough space...

'Have you time to come back to River Cottage for a cup of tea?'

'I daren't, really, Margie. I only came out for a bit of fresh air and a change. It's almost more than my life's worth to be late back. Cedric is a real slave-driver. He never misses a trick. He's even worse than Mrs French, his cook.' Chloe smiled. 'On second thoughts,' she changed the subject hastily, 'I will chance a cup of tea. I'm quite parched!' There was a slight, nervous pause. 'Have you seen anything of Mac?'

'No, but there was some talk of him getting engaged to Myra Mitchell from the hairdressers. They both belong to the rambling club.'

Chloe nodded silently, her short hair gleaming like a magpie's feathers in the sunshine. She tried to look unconcerned, but her heart had fallen like lead. She was no match for vivacious rosy-cheeked chatterbox Myra Mitchell, a born comic and almost twenty-four years old.

'Have you ever thought of joining the ramblers?' said Margie tactfully as they sat over a cup of tea. 'They get out on some really good walks, mainly in Derbyshire. Danny and I often went out with them when we were courting. They're a good crowd.'

'Chance is a fine thing, Margie.' Chloe finished off her drink. 'Anyway, it's been good seeing you.'

'Good seeing you, too. Pop in any time, Chloe, I'm never far away.'

That evening Chloe rang home to say she would be calling on Easter Monday. Lindi answered the phone.

'I'm bringing Father a very special present, Lindi. It's something to do with our secret about the IOU.' Chloe waited expectantly.

'Oh, yes...' There was silence.

'What?'

'Oh... Nothing.' Lindi had been caught off-guard. She had never given the secret another thought, now that Una had been told about it.

'Did you do much yesterday at Grange-beck, then? Did you get any time off?'

'I managed to get out for a bicycle ride. I saw Margie Renshaw from the *Gazette*. She said Mac's engaged to be married...'

'*Mac* is?' Lindi sounded quite stunned. 'Is it anyone we know?' Lindi had known Mac—even before Chloe had—before he had even worked at the *Gazette*. A group of them, as giggling schoolgirls, had admired him from afar.

'Myra Mitchell, from the hairdressers. They both belong to the rambling club. Margie said I should join it. She said I'd like it.'

'I'll bet you were surprised when she told you about Mac,' said Lindi, tactlessly. 'You were always going on about him when you worked there.'

'I never was. Anyway, he's much older. He's at least twenty-five. I'm really glad for him. Myra's very nice.'

'I wouldn't mind going out with them

on rambles,' said Lindi suddenly. 'If you get the full particulars, let me know. We could join together.'

Chloe's voice brimmed with exasperation. 'How *could* we? The hours we work?'

'But surely Cedric isn't as bad as Father? You might be able to arrange it? And as for me, I'm getting to the state where I'll be quite happy to go...and have a flaming row about it when I get back.'

When she'd put down the phone, Lindi was quite thoughtful. It was a sudden urge to join the rambling club, but it was better than nothing. She was ready for a battle with Father to get more time off. She smiled to herself with a sudden streak of determination.

With the full day off on Easter Monday, Chloe was intent on confronting her father with the IOU. She carefully placed the small decorated Easter egg into a cardboard box and put it into the carrier basket on her bicycle handlebars. It was a perfectly worked-out present for him. She set off from Grangebeck with strange feelings of excitement and fear. The morning was clear and perfect. Pink-breasted chaffinches and small grey sparrows hopped and chirruped in the hedgerows. The air was damp and sweet smelling. Chloe moved along quickly, her feet pressing on the pedals with unrestrained energy. She could hardly wait to get to Swansdown, and watch the fireworks...

At Swansdown that day Una was wandering down the aisle of the mossed glass greenhouses. White paint curled away from the putty around each window, next to the seed boxes.

Robby was in a foul temper.

'Honestly, Una, how can he expect me to do everything myself? Acres of wild garden. Seeds to propagate and transplant. Ploughing and weeding and hoeing. Paths to keep in order. Rotting fences and gates to repair. The boathouse and the rowing boats to paint and make good...and on top of it all, the horses.

'At one time there would have been an army of servants for all that.' He stared at Una miserably. 'You're certainly stuck in a hole here, Una.'

They walked outside and watched some rabbits scampering away to a thicket. Robby glared at them belligerently.

'And just look at those. Your dog Beech is as much use as a lame duck for getting rid of them!' He scowled at her accusingly.

Una couldn't bear it when he was in one of his moods. She hated him going on and on about the shortcomings of Swansdown, even though she agreed with every word he said. Sometimes, when they forgot about the hard work, it could be an absolute Garden of Eden. And Una did manage to hold her tongue about *his* family.

'I think I might start to look round for another job...'

Una stared at him in horror. 'Oh Robby... Don't do that!'

'They do say that Brent's the Bakers in Shale need a van driver. It'd be easier than this lot.'

'You'd *hate* it. You'd have to be trailing to Knutsford and even as far as Altrincham in all sorts of rotten weather. You'd miss the fresh air!'

Robby glared at her. 'It's all right for you to talk, Una. Your life bears no resemblance to mine. You're still at school. You have it smooth compared to me. If it wasn't for you, I'd have cleared out ages ago.' He looked at her mournfully from beneath a thatch of sandy brown hair.

Sometimes, when he went on for so long with his hardships Una longed to escape the whole place. She dreamed of being swept off her feet by someone like Ronald Colman, but without a moustache, and living in a castle, with constant trips to Hollywood on a luxury liner, calling in at Coney Island near New York on the way, as it seemed from what she'd read in *Film Fun,* to have big dippers even more daring than Blackpool's. At other times she tried to face reality. What was to become of her? Would she always live here in the village she'd grown up in? Or would it be better to launch out and go to Manchester where Great Aunt Mabel lived? Most of her mother's people were spread out in different parts of Yorkshire, so they didn't have many relatives close by. Her mother had been the only daughter among six children and although she had Yorkshire cousins, her brothers had all married and gone their separate ways.

Una thought seriously about Robby. Would he always be a grumbler? Or might he improve if they both went elsewhere?

Every day there was news of more and more people unemployed and down to starvation level in the cities. Not only in the cities: farms were suffering too, and one local farmer had suddenly given up the struggle and shot himself. Yes, village life seemed idyllic to some but there was always a dark thread of human tragedy woven in its fabric.

'Whatever's come over Chloe?' Ella said to Lindi, as they bustled about the hotel. 'She seems quite strange and nervous.'

'Can you wonder?' said Lindi wryly.

'It's a bit strange to have gone to work at Grangebeck in the first place. She obviously did it to spite Father.'

Ella's round face creased to a slight frown. 'Surely not, Lindi. It was probably the best way to get a new job quickly. After all, Cedric does know all the whys and whereabouts of everything where employment is concerned. He's got a finger in every pie, and to be perfectly fair to Chloe, what better person to go to for help?'

'Our very own Jack-the-Lad...' said Lindi cynically.

'Say what you like, but at least she's arrived with a special present for Father this morning. Surely she wouldn't have done that if she'd meant to be unkind.'

The Lamby family had always bought each other small Easter presents, which they traditionally kept until Easter Monday to exchange. This Easter was no different and they waited for Father to come in from the stables to open them.

Ella had bought him a cardboard Easter egg with a yellow polishing duster in it and Lindi had made him a horse's head egg cosy. Una had dyed and decorated him a proper Pace egg.

Constance Lamby had nothing for her husband aside from a rather cheap tobacco pouch with a transfer of a cartoon chicken

71

smoking a pipe on it which she'd bought at the market. She presumed he would give her the usual very small quarter-pound box of chocolates. The sort that had languished in some shop he'd chanced upon in a back street of his life. A shop where the faded box had rested for over a year in a jumble of goods in the window, with the snoozing shop window cat spreading its hairs on it for a few months. A place where fruit pies in cardboard cartons had fur inside as thick as the cat's beside them. The chocolates would turn out to be all discoloured and pale on top from the damp of winter and the warmth of summer sun.

Hubert Lamby disliked all ceremonies remotely linked with religious festivals. He suffered them in morose silence and nodded his thanks in a perfunctory manner, as and when required. Sure enough he presented Constance with a quarter-pound box of chocolates with slightly worn, bent corners, and had given each of the girls a small round package of marshmallows, complete with faded cover.

Chloe waited until he was leaving the living room to give him his gift.

'Father, I've brought you something, too.'

He stared at her, surprised.

She handed him the little parcel in

its loose paper bag. He took out the Easter egg and glanced at it, nodding his thanks.

'Aren't you going to open it?'

A trace of annoyance flitted across his face. He was sensitive to the idea that any woman should propose his actions. Then he softened and said: 'Must I?'

He opened the two halves of the egg casually, but suddenly he was alert. His eyes widened. His mouth was set and his face became entirely expressionless. With slow deliberation he placed the halves of the egg on the beer-stained oak table near his bookshelves and looked at the folded bit of paper sticking out of one half.

'What's this?' He knew already, that much was obvious.

Chloe hovered uncertainly, her heart thumping.

Hubert tried to laugh. 'Have you gone deaf?' I said, *"What's this?"* This scrap of paper?'

'Open it and see.'

He picked it up and slowly unfolded it, a strained, defensive smile lingering on his face.

'Is it a game or something?' He flattened out Chloe's careful duplicate but he glanced at it only briefly before pushing it away.

'What in hell's name's this got to do

with Easter? Where did you get it anyway?'

'Surely you can guess? Don't you recognise it?'

Hubert picked it up, and stared again. 'I didn't write this bloody rubbish. It's a clever forgery, a school-boy prank. That's not my signature and it wouldn't take an expert to find that out!'

He picked up the scrap of paper again and scornfully read out the words: *"'I do not owe you any thing...or any person from my family?'"* It's complete gobbledy-gook!' He seemed genuinely amazed and puzzled. 'Signed by *me?* Why should I want to sign all that bilge?'

Chloe began to waver. Had she made some terrible blunder? She'd purposely altered the words, confidently expecting her father to catch on to the meaning based on the first IOU addressed to Cedric Pawson. The true and awful message shone out in her mind: IOU CEDRIC PAWSON —MY YOUNGEST DAUGHTER—UNA CHRISTABEL LAMBY. SWANSDOWN HOTEL. MARCH 21st 1932.

She wondered whether to reveal every-thing to him right now, to describe how she'd found the real evidence at Grangebeck, and to plead with him to have nothing further to do with Cedric. But in her heart she knew the idea was pure romance. Her father and Cedric Pawson were as close as blood brothers.

'Where did you find it anyway? And what does it mean exactly?' He was perking up, and was less guarded. He knew he had won.

All the same, he stared at her coolly with a dangerous glint in his eye: 'I see it's on our own notepaper, but I don't reckon my signature's quite as bad as that, even in my worst moments. A very funny Easter gift, and no mistake. It certainly doesn't seem to be bringing out the best in *you*, Chloe, sheltering there at Cedric's, even if he does say you're a good typist.' Then with a sudden streak of genuine humour he said: 'I'll keep the two halves of the egg for putting back studs and cuff-links in.'

Chloe did not return to the sitting room. A sudden feeling of depression overwhelmed her as she cycled slowly back to Grangebeck. She was completely bewildered. Nothing had turned out a bit like she'd imagined.

There were some who suspected that the reason Hubert Lamby took to his bed in sudden bouts of illness and depression was because he was a square peg in a round hole. He was a man of energy and drive who had to curb his spontaneous and quick temper that could end with violence. This had served him well in the war of his youth but had to be well hidden in the world of polite hotels. But inevitably, at times when he was severely ruffled his latent anger rose. Just as it was doing now as he saw Chloe on her bike, going back to Grangebeck.

A sudden violent anger began to rise within him. The blood thumped in his temples. His ears went scarlet as he thought of the scrap of paper with which his daughter had presented him. *The indignity of it!* To have such an infantile and insulting trick played on him so insolently by one of his own daughters. The ingratitude. Did she think he had no feelings? Had she invented the whole bloody thing herself? Never would even he have dreamed he could breed such a damned little troublemaker.

The more he thought of it the more his rage grew. Then, picking up the small, tastefully decorated cardboard Easter egg, he thundered into the family living room, disturbing the afternoon calm like a raging bull.

'Does anyone here know about this parcel of evil your sister brought with her?' he roared. He tossed the scrap of cardboard to the floor disparagingly and in the same quick movement, picked up a heavy, handmade vase and hurled it like a hand grenade at the room's huge plate glass window.

There was a terrible doom-laden crash and then silence. The whole beautiful, spacious window was beamed in gigantic cracks from where the vase had gone through, leaving a dark central circular rent, like a menacing black hole vacated by the sun.

Constance and her three daughters stood there paralysed now with silent terror, their screams of alarm muffled by their fear.

He stared at them all like a glowering red-eyed animal then turning quickly he left the Swansdown with howls of blustering rage.

Chloe arrived at Grangebeck Manor and only a few minutes after parking her bike she was waylaid by Cedric's maid Susie.

'There's been a phone call for you only a few minutes ago, Miss Lamby. Your sister, Miss Una. She wants you to ring her back straightaway. She sounded in a real tizzy.'

Chloe nodded peaceably; she'd expected this. It was natural that Una would be a bit upset when she knew about the IOU. But it had all been done to help her. Una would realise that as soon as the fuss had died down. Chloe walked towards the phone, complacent and smiling.

CHAPTER 4

Broken Hearts

'Come back again? Whatever for?' Chloe could hardly believe the desperation in Una's voice.

'It's Father. God alone knows what you said to him. He's smashed the living-room window with a vase! It was awful...' Una's voice broke with agony.

'It's going to cost the earth to get repaired. He's gone quite off his rocker. He's been stamping round outside muttering all sorts of threats. He and Mother have had the row to end all rows. They've been facing each other like a couple of snarling mongrels.' Una's voice filled with sobs of despair and she struggled to continue.

'And now Father's locked himself in the stables and Mother is drinking claret as if it's the end of the world.'

'But they're always having rows,' said Chloe uneasily. 'And it's always the final one...' A guilty feeling began to creep over her. Surely Father hadn't actually mentioned the Easter egg to them?

Her worst fears were realised as Una's

voice broke tearfully. 'You're at the root of it, Chloe. Tampering with that terrible IOU. It's like a nightmare.'

'I'll come back right now. And *don't worry.*' Chloe hung up the telephone with trembling fingers.

'Something urgent's cropped up at home,' she called to Susie. And in a few minutes she was ploughing her way back to Swansdown with a thumping heart. All the way there she castigated herself. Why had she been such a fool to challenge Father with the false note? Why on earth hadn't she just tucked the wretched evidence out of sight when she'd found it in Cedric's desk, and said no more? When would she ever stop plunging into family trouble because of haste and lack of foresight?

Deep down she knew the truth. It was because of the way Father had treated her when she'd left the *Gazette,* and now her carefully laid plans were rebounding with a vengeance against her...

Cedric Pawson noticed immediately that Chloe had gone.

'Did she say why, Susie?' he asked thoughtfully.

'No, sir, but it was straight after she'd rung Miss Una and she said summat had cropped up at home. She looked all of a flutter...poor thing. I 'ope Mr Lamby's not nearly dead again.'

Cedric eyed her coldly and went into his sitting room. But no sooner had he settled down than Susie was tapping at his door to tell him that Mr Lamby himself had arrived on horseback. 'The horse is snorting like anything, sir,' she reported nervously.

Cedric scowled and went out to meet him. What the devil was up? Whenever the skin and hair was flying at Swansdown, Hubie landed here to escape.

A calm smile had surfaced on Cedric's face by the time they were together in his sitting room. 'Brandy?' He poured two small ones. 'So what's up, old son?'

'God alone knows,' gasped Hubert, gulping his drink. 'Chloe suddenly rolled up at our place and presented me with a very strange note with my signature forged on it. It looked as if it was based on the one you received some time ago.'

The two men stared at each other in silence, then Cedric said, 'Surely it wasn't worth this fuss?'

Hubert grunted angrily. 'I'm afraid I saw red. A window got smashed. It's all right for you, Ced. You don't know what you're missing, living here in bachelored bliss. Chloe must have found that stupid jape IOU somewhere here and copied one for me for Easter. A typical piece of dramatic, meaningless female nonsense. I thought you destroyed the bloody thing?'

Cedric looked up sharply. 'I didn't destroy it. Let's be quite clear on that one, Hubie. If you can remember back a couple of months we *both* decided to keep it, to try and find out who'd sent it. The last time I saw it, it was in my study desk.' He smiled very slightly. 'It was quite clever really, Hubie. Your Una is by far the best of your bunch, but she needs another two years of freedom yet. God bless the lucky bloke who manages to catch her eventually. The whole thing was such an obvious schoolboy antic...'

Hubert thought for a moment. 'Unless, it was Chloe?'

'Not the type, Hubert. Not the type.'

'She did the Easter egg one...'

'Exactly what did it say, Hubie?'

'That I wasn't going to let you have Una—a reiteration of that first load of guff. But it's shoved me up a real gum-tree, Ced. What the hell do we do next?' Hubert belched plaintively and continued. 'I didn't mince matters. I made no bones about it. And when the window went they all had bloody hysterics. Connie drained the decanter. Ella left the iron to fall on the carpet and it burnt a sodding big hole. Lindi began to blare like a fish wife. And poor little Una...naturally I felt a bit sorry for her. She was *very* upset...'

'I must say I wouldn't have liked my window blasted with a vase,' remarked Cedric blandly. 'You'd have been wiser to ignore the stupid note, Hubert. You should have torn up the damned thing then and there in front of Chloe and said nowt.'

They sat there for a few moments in silence, then Hubert said quietly, 'Trade's very bad at the hotel.'

'Trade's very bad everywhere old son... Even I'm feeling the pinch.'

'Sometimes I'm driven to thinking we might have to sell up.'

'Chance is a fine thing old boy. You'd hardly get a bean. You'll just have to stop the gambling and sit tight for a few years. After all, Hubert, to put it bluntly, you've got one asset some buggers would give their eye-teeth for.'

'Oh, aye, the horses...'

'Not the horses, you fool. The women! The labour force, Hubie. They're worth more than their weight in gold, especially in these hard times. There's all the makings of a rich revival on your spot, one of these days. But you'll need to hold on to them all. You miffed it a bit with Chloe. I'm reaping the benefits of that. She's extremely competent.'

Una had seen Father galloping off as she waited for Chloe to arrive back at Swansdown. She was down by the mere beneath a large oak tree explaining the fuss to Robby. But the more she said, the more tense and angry he became.

'I just don't want to hear any more, Una. Both your father and Cedric Pawson sicken me. They're tarred with the brush of meanness and selfishness.' He got out a chisel and began to scratch busily at the bark of the oak tree, gradually lifting out small portions of bark until he had carved an *R*.

She watched him silently. She knew he was right, but all the same one of the men was her father, and he'd had always been kind and loving to her. She really had nothing to complain about. She could see it was different with the rest of them. And Robby, he got the worst of her father from all sides.

Una watched as he dug hard into the surface of the tree. It disturbed her to see him doing that—if Father saw it, he would have a fit.

'Do you think it's wise to carve your initials, Robby? Father might...it would be awful if he got in one of his moods and gave you the sack.' Una spoke hesitantly and waited for his response.

Robby took not the slightest notice.

Silently he scraped and chiselled away with deep-seated, angry determination as the initials R.B. and U.L. intertwined within the outline of a heart appeared deeply in the brown of the bark, making pale buttery clefts.

He stepped back and looked at it in triumph. At last he was smiling. 'There you are! And if the tree's not chopped down by your father it could last another five hundred years as a record of *us.*' He dropped the chisel to the ground, wrapped his arms round her and kissed her.

'Take no notice of any of them, Una. We've always got each other and I'll never desert you, whatever tricks the rest of them get up to.'

They looked at each other warmly before Una turned to make her way back to the big house. As she walked, Una could see Chloe pedalling away along the winding drive. They waved to each other.

Robby saw her, too. And for an instant he felt a surge of panic. Trust Chloe to have found the IOU and to have retaliated, he thought, his panic turning to a burning sense of guilt. In a way she was a bit like him, with her hasty passion and prim resolve.

It was his own passion that had led him to the IOU idea in the first place. But now he'd never forgive himself for being such a fool as to send it.

His actions had been fired by hate, jealousy and frustration. But now he realised it had been sheer stupidity. It was obvious to any fool that Pawson had his eye on Una for the future.

And as for Hubert Lamby, with his perpetual play-acting while his daughters answered his every beck and call, well, he was just plain nauseating...

Forging the IOU had been a bit of a game at the time. He knew full well its message wouldn't be lost on Cedric and Hubert. Neither of them was a fool. It would let them know that someone else could see what they were up to.

The idea had sparkled in his mind, growing sharper and more searing every second. It was on a day when the greenhouses had flooded after heavy rain. The heating had petered out, and all the seedlings were drooping with cold. He'd sat there beside a small oil stove in the tool-shed, planning the forgery to his heart's content and revelling in his own artistic abilities. Never once had he imagined any real repercussions.

Chloe's face was flushed to dark rose within the frame of her short glossy black hair. She was sweating from the hasty return journey and she sat in the living room, still panting slightly as her three sisters stared at her accusingly.

'What a fool of a thing to do, presenting Father with such a sordid joke,' said Lindi. Her face was still streaked with tears. 'I never realised you had something as bad as that planned. You've escaped the worst of it! That window took ages to paste over with wrapping paper.' Lindi brushed back a strand of fair hair reproachfully.

Chloe was cooling off. She felt quite chilled. 'But it wasn't a joke. Call it a forgery, or what you will. I wrote it to try and bring Father to his senses, to show that I knew about the real IOU he'd given Cedric.'

'With me as the prize,' sobbed Una indignantly.

'I had to try and do something,' Chloe struggled to explain, angry tears forming in her eyes. 'I couldn't just ignore what I'd seen.

'Did you say anything to Cedric about finding the IOU?' said Ella, who was busily knitting a Fair Isle sock on four fine steel needles for Dudley Plume, a young writer who had just come to live in the middle of Pover village. He was another of her idle pleasant dreams, along with the firmly-married Monty Marqueson and his badly-matched wife. Ella's knitting soothed her in all catastrophes.

'How on earth could I say anything to Cedric?' exclaimed Chloe angrily. 'He'd probably have sacked me on the spot for prying into his desk.'

'Have you still got the one from his desk?'

'Of course. I couldn't just leave it resting there for the rest of the world to see. I've locked it in my deed box, now.'

'Father—he spoke to me later—reckons it was all the work of some schoolboy. A joke of the worst type and in very bad taste,' said Ella primly.

'He just would, wouldn't he?' said Chloe bitterly. 'Where is he now, anyway?'

'Galloped off in a fine temper to see Cedric,' said Una with slightly more composure. 'Robby and I saw him. It's a good job your paths didn't cross...'

When everything had settled down Chloe set off at last to Grangebeck.

About a mile along the winding lane she caught a glimpse of Robby. She slowed down as she reached him, and got off her bike.

'I think the whole thing's been sorted out at last, Robby,' she said cheerfully. 'I gave Father a rather silly Easter present, but it's all calmed down now, thank goodness All the same, I hope I don't meet him on the way back...'

Robby nodded silently, but didn't meet her eyes. Chloe looked at him with confusion. Whatever was the matter?

Then, in a sudden burst of passion, Robby looked up, face flushed.

'You aren't the only villain, Chloe. It was me who wrote the first note.'

'*You?*' She couldn't believe her ears. Had he suddenly gone mad? 'You? What on earth do you mean? How could you have written something of Father's?'

'The same way as you did. You aren't the only clever forger in these parts...' He glanced towards her briefly and then deliberately turned and walked in the opposite direction.

All the way back to Grangebeck Chloe's mind was in a whirl of indecision. What should she do? Was what he'd said true? Should she destroy the original note she'd found in Cedric's desk or should she give it back to Robby?

Perhaps she should tell Father she'd discovered the whole messy affair to be a practical joke against him by a person she could not name. And, most important of all, she wondered what she should say to Una.

The fresh air was sweet against her face as she neared Cedric's. It strengthened her resolve. Best to say nothing at all to anyone. Just bury the whole sorry situation.

Others would soon forget, and it wasn't as if she was living in the same house as Father these days.

No sooner had she put her bicycle in one of the old coaching houses and unfastened her windjammer when a shadow fell across the door. Cedric Pawson stood silently in the doorframe, his broad muscular frame barring her exit.

'So what's been going on then, Chloe? Hubie's been over here and he's very angry indeed.' His shrewd grey eyes glittered slightly in a shaft of light from one of the small, stone-clad windows.

Chloe stood like a captive pigeon. She stared down at the unevenly cobbled floor and shivered as she felt a sudden draft of cold air.

'While you were out I've been looking through my desk, and a small piece of paper is missing.'

She faced him silently, hardly daring to look up.

'Hubert seems to think it might have been your work? Congratulations on such a well-planned little epic.'

He waited expectantly, a stolid figure in his finely tailored tweed suit, hands resting casually in his pockets.

Chloe said nothing.

'I can tell you this much, Chloe.' His voice took on a more menacing tone. 'If I ever find out it was you who pinched that stupid nonsense in the first place, whether you wrote it or you didn't, you'll be out of here quicker than a flying bat!' With that he swung round on his well-shod, tan leather heels and vanished.

Chloe breathed with relief. She sensed he would never refer to it again. Please God, let it rest forever as a lesson to be learnt about never meddling in other people's affairs. And as for Robby Belmane and his part in it, she would never mention any of it to Una. They could sort it out between them, if the facts of the incident ever came to light...

Not long after Robby had blurted out the truth, he heard the sound of galloping hooves slowing down to walking pace. Hubert Lamby came to a halt beside him at the gates of Swansdown drive.

Hubert glanced down at him from aloft. 'Why aren't you working in the stables?' he barked.

'I am.' Robby looked back at him calmly. 'I never stop working in this place, Mr Lamby. You can rely on that.'

Lamby stared at him hard. 'You're an insolent young bastard, Belmane. You'll need to watch your step. There's plenty more young 'uns in Pover.' He gave the horse a jab with his heels and trotted away.

Robby's face crumpled in a picture of misery and frustration, his bold stance shattered. He was sick to death of being treated like some pathetic underling by Hubert. Oh yes, he knew he was only young and not properly qualified, but he reckoned his brains were as good as anyone else's. Yet there again he wasn't supposed to have too many of those where Hubert Lamby was concerned. A Hubert Lamby quota of brains meant enough to be able to carry out verbal and written instructions, but never enough to work out how badly paid he was. And, of course, he was expected to have brawn enough for ploughing a field single-handed, pollarding six willows, washing out all the stables, mending ten rotting doors, cleaning out a septic tank, carrying sacks of coal, and rolling beer barrels. And all in a morning's work.

Robby thought again of the IOU and his miserable mood evaporated. He felt a strange sense of pride, and of rebellion. Why should he be relenting? Cedric and Hubert deserved it a hundredfold. It was just unfortunate that it should have rebounded. A streak of unease crept in again. Maybe it had been rash to pour it out to Chloe, even though she was the most reasonable one in the place. More reasonable than Una. Una was different.

He loved Una passionately, but he couldn't exactly describe her as being reasonable.

He gave an involuntary shudder. God help him if Chloe said anything to Una. Then, wiping his worst thoughts from his mind, he strode away, whistling as if he hadn't a care in the world.

Hubert Lamby kept away from the women for the rest of that day. The sooner Easter 1932 was over, the better he was going to like it.

He was just strolling along, close to the gently lapping waters of the mere when his foot caught the edge of something lying in the grass. He picked it up and clucked with annoyance. One of his chisels. Money was short enough without that young lout leaving them carelessly to rust away. He looked up and froze in his tracks. *R.B. and U.L.* intertwined. His hand gripped the chisel, and he had an angry desire to stab it out as he stared angrily at the heart-shaped line round it. The insolent young sod!

Hubert Lamby rushed back to the house like a raging torrent.

'What is it, Father? Has something happened?' Una was watching him as he came up the back steps.

'Something happened?' He glared at her irritably and said breathlessly: 'I thought nothing much else could happen today after the Easter egg affair. But now I find *this!*' He brandished the chisel towards her. 'I don't know whether you realise it, Una, but Belmane has scratched both his and your initials on one of *my* oak trees. On one of the best bloody specimens we've got. That lad is completely irresponsible, and he's getting above himself.'

Una stared with fright. 'Fatherl He works like a slave all day long! And, if you must know, I knew about the initials. I was there. He carved them today. We *love* each other.' She gave a sob and ran quickly from the room.

Loved each other? Hubert Lamby was completely flummoxed. Never in his life would he ever expect such an outburst to come from his youngest daughter's lips. Surely she couldn't be so misguided as to think she was in love with that young lout, when she was still a schoolgirl?

And then, of all things, to be influenced by this ignorant, labouring simpleton. Hubert's heart raced with cold anger. God forbid anything really serious should develop.

He was just marching into the hotel office when the phone rang. It was Cedric.

'Everything smoothed out, old man?' Cedric carried on without waiting for an answer. 'Just thought I'd let you know Chloe's going on OK. I gave her a mildish warning about that IOU. Some bugger must have swiped it from my desk. Anyway, God knows where it is now, but the incident's over as far as I'm concerned. How's life at your end then?'

'Dreadful. Would you believe that young idiot Belmane has actually hacked one of my best oaks to bits scrawling his initials on it?... Oh aye but that's not the worst. He's made a real arty job of it and entwined his initials with Una's in a blasted heart. And as if that's not bad enough, Una's taken some peculiar emotional turn and says she loves him.'

There was a sudden silence at the other end of the phone, then Pawson said swiftly, 'You know what you've got to do then, don't you?'

'Of course, sack him. That's quite plain.'

'That's neither here nor there, Hubie. What you've got to do is make him fill in the bark on that tree from another of your oaks and get it bound up for a bit until it takes. Get him to do it right now. It'll serve two purposes. One—to make good what he's vandalised and two—make sure his grandiose ideas about Una are completely blotted out for good. Right?'

Hubert replaced the phone handle in thoughtful mood. He felt slightly better after what Cedric had suggested.

The following day Hubert had arranged to tackle Robby in an official manner about the tree carving. He had already decided that as soon as Belmane had covered up the offending damage he would sack him on the spot. There were at least three other lads in Pover who would jump at the chance of work. He'd arrange with Ced to get two cheap beginners for less than the price of one.

To his mind, Belmane had always been over-valued. He'd been employed without Hubie's knowledge, one day, a year ago, by Constance when old Bobby Olders had made a scene. Bobby got nasty about replacing broken tiles on the stable roof, saying that at eighty-five he was too old for both tiling roofs and removing moss from all the guttering. 'Them jobs is fit only for steeplejacks, Mrs Lamby. Just you wait 'til Hubert reaches my age. There's such a thing as dizziness comes about, and not from boozing neither!' This was followed by him having a brain-storm, whereupon he disappeared and got himself a job gardening in Pover church grave-yard.

By the time Hubert summoned Robby to his office that day he was in quite a good temper about the prospect of an overall improvement in his finances. The thought of removing this sharp thorn from his flesh was beginning to pacify him. He took a swift look at Robby as he came into the office. Aye, he was a fine enough specimen. A bit too fine... He decided to ask him to sit down so as to balk any idea of fisticuffs.

'Sit down, Rob. I expect you know why you're here.'

'No.'

'No? Come off it, lad. You mean to tell me there isn't anything you've done in the past couple of days that was distinctly wrong?'

'No.'

Robby looked away.

'What if I said I found one of my chisels lying around in the grass?'

'Yes?'

'Lying by one of the oak trees by the mere.'

Robby's face cleared slightly. 'Oh, *that's* where it went. I thought I'd left it there, but when I went back to search, it had gone.'

'It wasn't so much the chisel. It was what you used it for. You made an unholy mess of that tree, scratching all that bark away. Before you say owt else I want you to get it seen to right now. Fill the whole bloody thing in with some more bark from elsewhere and wrap it round tightly with some scrim.

'Go on then. Don't just sit there

gawping! Get on with it!'

(And then, thought Hubert, as soon as you get back from that job, you're in for the bloody sack.)

Very slowly Robby rose and left the office. He found a large roll of coarse hemp scrim, and taking a sharp knife to cut some bark, he made his way back to the oak tree.

He stood there in the still, hazy air. The oaks still held papery, crinkled, silvery gold leaves, survivors of winter wind and gale. The trunks were softly greened in parts and small fresh buds were clumped in four small buds of bronze at the tip of every stout twig.

Robby stared up between the bare branches at the freshly carved heart and its entwined initials. And then there was the sound of soft footsteps approaching—it was Una.

'Robby!' She looked at the chisel. 'You found it then?'

He shook his head and pulled a slight face. 'Sadly your father found it and there's trouble brewing. He sent for me. At first, I thought he was going to sack me on the spot for mucking up one of his trees.'

Una's face tightened with indignation. 'You haven't mucked it up. It's beautiful. It's there for all the world to see...' She forgot her earlier reservations about

97

Robby's labours and was overwhelmed by defiance and pride.

'He wants me to fill it all in with other bark, and bandage it round with this scrim.'

'Surely you won't do it? It's like destroying our own true love!' She flung out her arms to him. 'Don't do it, Robby.'

Robby shook his head slowly. 'I expect he's right in some way. If every visitor to his hotel carved on his trees they'd be ruined.'

'But visitors don't. And we aren't just visitors. This is our own sacred tree, Robby.' She gazed towards the swans on the mere. Tears were forming in her eyes; then, slowly, a small smile appeared.

'I've thought of something. Just *pretend* you've done it. We'll bandage it round and round with the scrim. He'll never know the difference.'

Solemnly, they slowly and carefully wrapped the loosely woven scrim over the heart, time and time again. Then they fastened the bandage in place and walked back towards the hut with the chisel.

'He said I was to report back to him immediately it was done,' said Robby.

'Hurry up, then. I'll wait here.'

She kissed him full on the mouth and they clung together for a few seconds.

Robby suddenly felt frightened. He didn't trust Hubert for one instance. 'Supposing he gives me the sack, Una, and I have to go elsewhere to find work?'

'If that happens, which it won't,' she said consolingly, 'I'll come with you! What's come over you? It's not long since you were threatening to give in your notice and go to Manchester. But don't alarm yourself, Father would never find anyone as good as you again.'

His bold words haunting him, Robby tapped fearfully at Hubert's office door. He knew he'd said all that about clearing out, but he hadn't really meant it. Things were all right here for him and Una and work was hard to find. His threats had been empty and he'd thanked his lucky stars that he hadn't carried them out.

Hubert Lamby, however, was made of sterner stuff. This episode was something more than puppy love. There was his daughter's maidenly honour to consider, and the insult to his property. And he had to take into account Cedric Pawson's views on the matter...

Both he and Cedric knew full well the value of a beautiful unsullied virgin as the prize for a man who'd shown he could make his own way in the world. A man who could provide a fresh rose of a bride with a life of luxury from the beginning—in a feathered nest ready to receive a multitude of children, and domestic duties to keep her well occupied during her most appealing and dangerously attractive years.

Robby's knock shook him from his thoughts.

'Come in,' he shouted, more gruffly than he'd intended.

'I've seen to the oak tree, sir.' Robby stood as tense as a tiger in the sudden silence.

Hubert looked at him, and sighed, unexpectedly experiencing sad pangs of nostalgia for his own youthful desires before the war, when life had no bitter edges. He glanced with guarded envy at the well-set, slim shoulders, the muscles so deceptively lean and baby smooth under the firm flesh. The eyes were sharp and bright and Robby's hair rippled with auburn.

Yes, he had to go.

'You did what I said then?'

Robby nodded silently. There was a sharp, choked note in Hubert Lamby's voice that he'd never heard before.

'You must have had very strong feelings to have hacked that tree in the way you did? The sort of feelings that need to be curbed in a lad like you.'

Robby felt his heart thudding and his temper rising.

'It wasn't exactly *hacked*, sir.' Then he added with ill-judged defiance, 'It was a token of shared love...in a place of beauty.'

'*Shared love?*' Hubert gripped the edge of his desk, his face dangerously red. 'What does that mean?'

'It means that your daughter Una and I love each other, and one day we'll marry.' Robby felt himself grow white with hidden terror. He'd never meant to say those words, never even faced them in his own mind. But now they were said he stood there like marble, awaiting his doom.

He came out of the office a few minutes later like a punch-drunk boxer, as he slowly found his way back to Una in the garden.

'What on earth went on, Robby?' She took hold of his hand. It was cold. 'Surely he didn't go into one of his rages?'

He looked at her in anguish and shook his head resignedly. 'I felt in my bones it might end like this. As far as *he* could see, Una, it's a question of getting us separated as soon as possible. And that has meant sacking me on the spot!'

Una paled with alarm. 'He must have gone mad. Carving our names on that one tree out of hundreds can't possibly have been the reason. What on earth's got into

101

him?' A cold shiver ran the length of her body, as Robby stood there with his head bowed in misery.

They walked down to the edge of the lapping mere in silence, and stared brooding towards the swans and little black and white dab chicks. Robby muttered under his breath, 'I wonder if he guessed that it was me who wrote that stupid IOU to Pawson.'

Una stood stock still. Had she imagined it?

'What did you say, just then, Robby?'

He looked towards her quietly. 'You might as well know the whole of it, Una. Everything's wrecked now. I shall have to leave and go elsewhere for a job. Yes, it was me who sent that false message. It was the daftest thing I ever did in my life. I knew he'd recognise it as someone getting at him over you, but I expected him to rip it up straightaway.' He stared helplessly at Una, begging her with his eyes to forgive him.

She hardly noticed. 'But what about Father? How could you have written such an awful thing, pretending it had come from him? Father has never done me any harm in his life!'

She began to sob, then, turning quickly, she ran blinded with tears back to Swansdown and her own small bedroom.

102

CHAPTER 5

Spring Madness

Una was in the village post office dealing with some parcels from the hotel. It was only a couple of mornings since Robby's confession to her about the IOU. She hadn't told any of the others the full story, but she had refused point blank ever to go back to school again now that Robby had gone. Part of her life had already been swept away. No longer would her future hold the *Gazette,* with Chloe there to show her the ropes if she stayed on at school. No longer was Robby there to greet her each day when she got home from school as they shared their secrets and their love. The misery of what she had discovered, and the fact that she'd never seen Robby since that moment when she'd heard his guilty secret was hard to bear. Her schoolgirl life was shattered.

'How can I pretend to be a schoolgirl again with Robby sacked by Father?' She had looked at her mother with wide-eyed anxiety. 'I'd sooner stay here to help out until you get someone else to take his place. I could never concentrate on studying again. I'd brood too much.'

'You'll make matters worse if you do that, Una. You'll feel better once the Easter holidays are over,' her mother had said, as she and Una, Lindi and Ella had nibbled at their boiled eggs. 'Father is very keen for you to concentrate on your school work, and you might as well take advantage of it before you are forced to become a total drudge, like the rest of us.'

A sudden gloom had descended on the room. They were all going to miss Robby. He was almost part of the family.

The village post office in Pover was the meeting place for everybody, from Lady Limpet downwards. If one happened to arrive when both Lady Limpet and Miss Trill the post mistress were there, one heard every bit of village news discussed with Town Crier propensity. At the moment, however, the place was peaceful as Una handed in her parcels.

'Looking forward to school again?' murmured Miss Trill innocently. 'I hear young Robby Belmane's leaving the village. His brother was saying he's left your place? Off to Bowdon, all of a sudden, to his Aunt Beth's. More prospects in a place like that with those houses needing gardening boys...' She glanced quickly at Una above her pince-nez then busied herself with stamps.

Una said nothing. As she stopped by some magazines on the way out of the shop she bumped into Dudley Plume. His brown leather briefcase was already open and full of fat fawn envelopes needing stamps.

Dudley Plume hadn't been living in Pover very long. He was the local writer and another of the village gentlemen on whom Ella had her eye. His home was Eagles cottage, two minutes away across the street.

Miss Trill forgot Una entirely. 'What a correspondence, Mr Plume, and all to publishers in London! What an exciting life you must lead and no mistake. I shouldn't wonder that one day you'll be the poet laureate, judging by that lovely little poem you penned for Lady Limpet's birthday. She was saying she's having it written out in special script by Mr Marqueson and hung in her library...'

Una left swiftly. She'd already heard enough about Dudley Plume and Mr Marqueson from Ella. Enough to last a lifetime. She could just imagine what a fiasco there'd be if Mr Marqueson wrote it all out in copper plate Gothic and made some awful spelling mistake in the middle. He was that sort of man, the sort who *never* admitted mistakes. It would be the headline of the week in the *Gazette*.

Una simmered slightly. Dudley Plume was only twenty-one and living in luxury in a cottage provided by Lady Limpet, right in the middle of Pover near Tessa Truett's Twinkle Tearooms. Not many people of that age would manage that in a place like this. She gave a deep sad sigh. Maybe it was as well that Robby had gone to Bowden, for it was plain you had to be someone's favourite before you succeeded in Pover. It was common knowledge that Lady Limpet had said Dudley Plume was a genius in embryo who needed nurturing, but most people thought it was a load of codswallop.

Robby had once told her that Dudley Plume claimed to be a very distant relation of the renowned author Mrs Gaskell, who had Manchester connections. But this was only half the tale. This background of literary nobility had caused a great fluttering in Lady Limpet's breast, as she swiftly recalled her own thwarted literary background—a cousin long dead who had once met William Wordsworth and promptly written a seven-verse poem about walking along a leafy lane in Pover and seeing masses of golden dandelions.

Originally, Dudley Plume had come from Navigation Road in Altrincham to

Pover to train as a junior footman with Lady Limpet. It had been a complete disaster. His mind, even at his age, was often on a higher plane.

He drifted round the corridors of Lady Limpet's vast domain at six o'clock each morning, halting clumsily at bedroom doors, carefully replacing expensive, badly polished shoes with black or brown boot polish smeared lavishly round the ankle edges. Many Limpet guests became tight-lipped and brusque as the trademark of the household hospitality appeared indelibly ringletted on their socks and stockings, often seeping through to the actual flesh.

Another time, with childlike energy, he put large quantities of beer instead of a teaspoon of vinegar in the water for cleaning the windows in Lady Limpet's silken boudoir.

'Just you watch how everything sparkles,' said Prudence, a housemaid full of evil intent, as the whole place began to stink like the local taproom of The Perch, Pover's village inn.

He constantly mixed up surnames and titles. He tripped over the two Pekingese and the small spitz Pomeranian every day; and he knocked over so many family treasures they had to have their cracks turned to the walls.

'Why is that Dresden shepherdess always facing the wall?' demanded Lady Limpet with fleeting interest as she whisked past it one day.

What saved Dudley from instant dismissal was Lady Limpet's secret sympathy for his predicament.

'Plume's a square peg in a round hole, Bobbo,' she boomed to her husband, Sir Robert, a man of few words.

From that moment onwards Lady Limpet became a happy woman. She had always been accepted as a champion of budding talent in young males, wherever it chanced to bloom and now here on her own premises she had a dream situation. For among all his gifts Dudley Plume had the ability to play very small tunes on the violin, to her piano accompaniment, and he had a certain, slight leaning towards writing. This last attribute came to light when he wrote Lady Limpet a poem for her birthday, signed: Anon, and on pale mauve note-paper.

With great respect I'm bound to say.
I know these hours are thine in every
way.
For those who serve and those who play
A tune of radiant happiness on thy
Birthday.

Lady Limpet sensed immediately that they had a genius in their midst.

Una was just walking back from the post office when she heard Dudley Plume's footsteps catching up on her. She turned slightly, in no mood for conversation.

'I say, did you hear what she said about Rob Belmane, in the post office,' he said breathlessly.

'I'm Dudley Plume, by the way, I know your sisters a bit. There's one who works for the *Gazette* at Shale, isn't there?'

'She doesn't work there now,' muttered Una, loathe to encourage conversation.

'She was at that meeting when I was the chairman,' babbled Dudley cheerfully. 'It was the first time I'd ever been one. Marqueson was giving one of his talks... Anyhow, what I was going to say was, maybe Belmane could help me out a bit if your father's kicked him out? Sort of general handyman. I've got carte blanche to make Pover into a place of literary interest, with the lost works of Lady Limpet's cousin, Maudley Montgomery the poet. She wants me to compile his works in any way I can and make Pover the landmark it deserves to be.' Dudley blundered on and on.

Una looked at him with horror and

tried to escape by walking more and more quickly.

Eventually he turned back towards his cottage.

'Let me know, anyway,' he shouted, oblivious to her disinterest.

Una ignored him and bent her head as she hurried towards the bus stop to wait for the country bus leading to Melmere.

About a week later when she'd begrudgingly gone back to school and was gradually recovering from all the fuss of Easter, she came back to find a letter waiting for her.

Ella had taken care of it for her. Una snatched at it fearfully. It had an Altrincham post mark and they both knew who it was from.

Robby.

Her colour rose as she opened it feverishly, then hurrying from the room, she dashed upstairs to the secrecy of her bedroom to read and re-read his words.

Hollofern Cottage,
Langham Road
Bowdon, Cheshire

Darling Una,

As you can see, I have moved to my Aunt Beth's. No doubt you will have learnt it all from local tittle-tattle. Unless you saw our Maurice. I have got a job as gardening boy at a big house owned by Meranto's the engineers. They are very nice people and are only a few minutes away. They also want a new tweeny. The last maid has just got married. You wouldn't have to do much at first until you got into it properly, and I'd be there to help you. Let me know what you think...

Una stared at the words and read them for the fourth time. A *tweeny? Her?* Had Robby gone out of his mind? All at once her school days became a haven of important work and essential to her future. No longer was it the awful place she'd grumbled about to Robby when they were both feeling fed up.

To leave it, right now, just to become a maid somewhere? Glory be! It would be a million times worse than being at home! Maids in any house were the lowest of the low. She hadn't been put on earth for *that...*

She carried on reading the letter.

I shall be calling back home. My cousin Jack is lending me his old Tin Lizzy... I will meet you at seven o'clock on Wednesday evening by the kissing gate at Pover Church, and take you back to

Mrs Lockley's at Bowdon to her board and lodgings.

Una was overcome with indecision. She had to meet him, to hear all his news, to see how he was getting on, and to tell him how much she was missing him. Yet she didn't want to go back with him.

And how could she possibly meet him late in the evening? Or even think of leaving home? Everyone would wonder where she was. They would all think something terrible had happened. It was just stupid to disrupt everyone's life to run off and be a maid.

Yet...

All that night she turned restlessly in bed, dreaming muddled dreams and always waking with Robby's plan still in her head. Should she tell anyone about it? Perhaps she should mention it to Chloe? She closed her eyes yet again and tried to rest. Telling anyone, even Chloe, would just add fuel to the fire. This was something she had to deal with entirely on her own. It was the first time she had ever been faced with a decision of such importance.

Wednesday arrived in no time. Father had already advertised locally for someone to take Robby's place and in the end, because there were no suitable youths available as full-time workers he decided to take on two fourteen-year-olds: a girl called Dinky Mitchell, and a boy called Norris Ribs. Both of them already had other work. Plump little Dinky helped her sister Myra in the afternoons at the local hairdressers, while Norris got up at five every morning to help his father with a milk round. They were a motley crew but they were the best Pover had to offer.

By late afternoon on Wednesday Una was wavering in a lather of indecision. Clearly, Robby had no chance of being employed again by her father and returning to Swansdown even if she pleaded for both of them.

With heavy heart she decided to go and meet Robby at the church. The kissing gate was in a secluded spot along a beech hedge, away from the main path. She would tell him she wasn't coming with him.

She lay on her bed and wept silently into her silky green quilt until it was wet with tears. Then she turned and lay motionless, staring at the bedroom ceiling, eventually getting up to go and meet Robby to break the news.

'Where are you going at this time in the evening, Una?'

She was just slipping out by the side door when she heard her father. She stopped in her tracks, heart thudding.

'Haven't you got any work to do? Only a few minutes ago, your mother said she needed you in the kitchen. Where are you off to?'

There was a puzzled frown on his face. She looked away guiltily.

'Just got to go on a message. Shan't be two ticks...' She breathed with relief as he turned away.

Robby was standing there by an ancient, overhanging cedar tree. He moved forward to the small wooden kissing gate, his face alight with joy. He seemed taller and he was wearing a dark grey suit. It wasn't often she saw him in his best clothes.

'Una!' He kissed her longingly. She returned his embrace passionately, clinging to his shoulders and nuzzling his neck, dreading what she was going to say.

He peered round. 'Where've you left your belongings?'

She distanced herself from him and looked at him in bleak misery.

'I haven't got any, Robby. The fact is...'

'Haven't got any?' He was genuinely startled.

'No... You see, I...'

'Don't say you're not coming?' His face became pale with desperation. 'It's all arranged The journey back. The digs at Mrs Lockley's in Bowdon. You can't just stay here after all we've planned.'

'I meant to come, I truly did, but...' she struggled to finish.

'If you don't come with me now, you mark my words, Una, you'll be a slave to this place for ever and ever.' His eyes were blazing with passionate warning.

'Look at the rest of them. Look at your mother. Never saying boo to a goose and forever drowning her sorrows with port and sherry. And your Ella with never a minute of her own, except for that endless knitting. And what about Lindi? Not daring to bring any boyfriends within a mile of the place. Even your Chloe found it so bad she stooped to work for that slimy Cedric Pawson. Surely you don't want to end up like them?'

'It's not *quite* as bad as that, Robby.' Una began to weaken. Everything he'd said was perfectly true. Neither Ella nor Lindi dared to go out courting. And poor Mother was the most restricted of all of them.

Perhaps Swansdown really was no more than a treadmill of misery.

Worst of all was the thought of a life without darling Robby to turn to for consolation. He was staring at her fiercely. She knew it was all or nothing. How could she bear to lose him for ever? It would be like death.

She took a deep breath and made up her mind.

'All right then, I'll come with you, Robby. I'll give it a chance. But you'll have to wait while I get a bag packed, and I'll have to be terribly careful not to be seen. I'll go to our oak tree and meet you there in about half an hour. If I'm not there, you'll just have to keep on waiting. I'll meet you in the end so don't worry.' Her mind was totally made up now.

Robby gave a deep sigh of gladness. 'Thank the Lord you've seen sense, Una. You'll never regret it, I swear.'

She clambered into the little Ford and they parked it along the lane, where the road was at its nearest point to both Swansdown and the mere. It was an open gravelly spot, secluded by huge oak trees and tucked out of view from the hotel.

Una's heart was thumping with nervous terror now as she hurried back to get her belongings. *Please God, don't let anyone see me or stop me... Please let it all work out all right...*

Una sped softly up the small winding back stairs to her bedroom, hoping against hope that none of the others was about. The bedroom door was shut and she hardly dared to open it in case someone was there. Often her mother was in her bedroom, maybe hunting for spare sheets from the old mahogany press, or one of her sisters, borrowing something. But she was in luck as she carefully turned the door knob and found the place to be silent and full of mellow evening light.

Hastily she packed a small suitcase and a rucksack, taking little except essential clothes, nightwear and toiletries. She packed her savings bank book, her only jewellery: a set of proper pearls given to her by Granny Lamby, and her small rather balding, straw-coloured teddy bear Rupert. She left her diary behind. There was no time to dither.

Una hardly dared to breathe as she came down the back stairs again. But she was lucky, and she gave thanks for the cool evening air meeting her once more at the doorway. Una hurried quietly to the carved oak tree, keeping well hidden by the shrubs and bushes along the hotel lawns which led down to the shores of the mere.

She could see Robby, now. He gave her a slight wave as he emerged from the shadows of the tree's huge branches.

'Una! I thought you were *never* coming...'

'I was as quick as I could be...I didn't even have time to leave a note. I hope they don't get upset. I'll have to ring them up when we get to the other end.' Anxiety was flooding her. What on earth was she doing?

She put her suitcase and rucksack down in the long grass, and tried to regain her composure. She was almost crying now. Robby took her in his arms to comfort her.

'It'll be all right, Una. Just you see...'

They clung to each other by the stout tree trunk in the very spot where Robby had carved the heart with their initials. The bandage was still on it. He drew out his penknife impetuously.

'No need for this stupid thing any longer.' Hastily he hacked away at the rag until it fell to the ground and revealed the clearly cut carving. They both looked at it in wonder. It seemed like a million years since the deed was done. Little could they have imagined the trouble that a simple token of love carved on a tree would cause.

Hubert Lamby was feeling restless and upset. Had he just seen that young devil Belmane in a tin lizzy with a girl or hadn't he? Had the swift passing glimpse merely been imagination? Hubert Lamby had managed to keep most of his family round him in constant servitude because he was jealous. They were property to be guarded.

As far as Constance Lamby was concerned, taking to the occasional bottle was by far the easiest way of blotting out Hubert's regime. She knew others who suffered far more than their family did.

'Constance?' His customary bellow echoed about the house.

'Yes? What is it, Hubert?' She looked up at him. She was making coffee in the kitchen, arranging it on silver trays.

'I've just seen Una sloping off somewhere. She said she was going on a message? Surely she should be in here, helping you?'

Constance breathed a small sigh. 'What should and should not be is not always what's happening, dear. Maybe she's gone for a quiet walk. She has lots of homework to get through, so she can't have gone far. She's only a schoolgirl, Hubert. She can't be expected to do quite as much as Ella and Lindi.'

Constance began to measure out some brown sugar crystals for the small white sugar bowls. All the hotel pottery sparkled with a thick serviceable glaze. At one time Constance had loved the kitchen, but now as the stock depleted and breakages accumulated the joy was dissipated by the mounting expense of replacements and refurbishing. Aspects of day-to-day life which seemed to escape Hubert entirely.

'Una's beginning to change, Con.' Hubert glared towards her accusingly. 'She's getting insolent. God forbid that she should become like Chloe. I sense she's getting deceitful. You should never have let Belmane come to her birthday party when I was ill. I can't be sure but I think I saw him near the mere just now in a small car.'

Constance said nothing. She was far too busy to interrupt what she was doing. She was used to being blamed for everything, and in a mild way she could see the funny side. She realised it was quite ludicrous for Hubert to blame her for Una becoming a young woman.

Hubert's voice hardened.

'I hope that young fox Belmane isn't sniffing round here...' He turned away with a huge grunt and plunged out of the kitchen, striding to the back door. His blood pressure was rising by the second, and by the time he got to the stone outhouses near the stables he was in a furious rage. Surely the young devil hadn't had the audacity to set foot in these grounds again? The more he contemplated it, the more the idea grew, until eventually he charged back inside.

His face was expressionless as he climbed the broad, thickly carpeted stairway from the entrance. He stopped on the first landing where the huge arched window with its borders of stained glass lilies looked out towards the mere. A cold hatred rose within him now. From here he could just see the top of the oak tree where Belmane had showed the temerity to carry out the mutilation. In another month its branches would be lost among the fertile leafiness of summer.

Hubert continued to stare. Then, with sudden determination, his face set grey as concrete, he went to his gunroom and taking his shotgun and field glasses, he tramped out of the hotel towards the mere. He stopped some way from the oak tree and looked through the binoculars. He could see Robby, even in this light. Hubert gave a slight shudder. Una was standing with him. She had a suitcase and rucksack close by. His assumptions had been correct. He gripped his shotgun, and with measured steps strolled towards them with studied casualness.

'So what have we here?'

They were both too startled to reply.

Una was overcome with panic and fear. The expression on her father's face was terrifying.

Robby was the first to speak. 'Una and I have arranged to go to Bowdon. We knew you wouldn't approve. She was going to get in touch by phone when we arrived.'

'Shut up!' Hubert began to raise the shotgun in Robby's direction. 'Una, get back home immediately!'

Una stood transfixed.

'Did you hear me?'

She remained frozen, her clothes clinging to her body with cold sweat and her young round face ashen. Hubert took a few paces back, then he levelled the gun directly towards Robby.

'Get going,' he said, with icy determination.

Robby glanced at Una. Then stepping sideways and still facing Hubert he moved towards the bushes then turned and ran full pelt towards the car.

'Robby, wait for me!' Una came to life. Hubert had lowered the gun, but no sooner had she spoken than he raised the gun again and this time the shots from it thundered through the trees. Crows rose from their roosts, cawing and croaking and flooding the darkening skies in disturbed clouds of heavy, flapping wings, as the eerie noise of the gun echoed and gradually subsided.

There was a silence as still as the end of the world.

Hubert Lamby turned towards the house and strode away, ignoring Una completely.

At first she was too shocked to even move. Then, turning slowly towards her luggage she surveyed the scene like someone in a trance. Her suitcase and rucksack had been blasted to hell. Bits of her clothing lay scattered across the ground, and some had even landed in the icy waters of the mere, to be quietly lapped back to the shore. A hairbrush lay in splinters beneath a young sprouting willow. Even her teddy bear was peppered with holes. She sank to the soft damp grass, numbed by grief and shock, unable to even think or move. For some time her brain refused to accept what had happened. Then she heard Robby's voice, seeping through to her consciousness. She was aware of him urging her to get up and go with him, but his voice seemed strangely distant.

'We must move, quickly, Una. He's a madman. It's not safe to go back.' He took her hand and tugged at her. 'Get up. It's our only chance.'

She allowed him to pull her up and drag her swiftly towards the car. A few minutes later with faces like ghosts they were on their way.

She was without a penny and with only the dishevelled grassy, mud-stained clothes she was now wearing, as they arrived, some hours later, at Mrs Lockley's board and lodgings in Bowdon.

CHAPTER 6

The Search

'Gone off with him?'

Chloe could hear Pawson bellowing down the telephone to her father. She was in the small antechamber leading to Cedric Pawson's study which had become her office. The door was ajar. Pawson never cared who heard him on the phone. He was not a secretive, brooding man like Hubert Lamby. At first she didn't take much notice, she was typing. Chloe was used to their constant dialogues. She presumed it was some sort of local gossip. Perhaps her father was complaining that two of the guests had eloped and taken all the hotel towels? Everything was repeated to Cedric.

'You did *what?*' Suddenly, Pawson sounded genuinely alarmed. 'What a bloody stupid thing to do. I'll be over there right away. When was it? The little swine!' Pawson swore under his breath and hung up the telephone. He came striding into her small office. Chloe had never seen him so upset.

'Just off to your place, Chloe.' He knocked the soft grey ash from his cigar into a heavy, lead crystal ashtray. 'Hubert's had a spot of bother with that young devil Belmane and your fair sister, The Lady Una...' He gave a derisory snort.

Chloe's heart jolted. What on earth had happened?

The minute he'd gone she phoned through to Ella. 'Yes. Cedric's on his way right now, Ella. Whatever's been going on?'

Ella's account confirmed her worst fears.

'Father fired his gun and ripped her luggage to shreds, Chloe. We heard the shots from the hotel; it was dreadful. Lindi's out there right now, still picking up the bits. Constable Broadacre came round from the police station, but Father told him there was nothing to worry about, that the gun had gone off accidentally. Goodness knows who spread the news. It certainly wasn't us.'

'So where's Una now, then?' Chloe gripped the phone with sudden tension.

'She rang us late last night. She's in lodgings. I hope I've got the right address. It's Bowdon...I've got the main details. She hasn't any belongings. She mumbled something about borrowing a nighty, poor child. She sounded awful. We're all tiptoeing around here, and Father has locked himself in his dressing room. Is there any chance you might manage to find her Chloe? Maybe take her some clothes and some money?'

There was a moment's silence. Chloe's brain was in a whirl. Would Pawson let her go? She needed to keep her job.

'I'll see if I can manage something when Cedric comes back, Ella. I'll give you another ring.'

Hubert heard Cedric's voice, and Cedric's sharp, irritable tap on his dressing-room door. He opened it immediately with a murmur of relief.

Cedric sat down close to Hubert. The stuffing of the high-backed mahogany chair bulged up through the frayed, faded tapestry. They both gazed towards the cast-iron fireplace. Hubert spoke first.

'What the hell do I do next? The threats didn't do an atom of good. She went off with the little blighter. But believe me, if he ever comes a step near here again in my lifetime, the gun'll be ready for its true work!'

'The main thing is to get her back as soon as possible, Hubie,' said Pawson calmly. 'You'll always have trouble in the offing while she's stuck away from home at her age. Even the best of 'em can slip. And if she's going to do that, better it's at this end with someone decent.' Pawson shrugged.

'I've *got* to get her back, Ced. She'll not be too fond of me after what happened, and the others haven't the time to fetch her. They've got this place to run. It's chaos at the moment. Constance is beside herself with shock, and there's that race meeting due...'

Pawson stood up and patted Hubert's shoulders.

'Don't worry too much, old boy. I'll send Chloe off on a reccy and she can report back. No need to look so disagreeable. She's extremely efficient. I shall hang on to her like grim death.'

Hubert gave a wan smile. He felt slightly better now. They began to discuss the horses and twenty minutes later they were both their normal selves, with Pawson warning Hubert on the pitfalls of gambling.

'Wormwood Scrubs isn't for you, old mate. But that's where you'll land up if you go too far into the mire...'

Chloe was on tenterhooks when she heard Pawson arriving back at Grangebeck. When would be the best time to approach him about going to see Una?

It seemed like hours before he came into her office, although only minutes had elapsed. She stared up at him from her small upright chair and stopped typing. Today he looked quite handsome. It was a pity he'd split with Tessa Truett. They were two of a kind. Both as hard-boiled as blazes, but quite charming when the need arose.

She wished she could be like that—able to switch the charm on and off at exactly the right time—but it wasn't in her nature. She tried to smile at him encouragingly, to broach the subject of Una, but she was forestalled.

'You can leave all that stuff you're typing, Chloe. I want you to get yourself away to Bowdon immediately and see what's going on. Ella had the details, she read them out to us.'

Had she heard right? He and Father must have agreed upon it. Pawson felt in his pocket and drew out a wad of bank notes. He handed her three five-pound notes.

'That's for expenses, just in case you have to stay overnight. The point is, Chloe, I don't want to see you back here without Una by your side. Understand?' The warmth of his charm evaporated and he fixed her with a cold, piercing gaze.

For a few seconds she was astounded by both the amount of money and the suddenness of his instructions. But she quickly recovered and answered quickly.

'Yes, yes, of course. I'll go straightaway.'

'And if you have any trouble with Belmane, let me know immediately by telephone.' Then, to her absolute astonishment, he added, 'I'll drive you to Altrincham station right now, then leave you to do the rest. No need to mention my name in all this. Just do your best, as Una's sister.' He narrowed his eyes slightly and a glimmer of a smile caught the sides of his mouth.

'Off you go then... Get some things together.'

Chloe hurried to her room and packed a small valise, just in case she should have to stay over. The whole episode was taking on a much more important role now. She felt a sudden shiver of unease at the way it was turning out. Was she becoming a sort of travelling wardress for Pawson, bringing back poor Una like some delinquent prisoner? And what about poor old Robby? When all said and done it was Father who was really to blame for it all. He had behaved abominably.

The huge silver-grey car came to a standstill on the half-moon of cobblestone outside Altrincham railway station. Pawson gave Chloe a cursory wave with his neatly gloved hand as she set off towards Bowdon Downs on foot. Her heart was filled with gnawing fear.

Una's address at Mrs Lockley's board and lodgings was folded into a small square and resting in the palm of her own gloved hand. She knew the address off by heart now, including the whereabouts of the Merantos' massive house, where Robby was working as a gardener. It was nearly four o'clock. Most people would be starting to settle down for afternoon tea. She could see now why Pawson had thrust the money at her, for there was no way she was going to be able to return tonight, unless by some chance Una agreed to come with her immediately.

She swallowed nervously as she walked on. Things never turned out as she hoped, and she was quite apprehensive about her meeting with Una. Sisters or not, Una could slam the door on her, and she was concerned about what might happen if she returned to Cedric empty handed.

She plodded her way up the long hall, wondering where to start. Perhaps Hollofern Cottage, the home of Robby's Aunt Beth, would be best. At least Robby would know she was here, and maybe she could find out the situation from his aunt. Chloe prayed to herself that his Aunt Beth would be in. She didn't even know her surname.

It took her far, far longer than she'd imagined to reach the cottage in Langham

Road. It was a very old place with rosy, slightly crumbled-looking brickwork, and small paned, leaded windows. There was a faded green front door with a heavy iron knocker shaped like the head of a lion.

The house came right up to the roadside. Small borders of marigolds and Virginia stock lined either side of the door and a bit of purple clematis was festooned up a rickety, wooden trellised porch. Inside the porch, little wooden seats were set on either side of the door.

Gingerly, Chloe raised the enormous door knocker. It gave one loud clonk, and she stood back expectantly in the warm mellow teatime sunshine.

The woman who answered the door looked sharply into Chloe's anxious face.

'Yes?' She was tall and gaunt, with very short frizzy ginger hair. Her thick lisle stockings were wrinkled and her florid red and yellow cotton dress added extra heat to the afternoon.

'Excuse me, but are you Robby's Aunty Beth?'

'Mi' name's *Miss Brimstone*, if you please. And what's it to you, if I am? Who might you be, anyway?'

Hastily Chloe began to explain the situation as tactfully as she could.

'It's nowt to do wi' me,' said Miss Brimstone acidly. 'But I'll mention you called. What was the name again?'

'Lamby—Chloe Lamby.' Then Chloe added, with all hope draining away, 'You don't by any chance know of any lodgings round here, do you?'

Beth Brimstone's face relaxed slightly. 'I don't know if Mrs Lockley's got owt?' She nodded towards some houses on the opposite side of the road. 'That place painted brown and cream, with the purple curtains and the cracked chimney pot. But I know nowt about owt where she's concerned.' She closed the door quickly.

A new surge of optimism swept through Chloe. A few minutes later she had climbed the three donkey-stoned front steps and rung the bell. Through the large, decorated door panel in the top of the door, she could see the blurred figure of an elderly servant waddling towards her to open it. The door swung open revealing a gloomy interior of brown oil cloth and the slight odour of tom cats.

The servant's complexion was mauve and her starched white cap was level with her eyebrows. Her hair was iron grey and cut off in a basin shape, along the tips of her ears.

'Yes love?'

'I came to enquire about lodgings for the night...' Chloe felt like fleeing. What a place to be. Her heart bled for Una.

132

'Miss Brimstone across the road said you might...'

'Just a minute, chucky. I'll see the mistress.'

A few moments later Mrs Lockley appeared. She was a huge woman in a voluminous, artificial silk afternoon dress with a lace inset, where stray biscuit crumbs rested across her bust cleavage. 'Was it just for one night?'

Chloe nodded.

'I do 'ev *won* small room. Will you want meals? Eye tea's at six-thirty. The beds all 'as one feather pillow and one flock. There's Doulton chamber-pots under all beds and the bathroom is on't second floor. It'll cost three and six if you 'as this boxroom, but keep your eye ont' mouse trap int' corner with bare feet. If you wants summat better you could 'ave a bed ont' first floor with its own wash basin, double bed, satin quilt and morning tea. But it'll be very dear.'

Chloe hesitated. Should she take the dear one? She had more than enough money from what Cedric had given her. But on the other hand, what a waste if it turned out to be as bad as the boxroom. Anyway, she wasn't afraid of mice.

'I'll take the boxroom,' she said quickly.

She followed Mrs Lockley inside, and signed the visitor's book on the hall table.

It was next to a large Bible, and on the wall above it was a framed, illuminated script which said:

There is a charge of sixpence for use of the hot water geyser in the bathroom. Spittoons can be hired from the store cupboard.
SWEARING IS BANNED IN THIS ESTABLISHMENT.
Isabella Murgatroyde Lockley

'Show her where to go, Franny,' said Mrs Lockley to the old servant.

'This way, love.' Chloe followed her as Franny laboured slowly and painfully up two flights of stairs to the boxroom. Lined with rumbling water pipes, it had a very small window overlooking a high brick wall. There was a photograph of a man in uniform on the wall, and the black iron grate was stuffed with faded red paper. The jug and basin on the washstand had ancient discoloured chips round the edges, as if even the mice had become desperate.

'Eye-tea is brawn and salad today,' said Franny. 'Would you be wanting it?'

'Yes, please.' Chloe hesitated and then she added, 'Do you happen to have any other young ladies staying here?'

Franny gazed at her solemnly with bulging, pale blue eyes. 'Oh no, Ma'am.

134

Not now we 'asn't. We'ad Miss Chol-
mondley, till last week, but she went back
'ome with an attack of the gripes.'

Chloe's heart sank. 'You haven't got a
Miss Una Lamby here, then?'

Franny wrinkled her brow. 'Oh no,
Miss... It's mostly gents we 'as 'ere.'

'Are you *sure?* She's a very young, rather
pretty girl with her hair in a long plait.
She was supposed to have arrived here last
night.' Chloe's face fell and she struggled
to keep the panic from her voice. What on
earth could have happened?

Then slowly Franny said, 'There was
some talk about last night, Miss. But it was
my day off, see? A young lady arrived in a
very bad state, but Mrs Lockley sent her
away. She never takes in girls who might
be street walkers or look troublesome. She
sent her to Mrs Prinn's in Altrincham at
the Twa Ducks Inn. Mrs Prinn's not so
perticaler.'

Chloe went white with the implied insult
to Una, but Franny went on, unperturbed.

'From what was told to me, Mrs Lockley
let 'er use the telephone first to get in
touch with 'er sick father who'd just shot
'isself in this country nursing 'ome. But
Lotty who told me always lards things
up so it might not be quite the truth.
Anyways, Mrs Lockley lent 'er a nighty
left by someone else. Then she shunted

135

'er off to Ma Prinn's.'

Franny stopped for breath, then said, 'I'll put you down for Eye-tea, then?'

When she'd gone Chloe flopped down on the lumpy bed. Poor Una. What an awful muddle. She lay there miserably, trying to think of what to do next. Should she call back at Miss Brimstone's, in the hope of seeing Robby? Or should she go straight to Mrs Prinn's?

After much deliberating, she decided it was best to get along to Mrs Prinn at the Twa Ducks as soon as possible. Her energy flooded back to her as she hurried to the small dining room.

After a watery cup of tea and a questionable-looking meal she set off.

The Twa Ducks was a small, plain-looking place but well patronised. There was a piano inside and they had four rooms for let. She went round the back and eventually found Mrs Prinn, a beady, bird-like woman with thin sinewy arms. She was dressed in black sateen and had her brown hair tied back in an untidy bun.

'Your sister has her young man visiting her at present, Miss Lamby. Wait here and I'll tell them you've arrived.'

A few minutes later she was back, nodding her head cheerfully. 'That's all right, Miss Lamby. They say you can go and see them. I'll show you the room.'

Chloe followed her upstairs with her heart thumping.

Mrs Prinn turned the small black knob on the painted wooden door.

'Your sister is here,' she announced grandly to Una, and she hurried away.

They were sitting in matching green wicker armchairs. Una looked tired and pale, and Robby had a defiant expression. 'So who sent you?' he said without ceremony.

'I'm not going back with you, Chloe,' Una interrupted quickly, beginning to look tearful. 'It's been bad enough escaping from Father, I could never, ever return now. I'd sooner die.' She reached out for Robby's hand and clasped it.

'Shh... Don't take on so,' said Robby, trying to soothe her.

The more Chloe looked at them the more she realised it was essential to get Una back home to some sort of normality.

'I'm staying at Mrs Lockley's, Una.' She turned towards Robby. 'I visited your aunt, Miss Brimstone.'

Except for a goods train rattling and clanking its trucks in the far distance there was complete silence.

Then Robby said, 'You won't be able to see Una tomorrow. She starts work at Meranto's early in the morning as a new tweeny. We'll be there together. I'm working there in the garden on shifts. She'll be living in. I've arranged it with Mrs Meranto.' He stroked Una's hand gently. 'You'll soon be happy again, Una. just you see.' He spoke to her as if she were a child.

Chloe looked at them both again. She was only a year older than Una but at this moment she felt she must be as old as Granny Lamby. They looked so vulnerable and so alone here in this humble-looking, bare bedroom.

Surely Robby wouldn't have... Surely, not yet at their age? Chloe was still a virgin herself and hoped to remain one until she married. She hastily tried to blot out her thoughts about Una's virginity. Una was too much of an innocent child to be left like this.

Oh yes, there were hundreds of young girls wandering round Manchester in a far worse condition, but often these girls became tough and callous. It wasn't what anyone would have wanted for Una, or any child who came from a decent family.

'You go home, Chloe. I swear to you I'll be quite all right. I'll write to you at Grangebeck and tell you all the things I'll need to get on with my life here. Robby's brother can come across with them. Tell Mother not to worry. It'll all work out.'

Opening her small handbag Chloe took

ten pounds from the money Cedric had given her.

'Take this, Una. Just to be going on with.' She thrust the money across to her sister.

With tear-filled eyes Una hugged her sister gratefully as they parted. And for one awful second, as they put their arms round each other, it seemed as if Una wanted Chloe to stay forever.

That night when Chloe was back in the boxroom at Mrs Lockley's she tossed and turned in the uncomfortable bed, racking her brains for the best path to take.

How could she possibly admit to Una that Cedric Pawson had provided the money to bring her back home to Melmere? Chloe realised now that Una would never again be able to fulfil the role of best-loved diligent schoolgirl daughter—particularly after the way Father had so brutally treated her.

On the other hand, something inside Chloe persisted with the idea that in order to blossom, Una needed to be back at Melmere. It was the only place where she could make up her own mind in peace and quiet about what she really wanted to do.

But where could she stay?

Una would never again want to enter Swansdown while Father was still there, and it was ludicrous to expect her to stay at Pawson's. Chloe was well aware of Cedric's wolfish intentions. But Pawson's will was as strong as steel when he saw the need to assert himself. He would never need to use a gun for he knew dozens of more civilised ways to get his own way...

The following morning, Chloe was up and ready to leave after breakfast. She walked to Altrincham post office and sent Cedric Pawson a telegram. It said: ARRIVING BACK BY BUS TODAY ALONE STOP CHLOE STOP.

As she waited for the bus back home she smiled sadly to herself and sighed. Surely she was the worst person in the world at rescuing people...

CHAPTER 7

June

Una bought herself a summer frock to wear for her interview with Mrs Meranto the next morning. She went to a small drapers at the Polygon in Bowdon as soon as the shops opened. Costing twelve and sixpence the frock was of pale blue cotton, and she bought some salmon pink stockings and a straw hat to go with it. She set off from the shop wearing her new finery. Her mud-stained belongings from her escape from Swansdown were left behind for the dust-bin collection.

The Merantos were a very rich family. Their engineering and organisational skills had been used in armaments manufacturing since the nineteenth century, before the Boer War. These days they were known as 'progressive' and liberal minded. The staff they employed at their vast home in Bowdon, which was sheltered from curious eyes by tall pine trees and larches, were treated fairly.

Una remembered delving into a rather forward-looking book which Mother had bought secretly to give to Ella. The book stressed that the efficiency of the servant depended on the understanding and kindness of the mistress. Understanding and loyalty were the watchwords. The book had gone on to point out the mutual interest of both servant and mistress in keeping the house beautiful, explaining that the servant was as much a craftsman as a writer or painter. The servant was responsible for bringing peace, well being and happiness to the home.

It was urged therefore that the good servant should have, if possible, one whole free day off per month, and be allowed a few simple pastimes such as reading or sewing in the afternoons, in between answering bells and carrying out household duties.

The moment Mrs Meranto opened her mouth it was obvious she had that same book on her shelves.

'We are all engaged in the task of running this house,' she said with bright eyes and a wonderfully radiant smile. 'There is no sense in quarrelling or bullying each other. No servant is of a lower order these days. The idea is preposterous. Your wages will be ten shillings a week to start off, and full board.'

Una nodded timidly.

'I believe you're from Pover, where young Robby comes from? Have you been in service before? Robby said little about your background but I know that country girls are always reliable. Did you leave school at thirteen?'

'I didn't leave very long ago,' said Una quietly, feeling more and more ashamed. 'There was no longer room for me at home. My father...'

Mrs Meranto stood up and put a gentle hand on her shoulder.

'There, there my dear. No need to say any more. We all know what it's like coping in a small cottage with growing children and many mouths to feed. I'm sure you'll be very happy here, and one day, you never know, if you work hard...you might become something as grand as head cook or housekeeper. Or even marry the butler!'

Una laughed politely. She knew Mrs Meranto meant well.

'I will introduce you to our housekeeper, Mrs Pepper. She will guide your work and keep you under her wing. She will give you a form to complete with your name, address and age, and your parents or guardians will have to sign it. And she will read out to you our Badge of House Loyalty about not spreading gossip or lies whilst you are in our services. If all is satisfactory with your form, you will be allowed to start work in a week's time as a tweeny.'

Una was taken aback. She hadn't realised she would need to have a consent form signed by a parent or guardian. Mrs Meranto left the room quickly and Una was joined immediately by Mrs Pepper who took her to the servants' quarters. In a small sitting room, she produced one of the forms to fill in.

Una sat there on a tough, black horse-hair chair and stared at it.

'You can use either pen and ink or copy-ink pencil, according to what suits you best, Miss. I advise the copy-ink in case you makes ink blobs on the table cover. We have to pay towards anything we damage. We leave pen and ink for the butler, and more important things.' She handed Una a short purple copy-ink pencil. It was very blunt and Una was tempted to wet it with her tongue, but she knew the awful purple tongue that would result.

She wrote her name in a large uncouth scrawl as the hard blunt pencil skidded about on the paper in deep indentations.

'Una Sanby. Perch Cottage. Pover Lanes. Pover.' Miss Pepper read it out aloud slowly. Although Pover had a pub called The Perch, there was no Perch cottage. But it all sounded possible.

Mrs Pepper seemed well satisfied with everything. 'We has to get the permission, Miss. Mrs Meranto insists. You're still a child really, even if you is sixteen. But don't worry about it. Get your Pa to sign it. Even if he can only mark a cross on it. All being well, we'll hope to see you with us next Monday morning.'

Una said goodbye and walked towards the long winding drive. However was she going to get permission from Father? And what was she going to do for a whole week? She still had just over nine pounds left of Chloe's money, which meant she could stay on at the Twa Ducks, but supposing she had to wait a long time before she got her first wages from the Merantos? God forbid if she was paid quarterly, like some places she'd heard of.

They hadn't mentioned anything like that at the interview; she'd have to ask Robby. Granted she would have the benefit of board and lodgings, but it meant she was virtually a slave if she had no actual money. Did she really want to work as a maid? This was what Chloe had escaped from when she first went to work at the *Gazette,* what her sisters did every single day at the hotel.

Una slowed her pace as she walked along. It was one of those warm, still June days with clear skies. Proud blue and cream lupins stood undisturbed, passively accepting the visits of softly buzzing bees in steady sunshine. Birds rustled amiably in the motionless bushes.

Suddenly there was the sound of a wheelbarrow on the gravel. Una looked towards the greenhouses and saw Robby. She hurried across to him, her face wreathed with smiles of relief.

He kissed her warmly. 'How did you get on? Let's go over by those white rhododendrons where we can't be seen.'

She quickly told him about needing parental consent to work.

'How can I possibly get that, Robby? I thought you said that I'd be able to start work today, but it's not so. There's a week to wait, and Father's signature to get. The whole thing's hopeless.' She looked at him with despair in her eyes. 'I gave the housekeeper a false address. Perch Cottage, in Pover. And I changed my name to Sanby, for safety's sake. Even if it is a bit dishonest.' She spoke quickly, frightened and desperate for reassurance.

Robby frowned slightly and wiped some sweat from his forehead. Then he said with a touch of irony, 'You're getting as bad as me, Una. You only need to write your father's signature as Sanby and we'll be quits.'

She stared at him in horror. 'I could never, never do that! It would haunt me forever.' There was silence as they stared at the gardens.

'Anyway,' said Robby lightly. 'I'll have to get moving or they'll think I'm swinging the lead. I'll see you tonight at the pub and we'll arrange summat.'

She waved to him as she reached the drive again, but he had already turned away. As she left the huge iron gates of Meranto's, Una felt an emptiness she had never known before. What should she do now? If she had been at home there would have been so many occupations—gazing at the swans on the mere included. She began to feel terribly homesick, and she had hardly been away two days.

'What was the general state of affairs then?' asked Cedric Pawson amiably, when Chloe arrived back. 'I noticed there was no urgent request for me to bring both of you home?'

Chloe didn't waste words. 'Una refused, point blank, to move. How can anyone blame her, after the way Father treated her? At least we'll know where she is, working at Meranto's.'

'Meranto's?' Cedric glared at her sharply. 'What on earth is she going to do there?'

'I—I'm not quite sure,' faltered Chloe, 'but they're supposed to be very nice people.'

'Very "nice" people? What the devil does that mean? Surely she isn't going slumming for them at her age? Believe me, Chloe, I know all about that side of life.'

Looking at his gold watch, he muttered, 'If you get any calls, I've gone over to see your father.'

Chloe sighed to herself and settled down in the office to catch up with her work. She felt completely unsettled after seeing Una and Robby.

The phone rang and she unhooked the receiver with trepidation. She was relieved to hear Margie Renshaw's cheerful voice.

'It's really to invite you to Oliver's

christening, Chloe. I don't seem to have heard from you for ages—but thank you for the lovely card you sent. It's been one mad rush ever since, and he's getting huge. Is Cedric still chasing you round with the whip?' She hesitated jokingly, then her tone changed. 'They're saying in Pover post office that Una's eloped with Robby Belmane.'

'It's a complicated tale, Margie. She's in Altrincham at present, but we all want her to come back. And yes, I'd adore to come to the christening.' They chatted on for a few more minutes.

Then Margie said, 'Mac Haley will be coming. He's always asking after you.'

Mac Haley asking after her. Chloe replaced the receiver with a sudden rush of curious, pulsing feelings. She was half pleased and half saddened, for Mac Haley was the only man with whom she'd ever felt completely at home. He was one of those people you could go to the end of the world with, and be protected forever. She had loved him desperately from the moment she'd met him at the *Gazette*.

He'd been so cheerful and helpful, and so concerned that she should enjoy working there. At first he'd seemed startlingly handsome, with his short dark curly hair and sudden quirky smile. His face was brimming with constant enthusiasm and his grey eyes were as sharp as needles as he worked away with pencil and pen. Oh, how she had loved him from afar, knowing that he always had his own women friends in the background.

She sat at her desk in Cedric's office, considering Mac's engagement to Myra Mitchell. To be quite fair, it was obviously a good and happy match. Myra was a person who everybody liked and she had an outgoing personality. She wore outrageously bright colourful clothes: Red and cream silk striped frocks and Georgette blouses with low necks and huge ruffles. The sort of clothes Chloe would never have dared to put on. In fact as the months went by Chloe realised she was getting drabber and drabber in her navy blue dresses with their small white Peter Pan collars.

With a sudden restless spurt of energy, she picked up the telephone again and dialled home. 'Lindi, it's me.'

'Hello, Chloe?'

'No need to sound so anxious, Lindi. But you know how you said you'd come with me if I was ever thinking of joining any of those rambling club outings? Well, I've decided to go on one set for a whole weekend in the Lake District in two weeks' time. Margie Renshaw is sending me details and enrolment forms to join!'

'Just like that? What will Pawson say? But, good for you all the same!'

'I don't care what he says. Even if he's awkward I shall go and see what happens. So why don't you do the same with Father at your end? Just tell him you're going with me and see what happens.'

'A marvellous idea! I feel ready for a showdown. I'm at explosion pitch at the moment.' Lindi's voice was alive with happy enthusiasm. 'You get it all worked out and I'll be there.'

Chloe replaced the receiver for the second time with a sudden glow of happiness. Something positive to look forward to at last. Her face flushed momentarily. And, maybe, maybe she'd have a sight of Mac Haley again, even if he was with Myra. It was the weekend before the christening of Margie's baby son, too. So there was a chance that she might meet him *twice*. Chloe stood up fully and went to make herself a cup of coffee. For the time being Una was forgotten.

By the time Cedric had been at Swansdown for five minutes, Hubert had begun to change colour. Perhaps it was the onset of one of his attacks, but whatever the cause Cedric Pawson's news of Una going to work as a common skivvy in someone else's establishment sent his face an ugly dull scarlet.

'Sometimes I give up completely, where women are concerned,' he said, head buried in hands. 'How could any schoolgirl want to go off with a dishonest little tyke like Belmane?'

'Perhaps because she was threatened by her father with a gun?' suggested Cedric casually. 'I must say I wouldn't take too kindly to having my suitcase blasted to bits. But it's all over and done with now. The main thing is to try and get her back home and settled down again, Hubie.' Pawson's voice was soft and reassuring now. 'Chloe did her best, but it didn't seem to be quite good enough.'

Hubert nodded grudgingly. 'I was a bit of a bloody fool. But *you've* never had to suffer life with a house full of women and all the nonsense that comes with it.'

Cedric had heard this lament many times before and he hastily made his exit.

Driving back to Grangebeck Manor, Cedric had a satisfied expression on his smoothly shaved face. His plans for Una's return were already taking shape. He could guarantee that once she was back and provided with some cosy little occupation, like helping Dudley Plume with his literary research, all this present business would be forgotten. Especially if he encouraged young Marcus Oliphant to take her out occasionally. Marcus had no option but to keep well in with Cedric, for there was the little matter of an unpaid debt...

Una had survived three more days of the week which lay ahead of her, before she was to begin work for the Merantos. It hadn't been half as bad as she'd imagined.

The weather was so good she had spent one day out at Castle Mills open-air bathing pool with Patty Moor, the newly married sister of one of her friends from school. Una had met her quite by chance in Manchester, and Patty had taken pity on her.

'I must say, Una, it was a terrible shock to hear you'd run off with Robby. Selina just couldn't get over it. And you were doing so well at school, too.' Una grimaced at the speed with which gossip from Pover travelled.

Her day out cheered her up enormously. She still hadn't signed the permission form and the thought of it lurked, unwelcome, at the back of her mind.

Finally she forced herself to face the issue. She drew the form from her pocket and stared at the dotted line. What had Mrs Pepper said? A cross would be acceptable if her father was unable to sign his name. Well, a cross it would be. With that decision made, Una found pen and ink and carefully scrawled a slightly wobbly cross. At least no one could accuse her of an actual forgery of her father's signature or the use of a false surname if it was ever found out. Then, to make it more authentic, she decided to go to Knutsford on the bus, and post the form back from there. She knew Knutsford well, and it was just far enough away from Melmere and Pover to avoid coming face to face with anyone she knew.

The weather was warm and wet. The red and cream single-decker bus trundled its way along lush emerald country lanes, thick with rain-dappled foliage and dripping greenery. People in the village lanes round King Street in Knutsford sheltered beneath large bobbing umbrellas. The wonderful aroma of baking hung in the air, and Una bought a small balm cake from one of the cakeshops.

After posting the envelope, she walked across to the village green and sat in the rain munching it. She ate very slowly for the snack had to last until she got back. Her money was dwindling dangerously.

At first, she did not hear the voice beneath the black umbrella, or even see the Burberry raincoat advancing towards

153

her. She didn't realise it was Cedric, even when he sat down next to her.

'Una! You're drenched. Come and dry out a bit and have a cup of coffee.'

She frowned back. 'How did you guess I'd be here?'

'I didn't. I'd just parked the car when I saw you coming in on that bus...'

'So you followed me...' She tried to look angry but her heart was racing and she began to tremble.

'Seems like it, doesn't it?' A spark of amusement lit his eyes. 'You seem to be setting the whole of Pover in an uproar. Chloe was saying that you never want to come back again? A bit drastic, don't you think?'

She looked away from him silently. A mixture of hate and heartache swamped her completely and tears came to her eyes. All she wanted now was to have someone on whom she could lean. Someone to carry her safely home to Melmere with the whole awful episode completely forgotten.

Sensing her distress, Cedric gently slid his arm round her and she suddenly collapsed against him, sobbing and burying her face in his thick damp coat with its lingering odour of cigar smoke. She found it oddly reassuring. He sat there silently as she regained her composure. Then he spoke.

'Come on, child. Let's get a proper meal.'

Hors d'oeuvres, fresh salmon, custard flan, fresh fruit, cheese and biscuits. Una demolished it all, and soon she was smiling happily, replete in a world quite alien to one in which meals were comprised of a solitary balm cake.

'I'll run you back to where you're staying,' said Cedric, with calculated casualness. 'It won't take long.' She tried to protest but the words wilted on her lips. She had no return ticket for the bus. He had saved her skin.

'So you've decided to work for Meranto's?' he said, as they drove back. 'When do you start?'

'Next Monday.' She was terrified he'd ask her about parental permission, but he didn't seem to notice.

'How will you manage financially?' She stared hard at the dashboard of the car.

'I shall probably have to ask Chloe for a loan...'

'Good idea.' He didn't say any more, but took her right to the Twa Ducks, and waved slightly as she got out of the car. He drove away swiftly.

'Who on earth was that, love? The Lord Mayor?' said Mrs Prinn.

'A man my father knows.' Una changed the subject quickly. 'Has Robby called?'

'He's waiting in your room, dear. He was just at the point of leaving.'

'Where the heck have you been,' Robby glowered as she burst into the room. 'I've been hanging around for ages.'

'I went on the bus to Knutsford to post the employment consent form back to Meranto's.'

Robby looked at her suspiciously. 'Whatever made you do that? You could easily have passed it on to me when you'd signed it. Do you want to come back with me to Aunty Beth's? I said I'd bring you for some supper. We'll be really late now and she hates people being late.' Robby sounded petulant.

'I'm sorry...' Suddenly Una felt tired. All she wanted was to lie down and rest. She began to wish Robby hadn't been waiting for her.

'Come on then,' he grabbed her hand. 'Don't just stand there.'

'There is boiled ham in the meat safe,' said the message scrawled on the back of an old envelope on the kitchen table. 'Help yourselves to tomatoes—jelly in the cellar, cream in the covered jug. Gone to my Bible class.'

Una was glad she was out. Together they prepared their meal and Robby wolfed down everything. Una wasn't quite so hungry after her marvellous meal at Knutsford with Cedric Pawson.

Robby wanted to just sit there on the sofa and fondle her, but she wasn't in the mood.

'I'm not just a doll to be played with, Robby.' She snapped out the words suddenly and stood up hastily. It was the first time in her life she had ever spoken to him like that.

'Going to Knutsford doesn't seem to have done you any good. Did you go on your own?'

'Go on my own? Of course I did. How could it possibly be otherwise?'

'Sorry—but it seemed such a silly, time-wasting thing to do.'

Una was puzzled. She had never realised how different they were in their views until she'd come to Altrincham. They had been twin souls in Melmere, but here they were chalk and cheese.

'How else would I spend my time with no money and no job until next week?'

'What about the sister of your pal at school? Couldn't you have gone to see her instead?'

He was just being awkward and deliberately argumentative.

'Take me back to the pub, Robby. I'll have an early night...'

'But it won't be dark till late, and the

rain's gone. Fancy wasting a beautiful June night. Let's go to the park for a game of clock golf and watch the bowls.'

Reluctantly she agreed to go, and by the time they were there she was enlivened by the friendly atmosphere. Free cups of tea were being handed round in honour of the park attendant's daughter's birthday and there were small, brightly coloured Japanese lanterns hanging in the trees.

The evening air was awash with romantic music as everyone joined in the chorus of 'Goodnight Sweetheart', played on a gramophone. Couples danced cheek to cheek on a small wooden square set on the nearby grass. The evening flew by, and soon the gentle, somnolent dusk took over.

'Somehow it's as if we were both back in Melmere,' murmured Robby, as they roamed together, arms entwined. 'Oh, if only it could all be what it was before...before he...'

Una put a finger to Robby's lips. 'We must just forget the worst bits. It'll be much better when I start work at Meranto's, then we'll be truly together again.' Her words were gentle, heartfelt, but inside she ached for the childhood world she had lost—the life she had taken so much for granted as she flinched from what might lie ahead. But her feelings were disguised by the loyal, warm smile on her face.

Robby gazed at her with unbridled joy as they wandered back along the country lanes. Neither of them took any account of time. The night was clear now and in the bright glow of the moon they drifted back into Altrincham, oblivious to everything except each other.

But when they reached the Twa Ducks, the place was like a silvery tomb. Not a soul moved and every door and window was shut tight.

'Don't you have a key, Una?'

She shook her head as a distant clock struck one.

'One o'clock in the morning... Whatever shall we do?'

'You'd better come back with me to Aunt Beth's,' said Robby. They both felt weak with longings of love. All they really wanted to do was lie out under the stars, clasped together for ever.

When they finally reached the cottage it was nearly two. The night had cooled and the walk had sobered them.

'You'd better take my bed, and I'll sleep downstairs on the couch,' whispered Robby, as they crept inside.

Early the following morning Una awoke to a terrible racket.

'You mean *she* is up there? In *your* bed? What on earth's come over you.

You'd better get off to work. It's nearly seven o'clock. Leave her to me.' Miss Brimstone's voice echoed up the stairs.

Una heard the door slam and then there was silence. She jumped up quickly, dressing and making the bed. Suddenly there were two loud knocks on Miss Brimstone's door. The dustmen had arrived to collect an old iron bedstead from round the back and as Miss Brimstone dealt with them, Una made her move.

Like lightning she was down the stairs, out of the front door and away down the hill before anyone could say Jack Robinson.

'Whatever happened to you, love?' said Mrs Prinn kindly. 'Did you decide to sleep at Robby's? P'raps I'd better give you a key for the last few days.'

Una nodded and settled down to breakfast. In a strange way she was glad to be back.

'I'll charge you one night less, dearie,' said Iris Prinn confidentially.

Una smiled. Perhaps things really weren't so bad after all.

Cedric Pawson had just finished his breakfast and was sipping his morning coffee. As soon as he'd returned from Knutsford, he'd called in to see Hubert at Swansdown.

160

'God knows what she was doing trailing round there on a wet day, but one thing's clear Hubie, you need to get her home as soon as possible.' Cedric had been more shaken by Una's tears than he cared to admit.

'She'll never come back here again,' said Hubert morosely. 'It's ruined her mother's life. If ever I see that young monster Belmane, the bullet'll hit him right between the eyes!'

'How would it be if I tried to find her digs in Pover village, Hubie? At least she'd be closer to home.'

Hubert shrugged and turned away. To his mind he'd been deserted by all his women. Chloe avoided him, Una was on the loose, and as if that wasn't enough, Ella had been out twice to archaeological lectures with Marqueson's son Monty who was estranged from his wife, and lived at home. And Lindi was twinned to an old school friend who did nothing but follow Lindi about the hotel, talking about all the wonderful jobs there were in Manchester at the new Wireless Studios. Hubert's voice brought him back to the problem at hand.

'I've been putting out a few feelers, Hubert, and I reckon we could get Una a job helping Dudley Plume with his research. Lady Limpet seems quite amenable, and Tessa Truett has a spare room in which she could put her up. What do you think?'

Hubert gave a great groaning sigh. 'What *can* I think? I expect it would make Constance a bit more agreeable. So long as she doesn't bring that young fiend back with her from Altrincham.'

As Cedric was leaving he said off-handedly, 'Oh and by the way, I'm getting Oliphant to help us out with the horses from time to time.'

'Oliphant?' Hubert looked alarmed again. 'Surely you don't mean that young scoundrel who ran up that enormous champagne bill then sloped off without paying? He's nothing but a womaniser who manages to spend half his life in Juan Les Pins hunting likely females with young Cadwallader Limpet!'

Cedric's eyebrows twitched slightly. 'He'll be well under my control. No fears on that account. He's very much down on his luck at present and I'm providing him with a roof over his head.'

'Surely not in Pover Village?'

'At Grangebeck, where we can keep an eye on him...'

Hubert looked completely bewildered.

'But...what about Chloe? Isn't it inviting trouble?'

'Calm down, old boy. You're becoming

over-wrought. Chloe has her own work to do and I'll be making damned sure he has his.'

Hubert was silent for some time after Cedric had gone. He almost took to his bed. He knew deep down that Pawson's power lay in taking advantage of idiots who'd made a mess of their financial affairs. He gazed out from one of the beautiful full-length windows towards the mere. It was the perfect view: calm, quiet and rural; a blissful haven for anyone with enough money to take advantage.

Hubert Lamby turned away from the window, and walked outside to the stables. Ahh, his horses. Both his consolation and his undoing, Hubert's horses meant more to him than any one of the women in his life. They were dependable, noble creatures. But what he never ever seemed to know, if the truth were known, was the surprising resilience of Lamby women.

When Marcus Oliphant arrived to take up residence at Grangebeck at the end of June, Chloe was in the midst of preparing to go to Oliver Renshaw's christening. She was looking her supreme best. A new Marcel wave at Myra Mitchell's salon in Pover, was accentuated by a small, petal-shaped hat, taken up on one side with a pink satin bow. Marcus Oliphant's eyes bulged at the thought of being under the same roof as this lovely creature.

He was tall and muscular at twenty-one and his dark hair grew back in a widow's peak from the centre of his forehead. He dressed immaculately, in navy-blue striped suits, courtesy of the Fifty Shilling Tailors, and he wore a large diamond signet ring. His teeth were bright enough to be seen in the dark and strong enough to rip the bark from trees should the need ever have arisen.

She was in good time for the service. Margie Renshaw had invited her to call round early.

'Mac Haley will be here,' she'd said. 'You could go together to the church. He's ever so keen to know how you are.'

Chloe nodded. She was looking forward to seeing him. It seemed years rather than months since she'd left the *Gazette*, and it was strange that their paths never seemed to cross in the normal course of things.

'Chloe! I hardly recognised you.' He greeted her almost effusively and with a broad smile he clasped her hands. Chloe felt a rush of pure happiness as he told her the news of the goings-on in the office, and the latest deeds of Mr Eldew. She looked into his lean, sun-tanned face and felt herself smiling into his laughing grey eyes. He was just the sort of man she would like to marry.

'Margie keeps telling me about the rambling club you all belong to.' She hesitated.

'Are you interested in joining?' For a moment he looked slightly surprised. 'I always thought you'd be too busy...I'll ask Myra to pass on the particulars. She's the local secretary. You'll see her later at the christening.'

Then, in a rather low voice he said suddenly, 'Did you know we're getting married in August? We'll be sending you an invitation.'

Chloe smiled and looked down at some delicate, tall blue columbines growing in a gentle leafy spray near the trees.

'I wish you both every happiness.' A sudden sadness filled her heart, for a few brief seconds she felt as if a friend had died.

Dudley Plume was busy in the small back room of Eagle cottage in Pover High Street, just opposite The Pond giftshop. His room was awash with secondhand books; the sort he deemed to be of epic importance were those that helped in his quest for any scrap of information about lost gems of lyrical wisdom concerning Lady Limpet's ancient and long departed (if ever existed, thought Dudley Plume) poet cousin, umpteen times removed.

He was in a depressed state, having been suddenly overtaken by the immenseness of the fruitless task ahead. It was a beautiful June day and the village street was full of life and colour. But he was missing it all in his cave of a cottage as the cobwebs of academia covered him like a choking shroud. There was also a gnawing gripe in his groins—a need for a beautiful maiden to arrive on his doorstep.

Suddenly there was a knock on the front door. He opened it with enthusiasm, only to see Cedric Pawson on the step.

'Could I come in and see you for a few minutes?' Cedric said with cool authority as Dudley ushered him in.

'I'm afraid I'm up to my eyes in all this,' said Dudley, gesturing to unopened parcels and battered leather volumes. 'The world is passing by. I doubt if I'll ever partake in another Pover cricket match at this rate,' he said dramatically.

Pawson gazed round at the clutter.

'You certainly need help. Don't you even have a typist?'

'Not a sausage. Everyone keeps away from me like the plague. I'm being driven to total extinction.'

'You look fairly fit to me.' A whisper of sardonic humour swept Cedric's face...

'As a matter of fact, I've just been having a word with Lady Limpet and she was saying you needed more help. She seems very keen to put Pover on the cultural map.'

'And so do I, Mr Pawson, so do I. But it's impossible for one snail to work its way through the ramifications of the lettuce kingdom in ten seconds.'

'Would you be interested in Miss Lamby coming to help you out?'

Dudley's eyes shone with sudden happiness. 'You mean the one who works for you, who was at the *Gazette?* Miss Chloe Lamby? It would be a miraculous gift from the heavens, Mr Pawson. Believe me.'

'I was thinking more of her younger sister, Una. She's away at the moment but is due back shortly. She's extremely capable and has just left school.'

'Marvellous, Mr Pawson. Marvellous. Any port in a storm.'

Cedric had already turned to go, but he paused and added, 'That's settled then, Dudley. She'll be here some time in July—or six weeks hence at the very latest. I'll tell Lady Limpet you agree.'

Dudley nodded speechlessly. When Cedric had gone, he sat down in a daze on the edge of an empty packing case, basking in the mysterious turn of fate and good fortune. What a stroke of good luck. Any sensible female help was better than none at all. He hoped she'd be pleasant, though, like her older sister.

A touch of reality began to tug at the back of his mind. He'd met that younger one once in Pover post office. Yes, she was mixed up with Rob Belmane, who'd escaped to Bowdon after being threatened by her father. He wouldn't have minded someone like Belmane to have helped him, rather than this youngest Lamby girl. He sensed she could be a bit uppish. He began to feel rather glum.

Pawson was however in a very good temper. He arrived back at Grangebeck that day, past swooping June swallows, winging complicated ribbons of air. He paused to listen to a skylark as it suddenly rose straight to the skies from ground a few yards away, trilling ever higher as it spun.

Yes, everything was going to work out. Exactly as he wanted it.

CHAPTER 8

The Catastrophe

Although the Merantos had gas fires in some rooms there were many others with normal grates, which entailed the removal of ashes from underneath the fire bars. Una had never realised so much cleaning equipment existed, despite having lived in a hotel herself.

In her own comfortable life, being the youngest and still at school, she had escaped most of the worst of the routine cleaning work. But now her main introduction to housework was sweeping and dusting. Dust, dust, dust, *dust*, for ever and ever, bedrooms, multitudes of intricate furniture, cornices, window ledges and window panes, standard lamps and light fittings, bookcases, hearths and mantelpieces, ornaments, pictures, doors and doorknobs. The list was never-ending: furniture polish, floor polish, metal polish, window cleaner, and black-lead.

'Lamby, you never dusted the rungs of that table this morning...'

'Lamby, I ran my finger along the back

of the piano and found...'

Una took it all with silent politeness. To her knowledge she'd dusted every scrap of the grand piano, even twisting her limbs into contortions to do the hidden bits. But always it was made to look as if she had been slapdash and untidy. Every day when she met Robby there was a longer list of woes. 'I've never had such a boring, thankless job in all my born days, Robby. I feel as if I'll be trapped for ever by the Meranto dust and my life will just wither away.'

He tried to console her, but after a while he became heartily fed up with her complaints. 'What about me, nagged all day by the gardeners and doing nothing but shifting manure about?'

'I'd sooner do that than dusting!'

Then, one day after the usual bout of quibbling, Robby said, 'You know, you're terribly spoiled, Una. People are desperate for jobs. There's many a woman with a half-starved family who would have welcomed this situation. I was talking to Matilda Brent, the parlour maid, and she said the last tweeny never grumbled once and never had to be reprimanded. Oh, and, by the way, she's invited us to a pie and peas supper in aid of Fallen Women at the assembly rooms after work next Friday.'

Una felt her colour rising. She had feared for about a week that Robby was no match for the wiles of the neat, little dark-eyed trollop who didn't know what truth meant. Matilda was all right on the surface, but her dusting activities were restricted to one vague swoop round with a feather duster in the bedroom of the most handsome man in residence, and large soulful expressions if ever faced with explanations: 'I must have missed that bit, Mrs Pepper. Master Ronald grabbed me by the skirt and tried to ping my garters. The long and the short of it is, Mrs Pepper, I cannot in all virtue go in that room again if he's there so you'll have to send Lamby.'

Una had been working at Meranto's for nearly a month when the accident occurred. It was a very wet day in July and she was cleaning ashes out of the drawing room grate. The Merantos were not the sort of people to do without fires between May and October, and they often stayed up late, stoking up the heat with logs.

Una had been brooding over Robby and that awful snake-in-the-grass Matilda. She feared the whole situation was going from bad to worse, especially since Robby had spent an afternoon out with Matilda, staying mum about where they'd been.

'Why are you so suspicious, Una? What does it matter where we went? Surely you trust me enough not to want a detailed report of my every movement?'

'Of course I trust you, so why are you so secretive? Surely you can just mention where it was as a matter of interest? You wouldn't like it if I waltzed off with Splodgy Moorfield from the kitchens and refused to say what we'd been up to.'

'Well, if you must know, she came over to Aunty Beth's with me because she said she was mad on stuffed birds and I was telling her about Aunt Beth's hummingbirds in the glass case.'

'Of all the cheek!' Fury flared up in Una's face. 'Your Aunt Beth'll think you've started to go out with her, now, rather than me.'

'I knew you'd kick up a fuss,' sighed Robby. 'Anyway you'll be delighted to know that darling Aunt Beth wasn't in. So stop harping!'

But the damage was done, and while Una was kneeling down at the hearth in the drawing room, clearing out the ashes, she went over and over the incident in her mind. Was Robby getting tired of her? Didn't their love mean anything to him? How dare he dilly-dally with Matilda when she—Una Christabel Lamby of the Swansdown Hotel—had sacrificed her life at beautiful Melmere for him, coming to work here as a drudge. Did their vows carved on the oak tree mean nothing? Had the estrangement from her father been all in vain?

Una knelt down to the hearth with smarting eyes, blinking back the tears and scraping away at the still warm ashes, shovelling them into a small ash can carrier. Just supposing Aunt Beth had been there when Robby and Matilda had called and had been completely caught up by Matilda Brent and her smarmy, lying ways. No wonder Matilda was being so suspiciously sweet to her; she had even mentioned Robby's name three times yesterday.

The thought of it all, and the enormity of being the jilted girl of Robby Belmane, with never a true friend of her own to turn to, so captured her imagination that she hardly noticed where she was shovelling the ashes. With the help of a slight breeze from an open window some of them began to smoke and glow red hot on the richly floral pink carpet.

Quickly, in nervous panic, she doused it all with water from the nearest flower vases, as roses and delphiniums lay scattered everywhere. Then, in her haste she knocked over two small rosewood tables and tripped over the wretched ashcan itself. Her heart was thumping with terror as even more of the carpet was covered in thick, gritty, burning sediment. Trembling with fear she scrambled for more and more flower vases including a Chinese one as big as an umbrella stand. The final resounding crash as she tripped, seemed to Una to shake the whole room. But as she lay there in the silent aftermath, with only the sonorous heavy tick of a large, chiming clock, she realised the house was still quiet. Water and bruised flowers were everywhere. A smell of burnt and smoking wool sickened the air.

She staggered to her feet and then flopped down again in a terrible haze as her head struck the huge marble fireplace.

When Una came to she was lying in a single bed in one of the small guest rooms with Mrs Meranto standing beside her.

'Thank goodness, child! I thought you were never going to recover. Dr Wallace will be here shortly. Meanwhile, I think we'd better find Mr Belmane and ask him to get in touch with your father as soon as possible. It will be no use taking a chance on a telegram if he only signs his name with a cross.'

Una stared at her in anguish. What sort of nightmare was this? 'Not that, please...' she mumbled. 'My father doesn't get on with Robby.' She sank back wearily against the pillows. Then she said weakly, 'If someone could get hold of my sister

Chloe, instead. She works for Mr Pawson at Grangebeck Manor.' A small glimmer of hope rose within her. 'I think I can remember the phone number, it's Pover 124.'

The minute Chloe received the message, she phoned her father. He cursed down the line.

'What the devil's she doing staying with the Merantos?'

'She's not *staying* there, Father. You know she isn't. She isn't a guest. She's working there on the domestic side.'

'And you mean to say they took her on without even consulting us? It's a damned disgrace It makes it sound as if they've picked her up from the streets. What does Cedric say?'

'I haven't told him, yet.' Chloe's voice went cold with anger. 'She's our *family*, Father. *Mother's* the one you should be telling. I only phoned you first because I was the one the Merantos got in touch with. Una must have given Cedric's number. Perhaps you and Mother should go down there to sort it out.'

'Never you mind trying to rule *our* lives, Chloe. Is Cedric there?'

'No, he isn't.'

'Ask him to call round when you see him, and tell the Merantos her mother and I will be round to see her some time today.' He hung up quickly, and went to find Constance in the kitchen.

'I've just had a call from Chloe. Apparently Una has had a slight accident. She's at Meranto's in Bowdon. They're looking after her. It's that bloody place where Belmane's employed as a labourer.'

Constance looked shocked. She left her work and followed him to their sitting room. 'That poor child. Whatever's been happening? We must go straightaway. I'll tell Ella and Lindi.'

'Not straightaway. I'll need to see Cedric first and get the full picture. I've also got someone coming to see me this morning about the horses. You go. Take the Jowett and go now. P'raps Mother could come over and keep an eye on things.'

Constance nodded silently. She was ready in five minutes and within ten she was driving to Bowdon to see her beloved daughter. In a strange sort of way she welcomed the visit. But at the same time she prayed fervently that it would be nothing too serious. Until now she had not dared to encourage Una to come back home. The terrible shooting incident had become engraved in their minds.

Mrs Meranto greeted Constance Lamby. 'I'm sure your daughter will be pleased to see you. Every girl needs her mother at a time like this.' Her smiling face masked the confusion she felt at the sight of Una's mother. Once the servants were employed, she took little interest in their personal lives. She did, however, remember distinctly that Una Lamby was a village girl whose father could only manage to sign his name with a large trembling cross, and that Lamby was the youngest of a huge brood.

Mrs Meranto looked at this small, very thin woman with hennaed hair who'd arrived to see young Lamby. The henna showed pink where it was trying to cover up white hair. Her face was pale and her skin delicately transparent. The two-piece saxe blue silk costume she was wearing fitted her to perfection. Mrs Meranto had seen something similar in Marshall and Snelgrove's. Perhaps she had been lucky with someone's hand-me-downs. Perhaps it was someone for whom she cleaned.

As they went upstairs to the sickroom, Mrs Meranto said gently, 'Your daughter will obviously need to get back home as soon as possible to recuperate. In fact, if transport could be arranged, she can leave any time. All she needs is a few days of complete rest. Do you know anyone in your village with a car who might possibly help you? Do you have enough room to deal with her at home?'

Constance looked both puzzled and relieved. She could probably take Una home immediately, but would she want to come, knowing all the trouble with Hubert?

'I could take her back with me immediately then, Mrs Meranto.'

Mrs Meranto hesitated in the thickly carpeted corridor. She looked at Constance with genuine concern. 'Oh no, dear. We couldn't think of allowing her to journey all that way on a bus. Dr Wallace just wouldn't allow it. And I'm afraid you could hardly expect us to pay for a taxi. It would be phenomenal But not to worry, Mrs Lamby, we'll find a way. Then as soon as she's better she can come back to us. We shall keep her place open for her. How does that suit?'

'I came in my own car, Mrs Meranto.'

'Your *own* car? Ah, I see. I hadn't realised you drove a car.' There was a sudden awkward silence. Mrs Meranto showed her into the room where Una was and hastily departed. Her system of categorising people had been strangely disrupted and she felt uneasy.

On the way to her sitting room she decided to pop along and see Mrs Pepper the housekeeper.

'Ah, there you are, Mrs Pepper. I've just

been having a word with tweeny Lamby's mother. She'll be taking her back home by car. And I don't think we'll need to keep her place open, so if you'd like to look around for another girl?'

'Very good, Mrs Meranto. I'll note it down. I only hopes poor little Lamby won't suffer too much with that oaf of a father, and I daresay young Belmane from the gardens will be quite sorry. Though he seems to be walking out a bit with Matilda Brent these days.'

'Oh? Is that so?' said Mrs Meranto in smiling conspiratorial tones. Then leaving Mrs Pepper's room briskly, she returned to her own busy world.

'Mother!' Una gave a heartfelt gasp of joy upon seeing Constance in the doorway.

'I've come to take you home, Una, love. From all accounts all you need now is a good few days of complete rest. I've spoken to Mrs Meranto. If you tell me where your bedroom is I'll go there and collect all your belongings.'

'But what about Father?' The suddenness of her mother's announcement left her in a daze. It was the last thing she had expected. She had resigned herself to never seeing home again. It was almost like a dream. 'I'll have to let Robby know...'

'They'll see to that. You aren't fit enough

to go trailing about looking for him.' Her mother kissed her firmly on the cheek. The main thing was to get her away from this place and back to Melmere. And as for Hubert, they'd cross that bridge when they came to it.

As the car chugged steadily back home along the winding country lanes, across small humped-back bridges, in a land of damp green lushness and hawthorn hedges with the sun shining through sudden showers, Una's spirits slowly began to lift. Ever since leaving home she had tried to blot out her love for it all, to pretend she wouldn't care if she never saw any of it again, and that Robby mattered more than everything else in the world. Now she realised she had been wrong.

When they drove through Shale Bridge she glanced with affection towards the *Gazette* offices and when she saw a girl she knew in her familiar school uniform going by she felt a strange glow of affection. She felt as though she'd been in prison for a million years and had only just escaped—yet it was only a few weeks away from it all. She took a deep breath of pure happiness.

'We'll take the road by the side of the mere,' said her mother. 'The swans are out with their cygnets.'

Swansdown was quiet and peaceful when

180

they arrived back. Granny Lamby was there to greet them. Nobody said very much, but her grandmother made her a drink of Horlicks, and she was packed off to bed.

What paradise to be back in her own room again.

Then, as she lay there with daylight sunbeams dancing on the wallpaper, she heard the gentle clop of horses' hooves, and she knew her father was home.

CHAPTER 9

Settling Down

The minute Hubert realised Una was back home and upstairs in her own bedroom, he panicked. He simply couldn't bring himself to face her, especially if she was ill and in need of rest.

He rang Pawson immediately. 'Una's home. Constance brought her. I've...I've got to go away to Thirsk for a few days, old boy, to see Tommy Formby about some racing stuff. I'll be staying with my cousin Frank. Keep an eye on things over here for me, there's a pal.'

'Going to Thirsk? Right *now?*' Constance

was flabbergasted. 'Aren't you even going to say hello to your daughter?'

'I'll see her when I get back.' Hubert glanced away guiltily. 'Something's cropped up that can't wait. Pawson's always there if you want anything.'

Constance went back to the living room and poured herself a sherry. Then she sat back and sipped it slowly, comforting herself with the wry fact that at least he hadn't appeared with his gun at hand. In a way it was a bit of a weight off her mind to have him away until things settled down.

Fate had dealt Cedric Pawson exactly the cards he'd planned. He would have made sure he got Una back anyway, but this stroke of good fortune made it sooner rather than later.

Immediately, his thoughts went to Tessa Truett. Una would need to be in her own lodgings. No point in her suffering under the same roof as Hubert. That evening he decided to chance a visit to Tessa's, and he waited until just after she'd closed her tea rooms for the night. She had removed her daytime regalia, her frilly gingham apron and was lounging on a leather sofa in her exquisitely furnished living room.

Tessa was quite surprised to see Cedric, inviting himself in. These days their paths rarely crossed. It was hard to believe that only a couple of years ago they had lain in each other's arms admitting tenderness. Both born fighters, full of calculating and stubborn determination, they'd found the balancing line too unpredictable in the sex game. That was why she had given him his cards and told him to clear off.

'No one orders me around like a puppet, Cedric. I'm no boudoir woman if that's what you're about. My tea rooms are a serious business. If I want a man I'll choose one who knows what equality means. And don't forget to take that pair of suede brothel creepers away with you.'

Cedric had immediately thrown away his favourite, most comfortable pair of suede shoes. And he never wore suede shoes again. It was a tacit example of Tessa's power over him: she was the only woman who had ever been able to make him change one iota of his lifestyle.

'I called to see if you had a spare room.'

'What does that mean exactly?' Her grey eyes narrowed. She opened a gold plated cigarette case and offered him a Craven A.

Cedric shook his head and pulled out a cigar.

'The Lambys are going to need a place for young Una. She won't be wanting to stay at home; she's outgrown it all. It's a bit in the air at present but I'd like to know whether I could count on you if the need for a place arises?'

'I expect she could have the boxroom,' said Tessa slowly. 'I'd have to clear some stuff out, but it's always there.' Then she looked him straight in the face and said coolly, 'Who'd pay the bill?'

He snorted angrily. 'You know it isn't like that! If she does come here it'll be because she's got a job working with Dudley Plume and she'll be paying for herself. All I'm doing is testing the water, so to speak.' He stood up hurriedly; Tessa still had the power to unnerve him. 'That's that then.'

'That's that, Cedric.' She smiled and showed him out. 'See you when I see you then. Bye.'

When he'd gone Tessa took off the long pewter gown she'd been wearing, and put on a plain quilted housecoat. She curled up on her settee to listen to the wireless. She'd been expecting young Cadwallader Limpet when Cedric called. Lady Limpet was having a summer 'do' in a marquee, and she often used the services of Tessa Truett. Tessa had a catering list of all things linked with light afternoon and evening entertainment, from cooks and waitresses to scones and chocolate eclairs, and Cadwallader was due any time to place his mother's order.

But tonight, Cadwallader never turned up. She wasn't really all that surprised; when he and his friend Marcus Oliphant got together, bun fights in marquees were the very last thing on their minds. The Champagne trail was more their line.

She shook her head. Young men of this generation were no match for the likes of suave old Cedric. Perhaps it had been ordained that she should have been wearing gun metal silk stockings and garters for Cedric Pawson rather than two callow, youthful playboys.

Tessa sucked deeply on her cigarette and exhaled slow rings of smoke into the mellow, glowing lamplight. She knocked a small grey piece of ash on to her chromium-plated ashtray thoughtfully, then stubbed out the half-smoked Craven A with long, delicate fingers.

Little Una Lamby, she'd never imagined having her as a paying guest.

Within a few days of being back home, Una had completely recovered from her ordeal. In a way she felt a bit of a fraud when she saw all the grind of the hotel going on as usual around her. No one asked her to help out, they just left her to recover. Even Chloe seemed to be ignoring her, for she made only one very brief phone call.

Una drifted about aimlessly as her misery grew. The magic of Melmere seemed elusive these days; perhaps she'd never recapture it. She had to admit that it was her day-to-day school life which she was missing the most. She realised now her need for it. There wasn't even the end of school days to look forward to. She hung about the hotel, or went for walks down by the mere and watched small yachts gliding across the water on gentle breezes.

As for Robby, he might as well have been gone for ever. There hadn't even been a message from him.

Then, a couple of days before her father was due back from Thirsk, Chloe rang her to say that Cedric would like to invite Una across for afternoon tea.

'For goodness sake, don't turn it down, Una. I think he's going to introduce us to this awful Marcus Oliphant he's got working here and I'd like some moral support!'

Reluctantly Una agreed, and that very morning Pawson himself arrived at Swansdown to see her.

'How are you feeling these days, Una?'

'Very well, thank you.' Una was guarded.

'Not made your mind up yet about what you intend to do?'

What she intended to do? Whatever did he mean? At the moment life was a complete blank. She was like a piece of property being shifted about from place to place. All joy had gone.

She sat with him in the garden in silence. There were slight rumblings in the air at home that she should go back to school. Her mother had tentatively suggested it last night. Yet how could she possibly bear such ignominy after all that had happened and after she was supposed to have left for good? Even though she missed it.

Ella had chipped in as well. 'You haven't been away from it all that long, Una. You've only missed a few weeks from the whole academic year. I knew a girl who was ill for six months and came back again.'

'Illness is quite different, Ella.' Una had spoken with tearful frustration.

'But you've been ill, too, dear, or else why would you have become so rundown at Meranto's? You were still in a state of shock after running away.'

Una set her lips together tightly. She hadn't been ill; as well as the accident with the cleaning, she had been furious and depressed about Robby dallying about with someone else. 'It seems like a million years since I left school, now. And it *is*, I'll have missed whole patches of study. It'll be absolutely impossible to catch up on it. It's like a bus that never waits for you. It's like reading a book with half the pages gone, or going to the pictures and missing part of the film.' Una had hurried away, more upset and disturbed than ever. Whatever was she to do?

Cedric Pawson was trying to catch her gaze but she stared gloomily at some poppies.

'I was wondering if you'd like to come round for tea this afternoon, Una? Chloe could call for you. There's a young man coming to live in, to help out with some of my business matters. His name's Marcus Oliphant. It would be nice for the three of you to get acquainted.' He eyed her quizzically. 'He's not very old, just nineteen. He's a pal of Cadwallader Limpet's. He's a pleasant young fellow.'

Una nodded reluctantly, as she thought of Chloe's telephone call. What a state to be landed in.

Cedric realised he would have to get her over to Grangebeck as soon as he could. She was in the sort of mood when she might decide stubbornly to stay at home after all.

'Quick-sticks, then,' he said cheerfully, as if she were a small child. 'The car's waiting. Might as well come now, then you and Chloe can have a real old natter.'

When they were in the car, Cedric added casually, 'Ever thought of getting a job in

Pover and living in digs in the village? Dudley Plume's looking for help.'

'Dudley Plume!' Una went scarlet. 'He's the end! He suggested Robby should go there and help him. He's got to be the most batty, boring person in the whole place!' She sat there simmering. What little game was Cedric trying to work on her now?

Cedric sniffed irritably. She really was a spoilt little madam at present. He began to wonder if he was doing the right thing getting her mixed up with Marcus Oliphant, even though it would be a strictly platonic affair. Oliphant would be well grounded in the rules of the game where young ladies like Una Lamby were concerned. There would be no hanky-panky. Oliphant was to be her escort and faithful beau in the old-fashioned sense, just until she had got Belmane completely out of her system. Marcus Oliphant was quite capable of grabbing other favours in places further afield. Cedric drew a deep breath. If he managed to get Una persuaded into working for Dudley and lodging with Tessa Truett, Una could settle down until she was ready for a proper marriage. Maybe one of these days she'd provide him, Cedric Theodore Pawson, with an heir for Grangebeck... He stopped himself guiltily. They were crossing the

189

bridge over the grassy moat and he could see Chloe in the distance, waving.

Una's face lit up into a smile at last.

Marcus Oliphant couldn't have looked more handsome as he stood there as if he owned the place. A white marble bust stood beside him on a shining pink and black granite pedestal. The polished floor planks glowed beneath the claret-coloured carpet runner. A huge black oak chest stood against wooden panelling. It displayed large Belamine jugs and pewter mugs and plates.

Marcus stepped forward to meet Una like a young cavalier. He had no intention of being removed from such idyllic surroundings because of surly behaviour.

'Marcus Oliphant, at your service,' he murmured.

As he bent his head and gently shook her hand, Una and Chloe exchanged a brief poker-faced look.

Chloe was rather puzzled by his over-exaggerated greeting. It was a far cry from the reception she'd had just before Cedric left for Swansdown. Oliphant had given her a cursory nod and said disdainfully, 'What's the old rotter like to work for? Will he expect me to hang on every worn and weary syllable?'

'I have no idea, I'm sure,' Chloe had replied rather coldly.

Cedric led the three of them to the dining room, and after a large meal of roast lamb, he headed for the drawing room like a scout leader. 'I want all three of you to get on well,' he said firmly. 'We're all in this together now. Marcus will be working for me and your father. So if either of you two girls needs a male escort, he'll always be here to oblige, won't you Olly?'

Oliphant nodded enthusiastically.

By the end of an afternoon spent wandering round Cedric's vast walled garden and vinery, they were getting on quite well. Chloe realised that Olly was a bit of a card, and Una was, against her will, bemused by his staggering good looks and panther-like gracefulness, as he set out deliberately to amuse and delight them.

'Did the old devil say something about your going to work for Dudley Plume and getting digs in the village?' said Olly idly, as he and Una gazed at a stone water nymph. 'Thought I heard some talk of it.'

Una was taken aback. What was going on? It almost seemed to be a foregone conclusion that she'd want this job, and to leave home, just after she'd got back.

'What Cedric says and what I plan to do are two entirely different things,' said Una stiffly. 'I don't think Dudley and I would get on very well. I find him extremely boring.'

Olly looked at her askance. 'Boring? Is that all? You ought to grab it with both hands. He's mollycoddled to death by Lady Limpet. He's so stupid, he'd never allow you to do much and you'd live the life of Riley. You want your head seeing to. Old Caddy-wallader Limpet reckons that any assistant who lands there will live in paradise, at old Limpy's expense.'

Una started. She hadn't thought of it in that way before. Maybe it wouldn't be too bad after all. She certainly wouldn't always want to stay at home, especially with Father still about. But if she could get lodgings in Pover she'd still be able to see her family. Perhaps it would be worth trying to suffer the charms of Dudley Plume.

Another thought occurred to her as she stood next to her handsome escort. Maybe she'd even be able to see Robby again when he came home? Perhaps his sudden passion for the wily Matilda Brent would end as quickly as it had begun. And if everyone thought she was busy being chaperoned by Olly, she was sure she could get things back together again with Robby. Her face suddenly flooded with smiles. 'Maybe I will give it a try after all.'

'Atta girl!' Olly laughed approvingly. 'And as for digs you can't go wrong at Tessa Truett's place. She's a real humdinger.' A wave of admiration passed across his smooth face.

'*Tessa Truett?*' Surely it was a joke. Una frowned. 'Whatever made you mention her?'

'Because I heard she's a room for rent, my poppet. Can't think where I heard it, but it's got to be the heaven on earth I saw in the gypsy's crystal. And let me tell you here and now that you wouldn't find a better place in the whole of Pover. Plus damned good food. The trouble with you, my little angel, is that you need a bloke like me to guide you in the ways of the world.'

Una said no more, but on the way back to Swansdown that day she realised she'd been completely won over.

When Hubert arrived back from Thirsk a few days later he was both surprised and relieved to find no sign of his youngest daughter.

'Comfortably bedded out in the village, old boy,' explained Pawson. 'She started work yesterday as Dudley Plume's assistant, so your worries are over.'

Hubert Lamby felt a surge of relief as they went on to discuss the racing world. Whatever would he do without Cedric?

CHAPTER 10

Eagle Cottage

Dudley Plume's brain was approaching bursting point with all the work he had to do. When Una arrived early one morning he was completely taken aback. It was eight-thirty and he stood at the front door of Eagle cottage in his yellow-striped cotton pyjamas, eyeing her blearily. 'Yes? What is it?' He tried to place her.

'I'm Una Lamby. I'm coming to work for you, starting today. I thought it was all agreed.' She sounded puzzled.

Una gazed at him, from beneath her straw hat, with doom-laden fears. She stood in his doorway in a new blue poplin frock which Ella had made her, and she carried an old leather despatch case given to her by Cedric. Dudley looked like he'd had a night out on the town. He was completely bog-eyed and his brown floppy hair was hanging down in an untidy fringe over his eyebrows. She could even see ink stains and dried egg yolk on his pyjama jacket.

She was to start at eight-thirty, from

Monday to Saturday and finish at three. She knew it was all correct because she had already moved into her room at Tessa Truett's.

Her wages were to be thirty shillings a week, and Tessa was going to charge her five shillings a week, board and lodgings.

'A lot more than I managed to grab when I was a kid.' Cedric's eyes had narrowed with a spark of good-humoured cynicism, when it had been arranged.

Chloe had echoed his remarks. 'It's all going to work out so well, Una. I'm sure you'll be happy staying with Tessa, and from all accounts, Father's taken it all like a lamb and just wants to forget the past and have everyone happy again.'

Her thoughts drifted on. Marcus had stressed how wise she was to have taken his advice. 'You'll never regret it, old bean. Dudsy boy'll treat you like a princess, and once you are in with old Limpy you'll rest in clover all your life.'

Dudley Plume was speaking, and she started guiltily, lost in her thoughts.

'Oh yes.' A slight dawning of recognition crept over his face as he peered at her closely.

'I remember now, you were in the post office one day. You're Chloe Lamby's sister! That's it, Mr Pawson called and arranged it all! You need a job and you've come to help me.' He stood there smiling at her as she grew more and more annoyed.

'Hadn't you better invite me in then?' she said icily. She could see the whole situation was going to be hopeless. This was what came of having everyone else organise one's life. She knew she should be grateful, but oh, how on earth was she going to stand being with Dudley Plume day in day out?

'Oh yes, come in. Mind you don't disturb anything. Every single scrap of paper or torn page lying on the floor *means* something.'

Una had never seen such a mess in all her life. The dust alone was enough to send a healthy person to their grave. Huge fat spiders hung in webs of all shapes and sizes, laden with dead carcasses ranging from common house flies to tiny midges.

'I was working late. Didn't get to bed till nearly four. Been tabulating some stuff concerned with Lady Limpet's esteemed cousin Maudley Montgomery. There are eighty-three Montgomeries in her library and none of them is called Maudley. I'm having to sift through the work of every Montgomery who ever lived to find a reference to him and his work. The only known copy of his work at present is a slim volume of poems entitled "Dandelions" which Lady Limpet has had rebound. It's vital for me to produce conclusive evidence soon or I'll be out of a home and a job.'

Una placed her despatch case carefully in a corner where she'd be able to find it again. What a waste of a lovely sunny day being stuck in here. Already the High Street was buzzing with happy traffic. Horses and carts were moving about. Two Fords and a Vauxhall had whizzed past the window panes. A dray carrying beer barrels was parked outside the Perch whilst Polly Mogson washed the steps.

'As you can see by the chairs,' droned Dudley, pointing towards some misshapen hummocks, 'this is really just the sitting room for visitors, and a place where I undo parcels. My real work goes on upstairs. We'll be upstairs most of each day. We're in a bit of a time warp, here. The only water supply is the cold tap in the back kitchen.' He coughed rather shyly. 'And the wc is a soil privy a few yards down the back garden. Would you like me to show you exactly where it is?'

They ploughed their way through the long grass and Una looked along the garden. It was a long narrow strip of wilderness, mainly full of deep blue lupins which had seeded everywhere. It was beautiful in spite of itself. There was an old pear tree, and pink cabbage roses rambled over the crumbling red brick privy. At this time of the year any stench from the place was disguised by the wonderful scent from rampant, creamy flowering honeysuckle.

From the narrow side passage leading back to the front she saw a large black and white terrier. He was Spot, the oldest dog in the village and he was staggering along the footpath with arthritic perseverance towards Mr Maler's, the butcher. Una felt a sudden glow of happiness. It was a far cry from Meranto's at Bowdon. She thought wistfully of Robby. Would he be wheeling a heavy barrow of steaming dung at this very moment in that other world? Or would he be talking to that hateful little minx Matilda Brent?

Six cats dotted about in sun traps looked at her as if they held the secret to all things. Idly they licked their paws, blinking occasionally with deceptively drowsy eyes.

She walked back with Dudley into Eagle cottage, and spent the rest of the day helping him to look for clues about the existence of Maudley Montgomery.

Robby Belmane was getting a bit fed up with Tilda Brent. She was all right in small doses and quite fun to be with, but there wasn't a spark of romance in her, and she spent much of her time flirting with other men. She was a far cry from Una.

'You mean to say you aren't going out with me on your day off, after all?' said Tilda to Robby. 'I've gone to lots of trouble to get my time off to suit yours. You're a real, mean devil. It's quite a different kettle of fish when you're feeling a bit passionate; you'll promise me anything. Then the next moment when it's all over you go back on your word. Every promise you make to me is completely forgotten—as if I don't even exist.'

Robby groaned inwardly. Yes it would be more than good to get away from Meranto's and back to Pover for a day. He had not been home since Una left. His brother Maurice had said something about Una working for Dudley Plume and lodging with Tessa Truett, and he wondered whether he would have a chance to see her. Maurice had said Pawson had one of the Limpet hangers-on employed at his place and from the description it sounded distinctly like Marcus Oliphant. He was a real playboy.

He got back home on the evening before his day off. As he walked along Pover High Street he felt a rush of relief. It never seemed to change. The night was humid and scented with cut grass. People nodded and waved when they saw him.

As he passed Eagle cottage he saw lights blazing from the upper windows. Then, by some stroke of luck he saw the sudden outline of Una. He frowned to himself. Fancy her still being there at this hour; it was nearly nine o'clock.

A couple of minutes later, just as he was going past the Perch, he heard her call his name. It was music to his ears.

'Robby, wait for me...'

He turned towards her full of joy and held out his arms, not quite sure of his reception. One thing was certain, come what may and in spite of the wiles of Matilda Brent, his heart would always belong to Una.

'What are you doing here?' Her face was a mass of smiles. 'Are you home for good?'

'No such luck. It's a day off at last, starting tomorrow. I just had to get away from that place for a bit. It's been very lonely without you, Una.'

'Lonely?' Her tone changed. 'Surely not as lonely as all that, Robby. What about Mat—'

'Forget it,' he said harshly. 'It was nothing. It's still you, and me...' Then quickly changing the subject he said, 'I hear you've got that job at Eagle cottage. In fact, I caught a glimpse of you, just now as I walked past. It seems very long hours.'

'It varies from day to day. It was

supposed to be eight-thirty to three each day, but it couldn't be more different. There are no set times. Today I didn't go in until this afternoon.'

Una had discovered pretty quickly that time was not important to Dudley Plume. She had started to make her own hours. He was the sort of person who would have been quite happy for her to arrive at six o'clock in the morning, clean up the cottage, give him his breakfast, and then stay until midnight sorting through books and portfolios to invent some sort of literary life for Maudley Montgomery.

To date they had come across two unsigned poems, which could have been written by anyone but had been ascribed to Lady Limpet's family bard. One was called 'The Duck Puddle'—seventeen verses describing village life in 1903, written in an old laundry book. The other was a ballad called, 'How We Brought the Good News from Pover to Knutsford'. Dudley dutifully copied this one out on a piece of vellum, and Lady Limpet was delighted.

'Are you on your way back to Tessa's?' Robby slipped his hand into hers. It was just like old times.

'Yes.'

'What's it like living there?'

'Very nice.'

'Do you have to be back at any special hour?' Their conversation was slightly guarded, very polite.

'I'm always in by ten-thirty at the very latest. She treats me just like an adult.'

He looked at her longingly. 'What I'd really like to do is to borrow our Maurice's car and to go down to Melmere and see our oak tree, before it gets too dark. Have you ever been back?'

She gave a sudden shiver. 'I was at home for a little time while Father was in Thirsk. But I've never ever been down to the oak tree again since that awful night. I just want to forget it all.'

'If we both went back together, it would stop us harping on the past,' pleaded Robby. 'It would be like a slain ghost.'

She began to waver. Perhaps he was right. It was stupid to avoid that part of Melmere, just because of what had happened on that one night. Especially now that everything was sorted out at home and Father had calmed down. 'All right then,' she agreed reluctantly.

Soon they were chugging along in Maurice's car to a small parking place under the beeches, a stone's throw from the oak tree, and were both standing beneath its rugged branches.

At first Una could hardly believe it was the same tree; it was densely covered with leaves, and they pushed them aside to peer at the gnarled tree trunk. Then, suddenly, in the fast fading light, she glimpsed the heart-entwined initials marked there. They looked small and insignificant. She could hardly believe, now, all the trouble the small carving had caused.

Robby took her in his arms and kissed her again. They clung together like orphans in a storm as she nestled against the warmth of his firm body, feeling his tautness, his straining longing, as he trembled slightly with restricted passion. Whatever was going to become of them if their meetings were always fleeting moments?

As they walked slowly back to the car, kissing and nuzzling one another, she said, 'Do you think you'll always be working at Meranto's?' A picture of little dark-eyed Pocket Venus, Matilda Brent rose inside her. Una's heart thudded with injured pride and growing jealousy. Robby never answered...she said no more.

'See you tomorrow then,' said Robby tenderly, as they parted. 'I'll call in at Dudley's and see what time you'll be free. Are you glad we visited the oak tree? It should only bring us sweet memories from now on.'

She nodded gratefully.

The next morning when she got up it was pouring with rain. She decided to go across to Dudley's extra early so that she would have more of the day to spend with Robby.

Inside Eagle cottage, she tidied up the masses of papers and books, left there on the floor from the day before, and noticed a note from Lady Limpet with the Drawbridge Hall crest. She looked at it with surprise. *'Expecting to see you early Thursday morning with Miss Lamby to discuss Maudley's grave. Letty Limpet.'* It was Thursday today and Dudley was still dead to the world in the boxroom.

She grabbed the letter and ran upstairs. 'I've just found this. We're supposed to be seeing Lady Limpet at the Hall this morning!' She felt like throttling him as he opened one eye then tried to turn over to escape her.

She dug at him sharply. 'You can't just *ignore* it Dudley.'

He groaned. 'All right then. But just leave me alone, can't you? I was up till three o'clock trying to find another poem and it seems to me, just between the two of us and in strict confidence, that we'll have to make up most of Maudley's output ourselves.'

'Never mind all that. Get up and be quick!'

Una tore downstairs. Against her better judgement she boiled him an egg and made him a cup of tea. Twenty minutes later they were setting off on their bicycles to Lady Limpet's.

Drawbridge Hall was set on a steep hill surrounded by a grassy sward and hundreds of ancient trees. As they pedalled through the warm drizzle to the side entrance, Una thought sadly of Robby. There was no hope now of seeing him today. He had to set off back to Meranto's at about six in the evening, and she suspected that she and Dudley would be tied up by Lady Limpet for the whole of the day.

Letty Limpet was well known for trying to put a million new ideas into action, all at the same time. The Limpets owned most of the land round the village, as well as many of the cottages and shops. So, despite rural district councils and other august bodies, the Limpets always did things their way.

'Lord Limpet and I each have our own studies to work in, as Dudley here well knows,' beamed Letty, as she led them to her own personal sanctuary.

Una could see now where Dudley had got his idea for spreading everything on the floors. Lady Limpet's study was exactly the same, except that her papers and manuscripts and scrolls were resting on a hand-woven Tudor carpet.

'One needs the space,' she explained, gazing across a room which seemed to Una to be the size of Pover High Street.

'The reason I invited you both here this morning was to broach an idea that has been haunting me for some time. I'd like to build a proper mark of respect to our native poet within Pover itself: a marble monument carved in the shape of an open book and set in a small circle of weeping willows.'

Una and Dudley sat quietly, nodding their heads. Dudley drew out a small notepad and jotted down a few particulars.

'A monument of this calibre would fit in very nicely where the Pond gift shop used to be. As you know, it's been empty and available to let for more than a year. It's hardly more than a wooden shed so I think I'll knock it down altogether and use the land for our mark of homage. I own all that part of the street.' She gave them a motherly smile. 'I shall organise a small museum, too.'

Dudley began to look slightly worried. Even so, he wrote MUSEUM in his notebook and underlined it.

'We must all start right now collecting every object that was even slightly connected to Maudley Montgomery. Excuse me just one moment.' Lady Limpet walked across to a tall glass-fronted cupboard and came back with a wicker basket. Two golf balls were rolling about inside it. 'As you will see I have already started. His initials "MMM" are on both of these, plus the St Andrews logo and the date, 1872, in tiny letters. If you can find further bygones it would be invaluable. I am hoping that one day he will be as famous as dear Mrs Gaskell, or even Wordsworth.'

Lady Limpet ordered some coffee and biscuits to be served while Dudley rambled on earnestly about poetry.

'I have found another one which might be his. It was signed "MMM" and tucked away between the leaves of a book on fly fishing.'

Whilst sitting at this village pond
Staring at the great beyond
Watching dragonflies on wing
Hearing all the breezes sing
Hoping for the pike to rise
From beds of streams 'neath cloudy skies
And give me such a great surprise

'The paper is torn off after that,' said Dudley apologetically.

'Never mind, never *mind*, dear boy. You are doing *wonders.*' Lady Limpet's face glowed with pleasure.

On the way back to Eagle cottage, Una hoped that there would be time to see

Robby after all, but she was disappointed.

'The afternoon off? What on earth's come over you?' scowled Dudley.

'Nothing's come over me,' said Una in sulky fury. 'And just you remember that if I hadn't been here early this morning when you were lolling in bed, you wouldn't even have remembered that note from Lady Limpet.' She glared at him accusingly. 'As for that pathetic poem you said you found in that book, I saw you writing it out yesterday, then tearing the paper yourself!'

'Shhh, for goodness sake, Una. Be reasonable. Our bread and butter is at stake here. This afternoon it's essential that we give that derelict shack a really good going over. You can help me to draw a good sketch of Maudley Montgomery's epitaph surrounded by weeping willows.'

Una felt a sudden rush of enthusiasm. Robby Belmane faded from her mind as she made them both some cheese on toast. Immediately afterwards they set off with notebooks, camera and measuring tape for the plot of rough pasture and decaying building where the gift shop had once thrived.

They were still fiddling and fussing about at six o'clock. Just about that time a small car went down the high street, as Robby's brother Maurice gave him a lift back to Meranto's. Una saw the back of it as she stood behind an old hawthorn bush squabbling with Dudley about the correct position for the grave. The car hardly registered in her brain. 'No Dudley I think it would be a stupid idea to bury a pair of old boots underneath it with his initials inside.'

By nine o'clock that evening she was finally back at Tessa Truett's eating her supper.

CHAPTER 11

The Hunt Ball

Constance Lamby called in at the Twinkle Tearooms for a cup of coffee. She went there rarely, but this morning she needed to sit quietly, away from Swansdown and all its problems, to think about what Chloe had said to her on the phone earlier.

Constance always chose quiet Monday mornings to escape, when everyone else was well occupied. Today Hubert was out somewhere with Cedric. Hubert had been a bit more mellow and even-tempered lately.

Chloe had telephoned to reveal that

209

Marcus Oliphant was taking Una to the local hunt ball. During the course of their conversation Chloe said: 'I received an invitation to Mac and Myra's wedding in today's post. It's the last week in August.' Chloe had got over the first shock of Mac taking the plunge, even though her stream of unspoken affection for him still lay deep in her heart.

These days, Chloe rang her mother quite frequently. There was a growing bond between them.

The mention of Una and the hunt ball hit Constance like a stone. She knew the reputation of Marcus and his friends. They had visited Swansdown occasionally when some of them were no more than schoolboys. The sudden spurt in youthful growth had not disguised their lack of maturity. They were all rich, polite, debonair and forever drinking too much of the hard stuff with their meals.

Constance was worrying for the safety of her youngest and most vulnerable daughter, as Chloe changed the subject. 'Yes,' said Chloe cheerfully, 'I must admit I was devastated when Mac first told me he was getting married. It was like the sun going out. But I've got over it now. Myra's ever so nice. I think I'll definitely accept the invitation.'

'Yes, yes,' said Constance impatiently,

drawing her back, 'but what were you saying about Una and that hunt ball?'

'Oh, *that*,' said Chloe disparagingly. 'It's all part of Cedric's grand plan to keep her and Marcus on the straight and narrow.'

Constance was completely bewildered. 'It sounds exactly the opposite to me, Chloe. In fact I'm still hoping to get Una back to school again. I met her in the post office and she said she's becoming fed up with working on all this complicated material for Dudley Plume. She's a mass of moods.' Constance's voice cracked nervously.

'She told me, but don't ever say anything, mind, that one day there could be a real dust-up because what they do is just make-believe. It's nothing but a sham. One of these days, according to her, all this stuff about Lady Limpet's renowned relation will be exposed as a gigantic fraud. So as far as I'm concerned the sooner she gets away from it, and back to reality, the better.'

'Mother! Surely you don't believe everything Una says? She can be completely over the top. And anyway, Marcus is being a thorough gentleman. They get along like a house on fire...'

Constance sat brooding about it all as she sipped her coffee and gazed through the leaded windows towards the high street. Then, restlessly, she looked away and idly surveyed the Tudor effect oak rack near the tea room ceiling, which displayed old pewter mugs and pieces of English slip-ware pottery. As soon as she'd finished her second cup of coffee and nibbled through a digestive biscuit, she'd pop her head round the Twinkle kitchen door and ask Tessa how Una was. Maybe Tessa knew something about the hunt ball arrangements.

'Hunt ball?' said Tessa, shaking her head as she wiped her hands on a kitchen towel. 'She's never said a word to me about it. But there you are. You wouldn't expect her to, would you? She's very much a law unto herself where her private life is concerned. And it's not for me to dig and delve.'

Tessa's words made Constance more worried than ever.

'Why don't you trot along to Dudley's right now and have a word with her yourself, Connie? I saw Dudley ambling off on his bicycle ten minutes ago, so she'll be on her own.'

Constance thanked her, and made her way to Eagle cottage. She went round the back, knocked at the door then peered through the window. She could see Una kneeling on a piece of folded cloth, scrubbing the floor. Her heart fell a mile. Was this what she had brought Una

212

into the world for? Although she and her two eldest daughters were forced to carry out such tasks, she had hoped desperately that Una would escape such torments, and lead an easier domestic existence.

Una glanced up at the window and caught a fleeting glimpse of her mother's thin pale face. She stood up hastily and came to the door.

'Mother? What's brought you here?'

Constance stared at the stone floor and its bit of rolled-up matting. Then she said earnestly, 'Couldn't you just be using a mop, Una? Surely it isn't part of your duties to be here skivvying for Dudley Plume?'

Haughty annoyance clouded Una's sun-freckled face. 'I don't want to seem rude, but it's really nothing to do with you, Mother. I'm a proper working girl now. And anyway I'm not really a skivvy. He accidentally tipped a whole earthenware jug of ink across the floor so I sent him out until I'd got all the stains scrubbed away. It would be awful if we got all our research covered in dark blue blots and blotches. Lady Limpet would never forgive us.'

Constance sat down on a lop-sided wicker armchair and stared hard at her. 'Don't you think it would be better if you went back to school? I'm sure Tess would still let you lodge there. Unless you decided to come home to us again. We all miss you so much, even though you are so near.'

Una gave a mock sigh. 'Mother, we've gone over all that umpteen times. I know you mean well. But it's no use.'

'And another thing,' said Constance persistently. 'I heard somewhere that you were supposed to be going to the hunt ball with Marcus Oliphant. I just want to warn you. He, well, he's the sort of person that might—'

Una's eyes blazed. 'Might what? Mother you really are the limit. I never realised how old-fashioned you are! Marcus is really nice. I couldn't be in safer hands. It strikes me that you and Father don't want me to lead a life with fun in it like other girls. Why don't you put my name down for the local nunnery straightaway? And whomever's been tittle-tattling about that hunt ball needs a good telling-off. I expect it was Chloe.' Una clicked her tongue in exasperation.

Her mother gave a wry smile. 'If you want to know, I think Lindi's going, too, but she's keeping it a secret.'

'Keeping it a secret? What about the work at the hotel? How will you manage?'

'She's getting two girls from the village to stand in. Perhaps she'll tell you later.

These days she insists that her own life is entirely private...'

Constance made her way back to Swansdown with a sense of foreboding. She was glad Una was happy and confident again, but the thought of her innocence in the company of young men like Marcus Oliphant filled her with dread. She knew she couldn't shield her forever from the world.

Marcus Oliphant had become fond enough of Una to call her his little Tiggywinkle. She could be very prickly with him when she chose and to his mind she behaved exactly like a hedgehog. He was looking forward to escorting her to the hunt ball. He was getting a bit fed up of behaving like a beautiful, dutiful puppet for Pawson. It was time he asserted himself a bit. In the best, and wisest way possible, of course. He didn't want to lose his job. It was paradise working so close to the luscious Chloe.

'The hunt ball?' Cedric Pawson had looked at Marcus with suspicion.

'Yes. Well it is rather a good place to go, don't you think? Surely you've been to a few yourself'

Pawson allowed himself a glimmer of a smile. He had in fact been to many in the past. It was at a hunt ball that he and Tessa Truett had decided to part when they'd both tripped up during The Lancers and she'd blamed him. He had sworn then never to go to another one. But now he was having second thoughts. He didn't trust Marcus Oliphant enough to encourage him to go with Una, unless he himself was around.

'I'll think about it and let you know.'

Later that day, after he had finished dictating some letters, he said to Chloe, 'How would you feel about coming with me to the hunt ball? To be quite candid I feel that it's up to me to keep a firm eye on Una for your father's sake.'

Secretly, Chloe was astounded, yet she had mixed feelings about accepting. Even if Una was still a bit of a child, surely it was nothing to do with Cedric if Una chose to be escorted to the ball by Marcus? Cedric's constant interference in Una's life quite took her breath away.

All the same, as far as she was concerned it was a welcome invitation to have a night out. She had a beautiful silk ivory ball gown with a big red sash that she'd only worn once. She'd also heard through the grapevine that Lindi might be there, which made the thought of being with Cedric all the time less daunting.

She drew a deep breath. 'Yes, I'd be delighted to go.'

He gave a sigh of relief. 'Settled then.

I'll let Oliphant know.'

Marcus took in the news with a feeling of gloom. 'We're going to be chaperoned by the Grand Master himself,' he announced to Una. 'He's bringing Chloe with him.'

Una was delighted that both Lindi and Chloe would be there, even if they were all twirling away in their own respective circles. 'You don't have to be quite so miserable about it, Marcus. We'll easily be able to keep away from Cedric in the crowds.' But Marcus didn't look at it that way.

The hunt ball often changed its venue and this time it was being held in the ancient barn and old hall at Cranston-over-Brook, between Knutsford and Pover, on the west side of Melmere. These gatherings were a mixture of grandeur and homeliness. Everyone thudded and rollicked about in the dances. There was a good mixture of all ages and local families. Generally, the men were on their best behaviour. Younger women were affectionately petted and pampered. Mothers and maiden aunts were glued to their seats with patient good humour ready for even one invitation to trip the light fantastic, or else they danced round together. Nobody succumbed to being an actual wallflower, especially if their own nearest and dearest had departed to the beer barrels, or was keeping well out of sight, hunting for the girl of his dreams during three secret fleeting hours, and escaping with her like a fox into the darkness.

Marcus was just tapping his foot with restless impatience when he saw Lindi. Their paths rarely crossed in normal day-to-day life. She was sitting with some other women, her hair shining like a golden halo. He gasped in disbelief. Why on earth hadn't he noticed her before? What a beautiful, blonde iceberg in that sea-green taffeta dress. He gulped with amazement.

Cedric Pawson sat with Chloe politely sipping a Pimms. He wasn't a family man. He wasn't a handsome young bachelor like Marcus. Marcus was careering at speed round the dance floor with Una, who was laughing hilariously, and Cedric glanced away jealously.

'Would you care to dance?' he asked Chloe.

'I should love to.'

As they stepped out on to the dance floor, Marcus saw them immediately. What a waste for Chloe in that wonderful ballgown to be tied to Pawson all night. It was diabolical At the same time he kept stealing another glance at Lindi. It was a sudden and electrifying obsession.

The lilting music of a waltz increased his zest as he deliberately steered an exuberant Una closer and closer to Chloe and Cedric in the heat and haze. He saw the sudden inviting sparkle of necklaces and tiny earrings, breathed the warmth from bare arms, revelled in the gleaming glow of gowns and Chloe's trail of scarlet satin ribbon. He was so close that his heel touched a shoe. Not her shoe, but Pawson's.

Pawson glared at him angrily. 'Look where you're going, can't you?'

Una began to giggle, but Chloe had seen the look of desire on Marcus's face, seen the pale passion in his gaze, and she was slightly shocked. She had never really been romantic in the true sense, except in her thoughts of Mac Haley. She glanced briefly towards Cedric's furious face and distanced herself from his powerful body as he tried to pull her to him with sudden force. Then the waltz ended and they all strolled back sedately to their seats, smiling and assured as if nothing had happened.

Towards the end of the ball, when Chloe and Una were in the ladies' room, Chloe said bluntly, 'I think Marcus has his eye on me, Una, and I don't quite know what to do about it.'

'His eye on *you?*' Una laughed. 'I think it's Lindi. He was besotted with her tonight.'

Chloe gazed at Una. Even in her own

mildly intoxicated state, she could see her sister was in a giddy mood from all the drink, music and dancing.

'But he was nowhere near her. It was me he stayed so close to when we were dancing. He's always telling me I'm the one for him. Of course I usually take it as a joke and ignore him.' Chloe's eyes were dreamy and large from wine drinking.

Una's pink dress clung to her tightly with the heat of the night. Her eyes shone too brightly and she looked like a delicately painted porcelain in the artificial light.

'I think I'll rouge my face a bit more,' Una said.

'You don't need to, Una. You'll just look common and awful.'

Una ignored her. She took a small powder compact from her pocket. 'I like Marcus quite a lot, myself. And he is supposed to be *my* chaperon, remember.' She spoke playfully, and her thoughts turned to Robby.

How could she be talking like this when it was such a short time ago that she had pledged part of her life to Robby Belmane?

'Marcus is too old for you, Una,' said Chloe earnestly.

'He never is! He's only nineteen.'

'Not in the true sense. He's only here to look after you and if you flirt with him too much Cedric might sack him. Neither of us would want that, even if I wasn't very welcoming to him when he first arrived.'

Una nodded. She had cooled down a bit, but all the same this heavenly night out had stirred her in strange longings. Feelings she had never quite known before.

For Chloe, Una and Lindi the hunt ball turned out to be a happy welcome night of festivity and relaxation. But it was a game of master and slave for Marcus Oliphant and Cedric Pawson, and Marcus swore to break away from Pawson's clutches.

After Marcus had seen Una safely home to Tessa's late that evening, and whilst Una was still full of energy and freshness, swearing all the time that she could have danced 'til dawn, she suddenly decided to write to Robby.

Oh how she missed him, now that the gloss of the hunt ball was fading. It had been a good night out with Marcus, but she sensed that Marcus just regarded her as a little schoolgirl and it upset both her dignity and the romance in her.

She took out her notepaper and pen and began to write.

Dear Robby,
It seems ages since we were together. I hope you aren't too lonely without me...'

She hesitated and re-read it. She knew it was totally dishonest. She hoped he was very, *very* lonely without her, though she could hardly imagine it these days.

'I am going along all right at Dudley Plume's but it gets very boring. Mother keeps wanting me to go back to school. Tonight I went to a hunt ball with Marcus Oliphant so I'm writing this as soon as I've got back. I am so lonely without you close by. Marcus just treats me like a little kid. Chloe went as well, with Cedric. I'll swear it was just to keep an eye on me. Chloe thinks Marcus has his eye on her but I'm not too sure. Let me know when you will be back home in Pover again.

Yours, ever lovingly,
Una

She put it in an envelope and drew a small heart on the back, hoping he would bring out the letter when Tilda might see it.

Then she went to bed and slept like a log.

'There's a letter for you, Robby,' said Matilda Brent a bit peevishly. 'I didn't bring it across to the greenhouse, but it seems to be from your home.' She had seen the heart immediately and had recognised Una's writing. 'Don't forget about us going to the pictures tonight.'

Robby opened the letter at breakfast time. The gardeners started work before breakfast, with just a mug of tea and a slice of bread and had a proper meal at eight. He was glad Tilda wasn't there to watch him. She seemed to be trying to rule his life these days. When he was close to her he was like putty in her hands.

He knew that as soon as they were in the back row of the pictures in the darkness tonight, he would have to exert great self-discipline, especially if she had left any buttons accidentally undone.

He had been to bed with her twice, wearing a French letter. And she had inveigled him to buy her a small eternity ring from the jewellers on a day out in Manchester. Everybody on the staff at Merantos regarded them as a courting couple, and kind Mrs Meranto had once asked him when they would be officially engaged. 'Matilda is a charming girl and you will make a lovely couple.'

'Couple of what?' said Alec Bradshaw, who was in charge of the greenhouses, as he joined in some general gossip. He had once been out with Matilda Brent himself, but he'd quickly found she was a devious two-timer. It was rumoured that Tilda kept seventeen-year-old Master

Mervyn Meranto well warmed on winter nights—for the price of a coney fur coat.

'Did she have much to say in that letter?' asked Matilda coyly, as they left the cinema that evening. The picture was called *Min and Bill,* with Marie Dressler and Wallace Beery, and was so sad that Matilda spent most of the time snuffling and dabbing her eyes with her hanky. Robby was forced to put his arm round her and kiss her once or twice, and she rubbed her nose against his ear in return.

He pretended he hadn't heard her asking about Una's letter, but she persisted.

'It wasn't much,' he said gruffly. 'Just bits about what was happening at home.'

'Happening at home?' mocked Matilda. 'You've left there for good, now. This is your home, with me. Then, one of these fine days, we'll go somewhere together to a proper little home of our own.' She smiled at him confidently and he felt queasy. He wasn't as gone on her as all that!

But the more he drew back the more persistent Tilda became, and by the time bedtime arrived that night he was burning his boats and chancing a bit of loitering in her cramped little bedroom. By twelve o'clock he had been completely seduced.

'Hurry up, honeybunch,' she murmured sleepily as he dragged on some clothes

224

and staggered away. 'Watch out no one catches you or we'll both be singing in the streets.'

When he was safely in his own bed at last, he swore to himself that he would never be tempted by her again. He must write back to Una and tell her he was coming home to see her again on his next day and a half. Maybe it would weaken Matilda's hold on him.

He took Una's letter from the envelope and read it again carefully. She'd gone to the hunt ball with that foppish young rake Marcus Oliphant. He gritted his teeth. It would never have happened if he'd been there. It was past one-thirty when he'd finished writing to Una.

'...and so my darling one—life just drags along at this end much as usual. Alec in the greenhouses has been on at me about the lettuces. He found a huge slug on one of them and promptly blamed me, but I think someone put it there as a joke. Tonight I went to see a rather boring film with some friends. I'm beginning to wish I could find another job closer to you and home but it's next to impossible. Keep smiling.
Your ever faithful Robby.'

When his letter arrived, Una read it avidly,

but with suspicion. Who were the 'friends' he spoke of? There was no mention of Matilda. She kissed the part where he had written his name and put the letter carefully back in the envelope, then into a small shoebox covered in blue patterned silk. This time when he came back they'd have a really special day out, and she, Una Christabel Lamby, would blot out that awful Matilda from his mind for ever and ever.

CHAPTER 12

Bylow's Tower

'I want you both to have a really nice day out today,' said Lady Limpet to Una and Dudley, as they walked round the site where the Pond gift shop had once been. 'As soon as we've finished inspecting this you can go to Bylow's Tower and see if any further improvements can be made.'

It was August and already the ground had been cleared completely. It had been freshly dug into important looking trenches with levelling markers of string and small wooden corner posts, to show the actual spot where Maudley Montgomery's edifice was to appear. There were plans for a new brick and timber thatched cottage said to have been based on the original design of a similar one from the past.

'When it's all finished,' promised Letty Limpet, looking lovingly at Dudley, 'You will be able to use Eagle cottage for storage and work, and live here as the official curator for Maudley and his works.

'It will be linked up to other locations of general literary interest, like Bylow's Tower.'

Bylow's Tower had been one of King Richard's shooting lodges. It was solid and stocky with a stone turret and very small slit windows. The old grey stone was coloured by small circles of orangey-yellow lichen. It was part of the Limpet estates.

Lady Limpet was having some of the interior walls refurbished with bows and arrows, and long wooden-shafted axes decorated some of the doors. The oldest pike in Pover was there, too. A fish in a glass case on top of a padlocked, carved oak chest. It lay there gloomily like some strange over-varnished, yellowing, stuffed sock—imprisoned forever.

'I have three keys,' Letty opened her red leather handbag and handed one to Dudley. 'Keep it *very* safe. It's over two hundred years old.' She looked at them both. 'An up-to-date inventory of everything here will be required, and we must find more items to display here. It needs to be given a new, exciting historical flavour. Perhaps Maudley Montgomery slept here, or something to that effect.' Her cousin seemed to achieve even greater notoriety as they spoke.

Una stifled a yawn, and gazed at the ceiling. Slavery at Eagle cottage: all her energy was dedicated to helping Dudley. The whole of her future being drowned in the fictitious life of Lady Limpet's current obsession. What on earth could she do to escape?

She quite liked Dudley, but she knew he was more than capable of paddling his own canoe. He was standing there now, smiling and nodding his head and promising Lady Limpet the moon in order to keep himself in comfort for the rest of his life. And that was the point, it was *his* life and certainly not Una Lamby's.

When they were alone together at Bylow's Tower and Dudley was prowling about with a joyful expression on his face, he was suggesting all manner of fresh objects which might suddenly be acquired for Maudley's past life.

Una said firmly, 'No Dudley, I do not think it would be a good idea for us to find him his own penny farthing bicycle. And I certainly don't think you should make up any more poetry. There was a girl in our class at school who was much better and she failed her English exams.'

Dudley was standing with the large key to the tower still in his hand. Stung by her words he dropped the key and Una picked it up and put it safely in her old blazer pocket. Perhaps, after all, he really did need someone to help him. She knew for certain that it wouldn't always be her.

Dudley was rueing the fact that it was Una who had been sent to help him and not her intelligent and more imaginative sister who had once worked at the *Gazette*.

'Anyway, I think we've done enough here for the time being,' he said defensively. 'We've taken an inventory, and we've got some ideas for further improvements. That's about it for the moment, so come on.' He stalked to the front door, leaving Una trailing after him to lock the place up.

When Una got back to Tessa Truett's that night, the key to Bylow's Tower was still in her pocket. Carefully she put a small folded silk headscarf on top of it, and then she wrote a letter to her darling Robby.

Dudley Plume was lying in bed bemoaning his fate. He was suffering a badly sprained ankle, caused by tripping over one of the marking strings at Maudley's Memorial.

He was supposed to be going out with Una to inspect a stuffed badger. He'd been toying with the idea of writing a poem called 'Badger', by Maudley Montgomery. It was only eight a.m., but Dudley had been awake for hours. Only yesterday his arch-enemy, the self-appointed historian Malcolm Marqueson had sent an angry letter of protest to the weekly *Gazette* about the plans for the Maudley memorial. Fifty-five-year-old Marqueson claimed the memorial would be an eyesore and a blot on the landscape. Dudley was angered by the opposition, and concerned that the letter might spark some kind of village outcry. Any unnecessary digging into the life he had created for Maudley Montgomery would not be welcomed.

His mind skipped back to the work at hand. Badgers. The only badger Dudley knew of was the one in *Wind in the Willows*. Wearily he hopped out of bed on one leg, balancing against ledges and chairs, and wincing with pain as he hunted for a pencil-stub and a scrap of paper. Then he hobbled back to bed again and sat there in a half-baked daze until inspired.

Badger striped is my delight
In the portholes of the night
His lordly living and his might,
His strength and grit, his fearless bite

Puts all his enemies to flight.
He fights to keep his ancient right.
He will not take the hunter's bait
But reigns supreme on this estate.
He will not flinch inside his sett.
Courage is his epithet.

Dudley flopped back, exhausted by his own brilliance.

He heard Una moving about downstairs and called to her. 'You'll have to go badger hunting on your own. This ankle's worse today. But I've found one of his poems for when we get a decent stuffed badger specimen. I suspect the one lodged in Mrs Peebles's outhouse will be a moth-eaten, maggoty monster.'

It was their habit now to refer to 'finding' more of Maudley's literary output, rather than admitting it was an invention.

Una wasn't listening; she was still thinking about the note in her pocket from Robby. He was coming home to Pover today, and he was arriving at midday.

Una went upstairs to see Dudley.

'I can't be fiddling about at old Ma Peebles today, Dudley. Especially without you. And you know what you said about it being a waste of time there anyway. She was a complete failure over that fifty-year-old owl she promised us. It had doll's eyes in it and I plainly saw some sea-gull feathers and a bit of ocelot fur collar on its chest.'

'We can't afford to ignore any claims about links with Maudley, Una. He's my bread and butter, now. So we must check everything.'

Una was firm. 'Robby has written to say he's got some time off. He'll be here by midday. So a better plan for me would be to go and get on with some work at Bylow's Tower. It will be easier for Robby to find me there.'

Before Dudley could utter one strangled syllable she dashed out of the bedroom and downstairs again.

'Yes, that's it,' she called. 'I'll nip back to Tessa's right now and let her know where I'll be in case he calls there. I've got the key.'

As she hurried back to Tessa's her heart nearly burst with childish triumph at her *fait accompli*. It meant that she could meet Robby at Bylow's in complete privacy; there were no other keys except for Lady Limpet's own. She would meet him and she would *make* him love her, her alone. For ever and ever.

In the bathroom at Tessa Truett's cottage there was always a bright orange silk kimono. It was embroidered with pale yellow chrysanthemums, and rested on a hook behind the bathroom door.

As soon as Una got back she removed it from the hook and tucked it into a shopping bag along with her navy-blue school bathing costume. Then she wrote a message to Tessa and left it on the living-room table. *'If Robby calls, please tell him to come straightaway to Bylow's Tower. I am working there today.'*

She cycled the couple of miles along Melmere to the nab where the tower was. The views were sublime. The tower was almost surrounded by the clear sparkling water of the mere, with sheltered little bays on either side of it.

She unlocked the door to the tower, and closed it carefully behind her. It swung heavily with a loud creak, and slammed shut with a medieval thud, echoing round the ancient building. Inside the air was cold and still above the stone floors.

Una looked around. She felt no fear. She welcomed its peacefulness and her own luck at having a safe sanctuary in which to meet Robby. She peered round happily, then went into the sunniest room, up some winding steps in the turret. The views from the deeply clefted windows were perfect cameos of azure blue and brilliant grey-green sparkling waves. There was a cheval mirror there and rush matting on the floor. The old divan had a hand-woven fine woollen cover which had been carefully darned in places. There were two angular wooden chairs beside it.

Una slipped off all her clothes and put them on one of the chairs. She looked at her image in the mirror. It was like being a water sprite. She put her sun-kissed arms straight up in the air, then bowed them so that each middle finger met the other to form a pointed arch. Then, she gazed at her slim perfectly formed outline, and put on Tessa's kimono, sweeping it round her bare body with a defiant gesture. She thought fleetingly of Matilda Brent, and smiled to herself. She would wear the kimono for Robby. She would have it on when he called, but first she would put on her bathing costume—then it would look as if she had been going to go for a swim.

She took off the kimono and replaced it with the sagging, homely regulation swim suit. Hastily, she put her frock on top. Someone was knocking loudly and trying the door. Surely not Robby? Una leant forward and peered through one of the windows. She could just see the top of Marcus Oliphant's head far below as he paced about on the gravel. What on earth did *he* want?

Then she saw him drift away again and heard the sound of a car engine.

The sun was shining relentlessly. The sky was clear blue and Pover village looked like a picture postcard as Robby left the Twinkle tearooms. He had received Una's message about her being at Bylow's Tower.

'You can borrow my old bike to get there, if you want,' smiled Tessa. 'She'll be looking forward to seeing you so much.'

'I'm looking forward to seeing her, too.' said Robby fervently. He would have given anything to be back here for good—if there'd been decent prospects and there hadn't been the trouble with her father. But he knew it was no good harping on the past, and nothing ever turned out the way he planned.

He was glad to be away from the clutches of Matilda, even though it was only for a day or so. She was becoming quite a nuisance and seemed to think she owned him. He had a slightly guilty conscience about the way he had accepted much of what she offered.

Even so, there was a deep, niggling fear inside him. He dreaded being caught in another assignation with Una after that horrific episode with her father. Even the thought of visiting Bylow's Tower made him baulk. He knew it belonged to the Limpets. It was the sort of place that ordinary people like himself admired from a distance.

'Tessa?'

'Yes, love?'

'I think I'll try ringing Chloe at Grangebeck, just to make sure it's OK for me to go to the tower. I don't want to make a fool of either me or Una.'

'Of course, love. Very sensible. I've got the number in my telephone book.'

Cautiously Robby got through and a maid answered the phone.

'Just one moment, please. I only started work here today.' His spirits began to sink. He should never have phoned. It was only going to complicate matters.

'I'm sorry, sir, Miss Lamby is unavailable. But—'

'Hello? Marcus Oliphant here. Can I be of help?'

Before he had realised, Robby mentioned Una at the tower, but he was quick enough to make it sound as if it was only to do with her work. Then he rang off hastily without leaving his name.

'Did you manage all right then?' Tessa looked at him brightly. He nodded, then quickly mounting Tessa's bike, he decided to take a chance on visiting Una.

The minute Robby had hung up, Marcus hurriedly got into his car and drove to Bylow's Tower. Chloe and Cedric were due back any time, but in their absence Marcus felt responsible for Una's safety

236

and decided to check up.

The place was as quiet as a tomb in the summer heat, and there was no reply when he knocked at the door. But as he was leaving he noticed a bicycle against the wall.

Marcus mentioned the episode apologetically to Pawson when he returned. 'Thought I'd better check, but it was really a load of fuss about nowt, I expect.'

He was quite surprised by the effect of his words on both Chloe and Cedric. He saw Chloe's face cloud over with a worried look. Pawson tensed up immediately.

'I think I'll just go round and see Plume,' snapped Cedric irritably. 'She's no right to be wandering round a place like that on her own.'

On the way to the Tower Cedric decided to call in at Drawbridge Hall. Perhaps Letty Limpet could advise him about who had keys to the tower.

He was lucky. She was at home, wandering round her lavender garden. 'They've both been absolute treasures,' proclaimed Letty, pushing a stem of lavender to Cedric's nose in a lavish gesture. 'Just smell it. Isn't it wonderful? Yes, I can let you have a key. But please let me have it back by four o'clock.'

Pocketing the key, Pawson drove to Dudley's. His eyes flicked over the chaos and he heard Dudley bellowing at him to come upstairs.

'I'm stuck here; helpless. My ankle's giving me agonising and indescribable gyp.'

'I came to see if you knew what Una was up to this morning,' said Pawson drily.

'She's supposed to have gone to do some work at Bylow's Tower,' groaned Dudley. 'We were both going to inspect a stuffed badger at Mrs Peebles', but due to this wretched ankle there was a change of plan.'

'Did she have a key?'

'Oh yes. It was her idea to go because she happened to have the key from when we were there before.'

'I'll give you a lift there, if you like, and bring you back here again.'

'I'd sooner not, if you don't mind. Una is quite capable of looking after herself.' Dudley stared him out with a cold gaze and Pawson realised there was more to Dudley than met the eye.

Pawson turned away. There was only one thing for it. He would have to sort out what was happening for himself. But before he got back into his car he strolled across to Tessa Truett's.

'How's business? I'll have a coffee,' he said casually.

'Oh, fine. Look, why don't you go into

my flat and I'll get Griselda to bring us some in. No need to show you where to go...' she gave him a flirtatious look and they both laughed.

He went through to the living room and as he sat down he idly picked up the message still lying on the table. Robby Belmane! So that was what it was all about. He sat back in his chair thoughtfully.

When the coffee tray arrived he said, 'I mustn't stay long, I've got something urgent to see to. I couldn't help calling in for old times' sake.'

Ten minutes later he was on his way to Bylow's Tower.

CHAPTER 13

Gather Ye Rosebuds

Una heard Robby give a low gentle whistle. She had heard his bicycle on the gravel and seen him from the window, and now she hurried to open the door. The hot sunshine greeted her as she stood in her bathing costume and kimono. He came in and she locked the door again.

His face was burnt red with the sun and his hair clung to his head in sweaty curls.

'What's this? A jail?'

'I'm just playing safe, Robby. Marcus Oliphant was prowling round here earlier, though goodness knows why. I thought this was a good place for us to be on our own. We can stay as long as we want. There isn't much for me to do. I only have to check out a few ideas for Dudley and put them in my notebook.'

'What are you dressed like that for?' He studied the vivid orange silk kimono.

She looked at him shyly. 'I was thinking of going for a swim.'

'Going for a *swim?* From here? What on earth's got into you? It's one of the most dangerous spots imaginable for swimming.'

'Well, anyway, a sunbathe and perhaps a paddle...' She saw his face spread with relief. Then he looked at her suspiciously. 'First you're saying we both have to stay locked up in here for safety and the next second you're talking about paddling and sunbathing. I'm absolutely sweltered. All I want is a cold drink and to cool off.'

She took him up to the sunny room where the old divan was and drew the blinds. He flopped down. He lay on his back and he watched her bringing him a glass of water. She really was the most perfect thing on earth. He gulped the water down gratefully.

'All right then, I'll come out with you

in a short while. We could walk further along the mere into Nab bay where the current's safe for bathing. Then if anyone comes here looking for you we shan't be around.'

She smiled and nodded. But there was a niggling doubt in her mind. For a start the only towels for drying themselves were two minuscule cotton teatowels and a small hand towel. And what would Robby do for a bathing costume? People did sometimes swim in the mere in their trousers, but he could hardly go back into Pover soaking wet.

'I'll just go and do my notes then. It'll take me about ten minutes. There's a tin of biscuits in the cupboard, if you're hungry.'

He nodded thankfully.

Una disappeared into the oldest part of the tower and wrote: 'This was the spot where Maudley Montgomery shot his first and only raven: The Raven of Montgomery Nab. It brought him bad luck for fifteen years until he saved a maiden in a snowdrift on Christmas Day in Nab bay. A poem was found about it in a locked chest in the tower.'

She quickly closed her notebook. That was enough to save Dudley's bread and butter for a while. She'd look for possible relics while they were out. They must try and find an old blunderbuss and an ancient book about ravens for the new museum, as well as a pair of snow shoes.

The lapping waters of Melmere felt cool and delicious beneath the hot sun. Robby had scoffed at the idea of not having a proper bathing costume; he stripped to the waist and bathed in his twill trousers. They clung to his legs as he and Una swam and frolicked about like a pair of young seals.

Later, as they wandered back along the bay to the tower, collecting bits of driftwood as souvenirs, Cedric Pawson caught sight of them and heard their laughter in the quiet summery air.

He'd already called at Bylow's Tower and found it empty. But he hadn't gone in. He guessed they must be somewhere about because of the bicycles, but he had neither the time nor the inclination to actually hunt for them. He'd begun to stroll back towards his Humber limousine.

He hesitated now, as he heard Una's voice so full of joy, and something snapped inside him. What did youths know or care about young virgins? It wasn't until a man rose to maturity that he understood.

Robby Belmane had caused more than enough trouble for him and Hubert Lamby.

Cedric suddenly turned away from his car. Swiftly, he went back to the tower, opened the heavy main door and shut it quietly behind him. With his jaw set like granite he retired to a small bare music room. Cedric left the door of the room slightly ajar and sat there on the old leather couch to wait.

About ten minutes later there was a loud rattling at the front door as Una and Robby let themselves in. Cedric could hear them splashing about in the stone-flagged kitchen trying to rinse each other with fresh water from the sink.

'How shall we manage to dry off properly, Robby?'

'Easy, we just take off our wet things and lay them out somewhere to dry in the sun.'

'But we can't just walk about with nothing on, and even Tessa's kimono is wet through. Supposing someone caught us?'

'How can they when we've locked the door? We'll strip right off and hang the lot out of the windows in the room with the divan. Then we'll lie on the divan until they're dry: the Two Bodies Beautiful.'

'Oh Robby, do you think I dare?'

In spite of her fantasy about greeting him in the kimono and inspiring him to love her forever, Una was beginning to get cold feet. Being here in this stout all-seeing stone tower wasn't like being in a small private room together—all snuggled up with hardly enough room to view each other properly. For Una it was almost a challenge to the whole world. Here in the seclusion of these vast stone walls—two frail human beings, more naked than Adam and Eve. But she agreed to his plan. Soon they were both reclining together on the divan: Venus and Adonis.

Cedric Pawson could sit still no longer. He rose from the leather couch in the music room and began to climb the winding steps to their room.

They heard the footsteps in frozen horror. Was it a ghost? An unearthly reminder of a secret past? Was it the truth of some ancient legend?

Robby darted to the open window to get his trousers and the bathing costume, where they were perched on an outside stone ledge to dry. But in his panic and haste he dislodged them, and before he could grasp them they fell to the grass far below.

Una and Robby stood completely naked and looked at one another with horror. Una recovered first. She dragged the woven cover from the divan and tried to shelter them, just as Cedric Pawson swung open the door wide to greet them.

'It's a damned good day for sunbathing,' Cedric remarked casually. 'I wouldn't advise you to lie quite so close. It increases the heat.' Then he looked at Una coldly and said, 'You're a bonny girl, Una. Your father must be very proud of you.'

Una flushed a terrible deep scarlet. His words were sheer humiliation. She was rooted to the spot, unable to meet his eye.

Then Pawson turned to Robby. 'You're a fine figure of youth, too. Very well endowed by the looks of it. You'll need to be a bit more cautious.'

Robby trembled with rage and fear, silent with dumb horror.

Suddenly Pawson turned his back on them and left the room. At the bottom of the stairs he called: 'Just got to take this key back to Letty Limpet. She reckons it's two centuries old. Bet it's never seen such a sight as I've seen today.'

They heard the slow swinging creak of the massive door as it shut, and they stood transfixed for what seemed like hours.

When the sound of Cedric's car had died away, Robby sighed and kissed her bare shoulders. 'I expect I'd better dodge outside and retrieve our clothes. I don't expect it much matters who sees us now.' He returned and looked at Una ruefully.

'One pair of twill trousers. One school bathing costume. Both dry. Where are your other clothes?'

'In that big cupboard,' said Una.

They stood in silence for a few seconds. The whole scene was in their minds now like an unbelievable dream.

Neither Una nor Robby made a move to dress property. They let them fall to the floor in a crumpled heap. They stood a distance from each other now: she, with firm, gently-curved young breasts and pubic hair more tight and curly than anything else on earth. He walked slowly towards her—slim and straight and vulnerable—his own pubic hair darker, curling in triumph like the watchword of a lion's mane to guard his only pride. Their two bodies met once more as they sank languidly to the divan again. Their limbs intertwined in passionate embrace and she felt him inside her.

'Make him love me for ever,' she prayed. 'Oh please, God, make him love me for ever.'

Later that day, after gasping and sweating, and dreaming and discovering, then quietly talking, they dressed again, leaving tiny traces of blood behind them.

'I am no longer a virgin...' she said wondrously. She felt a mixture now of anguish and relief that the days of myth and mystery were over.

This was the way she herself had chosen it should be.

Seeing the two young bodies had disturbed Cedric Pawson far more than he cared to admit. But he veiled it all in a caring concern for Una.

'To put it bluntly, Hubie,' (for Cedric had driven straight to Swansdown after the incident) '...Una is in danger of becoming a common harlot. Wouldn't you sooner she was a wealthy, respectable, happy partner to a man who would love, care and nurture her for all her days?'

Hubert Lamby was pacing about in an agony of fury about what Cedric had related. His youngest daughter was *naked* with that young hound!

'You're absolutely right, Ced. He'll damned well ruin her without so much as a second thought. Quite frankly I would sooner see her married to an older man. The type you've just described.' They eyed each other knowingly.

'And as soon as bloody possible, before I have a heart attack.'

Cedric suddenly smiled briefly and patted Hubert's shoulder.

'Anyway, don't worry about it too much, old boy. I think we both know the solution.'

Hubert was now in a complete panic, as the full implications sank in. 'God save me from that young brat completely ruining Una's life. Am I to hang from the gallows in order to protect her?' He put his head in his hands and gave a terrible groan.

Cedric's face grew bland and happy. 'I'll make sure it doesn't come to that. Here's to a happy future for all of us.' His voice dripped with satisfaction.

Chloe Lamby was having an earnest conversation with Marcus Oliphant about the phone call earlier that morning.

'I can't imagine who it was. Fancy not leaving his name.' Suddenly the realisation dawned on her. 'Unless it was—' She stopped quickly, sure now that it was Robby. She could have kicked herself for not catching on earlier. What on earth was Una up to?

'That sister of yours can be a bloody nuisance,' grumbled Marcus. 'I was all set to watch some cricket today while old Ced was out of the way, and then it was all ruined by traipsing over to the tower.'

Chloe waited uneasily for Cedric to return. If it really was Robby who'd tried to get in touch with her, it wasn't going to make things easy for Una to settle down quietly again in Pover. Especially if they were going to start meeting in

248

secret. Chloe gave a small hopeless sigh. It was quite obvious that Una and Robby were destined for different worlds, now he was permanently based at Meranto's and Una was doing so well with Dudley.

Then her mind jumped to her own life instead. She was due to go to Mac and Myra's wedding at Pover church in a few weeks. According to Maggie Renshaw there had been a rumour that Mac and Myra would be living with Mac's mother temporarily when the honeymoon was over.

'Don't mention it to anyone, but he's got this new job working for the *Manchester Guardian*. They're supposed to be going to Disley to do up a small cottage.' Maggie had smiled cheerfully. 'No doubt they'll keep in touch, but we'll be losing a good hairdresser in the village.'

Chloe nodded. Her face masked her real feelings. Things were different now, after that Lake District weekend with the rambling club.

People often spoke about broken hearts, but hers was being worn away by the steady drip of her secret tears. That weekend haunted her still and she bravely fought back tears as she remembered it. Both she and Lindi had had a struggle to get a free Saturday and Sunday, in the first place.

At the rambling club meeting beforehand

there had been much confusion about transportation. Everyone seemed to be making their own way there and Lindi and Chloe's hearts had sunk. They certainly couldn't arrange anything at this late date.

'What a terrible jumble,' laughed Mac Haley to Lindi and Chloe, as he gave them a lift home to Pover after the meeting in his new Riley. 'I expect Myra will be glad now that she won't be coming. She's away looking after her mother in Conway. Would you two like a lift with me? There'll be loads of room.'

They both nodded enthusiastically. Chloe squeezed herself in excitement. What luck! Mac without Myra was a small dream come true. Lindi had also been won over by Mac's charms. She could see why Chloe had gone on about him so much. With his tall, easy movements and casual good looks he was a man worth fighting for.

One of the rambling club members knew the owner of a grey stone farm where they could stay. It was a lonely looking place, with its heavy green slate roof, set along a winding muddy, stony track among the mountains.

The weather was beautiful when Chloe and Lindi set off with Mac. They both wore navy blue shorts with corduroy wind-jammers. Their feet were clad in huge brown brogues.

When they'd all gathered in the camping outhouse on the outskirts of Keswick, they found to their dismay that there had been a complete misunderstanding about the numbers of people who would be camping overnight there.

'We understood it to be ten bunks for ten men,' said Ely Strong, the farmer. 'We niver expected five lassies added on.'

'We can take three lassies in t'ouse at a push. But that's eet.'

Dainty little Shirley Gobbins was delighted by the turn of events. The less rustic the better for her. She had secretly hoped for something more central, with a few walks round the shops in Keswick, and perhaps afternoon tea in the Royal Oak Hotel.

'I vote we go to the Nunnery Guest House, in Bracken Street,' said Mac, in undertones to Chloe and Lindi. 'I've been there with Myra. It's quite cheap and very comfortable. We can easily meet the others at Moot Hall for the start of the walk in the morning.'

That evening the whole group met together in a nearby village hall. There was dancing till two a.m. with Jack Ritchard's Orchestra. Tickets were two shillings and sixpence each (supper included).

The evening was laden with good cheer, as the wooden floor rocked to energetic dancing. The air was richly scented with hot pies and potatoes and gravy, and there was tea, homemade cakes, and trifle thick with fresh, farmhouse cream.

Mac Haley danced with both the girls as they mixed with the other revellers, but he found himself dangerously attracted to Lindi, with her soft golden hair shining like spun silk in the electric light. Her simple white cotton Hungarian blouse was fit for an angel; it had red and blue embroidery all round a low gathered neckline. They gallivanted to the music of sweating polkas, breathless highland reels, and general 'Excuse Me's' and 'The Paul Jones', which were intermingled with fox-trots, waltzes and quicksteps and 'Walkin' My Baby Back Home', 'Goodnight Sweetheart' and 'Blue Skies'.

Lindi was a very good dancer, graceful and supple. And she pressed herself with unladylike passion against Mac's body and let her forehead very gently brush his cheek.

As the evening wore on into the small hours Chloe noticed that Mac was enthralled by Lindi; by the time the last waltz arrived they had vanished completely.

'Can I see you back to your guest house?' said Alfred Parks, with whom she'd danced much of the evening. He was large and friendly, and knew the Lake District mountains off by heart. He talked about them the whole time as music thundered in their ears.

'No thanks, Alfred. I'll try and find Lindi and Mac. We're all staying at the same place.'

As she waited for them, Chloe grew increasingly defiant. She was determined not to let Lindi spoil her relationship with Mac. Tomorrow on the walk she would stay close to him the whole time.

Tears slowly gathered in her eyes. She suddenly felt tired. Would she ever be able to get up fresh for an early start?

'Are you still waiting, Chloe? Are you sure I couldn't see you back to your digs? It'll soon be time to get up again!' Alfred's voice was kind.

Reluctantly she allowed him to run her back in his small two-seater car. They had all been given keys; Mrs Telford, the owner, knew they'd probably be very late because of the dance.

'I'll be away to bed early myself,' said Mrs Telford, 'but you needn't worry that you'll disturb me. I always have a good night cap. Third-floor visitors can move about normally without being heard.'

Chloe crept quietly up to the bedroom she was sharing with Lindi. The other single bed was still empty. What on earth had happened? Then, with leaden eyes she flopped into her own small bed and fell asleep.

The next day when she awoke, Lindi was lying under the pale pink eiderdown, fast asleep. Chloe did not disturb her. She washed and dressed and went down for breakfast. Mac joined her shortly afterwards. He seemed only half-awake and smiled ruefully.

'What happened to you last night, Chloe? The last time I saw you that bloke Alfred Parks had you in his clutches.'

'What happened to *you?*' retorted Chloe, jokingly, as she ate some toast, and sipped her tea. 'I had to rely on Alfred to bring me back in the end.'

Mac didn't reply. He stared down at his poached eggs and said finally, 'Where's Lindi?'

'I didn't like to wake her. I was asleep when she came in. I thought it might have been a very late night and she'd need the extra bit of rest.'

Lindi suddenly appeared in the dining room. She looked as fresh as a daisy. She always seemed to look like that, thought Chloe enviously.

Lindi smiled briefly at Mac, but said nothing, remaining silent until they met the other ramblers outside Moot Hall. Then she wandered away to join some of the others, leaving Chloe with Mac.

Chloe was happy at last. Mac was attentive and pleasant, and it was just like the old days. Oh, how she wished she was still there in the newspaper office. Perhaps if she hadn't had to leave Mac might have fallen for her instead of Myra. But she knew it was a bit late to think of such things now.

At first the air was clear and fresh, but as they climbed higher and higher among the mountains a blanket of thick white mist came from nowhere and completely enveloped them. There was anxiety and dissension within the group. Some wanted to turn and go back. Others wanted to go on very slowly, saying it was a moving cloud which would soon clear. Others insisted on not moving from where they were in case they got lost. And many started to worry about being stranded and not getting back in time to catch their transport home.

Then suddenly, the worst happened. Chloe tripped and fell forward over a piece of rock, bending her leg beneath her against the hard mountain crag. She collapsed helplessly with a sharp cry of pain, and Lindi and Mac rushed to help her.

By the time the group had carried Chloe down to the lake again, the mist had cleared and the sun was shining brilliantly.

Mac went to fetch his car to take her to the local hospital. The doctor there said he was almost sure it wasn't broken but was a very bad sprain. He told her to see her own doctor the moment she got home.

Mrs Telford was very upset when she saw them, as they settled their bill. Then, just as they were leaving she hurried towards Chloe, who was seated in the back of Mac's car. She thrust a delicately embroidered handkerchief towards Chloe whispering: 'This might be yours, dear. I found it in Mr Haley's bed.' Then she waved, ran inside and closed the front door quickly.

Chloe stared disbelievingly. It was Lindi's handkerchief.

Since that time, Chloe had tried to forget those memorable two days with the ramblers, which had resulted in a broken ankle. She sat at work in Cedric's office with the lower part of her leg encased in plaster of Paris and her crutches resting against the wall.

Lindi never went on another ramble. She was moody and silent and secretive these days, and Ella and Una just couldn't make her out. Chloe had never given her back the handkerchief. She had laundered it and used it for herself.

Ella was unaware of what had happened on the lakeland weekend (apart from

Chloe's accident). She was enjoying the rambling club very much, and had already been out twice on walks round Hayfield in Derbyshire.

Monty Marqueson, Malcolm Marqueson's son, was there too. A rather glum soul, he lived with his widowed father under the auspices of a domineering housekeeper called Mrs Hornbeam.

Chloe was brought back to the present by the sound of Pawson's car. She took one look at his face. There was a strangely mixed expression of triumph there. He ignored her, and went hurriedly to his study. She heard a muffled thump from inside. He had been known to throw a chair across the room on occasions, but today he looked amazingly calm. A few minutes later he was out again, demanding to know where Marcus was.

'He was here only a few minutes ago.' Chloe paused uncertainly.

'He should be here, now!'

She had never seen him suddenly look so angry. His face was a mass of drawn, grim lines. His eyes were narrowed with fury. She reached for her crutches and went to find Marcus.

Marcus was tucked away in the kitchen drinking a small whisky and ogling at one of the maids, whilst he idly thumbed through the pages of *Strand* magazine. He looked up and smiled at Chloe.

'I was just saying to Cora, here: I think it's time for me to get the skids on and move away from this rather jolly life. The trouble is I haven't thought of anywhere to go yet.' His eyelids flickered. 'Especially, with the woman of my dreams so close, in spite of her present disability.'

For a brief instant the eyes of Cora and Chloe met, then Chloe said, 'Cedric's back and he's as mad as the devil, so you'd better go and see him.'

Marcus gave a weary groan. He buttoned up the open neck of his shirt, put his hand in his pocket, drew out his navy silk tie and tried to smooth it. As he tied it he said, 'Tell him I'm working out the pedigree of that mare he was looking at the other day...and washing the dogs at the same time.' Reluctantly he got up and trailed after Chloe.

His private interview with Cedric lasted nearly an hour. 'For God's sake—shut up can't you? And let ME talk!' bellowed Cedric. 'The reason I'm employing you is to keep your eye on Una Lamby and see that she doesn't get involved in anything unsuitable. It's not much to ask from a lazy young lout like you. Yet here you are lounging about, and there she is on her own at Bylow's Tower, completely unchaperoned!'

'Come off it, Ced, let's be fair. I bally well went there straightaway after the phone call came. There wasn't much point in pussy-footing round there when the place was empty. My main job was supposed to be here, especially with you and Chloe out.'

'My God, Oliphant, you aren't just here as a pretty face. I'm not a goldmine for poor little rich boys.'

At last Marcus began to bristle. 'No one ever thought you were, Pawson. But you have an undue interest in poor little rich *girls*. You're a bloody swine, if you want to know the truth.' Oliphant turned and stamped to the door.

'Come back here!'

'Oh, go to hell you miserable bastard.'

When he'd gone Cedric sat in silence. He was quite surprised that Marcus had turned on him; perhaps he wasn't as tame as he'd imagined. Cedric vowed to close the matter of Una and the tower, and not say another word about it—especially if he had a young enemy in his own camp.

'What did he say?' Chloe asked Marcus some time later. She tried not to show her anxiety.

'What *didn't* he say?' said Marcus nonchalantly. 'I could hardly get a word in edgeways. He was extremely insulting. Yes, I fear that I must cast a few feelers around for pastures new. I'd thought of training to be a vet,' he added seriously.

Chloe was dumbstruck. 'Isn't...well, isn't it a bit like—'

'Hard work?' Oliphant smiled. 'Yes it is, in a way, but the Oliphants aren't a load of pansies you know. There comes a tide in the affairs of man...and all that rot...' Then he added, 'My beautiful Madonna...'

Chloe groaned and got back to her typing.

A change had come over Una. It was caused mainly by a constant, lurking fear that Cedric Pawson might bring her secret to light.

Every day she half-expected someone to refer to the episode in the tower, but no one seemed to have heard about it. Then one day it occurred to her that perhaps the balloon of gossip would never burst, since it hadn't already.

But the memory of it had seared her soul.

She was unaware that except for telling Hubert, Pawson had decided to keep the incident to himself. Dudley Plume was completely oblivious to the truth about what had happened that day as he studied Una's notebook with its written suggestions.

Even so, Una's work with Dudley became more and more ridiculous nonsense to her, as Dudley bloomed with pride and joy to see all the plans growing into reality.

Then, one day, driven to sheer desperation after he had read one of his poems that linked Maudley with an ancient tin of corned beef and a box of wax matches in the year dot, Una walked straight out of the door, got on her bike and cycled back home to see her mother.

'Yes, Mother. I truly mean it. I *would* like to go back to school again. I could start in the Autumn term.' Una looked firmly at her mother. Constance was startled. 'No, it wouldn't worry me in the least about having to catch up on lots of work. I'm used to academic stuff now, Mother. I have notebooks full of it.'

Constance sighed wearily. 'Isn't it a bit late to be thinking about school now you're settled in that steady job helping Dudley? And so well fixed up at Tessa's? You can't just chop and change, based on sudden whims. And quite frankly I've had just too much of it.'

Una was close to tears. She had never known her mother to be so firm.

'Please, *please* give me one more chance

and see if you can get me back again for next term. I swear I won't let you down.'

Constance looked reluctantly at her distraught daughter and relented. She put her arm round Una's shoulder. 'Very well, then. I'll ring Miss Houseworth and see what she says. But if she doesn't agree, you'll just have to knuckle down and continue working at the research with Dudley Plume.'

Una hugged her mother and nodded gratefully. She knew however that what ever transpired she would not be staying as Dudley Plume's helper for one second more than she had to.

A week later Una was wild with joy. Her mother had arranged for her to return to school in September. 'Your father has managed to find some money from somewhere to pay the fees, please don't let him down,' Constance guessed Pawson had a hand in it, although Hubert hadn't actually said so. 'And Tessa says you can still lodge with her. Perhaps you'd better come back here until the beginning of term. You aren't going to be very popular with either Dudley Plume or Lady Limpet.'

Constance took a deep breath and looked seriously at Una. Una waited expectantly. 'There is just one thing, though, Una.

You will not be able to have Robby here to see you again. We can never have a repeat of what happened before. Is that understood?'

Una's heart sank. 'Yes, Mother.' She bowed her head. She had been so busy working out how to escape from Eagle cottage that she hadn't thought very deeply about Robby. Now that she regarded herself as truly his girl, and had made him love her enough to be man and wife, all of that was sure to look after itself.

But one thing was certain, Matilda Brent had been vanquished for ever that day at Bylow's Tower.

CHAPTER 14

The Merry Go Round

Robby Belmane went back to Meranto's happy and contented after his day at Bylow's Tower. Surely he would manage to find a job nearer home to be closer to Una again. She was his girl for ever. Nothing would change that.

But the next day, as rain poured down and he was stranded in the greenhouses, he began to see that life was going to be more complicated than he had imagined. Matilda Brent was peering at him between the aisles of tomato plants. She was smoking a cigarette.

He glared at her fiercely. 'Get out! Nicotine is banned in here. It plays havoc with tomato plants.' Quickly he moved towards her and stubbed out the cigarette.

'But I've just *got* to see you, Robby. You keep avoiding me. I only smoke when my nerves are bad.'

He pushed her outside and followed her. It was more than his job was worth to have her found there.

'It's bucketing down,' she wailed. 'We'll be drenched and I have to be back in the house in a few minutes.'

They went towards one of the shelters among the trees where timber was cut for logs. It had a large corrugated iron roof which rattled with the sound of rain. The air was heavy with the scent of cut wood and damp new sawdust.

Robby felt himself weakening. They'd had some good outings together. She was easy to be with. She prattled enough for ten and was pretty free with her favours towards him. Sometimes he gratefully considered her to be ideal for someone as lonely as himself. He was sure that if it hadn't been for Una he might have, well, not exactly *married* her, but kept her as a

264

regular and very special friend just to see how it worked out.

Whilst they were still sheltering, Matilda stood very close to him. Then she turned, looped her arms round his neck so that he bent down towards her slightly, and gave him a warm leech-like kiss, pressing at his mouth so that he felt her small sharp teeth. A slight tremor ran through him.

'Steady on, Tilda. We can't start that here...'

She put her arms down and turned away, pouting. 'You were really mean to me in the greenhouse, Robby. I almost thought you didn't love me anymore.'

He remained silent, then he said: 'Look, it's time we both got back to our work, or someone'll notice.'

Tilda ignored him. Turning back she suddenly put her arms round him and clung tightly, pressing the side of her face against his chest and murmuring in a muffled voice, 'What would you say if I told you we were going to have a little stranger?'

'A little stranger?' He frowned. 'What on earth do you mean? Look, we really must go. I'll see you after supper, tonight.'

'Our baby, Robby. I'm expecting *our baby.*' She looked at him brightly.

He loosened himself from her embrace. 'I d-don't understand. You can't be. We hardly ever, and even then I always withdraw... It's impossible. The last time...I even used a...' He fumbled for words, sickened by her news.

'It's true anyway,' she said. Her whole manner became brisker. 'So just you think about it while you're in those greenhouses gawping at the tomatoes. See you tonight then, my beloved.'

Robby felt weak with fear. It was a complication he had never expected and he still couldn't believe it. Then his common sense told him to calm down and just see what happened in the next few weeks. He would just pretend she'd never said anything. Maybe he'd check up from his brother about how girls or women knew they were pregnant even before the doctor told them. Anyway he certainly wouldn't be asking Matilda herself for more details or it would look as if he was accepting her announcement, which would mean he'd be trapped for evermore.

He walked back slowly to the greenhouses. Some of the leaves on the tomatoes were looking a bit yellow. It was not a good sign. Supposing he lost his job for not looking after them properly? He brightened a bit. Maybe that wouldn't be a bad thing—at least it would be a quick, painless escape from Matilda Brent.

The only thing was, of course, that she might follow him back to Pover, and that would be ten times worse. He'd have to go elsewhere, and as far as possible.

For the next few days Robby did everything he could to avoid meeting Matilda. That very evening he went out with Alec Bradshaw and two other gardeners for a quiet drink and a game of open-air skittles at the back of the local pub. After a couple of hours in their company the problems of Matilda Brent's news had vanished almost completely.

As soon as his next day off arrived, he was back to Pover in an instant, determined not to get waylaid by her again.

But it was different this time. He was surprised to find that things had changed as he strolled round to Tessa's to enquire if Una was about.

'Didn't she let you know then?' Tessa looked at him sympathetically. 'She's gone back to live at home.'

'Live at home? You mean back at Swansdown?' He was astounded. How on earth was he going to manage to see her now?

'Her mother persuaded her,' said Tessa, smiling reassuringly. 'I'm sure she'll get in touch with you, when she has settled in properly. It does seem to me to be a better idea to be living back there when it's so close.'

'Is she still working at Dudley Plume's?'

'Mmmm, but she's even been doing some of that work at home. And I know for a fact that she's not there today because both of them have gone to look for some ancient tennis rackets, near Knutsford.'

Robby spent the day wandering about Pover restlessly. It wasn't the same without Una there. Everything seemed so much more ordinary, and even his own family were busy with their own affairs.

With a heavy heart he returned to Bowdon and wrote Una a letter.

Sorry I missed you today, my darling one. I never knew you were back home again till I called at Tessa Truett's. It was awful wandering around Pover without you, and of course I could not possibly get in touch with you at home. What on earth are we going to do? Don't keep me too long in suspense. Your faithful lover Robby

Una read the words over and over again, and then she burnt the letter. He was right. What on earth were they going to do?

It was getting more and more unbearable working at Dudley's. She longed to leave and settle down properly to her school studies again.

The family had welcomed her back as if nothing had happened, and even Father had been quite pleasant. He had talked to her for ages about a new foal which he was sure would bring him fame and fortune. He promised Una a ride when it was broken in. He had urged her to practise more. She had nodded, but his words meant nothing. All the same she was glad he seemed so happy again.

As she sat there in the living room gently fondling Beech, she felt as if she'd never been away. She wanted it to stay like this for ever. She didn't even mind the kitchen work.

'Now Una's settled at home,' said Pawson to Hubert, one day, 'she could get a bit of practice in, riding with Marcus. He's pretty good. I'll send him round to see her.'

Cedric had patched things up with Marcus Oliphant. In fact they were getting along really well at present. Cedric was entirely unaware of Marcus's vague plans to up and leave him and go off to train as a vet.

'I shall probably toddle off to Edinburgh for the vet stuff. It's *the* place,' Marcus had said to Chloe. 'You can explain it to the S.O.D. when I've gone. But meanwhile I'll cling on here until my great Aunt Portia snuffs it and we all delve into her coffers.'

Hubert and Cedric walked from the stables and stood admiring the copper beeches. Hubert had complete faith in Cedric's judgement of young and suitable companions for Una. It had been a huge relief to him, after all that past trouble when she had run off with that little cur Belmane.

It was the end of August when Una broke the news to Dudley that she was leaving to return to school.

'Back there? You must be raving mad. Most people can't wait to escape!'

'You liked yours, Dudley. You told me—'

'But you never liked yours...'

'I used to say that,' admitted Una. She was nearly going to add *before I came to work here*, but stopped just in time.

'How am I going to manage on my own with all that work Una? All those poems to write. All the memorabilia to find and catalogue. All the filing and research. All the parcels to wrap and unwrap.' He looked at her woefully. 'What did Lady Limpet say?'

'I haven't told her yet. I'm sending her a letter of resignation tomorrow—on pale green paper with purple ink.'

'What about your boyfriend?'

Una looked at him suspiciously but his

face was as serious as always. It was hard to tell whether Dudley Plume was brilliantly intelligent, or completely stupid.

'If he's looking round for a post nearer to home, he could take your place.'

'I'm not really sure. He *might* be.' Una looked uncertain. 'He wouldn't want to be paid as little as me.'

That evening Una got through on the phone to Robby. She was beginning to pine for him. It seemed like years since they'd been together.

'Robby? I'm missing you terribly. Did you know I'm leaving Dudley's this Friday? He'll need someone else to help him out and he suggested you. He seems to think Lady Limpet will pay you a good wage.'

A few weeks earlier Robby would have dismissed the idea out of hand. But now, with Matilda convinced she was pregnant, there was nothing he wanted more than to escape to another job miles away. 'Tell him I am very interested. Give him my address and ask him to write to me here.'

'I'm glad to be back home, Robby. If only it was like it used to be when you were here.'

'We can never go back to what has been, Una. But there's always the future.' His voice broke slightly. He tried to blot out the future which Matilda was planning for him. 'When shall we meet again? It will

271

have to be in secret. Could you get to Castle Mills to go swimming?'

A ray of happiness filled her. 'I could find out if Chloe would bring me over by car on her next day off.'

Una put down the phone with elation. Perhaps everything would work out in the end, especially if Robby managed to get the job with Dudley. And as for her fears about Matilda Brent, she could see now that she'd been wrong about her.

She smiled to herself in sweet contentment. Yes, everything was going to be happy from now on.

Just before she went to bed Una looked through a few of her school books. She accepted that when she returned in September she would not be in the same group as when she'd left. This time all the other girls would be a year younger than she was.

'It's the only way to catch up on the syllabus,' her house mistress Miss Clarkson had warned her with brisk cheerfulness. 'But once you've got over that initial hurdle it should be a straight run up for the sixth form next summer.'

Miss Clarkson had been kindness itself. She had been assured that returning to school was the right thing to do.

'Almost everyone has a dread of going back to school once they've left,' said Miss

Clarkson. She was a small neat woman, with her dark hair parted in the centre. It was impossible to guess her age. 'Rarely do we meet a pupil like you, prepared to take the plunge and return to pick up the threads again.'

Chloe was pleased to give Una a lift to Castle Mills bathing pool to meet Robby. But after weeks of anticipation, Una was somewhat disappointed by their meeting when the day finally arrived.

'I won't come in with you to the pool,' smiled Chloe. 'I'll go into Altrincham and call back later.'

It was a warm but greyish sort of day, with a touch of thunder in the air as Una rushed towards Robby to greet him. Although he smiled and seemed genuinely pleased to see her, he was also peculiarly off-hand. There was a sort of inexplicable distance between them.

Dressed in their bathing costumes it was almost as if he were trying to ignore her, diving quickly into the water and swimming purposefully away.

Una began to feel frightened and frustrated. What on earth was going on with him?

After about half an hour of being ignored almost completely, she climbed out of the pool and got dressed. She sat beside the pool mournfully licking an orange Walls Snofrute, waiting for him to come out.

When Robby was dry and dressed again he was much more his old self He looked at her apologetically and said, 'Una, there's something I've got to tell you. And I can't pluck up the courage. It's not very good news, so if you'd rather not hear it just say so right now. We'll forget all about it.'

Her heart sank. He was looking at her with almost agony in his eyes. She did not know whether the redness there was from the chlorinated water or from tears of real despair.

They both fell silent. The noise of people splashing and laughing in the pool echoed around them.

Then, summoning up all her courage she said, 'Is it something to do with Matilda Brent? Have you decided you like her more than me after all?'

Robby gasped with amazement. 'No, no! I love *you*, Una. I worship you. That's what makes it all so much harder to explain. But it is something to do with Matilda Brent.' He put his arm round her. 'Let's walk across to the trees where it's more private.'

Una suddenly felt dizzy and ill. Whatever was he going to say?

Robby put down his jacket on the grass, and she put her cardigan beside it.

'I've been in a turmoil for days, Una. It's about Matilda expecting a baby. She says it's mine, but I swear to you on the Holy Bible it isn't.'

Una gave a small quiet sob. 'Oh Robby, Robby. How could you?'

'It was so lonely at Meranto's without you,' he pleaded, 'and I admit I went out with her once or twice.' Then he said, 'Apart from anything else the dates don't tie in with the times I went out with her.'

Una's face flushed deep red. 'So you've suddenly got yourself all brushed up on dates and things, have you?' she gulped with tearful anger. 'You've suddenly sought out all the information you can, to try and prove her child-to-be isn't yours. But what you are truly saying is, Robby Belnane, that it could have been. Because you *went* with her. Just like you *went* with me at Bylow's Tower.' Una began to weep bitterly. She never would have dreamed he could be so unfaithful.

'Una, oh, Una, my darling. You just don't understand. I swear to you that Matilda Brent means nothing to me except a sort of friend. If only you knew how hard it is for a man not to get carried away in a moment of weakness.'

Una sat like stone, hardly listening to his protests. If it was so difficult for him not to get carried away how could she ever be sure of anything to do with their love? And could she ever trust him again?

Suddenly she thought of Marcus Oliphant. She quite liked him, but never did Marcus try to tempt her, or she him. He seemed to be a perfect gentleman. She blinked back a few tears in the continuing silence. And what about Dudley? Quite frankly she couldn't imagine Dudley even daring to shake hands too long with anyone, except Lady Limpet, never mind kiss them.

Then Robby said slowly, 'I know you'll think this is just making excuses and trying to pass the buck, but I pretty well know for a fact that Matilda's baby, when it arrives, will be the child of Mervyn Meranto. It's common knowledge in the house.'

When Chloe called back from Altrincham to collect Una she was puzzled by her pale face and by Robby's apparent nervousness.

'Have you had a good time?' she asked cautiously.

They both nodded.

With a kind of strange timidity Robby kissed Una goodbye on her cheek.

When Una and Chloe were on their way home to Pover, Chloe said, 'What on earth happened? You look awful!'

'Just period pains,' mumbled Una in

a low voice. 'Either that or a bit of cramp from swimming. The water was quite cold.'

Chloe said no more, but she felt a sudden wave of sadness. She had hoped so much that they would enjoy themselves.

Una was lying in her bed at Swansdown clutching a hot water bottle to her belly. Ella offered her a cup of tea, and she looked across at the large unopened sturdy blue paper package on top of the chest of drawers.

'Anyway, at least you've got some sanitary towels if you need them. You should have given it the benefit of the doubt and never gone to that pool. You're swayed far too much by Chloe. Just because she can ferry you around doesn't mean you've always got to go to places when it's convenient for her.'

Ella was unaware of Una's real reason for going swimming. Her own life was quite pleasant at the moment and she wasn't particularly interested in all the fuss over Una and her return to school in the Autumn term.

Ella spent most of her spare time these days knitting pullovers for Monty Marqueson and his father Malcolm, and immersing herself in their gossip about local archaeology, which often included a tirade against Lady Limpet and her various schemes.

'Letty's destruction of that bit of land where the Pond gift shop used to be was a disgrace It's clearly part of a Roman settlement. The rutted stones of a bit of Roman road were found there forty years ago. That's why that gift shop always remained a wooden building.'

Ella nodded in sympathy, just as she tried to do with everything Monty's father said these days. But she had once been told by Chloe, when she worked at the *Gazette*, that old records revealed nothing in particular except a few eighteenth century terracotta drain pipes. All the same, one could never be too sure. Ella would think about such titbits deeply as she knitted another row of complicated Fair Isle.

The following day, Una felt completely fine. Even Robby's awful revelations had become less horrible in brilliant sunshine, and she strolled along the shore of Melmere and its sparkling water, drinking in the fresh air. She knew he had meant every word he said about Matilda Brent, so the sooner Matilda Brent acknowledged that her child-to-be belonged to that spoilt creature Mervyn Meranto, the better. And then if Robby managed to come back to Pover and take over her job at Dudley's, it would all be plain sailing. She was convinced now that Father had got over his awful hatred. Hatred could not last for ever, surely. And now she was at home and going back to school there was nothing for him to grumble about.

As she idled along on her own, feeling at peace with the world, a peculiar and disturbing thought entered her mind, completely out of the blue.

Today was the day her menstrual cycle was due to begin. Normally she wouldn't have bothered at all as she always knew it never varied within a day or so of its regular date. It was just that today she felt so carefree, almost as if it had already been and gone again. She frowned to herself, but then laughed aloud at her own nervousness. Time to worry about things like that when you were a married woman or a lady of easy virtue like Matilda Brent. The trouble that awful girl was causing was nobody's business. And now she was even making Una nervy herself. It was almost catching!

By the end of the week, Una's spirits had sunk to rock bottom. What on earth had happened to her period? Surely she couldn't be as late as this? She raked up all the reasons of an innocent nature that might have caused it. Moving to live in a new area? No. Family grief or loss of a loved one? No, thank heaven. She sighed.

She needed to wee the whole time, and there was no sign of her period. She was in a secret panic as she got ready for the new school term.

CHAPTER 15

Showdown

Chloe Lamby had never even set out to go to Mac Haley's wedding at the end of August. She was suffering a bilious attack. But in a way it was just as well, for there was to be no wedding, a fact which became the gossiping point of the whole village.

Mac did not turn up.

To say Myra was broken hearted would be an understatement. She lost weight, and suffered a nervous breakdown. For over six weeks she left her younger sister to carry on with the hairdressing business while she went back to her family home in Conway to try and get over it.

'Something happened in the Lake District, I swear it,' she said tearfully to anyone who would listen. 'Mac changed towards me from that moment. Something cooled him off and caused him to have second thoughts. I just put it down to the strain of moving to Disley.'

Mac went to Manchester, to his new job at the *Manchester Guardian*, and little was seen or heard of him.

Lindi Lamby often heard mention of the great saga as it was told and retold, but no one ever guessed her involvement, except her sister Chloe.

Lindi's night of love with Mac Haley had been a perfection. She knew that now. And at the end of it they had both laughed and collapsed into each other's arms groaning with relief and joy at such a well-timed union. Both of them had accepted that in reality there could only be this one perfect night.

But the memory of that one night strengthened Lindi's resolve to move to Manchester as soon as possible.

Robby Belmane felt heartsick when he got back to Meranto's. Even though he had been honest with Una about the real situation, Matilda Brent was always close by, still proclaiming in hushed tones to the underworld of secret gossip that if ever she *did* happen to become pregnant, which was extremely unlikely, Mr Belmane in the gardens would be the proud father.

If such a happening were to occur she would leave and live in a rose-covered cottage with him. The child would be called Sylveen if it was a girl, and Brently if it was a boy.

Robby was so overwhelmed by reports of this underground grapevine that he grew thin and worried, and spent far too much time in the local pub with his mates.

Then, one night, there was a terrible hullabaloo in the part of the attics where some of the servants slept. Robby knew nothing about it until the following morning.

It was midnight and most of the staff were sound asleep, due to be up again before dawn. In spite of this, they were awakened by Mrs Meranto. She was going round knocking on all the doors and then popping her head round to look in. Servants were not allowed to have locks on their bedroom doors. It was a safety measure in case of fire, though one or two did put chairbacks against their door knobs at night. Such measures were also undertaken by Mrs Pepper, the housekeeper, but she had narrowed it down to a specially made wooden wedge.

Mrs Meranto was a quite liberal-minded, employer who normally never came near the rooms of her staff, except in their absence. So it was a great shock to everyone to see her anxious face peering in at them, and to hear her apologising for the disturbance. Her excuse was a muttered tale about a search for Pom-Pom, her Persian cat.

Mrs Meranto was just beginning her story for the umpteenth time when she reached Matilda Brent's room.

'Excuse me, I'm looking for my...' Her voice faded. The bed was completely empty.

Cautiously Mrs Meranto went to the bed. It had obviously been slept in. She leaned over and felt it to see if it was warm. It was stone cold.

Mrs Meranto stood there expressionless. Reluctantly she went back down the winding attic stairs to the second floor. Without a moment's hesitation she tapped at Master Mervyn Meranto's door, then walked in quickly and put on the light.

There was a great storm of billowing white sheets on the huge double bed. When they'd subsided, Mervyn peered out.

'Mother! What in heaven's name are you doing here at this time of night?'

She looked at the bed in silence. Her sharp eyes had caught a brief glimpse of Matilda Brent's head. Without mincing words she said, 'I was just looking for a *servant* called Matilda Brent. I shall call back to this room in another five minutes to see if she's anywhere about. She will be receiving her notice first thing tomorrow morning.' Mrs Meranto turned on her heel and left.

The next morning Matilda put on the most dramatic display of her whole life. 'I swear to you, Mrs Meranto, by Holy God, and all His angels, that your son Mervyn is the father of my child. I wouldn't take the Lord's name in vain. It's common knowledge—Mervyn's been at me since the day I arrived. Out of respect to you, Mrs Meranto, I was keeping it secret. But you'll soon see when it's born. You'll see the likeness, all right. If it wasn't with me being a servant, we'd be proper man and wife by now. Mervyn knows it all too well.'

Mrs Meranto was more concerned than she was willing to show. It wasn't uncommon for servants to accuse the sons of their employers, but the girl was usually dispatched as soon as possible. In this case, however, Mrs Meranto had suspected something might be going on for quite a while now.

Matilda's words rang in her ears. And the fact that this might be her own first grandchild put a different complexion on matters.

'Very well,' said Mrs Meranto slowly. 'Far be it for me to question your story, Miss Brent. I am a reasonable woman. I shall allow you to stay on here and work until you are closer to the date when your child is due. Then, if you so desire, I shall arrange for you to go into St Evangelina's nursing home for unmarried mothers. After the happy event we will review the situation again.'

Matilda left the confrontation in a cloud of confident joy. She knew the baby was Mervyn's, and within seconds she was planning her new lifestyle. No rose-covered cottages for her: she'd have a new house in Sale or Hale Barns, holidays in Bournemouth, and a large six-seater Humber.

From that moment onwards she ignored Robby Belmane completely, and every grapevine in the place trembled with the news of Matilda Brent, who was carrying Mrs Meranto's first grandchild. Mervyn was promptly enrolled at Fresh Fields Agricultural College to study dairy farming, and he disappeared to work on an unknown farm until the college term started.

Robby couldn't believe his luck. He immediately wrote to Una, via Chloe, to tell her what had happened.

On his next visit home, he said, 'So now do you believe me, Una? Am I forgiven?'

Una had nodded and smiled serenely. But she seemed to Robby to be strangely quiet. Even when he kissed her passionately, she hardly responded.

'It's nothing really, Robby. It's all to do with going back to school again. It's going to be quite a change. I feel so grown-up now.'

Una hugged herself and smiled again. More grown-up than he'd ever know.

'Will you be wanting the STs yet?' said Lindi, glancing towards the blue packet still lying unopened on the chest of drawers.

'Mine's arrived early. And just on the day when I've managed to get an evening off to go the village hop. They've got a proper band tonight. I'm going with Tabitha Karlow, whose brother works at the BBC in Manchester.'

'Take them all,' said Una, adding quickly, 'I've got another packet in the wardrobe.'

When Lindi had departed Una lay on the bed and thought about her predicament. It was the beginning of September and her own periods had vanished. In just under a fortnight she would be starting school again.

She hadn't mentioned her worries to a single soul. She comforted herself that, even now, it might just be some sort of fluke, and nothing to do with her day at Bylow's Tower.

Whatever the case, she knew one thing for certain, she must not breathe a solitary word to anyone about it. She knew from experience that even the most trivial secrets could cause mountains of family drama if blurted out by accident.

Una looked across to the flowered curtains and then up to the ceiling. Tears came to her eyes. How was she going to bear it all? She knew deep down that she was expecting a child. Even though it seemed completely unbelievable.

She was curious about what it would be like to have a baby of her own. It was something she simply could not imagine. There had been occasional cases of certain older girls at school who had suddenly left.

And here she was, actually going back to school with the same thing happening to herself. She began to feel ill at the thought of it, and got up to make yet another trip to the lavatory. She willed herself to put all this completely out of her mind and act as if everything was entirely normal.

Una went downstairs. She made her way outside, and breathing deeply, gazed at the gardens and the vivid beds of snap-dragons overhung by late trailing pink and lemon roses.

She was just in time to see Marcus Oliphant dismounting from one of Cedric

287

Pawson's horses. Whatever was he doing here? He waved to her cheerfully, and her heart lifted.

'Just the girl I was coming to see. About these horse-riding lessons. Better late than never.'

'Riding?' She stared at him, bewildered. 'Are you sure you've come to the right place?'

'Quite sure, my dear. One of Cedric's latest brainwaves. "Get round there," he said, "And get Una Lamby into the saddle as soon as possible. It'll be the making of her!"'

She began to laugh. 'It certainly won't. I did once ride a pony when I was about four, but I just never took to it, and I've no intention of starting again.'

'Not even for Ced's sake?'

'I'd be less likely to do it for his sake. Any one would think he owned us all.'

Marcus began to look quite downcast. 'You can say that again, sweetheart. But don't let him get you down. Nil Bastardus Carborundum and all that jazz. Am I to return with the message that the lady has declined his generous offer?'

'You certainly are.' Then before she could stop herself and as if some devil had forced the words into her mouth, she said, 'And anyway, horse riding isn't very good for pregnant women.'

Marcus Oliphant started, and gave her a penetrating look. Then he said lightly, 'Too damned right, old bean. Jasmine Johnson went head over heels on hers and the air was pregnant for hours. Mum's the word old sprout. Bye for now.' He waved to her then cantered away thoughtfully. One thing was certain, no one would ever learn of this from him. She was a good kid and he wished her well.

Una walked slowly back to the living room. What a crazy thing to have told Marcus Oliphant like that. But she'd trusted him somehow, and by blurting it out she'd suddenly felt much better, as if the weight of her secret was shared. But for whatever reasons she'd told Marcus, she must never ever get carried away like that again.

She wandered around, restlessly, ill-at-ease and lonely. Things were going to be hard with such an awful secret to contain, but what other way was there? She couldn't bear another confrontation with Father. And with Robby being involved for the second time, Father's gun might damage more than just suitcases.

Eventually she left the hustle and bustle of the hotel and returned to her bedroom, lying there on her bed listlessly. Her brain refused to consider whether she should tell Robby the news. She turned and looked towards the small bookcase Mother had placed in the room for all her school books. She cheered up slightly. If she concentrated on her school work maybe it would help to blot out all her worries.

Although Robby was no longer pestered by Matilda Brent, he missed having a love life. Una had been in touch with him and had explained that for the time being they must not meet again. She was completely overloaded with getting back to her studies.

'This time next week I shall be back in school uniform. I'm going to need a bit of time to get dug in again properly,' she took a deep breath. 'I'm sure that by Christmas everything will be back in swing.'

'*Christmas?*' Robby could hardly believe his ears. 'But that's five months away. It's almost half a year!'

'I know it seems a long time, but it'll soon go.' Una bit her lip to stop it trembling.

'And you don't want to see me again until Christmas? Una, what on earth's got into you?'

Suddenly she felt like weeping. *Your baby, Robby Belmane. That's what's got into me. Your baby and I just don't know what to do.* She longed to tell him, but instead her voice quavered slightly and she said, 'It's not that I don't want to see you. It's just that it seems to be the best way of...'

'The best way of what?'

She heard his voice rising to anger and she couldn't stand it. She put down the phone receiver. She was quite numb with fear. Would he cast her away? Was she going to be cut off from everyone just because she thought she was having a baby?

That night in bed she cried again, but even the act of crying depressed her more. She seemed to do nothing but sob in secret and smile brightly in public. All she had to pin her hopes on was getting back to school, where no one would be concentrating on her moods. She would be only one of sixty senior girls. For once in her life she was beginning to welcome it.

Elbreeze High School at Shale Bridge was a day school with a good academic history. The headmistress, Miss Houseworth was always regarded by the girls as a bit of an eccentric. The only subject she taught was Ancient History, and only to the five sixth-form girls who were marked out for dazzling university careers.

Una fell back into the Elbreeze routine much sooner than she'd expected, and within a month it was almost as if she'd never left. To her surprise she was not the only girl who had been set back for a year. There were three others and they all became lifelong friends.

By October Una had managed almost to forget her pregnancy; it was easy to blame nausea on school dinners. And those second helpings of jam rolypoly.

'You are absolutely incredible,' drawled her new friend Dolores one day. 'You'll just get fatter and fatter, and no decent man will look at you. The castles of Britain will never see your face gracing the banqueting table, my dear, unless you cut out school rice pudding and tone down all that stodgy, jammy mess. One small chocolate liqueur and a tiny cup of black coffee in that darling new little place in Shale, with the dark green blinds, is all one needs.'

Life was good. It wasn't until Christmas, when her first term back at Elbreeze was over, that Una was forced to face the reality of her situation again. And this time there could be no denying it.

CHAPTER 16

Christmas

When Una finished her first term back at school, she was astonished to discover she'd come top in botany, Latin and mathematics. Before her time off, she'd had only mediocre grades in these subjects.

'You're a dark horse, Una Lamby,' laughed Dolores, as they gazed at the school noticeboard, framed with garlands of silver tinsel for the Christmas season. 'Whatever will you do with a selection like that?'

Una shook her head. She hadn't the faintest idea, but she was glad she'd made some progress, if only to show everyone she wasn't just wasting time.

'I'm positively glowing,' said Dolores, with a droll look. 'That's me. Second from bottom in everything but scripture and singing. I shall probably become a chorus girl.' Dolores gazed at the list, polishing her shapely fingernails with a small kid buffer. 'I notice Delia Hornbeam did jolly well in chemistry and physics. And Renata actually got a distinction in

English. We're not such a bad old bunch.' Then Dolores looked Una over carefully and said: 'You've not taken a blind bit of notice about not stuffing yourself with stodge. You're beginning to lose your waist-line. By the time the Christmas hols are over, you'll be like a turkey.'

Una smiled affectionately. She had never mentioned her secret to anyone; and it was fortuitous that she could blame any changes in her shape on Christmas mince pies or too much chocolate.

She felt so normal; it was hard to believe she was really pregnant. Maybe it was all some kind of mistake. She tried not to think about it.

And there was better news to think about anyway, Robby was coming home for three whole days just before Christmas. She felt a slight twinge of guilt. She had hardly missed him and the Autumn term had flown by.

Robby had found their separation very upsetting. 'It's getting so wearisome, Una. Time's just dragging along.' Their phone calls were always made from Chloe's office at Grangebeck. They had worked out a weekend system whereby Una would go along to see Chloe when Cedric was out of the way, and ring Robby from there.

'I can hardly wait for us to be together again,' he groaned. 'It's awful. It's like being a monk.' Una felt reassured by the mention of monks, now Matilda was out of the way.

Cedric Pawson was helping Hubert arrange a Christmas Eve ball at the Swansdown. They had been a regular event in the past, but because of Hubert's health the last few Christmases had been quiet.

'You need something to buck up Swansdown a bit, Hubey. Show everyone that your place is still alive and kicking. I'll see to most of it and get the cash moving.'

Cedric was paying a fantastic amount towards all the arrangements, including extra Christmas staff. It was to be the final celebratory mark for 1932, and afterwards the hotel would be closed down until the end of January 1933 to allow for decorating and refurbishing.

Una was more excited than she'd been in months.

Robby was packing his things to take back to Melmere. He had bought Una a very special Christmas gift. It was a large glass swan, shaped with a small hollow in the middle to form a bowl with glass feathers round it.

He put a beautiful embossed Christmas card inside the bowl with a scarlet corded bow, with fluffy silk ends to it. Inside were the words: *'Cygnet of Melmere. Loving you always. A very merry Christmas. Robby.'*

The glass swan had cost him nearly two weeks' wages.

He wrapped it carefully in tissue paper, then newspaper, and then brown paper. Then, tying it with string, he wrote MISS UNA LAMBY on it, and put it in a black leatherette shopping bag along with other gifts.

Before he went back home Robby looked at himself in the shaving mirror. He was growing a moustache to make himself look older. He trimmed it carefully with a pair of small nail scissors. Deep down he hoped that it would act as a disguise, so that if he ever bumped into Hubert Lamby, he wouldn't be recognised.

Just before he was due to set off, he was walking round the greenhouses, checking that everything was in order, when the most amazing thing happened. A message arrived from one of the servants saying that Mr Meranto wanted to see him straightaway.

'You're to go to the library. He's waiting there.' The girl's face was gloomy and Robby's spirits dropped like lead. He had never actually spoken to Mr Meranto, except to touch his cap to him. He was out of the country a lot on business but

296

rumour had it that he still knew what was going on in every corner of the estate, even when he was away.

Robby tapped at the library door, his heart thumping. Trust something to happen now, the last days before Christmas and just when he was due three full days off work. It was unbelievable. He remembered a terrible story about old Claude Bamborinee who had accidentally steamed the greenhouse at the wrong time and was summoned in this exact way to see Mr Meranto. He'd been given the sack without a moment's hesitation.

'Come in.' His tone was crisp, business-like, but not unfriendly.

Robby went in and stood silently. He was wearing his one and only suit, a hand-me-down of good-quality striped grey wool.

'You wanted to see me, sir?' He tried not to show his nervousness.

Charley Meranto stood there with his silvery head bowed for a few seconds. He was perusing a large open volume resting on the library table. Robby could see it contained a coloured plate displaying exotic plants and birds.

'What I'm going to say will probably come as a bit of a surprise, old chap.' said Mr Meranto.

Old chap? Robby could hardly believe

his ears. He wasn't used to such familiar language. Was Meranto trying to soften the blow of the axe?

'I won't mince matters. I want you to pack your bags right now and come with me to Patagonia.' He looked up and fixed Robby with a steely stare. 'I mean it, my boy. No mucking about. I've heard good reports of you. I want you to help me out with a few plant specimens and a bird photograph or two. Naturally there'll be other business matters as well. But that won't concern you.'

Robby's mind worked like lightning. He knew it was the chance of a lifetime. It also dawned on him that if he refused he would probably get the sack for not showing initiative.

'I'll get ready straightaway, sir.'

'You'll probably need a medical, but I'll arrange it for you. I'm calling at a doctor pal's place first, in Liverpool. The ship won't be sailing just yet. I'll see you're well looked after, my lad.' He gave Robby a fatherly pat on the shoulder. 'I was going to get my son Mervyn to help me on the job, but he's otherwise engaged.'

Robby was astounded by the way Charley Meranto was coolly ignoring the fact that Christmas was coming, and the household was buzzing with preparations for the impending festivities.

People in Pover, too, were astounded when a Rolls Royce drew up in the village and Robby Belmane got out of it carrying a black leatherette shopping bag, which he deposited at his home.

Ten minutes later his relatives were waving him off on a journey to what seemed like the end of the universe.

Constance Lamby was surprised to receive the parcel addressed to Una.

'He's gone away for a while,' said Robby's brother with a smug, secretive look. 'Your girl won't be seeing him for quite some time, that's for certain.'

When he'd gone Constance was overcome by a terrible fear. Surely Robert Belmane wasn't in jail! You never could tell these days. She knew from Chloe that Robby'd planned to be back for three days at Christmas. She had never mentioned a word of it to Hubert, and she was glad now that she hadn't. Perhaps the romance was now over.

She decided not to give Una the parcel until Christmas Day. It would cause less upset that way. She would just tell Una that Maurice had called and left the message that Robby wouldn't be home.

When Una was helping to decorate the huge Christmas tree after tea for the Christmas Eve Ball, Constance decided to raise the subject. 'Morry Belmane's been round. He said Robby won't be back here after all.'

Una's face fell. 'Not coming? Not coming back home to Pover? Are you sure?'

Her mother nodded. 'Anyway, don't worry too much.'

'I'm not worrying, Mother. I'm very disappointed, but I'm certainly not worrying. I expect he's had his hours altered for the sake of someone in a more senior position. It's a terrible shame.'

When her mother had gone Una began to worry in spite of her own protests. Why hadn't Robby told her personally? Surely he wasn't carrying on again with Matilda Brent? That would be too awful for words. Maybe he had got in touch with Chloe and she would know what had happened?

Every day until Christmas Eve, Una worried. Then to make matters worse, she called in to the post office and heard Miss Trill twittering on to her usual captive audience: Dudley.

'Oh no, I don't think you'll see much of him again. There's not a chance of him settling down and looking for a job here. He was back here in a Rolls Royce with Mr Meranto t'other day. And now he's gone off to the ends of the earth. It's all very strange indeed.'

Una turned quickly and left the shop.

Una was getting ready for the ball. Her long lavender frock had once belonged to Ella, but Una had removed some small georgette roses and stitched small diamantes to the bodice instead. It took her ages. The small paste diamonds had come from an old necklace and each one had to be released from its minute metal-clawed clasp. Then she had sewn the metal clasps to the bodice and pushed back the diamonds. The effect was stunning.

Even Ella was impressed. 'It fits you perfectly,' she said. 'I was afraid it would be miles too big with that huge flowing skirt. You seem to be getting bonnier by the minute.'

Swansdown had never been lit up so much as it was that night. The place was ablaze with laughter, music and dancing. The wine flowed, and the band played on. The largest of the Lambys' two barns, which had been converted years ago and had windows added, was normally a store for broken furniture and an old billiard table. But it had been transformed. The specially sprung wooden floor had been sanded and polished to perfection. The wooden chandeliers had reappeared, and the huge ceiling was festooned with paper garlands. There was red-berried holly round the arched windows and bunches of mistletoe were suspended from the ceiling on ropes of gold and silver.

Hubert was there in a honey-coloured satin waistcoat, looking cheerful and prosperous. Cedric Pawson, wearing a cravat with an enormous emerald, was smoking a cigar and looking around with satisfaction.

'Do you fancy a dance?' said Marcus Oliphant to Una.

She fell into his arms with excited joy as they swept energetically round the floor until she was quite dizzy.

'I think I'll have to sit down, Marcus.' She took a deep breath as a feeling of faintness overwhelmed her. 'I'm not usually like this,' she gasped.

Marcus led her to her seat at the table where Chloe was sitting, chatting to Mac and Margie Renshaw.

'You're back soon,' said Chloe.

'I'm just going to get her a lemonade,' said Marcus, moving away.

While everyone sipped their drinks and continued with bits of conversation, Chloe looked surreptitiously towards Una. 'Are you enjoying it?'

'Oh, yes.' Una nodded her head vigorously but she looked very pale.

'Maybe you should sit the next dance out,' said Chloe with concern.

Marcus came back with the lemonade. It

was cool and sparkling with a thin slice of lemon in it and a lump of ice. He sipped his own drink very slowly.

The music started up again and this time Cedric came over to Una and bowed. 'Are you going to try again?'

She shook her head. Pawson looked sharply at Marcus. Then he said in slightly bullying tones, 'Come on now. A young girl like you...'

Marcus bristled. 'She isn't—' But before he had finished the sentence Una was up and dancing. Anything, she thought, to avoid a scene.

Cedric gripped her tightly, almost carrying her along, and by the end of the dance she was beginning to feel better again.

'What was all that nonsense about not dancing with me?' said Cedric as they walked back from the floor. 'I hope Oliphant isn't getting above himself.'

'Oh no, certainly not.' She glared at him. 'I just felt a bit unwell.'

'A bit unwell? A strapping young girl like you?'

Una felt a flood of rising anger. 'Nobody is on top of the world all the time, Cedric. You should know that from Father. Maybe I take after him. I'm telling you here and now that I'm not having another dance anyway. So there!' She gave him a defiant look and walked straight out of the barn hall.

He watched her go quizzically. He liked the frock with the diamonds on. It always amused him when she got aggressive. She'd had that tendency ever since she was a small child; it suited her. She would make a fitting wife for any grand house in the land.

When he got back to his own seat he noticed that Oliphant had left the hall, too. His buoyant mood changed to one of simmering fury. Oliphant had another think coming if he imagined he could override Cedric Pawson where Una Lamby was concerned.

It was after two a.m. when Cedric happened to see Marcus in the entrance hall of Grangebeck, bidding good night to Chloe. He confronted him immediately.

'Another bit of cheek like that dancing episode Oliphant, and you'll be out in the gutter on your ear. You're just a beggar, and don't you forget it. If it wasn't for me you'd be nowhere.'

'What a charming Christmas greeting,' sighed Marcus to Chloe, when Cedric had stormed out of sight. Then he said under his breath, 'He's going to get quite a shock over your fair Una one of these days. I know that for certain.'

As she stumbled into bed Chloe wondered

vaguely what Marcus meant. Surely he hadn't got his eye on Una as well?

On Christmas Day Una dutifully opened all her presents. She recognised most of the parcels, but when she came to the rather bulky one, she was puzzled. Her name was written in block capitals.

Constance watched from across the room, hoping there wouldn't be bad news inside. She was still unsure where Robby had gone. Unlike the rest of the family she rarely picked up news in Pover, and Una had never mentioned the few words she'd heard relayed between Miss Trill and Dudley.

Una gasped with wonder when she saw the beautiful glass swan and read Robby's card. A postscript had been hastily added, and her heart leapt with joy. *'I have had to reopen this parcel to tell you what has happened. Dearest one, you will never believe it. Mr Meranto is dragging me away with him to South America* right now. *I will write to you as soon as possible with the proper address. Your ever faithful, Robby.'*

Una read the message aloud. 'To think I never even knew where Robby was until now. How did the parcel get here?'

'His brother brought it earlier in the week,' said Constance guiltily. 'But I had no idea what was inside. He just said

Robby wouldn't be here for his days off after all.'

Hubert Lamby scowled at his wife. 'How long has this been going on? I thought I made it clear that boy was not to cross our doorstep again. Una, you've been forbidden to see him.'

Una went scarlet.

'For goodness' sake, Father,' interrupted Ella. 'Can't you just drop your tirade against him for once? It's Christmas. Good will to *all* men...'

'And all women,' said Lindi piously.

Constance looked round apologetically. 'I thought he might have been in prison. His brother was so mysterious about it all. I wanted to keep any bad news from you for as long as possible,' she pleaded.

'Oh, Mother. How could you!' grumbled Una. She smiled to herself, secretly delighted that Robby still cared, that he was doing so well in his job, and most of all that he hadn't gone back to Matilda Brent again.

Matilda's pregnancy continued to irk her. Was *she* pregnant, too? Perhaps it was because it forced her to come to terms with her own condition. She looked around guiltily. She really should go to a doctor. A doctor who didn't know her, perhaps.

That night at bedtime she stood in front of the long mirror on the wardrobe

306

door and looked anxiously for a sign that she was definitely pregnant. Whenever she saw pregnant women they seemed to be monstrously huge. She looked more closely at her body. Her stomach was smooth and firm with maybe just a very slight outward curve to it. Her waist had thickened a bit and her bosom felt the teeniest bit heavy, but then again she had been eating far more since she was back at school.

She stood sideways. No, there was nothing to see but a slight outward push to the lower part of her stomach. Not a curve but a sort of straight line sloping slightly outwards and hardly noticeable. She had seen girls with nothing on at school when they went swimming and some of them were huge. Even some of the thin ones had bulging bellies once they had removed their elastic Roll-Ons, even though the rest of their scraggy bodies were as flat as pan-cakes. She looked at her ankles. Sometimes people said you got swollen ankles, and Mrs Ford in the village who had seven children, always said she got them. She looked down at her own: they were slim and perfect.

She clambered into bed. It was awful not quite knowing.

She closed her eyes and fell asleep.

On Boxing Day morning Marcus called round with a letter for her father, and he invited Una for a walk by the mere.

'Cedric has cleared off for a few days. Just as well, he's getting to be a real pain. He was on at me again only this morning—to try to get you riding round on a cuddie.'

It was quite warm in the sparkling sunshine as they wandered along the gravel of the shoreline.

'If ever there's anything you want to tell me, Una, I'll respect your confidence. Sometimes life gets hellishly lonely. What you do is your own business, but...I just wanted you to know that I'm here and I won't breathe a word...'

Una looked down at some driftwood and smiled with sudden shyness. 'It's awfully kind of you, Marcus. I do have a secret, but I can't tell it to anyone. Not even you. Thanks all the same.'

'Think nowt of it,' Marcus sounded relieved. 'I sensed you had some sort of trouble swelling away in the background. Anyway, you know what to do. Anything unusual and you can count on me.' He picked up a small flat pebble and skimmed it across the surface of the water. It bounced three times. They both watched it. 'Quite made my day that has,' he said as it disappeared.

As they walked back to Swansdown laughing and talking, Hubert watched from an upstairs window. He drew in an exasperated breath. Was he ever going to get her sorted out? Surely she wasn't setting her cap on that penniless ne'er-do-well, scrounger Oliphant. He could see quite plainly now that the only solution was for Cedric to take her on as his bride. At least in that way she would be safe from harm and would have a civilised, comfortable existence. Age gaps never mattered, when you got down to it, as long as the woman was younger. All he'd ever really wanted was a bit of peace with his horses, a pal like Cedric, a bit of spare cash, and complete peace from all the females in the place.

He turned away from the window, grunted and stared morosely into space. Little did he know that on that same evening Marcus Oliphant had secretly proposed to Lindi.

CHAPTER 17

Alarm Bell

Miss Torus, the physical training mistress was in a vigorous mood. The gymnasium was awash with climbing ropes, padded, leather-topped, oblong wooden horses, and huge square coconut mats. She was a trim, well-formed woman with a face like a friendly lion. Her gym slip was navy blue with a top border saddle of velvet, and she wore feather-thin brown leather pumps. Her legs belied such daintiness. They were clad in thick lisle stockings, and their bulging muscular curvaceousness would have honoured the body of a wrestler.

She nodded her Eton-cropped head towards the walls lined with rows of shining wooden bars reaching from floor to ceiling.

'Bars first, then the horses,' she said in a gruff voice. 'Small horse first, then large. Then up the ropes. Down and stand to attention by the piano if you manage to reach the top of the rope.'

She eyed the group impersonally. They were arrayed in blue interlock cotton tunics and navy bloomers.

'Start when I blow the whistle. Those of you who don't master all the equipment, stand over by the yellow beanbags,' she said crisply.

There was a shrill piercing blast on her small silver whistle, and ten girls began to go through the torment.

Some made no pretence of trying and others were like flying monkeys as they moved quickly along the equipment. Una Lamby had been quite good at PT, but ever since she'd come back to school she had been one of those who always ended up by the beanbags. As the weeks of the term wore on, she began to feel more and more lethargic, especially climbing the ropes; and she usually gave up after about two pull-ups.

'You're absolutely terrible, Una,' remarked Dolores. 'You're almost as bad as me, even though you do try.'

Una smiled woefully. 'I expect it's our age. They do say that once you hit your twenties your energy all comes back.'

Dolores nodded. 'And of course it makes a heck of a difference when you've got the curse. I just feel like flopping about like a lettuce when I have that.'

Una nodded. She'd almost forgotten what the curse was like.

'I can see that some of you are getting a bit lazy about those ropes,' said Miss Torus, after they had put away the equipment. She gazed at their flushed faces and the delicate perspiration on their foreheads. 'I think we'll just have one more try on the ropes before we go.'

Una gave a low groan. *Not again.* She saw Celia Suter put up her hand and plead for mercy. 'Please could I be excused this time, Miss Torus? I've got a boil developing on my knee.'

Miss Torus raised her eyebrows and

gave a cursory nod. 'I hope there aren't any more excuses. Right then, the rest of you. As soon as I blow the whistle.' She looked briefly at Una. 'Una Lamby, pull yourself together and show a bit more enthusiasm.'

Dutifully, Una applied herself. You were supposed to let the loose end of the rope near the floor lie in a certain way against your body. Then stretch up your arms and grasp the rope with a special grip. Then you pulled yourself up it with your arms, using your feet and bent knees as levers.

Her arms didn't have an atom of strength as she dragged herself upwards on the sisal snake. The actions varied between being a cross-legged Rumpelstiltskin, and a pinned-out frog.

She gave a last-gasp pull upwards with all her strength.

'That's bet...*err*...Lamby. Good!' exclaimed Miss Torus. But no sooner were the words out of her mouth than Una lost her grip and fell to the floor. There was a panic-stricken silence. She lay motionless.

Miss Torus hurried over to her. 'What on earth made you do that. Get her a drink of water, somebody.'

Delia Hornbeam rushed to the changing room and came back with half a cup of water.

Una sat up slowly and her hand trembled

as she sipped from the cup. She blinked round at them all, smiled apologetically and got up slowly. 'I feel all right now.'

'You'd better have a rest during morning break,' said Miss Torus briskly. 'Meanwhile, I'll see if you can lie down in the sick room for a few minutes.'

The bell sounded.

'Right-o girls,' smiled Miss Torus, with a sigh of relief. 'In our next session we will practise our rope grips. When you're hanging on, always imagine you are dangling over the Manchester Ship Canal and *never* let go. Some of you are getting far too slap-dash and careless. I hope this morning's class has been a lesson for everyone.'

When Una arrived home from school that afternoon it was dark and raining steadily. The hotel was as quiet as a tomb. Some of the heating had been turned off as an economy measure.

She still felt sore from falling so hard on the gymnasium floor.

'I think I'll go and have a lie-down, Mother,' she said quietly, after hanging up her coat.

'Aren't you going to have your tea first?'

Una shook her head. 'I fell from one of the ropes in PT. It's made me a bit dizzy. I'll be much better tomorrow.'

313

'I'll bring you a tray to your bedroom,' said Constance comfortingly.

Never had Una been so thankful to rest: her bed felt as soft as a cloud. It was nearly half-past seven that evening before she woke again.

A tray was lying by the side of her bed with egg sandwiches and a glass of milk. She sat up sleepily. She felt warm and comfortable. She drank the milk thirstily and began to gobble down the sandwiches. Finally she washed her face, combed her hair and decided to go downstairs to listen to the wireless.

There was homework to do too, but she knew she just couldn't be bothered in her present state.

Before going downstairs she went to the lavatory. She turned and glanced towards the pan with genuine amazement: 'My periods! They've begun again at last!' Then slowly she sank to the lavatory floor and knew no more.

Dr Frodsham, one of the three doctors in Pover was sitting downstairs in Swansdown library with Hubert and Constance.

'She must have complete bed rest. She must not get up even to pass water. I have a bedpan in my car which you can borrow, and the district nurse will deal with it further. There wasn't much loss of blood, but you never know in a case like this. She did say she'd had an accident today at school?'

'Yes, she fell down a rope in PT. But surely it wouldn't bring on a menstrual period?'

'It might...' He looked at them cautiously. 'But you see, Mr and Mrs Lamby, this is a show of blood associated with something more serious. I suspect your daughter is a few months' pregnant.'

Constance and Hubert stared at him uncomprehendingly.

'The main thing now is to keep her completely quiet, with the foot of the bed raised. If there is any further blood loss, you must get in touch with me immediately and I'll send for the ambulance. I'll call back in another hour or so in any case.'

Constance and Hubert looked at each other askance.

'Whyever didn't she tell us?' said Constance softly.

Hubert shrugged his shoulders. His face had yellowed to the colour of weathered straw.

'It'll be Belmane's brat. Just as well if it comes to nowt.' There was anguish in his voice.

'Hubert! How can you say such a thing? Our very own daughter. We must help her all we can. I'll go now and see how she is.'

Constance went quickly to Una's bedroom again. Una was lying in the upended bed which now had wooden blocks under the foot of it. Her eyes were closed.

'Are you all right, dear?'

Una smiled bleakly and put out her hand. Her mother took it and held it gently.

'Your father and I have just had a word with Dr Frodsham. He'll pop back and see you a bit later, but you must let us know if there are any more signs of bleeding.'

Una opened her eyes suddenly. 'Seeing as I haven't had periods for such a long time, Mother, I expect there might be some more. It might all be stored up.' Una's voice was expressionless.

Constance looked at her with a worried frown. She had no idea about the actual workings of the womb, but somehow she knew it wouldn't be like that. Especially in this case.

'Didn't Doctor Frodsham explain anything to you, dear? Didn't he say...'

'He only asked me when was the last time I saw my monthlies. And he felt my stomach while you went for that extra blanket.'

'But nothing else?'

Una shook her head. 'Except he asked

me about the fall in a bit more detail—'

'He didn't say you were...'

'Yes. He did say I was suffering from shock, if that's what you mean. But he seems to think that a week off school and plenty of rest should see things back to normal.'

Una had no trouble that night, and next morning she was quite sorry to have to stay in bed.

'Never mind,' said Dr Frodsham, when he saw her again. 'You're a good healthy specimen and hopefully this one small accident won't affect your expectations. The amniotic fluid surrounding your small baby will keep it safe from too much buffeting, but you'll need regular check-ups from now on.'

Una looked at him in disbelief 'B-but my periods. They were coming back. They stopped because of all the changes I had, like going back to school again.'

Dr Frodsham saw her young, pleading face. The situation wasn't new to him and he braced himself. 'Hopefully you can say goodbye to those for a bit longer, my dear, after that slight disruption. Have you a regular boyfriend?'

Una shook her head miserably. 'I did, but he's abroad. I just can't understand how anything could have—'

'I would think you'll have nearly another

six months without a sign of menstruation. Your infant should be born some time in May, but we'll go into that later.' He patted her head lightly. 'Plenty of time to get everyone knitting for you and to decide on names. You're luckier than many young girls your age. There are caring people round you. Nurse Farrow will call in the morning and take your particulars.'

He had vanished before she could even blink.

Within two days the news of her predicament had spread like secret wild fire. It was discussed behind her back at length by her sisters and her grandmother, her mother and father, and by the headmistress at school, who agreed to allow her to continue with her education.

Miss Trill knew about it in the post office but she did manage to keep fairly quiet about it, even though she ruminated on who the father might be. Was it Marcus Oliphant's? He was often seen with her.

Dudley Plume was vaguely aware of it, but wasn't the slightest bit interested. Tessa Truett was extremely interested, but she kept quiet and felt very sorry about it.

The person who thought about it the most, besides Una's immediate family, was Cedric Pawson. Naturally he was very sad, too. But there were solutions to every problem.

The strangest part of the whole situation was that Una herself never spoke of it to anyone at all. She just carried on as if nothing had happened. As if the doctor had never confirmed what she'd known all along, as if she had not even remembered his words.

Vainly her mother tried to broach the subject, only to find Una had moved swiftly out of hearing range. Una faced them with a serene face. If they wished to talk about her, let them do it behind her back, she mused. She knew that she must never admit anything until she had been in contact with Robby.

Only at school, two weeks later, was she entirely open. She had no real option.

'Is your father suing the school about your falling down that rope?' enquired the worldly Dolores, as they waved their test-tubes over Bunsen burners during science class.

Una shook her head and smiled. 'He'd never do that. His life's too complicated with his horses as it is. If it had been one of his *horses* who'd fallen down a rope he'd probably have got his friend Cedric to help him sue for a massive amount.' Una bit her lip and pressed on. 'But it was all my own fault in any case, because I kept trying to believe I wasn't pregnant at all.'

Her test-tube was getting blackened with smoke and a pungent odour was coming from its yellow fumes. The experiment was saved just in time by the visiting science master turning off the Bunsen burner, and telling them both to write down the results of the experiment immediately.

At morning break Una sat with her three best friends drinking cocoa in the crowded dining room. With a courage from deep within, Una furnished them with the full details of her condition. It was easier than she'd thought, and she found it was a relief to be able to confide in someone at last. 'And Robby's now in South America, and doesn't know a thing about it.'

'So what on earth will you do?'

'If it was *our* parents they'd go completely mad,' said Renata Hornbeam in lowered tones, as she nibbled a biscuit. 'In fact, I can hardly dare to imagine it. Can you, Delia?'

Delia shook her head solemnly. 'We've never even done it. We shall probably grow up to be old maids. It's more than our lives are worth even to admit that a boy has tried to kiss us. Not that I'm very keen on kissing anyway. George Jonson dribbles.'

'So what will happen next, then?' whispered Dolores to Una. 'One of my cousins *nearly* had a baby out of wedlock, but she was sent on a cruise with my aunt, and nobody ever quite knew what happened after that. She's married now with loads of children.'

On the way home from school, Una brooded about her fate. Whatever would happen? Time had started to speed by and soon it would be May. She could hardly believe she might be a mother by then. How would she mange with all her schoolwork and a small baby? Her lips went dry and her throat ached.

It was a marvellous day and water rushed and gurgled along a bubbling brook towards the mere. The grasses and water weeds flattened into speeding streaks. The meadow grass by the muddy path was a new green beneath last year's washed-out, overgrown surface. Bare trees were bathed in sunshine. The swans had returned again. Everything was lush and familiar to her but her life was so different now. Everything had changed in her.

As she turned to go in the house she could see Cedric's car outside.

'Have you thought carefully about what I've said, old boy?'

The air in Hubert's study was thick with cigar smoke as he and Cedric Pawson sat languidly in leather armchairs. They'd been there for over two hours. It was a waiting game and hardly a word was spoken.

'She's so young, Ced. That's the trouble.' There was another long silence. The only sound apart from the ticking of a grandfather clock was Hubert Lamby grinding his teeth.

'I'm in this bloody mess because of that little bastard, Belmane.'

'Does he know?'

'Don't ask me. I don't want to think about him.'

'You are absolutely convinced it's his child, aren't you?'

'Who else's could it be?'

'Have you asked Una?'

'*Asked her?*' Hubert roared. 'How could I ask her? I've hardly spoken to her. Constance is in quite a state about it. Una just goes silent on the subject.' He gave a sour, tense smile. 'If it had been Chloe, I expect she'd have gone round blurting it out to the nation.'

'You don't think it could be Dudley Plume's.'

Hubert gave an exasperated sigh. 'The damned truth is it could be anyone's. How can I ever trust her again?'

'There is quite a simple way out of it all, Hubie.' Pawson gazed at him steadily through the smoke haze.

'You mean termination? No Ced. Apart from it being unlawful—I—'

'Not *that,* you idiot!'

'What then?' Hubert looked away.

'Marriage, of course!'

'I wouldn't entertain it.' Hubert Lamby shook his head fiercely. 'If that young devil ever enters this place again it could be true murder. The very mention of his name...' Hubert went white.

'Not marriage to him, you fool. Una's marriage to me!'

Hubert looked at him blankly.

'We've discussed it before, old scout,' said Cedric. 'Don't try to pretend you don't know. She's your daughter and she's underage...' With the speed of a panther Cedric plunged. 'You can't do without me, Hubie. We're tied to one another, come what may.'

He looked at Hubert with a long, pressurising gaze. 'So why not make Una's state official by honouring me as your son-in-law? All your troubles would be over. Una would be married to a reliable man who loves and cherishes her. She would be rich. She would be a positive anchor to you where finance is concerned. All her earthly goods would be willed to you if I were to suddenly die. You couldn't have it better.' Then he added with swift practicality, 'It will all have to be arranged as soon as possible by special licence. Apart from the pregnancy itself needing to be made respectable, there is always the chance that the news will reach the wilds of Patagonia. Speed is of the essence, old fellow. We don't want to leave anything to chance.'

After half an hour of solid silence Hubert Lamby gave his assent. They solemnly shook hands and agreed that a man's word was his bond.

'I'll invite her round to my place at the weekend,' said Pawson, with barely concealed delight.

'Supposing she won't go?'

'Just you leave everything to me from now on, Hubert. The details of the wedding will be finalised within weeks.'

Una saw them from the window as Cedric waved goodbye and disappeared down the drive in his car.

Her mind flew again to Robby. She had never received a word of reply to the letters she'd sent. It was an awful feeling, writing letters of love which never got a reply. She knew this next one was going to be the most important of all. Until now she had not worried him. But now her full and undeniable state of pregnancy was established for all the world to see. It was vital to inform Robby that he was the father.

Oh yes...she knew she'd told her best friends at school, but that was entirely different. They understood... She knew that their lips were sealed. That was what best friends were for.

'I want you to ring Una and invite her here this afternoon,' commanded Cedric. 'I shall be taking her out for a run in the car. There's no need to be too detailed about it. Just say there's a wonderful surprise in store.' He fixed Chloe with a cool stare then suddenly smiled and rubbed his hands slightly, as she jotted down his instructions in shorthand.

Chloe frowned. What was he plotting this time? Surely poor Una had enough on her plate without him adding to it?

'You'll be able to get a bit of time to yourself, this afternoon,' said Chloe to Marcus Oliphant a bit later. 'His lordship's got some sort of outing arranged with Una. Goodness knows why? He's in a strangely ebullient mood. He's got his best suit on.'

Marcus scowled. 'That sister of yours does pretty badly with him always swanning around. I'm getting a bit fed up with it all. The time is fast approaching when I shan't even be waiting for any wealthy ol' beans to peg out. I'll just take to the jolly old road with a billy-can. Goodbye for ever to thoughts of being a vet.' He hesitated, then added, 'Unless you have any better ideas that might entwine us?'

She shook her head firmly. 'Not unless fate placed us outside the same dosshouse. You never can tell what the future might hold with an employer like Cedric...' She smiled at Marcus ruefully.

A few minutes later she was phoning Una to come over to tea, and to suffer Cedric's wonderful surprise.

CHAPTER 18

Cedric's Surprise

'But I don't want to go to Cedric's this afternoon, Mother. Whyever should I?' Una's eyes flashed with tearful anger.

'It's just that your father seems so set on it, dear. Couldn't you just go, to please me and save a lot of fuss? Chloe said on the phone that it's something very special. A nice surprise. Don't be rude about it, Una. He probably means well...' Her mother's voice faded a bit. Constance was just as suspicious of Cedric as Una was. She knew there was always a certain ruthlessness or at least self-interest in any of Cedric's seemingly kind acts.

'I'm just not going, and that's the end of it. It's a weekend spoiled. Dolores said she might get a lift here this afternoon in her sister's car.'

'You'll have to go, dear,' Constance said gently. 'You know what your father's like with his tantrums. Please be a good girl.'

'You all treat me as if I were still a little child. In spite of—' Una bowed her head. She knew she would give in. She would put on her school gaberdine and wait for Cedric's monster of a limousine to appear. She would idle away hours of her precious life perched meekly on one of his ornate chairs, all dressed up in her most voluminous and shapeless dark green frock.

Una wiped her eyes with her handkerchief. The indignity of it. Waiting here to be fetched by him and carried away at his whim. Never had she hated Cedric Pawson so much. Why on earth was he starting all this fuss again, like he'd done when she was younger?

Una sighed with anguish. Robby would know what to do. But when would she hear from him? Where were his letters? Supposing she never saw him again and the baby was born without a father?

She cooled down a bit. Perhaps she was jumping to conclusions after all. Cedric

Pawson was just being kind because of her present condition, she thought.

Whilst she waited for Cedric to arrive her father came into the living room.

'Oh, you're all ready then?' His voice was gruff and embarrassed.

She nodded silently.

'Cedric's a good friend of the family. Always has been. He's treated you girls well from the very start. Anyone who marries him can be sure of an honourable and comfortable life with no financial worries.'

'Tessa Truett should have married him, then,' muttered Una sharply.

Why on earth was Father drivelling on about Cedric's love life?

'Anyway, dear, have a nice time. I'm quite sure you will. I think he's here now.' He left the room hurriedly, and a few minutes later she was sitting next to Cedric on soft leather upholstery as they sped back to Grangebeck.

'I had thought we might go for a run somewhere. Perhaps round Tatton, but on second thought I think we'll just have a nice afternoon tea at home. Just the two of us, where we can enjoy ourselves in total privacy and comfort,' murmured Cedric.

Una said nothing. At least, she thought, it wouldn't be quite as bad as having to trail round on a wintry afternoon pretending to be amused.

She was surprised to find that he took her to a room on the second floor, a place she never even knew existed. It was a small room with six walls and windows in four of them looking out on to the gardens.

There was a log fire burning in the grate.

'It used to be a tapestry room,' he said, noticing her interest. 'Two hundred years ago the ladies in this place spent much of their time sewing.'

'Thank goodness I wasn't alive in those days,' said Una spiritedly.

'Oh, I don't know. After all, they were living in beautiful surroundings and were well clothed and fed. Many women still enjoy doing sewing and embroidery.' He looked at her sagely.

Una closed her lips tight to avoid the retort that was on the tip of her tongue, and was saved by the arrival of afternoon tea. It looked delicious. Creamy butter was oozing through the pikelets, and the black cherry jam gleamed in the half light.

When they'd finished, and it had all been cleared away, Cedric said softly, 'Excuse me a minute, I've got rather a nice surprise for you.'

Una felt more settled now, and when he'd gone she sat comfortably by the fire and stared into the depth of the glowing logs. The flickering orange and yellow flames fascinated her. It was a lovely room, and for a few minutes she felt at peace with the whole world.

Cedric came back and stood by her side, hesitantly holding a small oblong parcel wrapped in plain tissue paper.

'I want you to have this, Una. I bought it especially for you.' His strong firm hands opened out towards her as she took the parcel from him.

'Thank you very much, Cedric,' she mumbled, a trifle shamefacedly. 'It's ever so kind of you, but really, I'd sooner not.' She held it awkwardly, and with inner foreboding. 'I'm just not the type for presents anymore.'

'Open it anyway, you might change your mind.'

Curiosity overtook her as she slowly pulled off the tissue paper and stared at the fine, maroon leather box. Her own name was engraved in gold on the top. Inside, on padded ivory satin was the most perfect necklace of garnets and pearls interlinked with six gleaming diamonds. She stared at it in awe. She was speechless.

'Try it on.' His voice had softened persuasively, and his expression was quite boyish and earnest.

'Perhaps not...' She placed her fingers

tentatively towards it. Then added jokingly, to hide her embarrassment, 'Not in this frock anyway. They just don't go together.' Gently, she closed the lid. 'It's very kind of you, Cedric.' She handed it back to him, and rose to leave.

He took it back from her without a word. His face was calm and expressionless. Then, after placing it inside a small glass-fronted cupboard he said, 'It's not just kindness, Una. It's a token of love. I'm asking you to marry me.'

Una sat down again in dread as he stood there.

'Yes, you did hear me correctly. I said marry. It isn't unusual for men to propose.'

She felt herself growing hot as Cedric stood there impassively, a slight smile on his face.

'I think there's some mistake.' She gulped and blinked nervously. 'How could I possibly marry you, at my age?'

'People have married at your age before.'

'But you're so much older. You're more the age of Mother and Father and Tessa Truett. You'd hate to be married to someone as young as me.'

There was silence for a few seconds. Cedric could see he was losing. He knew there was a huge age gap, but he was determined to ignore it. There were no real reasons why they shouldn't be man and wife. Many a man was fertile into his eighties.

And what a wondrous thing for a man in middle years to be blessed with a fair young bride. What a blessing to rekindle youthful memories. What a bed mate! And how good to be able to reward her properly with property and wealth, and give her child a good start in life, he thought.

'You'd soon become tired of a schoolgirl, Cedric.' She fumbled desperately for the right words. 'I mean, I'm honoured, but it wouldn't work. We aren't the right sort of pair. We don't need each other. I could never bear to be a wife! Not your wife, Cedric. It would be ridiculous!' The more she said, the greater her tactless blundering.

Cedric was quiet as she continued to stammer her excuses. Then, when she had talked herself silent, he said, 'There's your baby to think about, Una. It'll need a father.'

She felt her mouth parched and her heart begin to thud wildly. Involuntarily she put her hands to the sides of her belly and stared at him fiercely. 'My baby's got a father. All babies have them.'

'You know full well what I mean. Surely you don't want it to be illegitimate? From the very moment it's born, you'll have two human beings to think about. And it's not all that far off either. Next May by all accounts.'

Her eyes sparkled with defiance. Father was clearly at the bottom of it all, as she'd suspected.

'As you said yourself, Cedric, people have married at my age before. I'm not a complete dimwit. I prefer to wait and marry the baby's real father. Even if I have to wait till the end of the world.'

'No doubt you mean Robert Belmane,' Cedric said drily. 'You might need to wait for ever if you're hoping for that!'

She went pale and a feeling of faintness overwhelmed her. She said nothing, but the words pounded at her in her brain. *Oh Robby, darling Robby, where are you? Please God, send Robby back home.* Tears filled her eyes and then suddenly she began to weep uncontrollably.

Cedric stroked her head and handed her a handkerchief, but she brushed his hand away angrily. 'Take me home, and never invite me again. Take me back to Swansdown this minute.' The sobs rose in her breast and she struggled for breath.

Silently, Cedric did as he was bid, but as she got out of the car at the hotel he said, 'I'm not an ogre, Una. I love you and I want to help you. You could do a lot worse than be married to an older man like me, and your child would at least have a father who would care for it properly.'

She looked at him as if she hadn't heard a single word.

When she got inside her mother greeted her cheerfully. 'That was a quick visit. What happened?' She looked more closely at Una. 'You've been crying?'

Una nodded. They went into her mother's bedroom where Una lay on the bed and sobbed her heart out. 'He wants me to marry him. He tried to give me the most beautiful necklace in all the world. It was terrible. Awful. Whatever shall I do?'

'I'll make you a nice drink,' said Constance soothingly. 'Then off you go to your own bed to have a complete rest and sleep it off. You'll feel much better in the morning.'

'The lovely surprise at Cedric's didn't turn out too well, dear,' said Constance to Hubert later that night. 'I think you'll have to forget about Cedric and Una.' She spoke mildly but the effect on Hubert was like red rag to a bull.

'*Forget* it? What's up with you, woman? Do you mean to say you'd be happy to see your daughter having a baby without a father to claim it?' He began to laugh bitterly. 'Oh no, the little devil's not getting away with that.' His face was flushed with fury. 'That girl is going to

334

marry Cedric Pawson whether she likes it or not, and I'll move heaven and earth to make sure it happens within the next few weeks. She's my child. She's under age. And she'll do what her father tells her. Is that clear, Constance?'

'Perfectly clear, Hubert.'

When he'd gone Constance took two tablets and sipped some water very slowly. She couldn't see it working out at all, but what options were there if Robby had vanished from the country and deserted Una? The thought of it wounded her to her very soul. Why should her precious daughter have been treated so badly? Was it better for Una to remain single? Or was it better for her to marry Cedric, even though it was against Una's will?

With a heavy heart Constance went to bed that night, fully resigned to the wedding Hubert was planning. Already she had blotted out the serious side issues. She juggled instead with future wedding arrangements, and how it could all be fitted in with running the hotel.

Una felt terrified now. What on earth could she do? Her nights were disturbed and in the mornings when she woke she was sick. Not with the ordinary morning sickness of pregnancy, but from a terrible feeling of foreboding. Every day she pleaded passionately with her mother not to let the marriage happen.

'All I can say is no, Mother. Surely it is enough for me to refuse?' But she knew in her heart it was not.

It was a nightmare for Constance, too. She felt that she was torturing her own daughter by conforming to Hubert and Cedric's wishes. But she herself was tied like a prisoner. She feared that not going through with it all might be even worse. And with a sense of helplessness, she struggled to comfort her youngest child.

'Mother, I'd sooner kill myself than become Cedric's wife! I'm already Robby's chosen partner. We pledged ourselves in Bylow's Tower. I allowed him because we love each other. I planned for him to *love me for ever.*' She shouted out the words in a mad, tearful frenzy.

But her cries of young anguish made no difference. The decision had been made and her tears only served to bring her mother's own heart to breaking point.

Within four weeks a pale, unemotional Una Christabel Lamby, drained of her youthful exuberance, was wedded by special licence to Cedric Theodore Pawson.

It was a quiet affair; so quiet that only Tessa Truett came to wish Cedric good luck. Horrocks, Cedric's butler, tactfully acted as his second. Hubert and Constance were there and Chloe came. But Ella and Lindi refused point blank in protest.

Una wore a tunic of cream wool, and a coffee-coloured coat with a dyed squirrel collar, chosen by her mother. It did not suit her, and she had tried to rip off the squirrel collar just before the ceremony. She was in a state of heightened perceptiveness as she equated herself to the scrap of animal fur trimming her outfit—another trapped creature. To everyone's horror she had insisted upon wearing a black veil over her coffee-coloured hat. Constance feared for her sanity.

Una's best schoolfriends stood loyally outside the register office and waved to her.

'She looks as if she's in mourning, in that awful black veil,' said Dolores sadly, as Una and Cedric came out of the building. They stared at her white face and saw her hand flicker towards them as she sat in Cedric's large closed car.

Una was glad they'd come, but it required too much energy, and emotion, to summon up a smile. The whole short ceremony had been like a ghastly charade. Her life had drained away from her days ago, when she'd been informed that she would no longer be able to return to school. It was the final nail in her coffin and she felt empty.

Botany, Latin and maths—the three feathers in her cap would be mere childish excellence and soon forgotten.

'You won't need all that,' Cedric had said with a gentle pat on her head. 'You'll get more than enough education being mistress of Grangebeck and preparing for the baby to arrive.'

There was no honeymoon, but the staff at Grangebeck had reorganised Cedric's master bedroom into a place fit for a young bride. There was a new hand-embroidered white satin quilt, and there were greenhouse flowers everywhere including yellow mimosa and orchids.

Cedric had given both Chloe and Marcus a full two weeks' holiday and told them that on no account were they to call back during that time.

'Una will need to settle in peace,' he said briefly as he dismissed them.

'That's the first decent break he's ever given us, and trust it to be in the depth of winter,' said Marcus morosely. 'I shall spend my time looking round for another job. Don't expect ever to see me back here again. I couldn't bear it. I'm beyond his threats now. Your poor little sister is taking my place as a pawn on his chessboard. Anyone can see it's all going to be a terrible disaster.' For once there was no flippancy in his tone as he and Chloe said goodbye and went their separate ways.

Although she hated to admit it Chloe was out on a limb. Where was she to go for two weeks in the worst part of the year? She could hardly go back to Swansdown, nor would she have wanted to. It had been agony enough attending the wretched marriage and she had only done it to show Una some support, and because she worked for Cedric. Her only real option would have been to go and stay with Granny Lamby until things were sorted out. She brightened at the thought, but it was short-lived. Granny Lamby had fled to Harrogate two weeks ago to visit an old friend. She had said that the whole episode was enough to hasten her into her grave.

It was Una who came to Chloe's aid.

Chloe had returned to Grangebeck to get her suitcase, after the wedding ceremony. She had arranged to stay for a couple of nights with her friend Margie Renshaw. She was just about to hurry through the servants' entrance when she met Una.

The two sisters clung together in a sad embrace.

'I'll have to go, Una. I shouldn't really be here at all today. You were very brave at the ceremony. Good luck. Cedric's not such a bad old thing when you get to know him.'

'But you're not *married* to him, Chloe,' cried Una. 'I'm his wife, now and for ever more.' Then she said in a small voice, 'I'm absolutely dreading tonight. Suppose it brings on a miscarriage?'

Chloe's heart sank at her words. 'It won't be half as bad as you imagine, I'm sure.' Then she added, 'I would promise faithfully to keep in touch over the next two weeks, if only I could find somewhere to stay close by. But as it is, I only have these couple of nights with the Renshaws.'

'Tessa would put you up,' said Una pleadingly. 'I know it for certain. Try there. I'll ring her tomorrow for you, Chloe. If I'm still here.'

'Don't talk like that. Of course you'll be here! And I'll try Tessa's myself.' Hurriedly Chloe gave her a kiss and escaped. What a fiasco it all was. What a stupid, stubborn man their father was to hand Una over to Cedric in such a callous way. Thank God she had escaped the family clutches.

As soon as possible she, like Marcus, would try to find another job rather than see Una wilting away.

Game pie had been prepared for dinner that night, followed by pear Hélène and crème meringue. The food looked sumptuous, but Una could hardly swallow a mouthful. Later there was Champagne, but she only took two small sips and then left it.

Cedric noted her absence of appetite with a mixture of anxiety and irritation. Hopefully by the morning she would come to her senses. Obviously the day had been a great ordeal, not only for her but, for others, too. It had not been a particularly jolly occasion. He wondered now how to approach this first night with his young bride. Should he tactfully leave her until she recovered her spirits, and perhaps her former shape? Or should he gently insist that they shared the marriage bed together? After all, it didn't really matter if they lay together, not touching to begin with. He knew a modicum of patience would be required. And there was a lifetime from now on.

Constance had insisted that Una should have some really pretty nightdresses.

'You can't wear those old wincyette pyjamas, Una. It would be an insult to any man.'

'I don't care for any man, Mother.' She had dissolved into yet another flood of tears. Eventually she had settled for pale pink georgette, inlaid with handmade lace round the neck and shoulder straps. 'But I insist upon my bedsocks, Mother. I *insist.*' There was a new note of resolution in

341

Una's voice and Constance didn't argue. She swiftly packed the bedsocks, and bit back her own tears.

On her first night at Grangebeck Una stood staring at the huge oak four-poster with its tapestry canopy.

Cedric had left her alone to get ready for bed, and she had bathed and powdered herself with a huge fluffy powder puff. Then she had put on the new nightie and her woollen bedsocks.

She clambered into bed and lay there, tense—like someone waiting on the doctor's couch.

After about five minutes she got up again and began to prowl about restlessly. She peeked into Cedric's dressing room. There was a small neat single bed there, already made up. It had a plain white fringed damask counterpane, and she climbed in, slipping between the cold white starched sheets and pretended to sleep. Then with the pure weariness of it all she slept at last.

Half an hour later, Cedric found her. He gazed down at her fresh young face, and saw the soft unlined eyelids and the curving eyelashes. He drank in the innocent, pouting young mouth and soft wavy hair spread so loosely on the pillow. Her slim bare arm was lying across her abdomen, as if even in sleep she was protecting her unborn child. He saw her small hand complete with its new wedding ring.

How had he managed to be blessed with such luck at his age?

The following morning Una was awake at seven o'clock, and at half-past, when the maid arrived with early morning tea, Una was back in the four-poster bed next to Cedric.

'At least make a show of it,' Cedric had pleaded. 'Come and lie next to me while they bring in the tea.'

At first she had turned away in the small white bed, pretending not to have heard him.

'You can't do that for ever, Una. You might as well get used to being my wife.' Then he said bitterly, 'You don't know how damned lucky you are not to be in the gutter. In my day, many a girl in your condition had nowhere else to go.'

Dutifully she obeyed, and she sat next to him like a model bride in her night dress and a satin and lace bed jacket. She wondered if everyone knew she was pregnant. Her brain was in a tired, hopeless whirl.

When the maid had been and the tea was drunk, she turned away from him in the bed.

343

She felt a stiff rod pressing against the back of her thigh and she got up quickly. Not *that*. How could she allow such a thing, when she and Robby were true soulmates, and Robby's child was within her? Surely there could be no greater reason than that? How could she possibly submit to another man? How could she give false kisses and have that thing pushed inside her? Especially when there was a baby there as well?

No, not with Cedric *ever!* Even if he turned out to be the kindest person in the world.

She had been forced to marry him in her most helpless and vulnerable state. She brooded on it all again with heavy sadness. Her happy life with school friends and her dreams of a life with Robby wrenched away from her.

But no one could force her to actually do *that* with Cedric Pawson, even if her name had been changed to his on a scrap of paper. Every day that week, Cedric never left her side. Always he was there, trying to fondle her, trying to catch her unawares.

By the end of the week she could see that Cedric was being driven mad by some sort of secret passion. His jaw was tense and he spoke to her in clipped tones. Then one day he said: 'You know, Una, this state of affairs just can't go on. Man is a noble animal. He can't stand being trifled with. It inflames his senses. This marriage is my first, even though it has come late in life. Your marriage has come early in life. Why can't we make a proper go of it? No man can accept a bed with a frigid bride.'

Una didn't know what to say, but it occurred to her that Cedric had been in the world a lot longer than she had. Men like him didn't wait to get married before they tasted the fruits of womanly contact, and Tessa Truett was a case in point. Cedric could find his comforts elsewhere, whenever he chose. He'd been doing so for years and years, even before she was born.

She looked away sadly, and prayed from the bottom of her heart for Robby to come back home.

Tessa Truett smiled at Chloe. 'Yes, as it happens, I can put you up, although I can't guarantee for how long.'

'It's only supposed to be for this fortnight,' said Chloe with heartfelt relief. 'I wanted to stay close by in case Una needed me. It's quite a change in her life to be married so quickly.'

Tessa nodded tactfully. A real bit of skilful manoeuvring by Cedric, she thought. So what had happened to Robby? From all accounts in the village post office, even his family hadn't heard a word from him. Robby Belmane seemed to have vanished from the face of the earth. She looked at Chloe pleasantly, but her mind was still on Una. How would old Ced take to a squawking baby that didn't even belong to him? She was quite surprised that he had taken it all on board. She would have imagined that Cedric would have regarded taking on a young boy's child, especially Rob Belmane's, as a task well beneath his dignity. But then again, maybe the prize of such a beautiful young bride was worth it.

CHAPTER 19

The Greenhouse

Cedric was being driven to his wits' end over Una. He was in a complete dilemma. He had no one to turn to, and he knew it would be the worst thing possible to mention any problems to Hubert Lamby. Hubert was the sort of friend who relied on others where his own daily life was concerned, but folded up completely if it was the other way round.

It was the beginning of May now, and the baby was expected any time.

He could tell that Una had resigned herself to the situation; in fact, it frightened him slightly to see such a change in her. Apart from the pregnancy, which had now fully taken over her young body, she had lost the energetic liveliness she once had as a schoolgirl. She was years away, rather than a few months, from the personality he had once been attracted to. It was worrying.

But she had lapsed into polite passiveness. She would let him do anything to show affection; anything, that is, except the act of consummating their marriage. She accepted his kissing and his petting with such indifference that he felt ashamed. As the weeks wore on he knew that their marriage was a complete sham, and was always likely to be.

The only time she became animated was when her three school friends visited her, and they prattled on about babies and baby clothes. Then, about ten days before the baby was expected, Cedric took it upon himself to admit he had a dire problem to face. This baby would be Robby Belmane's; both he and Una knew it. Yet they never said so. He realised now, seeing the dangerously pining state of her and her entrenched resistance to his pressure for the connubial rights of the marriage bed, that he had better check up on Robby Belmane. Una's baby wasn't some little orphan from the storm, sent to him by fate to treat as his own. Maybe Belmane was not aware of any of it?

Forthwith, he phoned Mrs Meranto to enquire about her husband's expedition. '...As you know, Mrs Meranto, we aren't complete strangers. We met about eighteen months ago at the Mayor's banquet.'

Mrs Meranto was extremely vague. She met thousands of people.

'Look here,' Cedric said in his casual and most persuasive manner, 'Why don't you and I get together for a spot of lunch somewhere?'

'I really can't spare the time for lunching out at the moment, Mr Pawson. But if you'd like to come over here for a bite?'

'Ideal. And please, please call me Cedric. What day had you in mind, Mrs Meranto?'

'Would tomorrow do? Please call me Morna, it's so much less of a mouthful.'

The following day Cedric was ensconced in what Morna Meranto referred to as her plantenarium: a large secluded room with a black-and-white marble floor. French bay windows led on to one of the lawns, and it was rich with exotic plants from warmer climates. They sat at a white wrought-iron table with cushioned cane chairs and sipped lemon soup, followed by sirloin and horseradish sandwiches.

'We'll take coffee in my private sitting room,' murmured Morna.

Cedric hadn't felt so relaxed in years. In no time at all he was explaining the reason for his visit, in a convoluted way. 'There's this young village girl, you see. I was concerned for her welfare when Robert Belmane went away, as she told me she was pregnant by him. She got in touch with me, looking for temporary work of a light nature, and when her problem surfaced, I realised that I would have to try and get in touch with the assumed father. There's no doubt about it, Morna, these young women can sometimes be quite a nuisance, and the young men also,' simpered Cedric.

By now they had drunk a bottle of wine and a number of liqueurs. Their tongues loosened by drink, they shared a rush of sentimental confidences. They had moved closer together and they were now seated on Mrs Meranto's small Georgian two-seater sofa, with their arms touching gently.

'Oh, how I agree with you,' sighed Morna earnestly. 'I must admit I have had various sorts of trouble concerning a girl pregnant by my own son Mervyn. They're so headstrong, the young ones these days. And after the seed has been sown, that's it. One can only accept God's will in these matters, I fear. We sent our boy away to agricultural college, to let him come to his senses, but this servant girl has followed him there. She has left her baby with her grandmother, has changed her name to *Meranto*, would you believe, and is working her way up to become a manageress. I fear she will follow him to the ends of the earth and we will be left with no choice but to disown him, especially if he actually marries her.'

By the time their meeting came to an end at around three-thirty, Cedric had managed to prise Charlie Meranto's Patagonian address from Morna.

'The mail often takes months to get there,' she said. 'In fact I haven't heard a word from Charlie and the boy since they went. My husband rarely stays away on an expedition for more than six months. I expect him back by the end of June at the very latest.

'I met someone three weeks ago who's seen Charlie, and he assured me they were extremely well. The boy Belmane has discovered a new species of a bog plant.'

Cedric gulped appreciatively, and returned home. He decided not to mention his visit to anyone.

Neither Chloe nor Marcus Oliphant returned to Cedric's after their two-week holiday.

Marcus had vanished completely.

Chloe had stayed on in her lodgings with Tessa Truett. They got on extremely well, and within two days Tessa had in a roundabout way spoken to Lady Limpet while discussing some forthcoming catering details for Drawbridge Hall.

'I think Chloe Lamby is looking for a change from working at Cedric's. It's made it a bit difficult with her younger sister marrying him. Chloe's such a talented young person. All that experience at the *Gazette* when she left school and she knows the area like the back of her hand...I often think she would be the perfect answer for your Maudley Montgomery Centre. She would get on perfectly with Dudley...'

Lady Limpet nodded cursorily. Her mind was on liver pâté, but she always snapped to attention with even the slightest mention of Maudley. 'Yes, yes. A very good idea. Very good. I'll ask Dudley what he thinks.'

Dudley Plume was absolutely delighted. The proposition was like a dream come true. But when Tessa approached Chloe she was met with a far more cautious reaction.

'I'm not sure, especially after Una being

351

there. She did say Dudley required rather more of a nanny than an assistant.'

'He's improved,' laughed Tessa. 'He had no option. It's a wonderful chance to escape from Cedric. You should grab it while the going's good, Chloe. You could always use it as a springboard to something else later.'

After some consideration Chloe agreed, and within a few days she was employed as Dudley Plume's new assistant.

Cedric was furious. He tried to keep calm because of Una. He immediately got in touch with an agency, and employed an elderly woman from Knutsford to travel in each day. She was called Miss Antrobus, was extremely efficient and wore bright orange artificial silk stockings. She was always bending over low tables to expose navy blue garters and an expanse of fleshy white thigh, which annoyed Cedric intensely.

He never replaced Marcus Oliphant.

Una had been feeling a bit queasy. She knew the baby was due, and the midwife had warned her not to stray too far away. Oh, how she longed for it all to be over. The waiting of these last weeks was terrible and she couldn't even see her own feet. Would she ever become an ordinary slim girl again?

The only consolation in it all was that Cedric had stopped trying to force his attentions on her. She had never allowed him to consummate their union as man and wife, a secret she'd kept from everyone.

These days she had a large sumptuous bedroom entirely of her own, with a double bed and a white satin bedspread and eiderdown, embroidered with pink taffeta cyclamen flowers. The room looked out across Melmere. Sometimes she sat and stared for what seemed like hours towards the water and the fairyland of new life blooming with the spring. She watched the swans and dab chicks, or gazed at the trees in the garden with their red squirrels and chattering birds. Sometimes, she felt like a prisoner in paradise here at Grangebeck.

At other times the beauty of it all soothed her and quelled her constant yearning to see Robby again. Would he ever be back to claim his child? God forbid that she should die when it was born and would never be able to tell him. She tried to pull herself together. She felt guilty for having such morbid thoughts.

The moment she felt the first twinges of labour, the midwife was to be notified. Then Cedric was going to drive Una to Parklands private maternity home at Shale Bridge.

All her clothes were packed and the

baby's things were ready.

A sort of madness came over her while she waited. Early one morning she looked out to see the sublime May weather once again. Birds chirped in the trees, doves were cooing and in the distance like a strange echoing sound the cuckoo called in the early morning stillness. The regular sound of horses' hooves carried up the path as Isaac Crackledown's daughter Maria arrived to deliver the milk.

Today Una was waiting to greet her in the drive.

They saw each other quite often, for Una was usually up early with the restlessness of full-term pregnancy upon her.

'Glory be, Una. You're up early again.'

'Yes. I wanted to ask you a favour, Maria. I want you to take me over to Swansdown with you on the cart, while everything's quiet. They'll give me a lift back later, and I don't want to fuss Cedric. It's such a lovely morning. I don't want to waste a second of it.'

Maria hesitated. She was thirty-five and had four children of her own, so she understood the whim Una had to get out for a while.

'Will Cedric mind?' She knew what a task master he could be, but she also realised that young Una was now his wife and had some authority.

354

'Gracious, no! He'll be really pleased to see the back of me for a few hours, and pleased that I'm going to see them all back at home.'

Maria smiled understandingly. She helped her to climb up into the milk cart and sat her next to the churns.

Just before they approached the gates at Swansdown, Una said, 'You can put me down here, Maria. I'll go through the little wooden gate towards the mere. I just want to look at everything in this glorious light.'

'Are you sure you're quite all right, dear? I hope I've done the right thing bringing you here and leaving you to roam, in your condition.' Maria's face crinkled into lines of worry.

'Absolutely fine. You've done me a real favour,' said Una reassuringly.

Maria helped Una from the cart, and the horse was soon trotting off towards the kitchens at Swansdown. Una, with a sigh of rapture, wandered down in the first beams of early morning sunshine to where the oak trees stood.

She looked at the special one, and breathed deeply with relief and pleasure. The hearts were still there. They had even spread a little in the cuts of the bark, beneath the newly sprouting, slightly golden twigs. It was the first taste of her old life since being tied to the vast domain of Grangebeck. She had rarely been home in the past months, even though she did keep in touch by phone. And she saw Chloe in Pover from time to time.

She looked across to the greenhouses where Robby had once worked and walked over to see them. They looked a bit shabby, and needed a coat of new white lead paint round the frames. There were some window panes cracked and broken. It saddened her.

The door was wide open in the first one, but it was almost empty, except for the mossy, weed-strewn brick path down the centre, and some stacks of darkened, damp, empty wooden seed boxes strewn on the flattened earth.

She knew there was one old, stout wooden kitchen chair there. She had often sat on it, surrounded by all the plants while she talked to Robby. She sat on it gingerly this time, in case it was rotten, but it was as sturdy as ever.

Suddenly a sharp gripping pain shot through her abdomen, as if she had been caught short and needed to go to the lavatory urgently. Then it faded away.

Surely it wasn't the baby? Was this the sign the midwife had referred to? Una began to shiver slightly in the damp air.

How could she possibly get back to

Grangebeck again now?

It was not even eight o'clock in the morning. She simply wouldn't go and reveal herself to Father and Mother at this time, especially with all the guests being here. Imagine all the fuss and palaver. They would probably have Cedric summoned like a warder, and she would be removed in his dark limousine to the nursing home. She shuddered with fright.

But how could she stay here?

She decided to take a terrific chance. She would go to the kitchens and if no one was about she would slip into the larder and find some food and maybe fill a thermos flask with water. They had flasks they kept for energetic visitors who wanted packed lunches.

Never was God so kind to her. The kitchen was entirely empty, and on the side bench by the racks of cup and saucers there was a packed lunch just being finished. There was a packet of freshly cut egg, and cheese and tomato sandwiches, fruitcake, a large white folded cotton napkin, and a flask of coffee. Manna from heaven.

Without waiting a second she tossed everything into a carrier and slid out again as quickly as possible. Another wave of cramp took over her body and she rested panting against a wall by the window. As the wave diminished she heard Lindi's voice.

'Where's that food gone?'

Una turned and hurried down towards the mere where the old boathouse lay. Was there any chance of being blessed again? Would the door be unlocked?

The door was wide open and there were some tins of paint standing there. Someone had been painting a row boat outside, close to the shore.

On a hook in the boathouse itself she suddenly noticed something amazing. It was Robby's old dark blue jacket. It must have been on that hook since he'd gone! She went across, stretched up and was met with another sudden wracking pain. She waited until it had ceased and then, taking the jacket and her small carrier bag, she left and walked back to the greenhouse. At least she would have the old chair to sit on. She could place it in a sunny secluded place and have something to eat and drink. She knew now that if she didn't have some food soon she wouldn't have the energy to get through this. Something inside her told her she must do all she could now to help her unborn child—anything, that is, short of sending for Cedric or telling her mother she was here in the Swansdown gardens.

The sun was getting quite warm. The newly mown lawns were soft and the night dew was evaporating into the morning air. Between the quickening arrows of pain, Una demolished her sandwiches and cake, and drank some of the coffee. There was an apple and a banana there, too, which she left as reserves. She was puzzled that the pains were coming so regularly. She had no idea how long they would go on for, and she had heard awful tales of women being in labour for days. The pain took her by surprise; she hoped it wouldn't last that long. Nothing had prepared her for the agony of the prolonged relentless contractions pulling at her belly from all sides.

How much worse could they get? She comforted herself with the thought that she could go to the house, find Mother and plead to have the baby there, whatever Father might think or say.

She took the chair, and found a good spot to sit, where she could rest her feet on a log and gaze at the sparkling waters of the mere. Sometimes she got up and walked a little but always she came back to her chair. She carried Robby's jacket with her. Occasionally she sat on it, on a grassy bank, and sometimes she clutched it fiercely as another contraction took over.

Early in the afternoon, and beside herself with weariness, Una steeled herself to go for another short walk, to take her mind off the pain. But she was unable to move. The pain ripped through her body, in wave after wave and she fell helplessly back against a hummock. She needed help. Sure enough, the contractions waned again and she regained some energy. She edged her way back to her chair, and then stopped dead with shock.

Granny Lamby was sitting on it, shading herself with an opened garden parasol. She was talking to Father, who was standing close by and their voices carried towards her as Una stood in the shadow of the bushes.

'I'm surprised that Cedric let it happen,' said Granny Lamby briskly. 'How on earth could she possibly disappear with the baby due so soon? Surely someone will have seen her? She can't be far away.'

'Probably gone along the mere to try and drown herself,' said Hubert with gloomy fatalism. 'But I'll tell you this much, Ma. If anything happens to that girl I shall blame that young bastard Belmane for every bit of it. From what Ced said, he's alive and kicking and still enjoying himself with Charlie Meranto in Patagonia. They're expected back in about a month.'

Una froze. Alive and well? And never a word! With Cedric and her father knowing it all the time and never even breathing a word to her?

She turned, and taking a narrow overgrown track among some massive, shell-pink rhododendron, she went back to the bare greenhouse.

The nearer she got the angrier she became. Her next contraction was hard and sharp, but she mastered it now with a rising determination. Minutes later she felt a warm rush of liquid escape from her. She guessed it was what they called her waters breaking, and she knew it would not be too long before the baby was on its way. It was warm in the greenhouse, and as the afternoon wore on and cooled off, she was glad of it.

Una wished she had the chair again, even if it was just to cling to. But by now she had not the energy to trail back and get it without being seen.

The next minute she heard her father's voice. He was approaching the greenhouse. Quickly she left it and hid again.

He was with Cedric this time, and he was carrying the chair. He dumped it back in the greenhouse, and muttered about guests borrowing things and not replacing them.

As they made their way towards the stables, Una heard Cedric say, 'I wondered if she might have come back here, Hubie?'

'Come back here? She'd never do that! Why should she when she's your wife and living a civilised life with every comfort an expectant mother could hope for. No, old boy, she'd never do that.' Their voices faded in the distance.

Una went back inside the greenhouse and sat on the wooden chair with a gasp of relief She had contractions of such force now that they made her feel quite powerless. They were taking over her whole body, and she had an uncontrollable urge to bear down.

In hasty panic she began to remove her underclothing, leaving only her tunic-like outer frock. She felt like squatting on the floor but her body was so huge that she just stood by the side of the chair and gripped it as she grunted with pain and effort. Then, exhausted, she lay on the floor, leaning slightly to one side with Robby's jacket under her shoulders and her small carrier bag containing the white unused cotton napkin by her side.

Her face was bathed in sweat and her hair clung in damp curls round her head. At about seven o'clock that evening, by the sounds of bells from a distant church clock, she knew the baby was arriving. She was standing by the chair again and she let out a terrible howl as she felt the contractions push the bundle from inside her down the birth canal towards the outside world.

She stood gripping the back of the

wooden chair. *Please don't let this old chair be rotten and give way,* she prayed silently. *Don't let it collapse. Help me Lord.* Holding on to the chair she sat back on her haunches, bending lower and lower over Robby's jacket until she was almost touching the floor. Slowly she rested on her buttocks, lying there with knees pulled up, panting and pushing with instinctive motions. At long last she felt the child slip out in a rush of warm fluid. And the pain miraculously stopped. She struggled to sit up properly and pulled the baby towards her, realising only now that it was still attached by its navel to a long blue, glistening cord which was still leading from inside her. She picked up the small, bare, child and laid it close against her belly. It was quite purple at first, and silent. Her heart stopped. What had she done?

Then, after a sudden gasp of the new world, it began to bawl relentlessly.

Una was dazed by the marvel of it. Taking out the small white napkin she tried to wipe its face and mouth, after which she tied the cotton napkin tightly round the rope of cord, and wrapped the child in her underskirt. She hadn't even seen what sex it was.

With a gasp of complete exhaustion, and confident that her baby was warm and safe, Una flopped back and closed her eyes.

Constance was the first person to hear the new baby's cry. She'd been standing on the terrace talking to a visitor when she flushed bright red.

'Excuse me, I think I'm needed.' She rushed madly towards the greenhouses, and was just in time to see the afterbirth appear. Una was lying like a ghost, and the baby was very quiet.

Ella had seen her mother rushing away and was close behind. They stared at Una, mouths agape before coming to their senses.

'I'll stay here with Una and the babe, Mother. You get the doctor and tell the others.' Constance leapt into action, hardly daring to look in the direction of Una and her new grandchild.

Within fifteen minutes an old bamboo stretcher had been erected and Una had been put to bed in the house. The baby was next to her in a dressing-table drawer.

Hubert Lamby's face was ashen as he got through to Cedric an hour later.

'Yes, she seems to be quite well now. She's asleep at present. Both the doctor and the midwife have been. It's a little girl. Six pounds, five ounces, and Una wants to call her Ramona.'

There was an awkward silence, as Hubert listened to Cedric talking. Then he said,

'Not ten days, *here?* We've got the hotel to think of. Surely she can be sent back to your place or to the nursing home?' There was silence.

'Yes. I expect you're right.' Hubert's voice faded. 'It'll all depend on what the doctor and midwife say. Mmmm. All right, then.'

Hubert put back the receiver. His face was a picture of misery.

CHAPTER 20

The Usherette

Chloe was torn by feelings of envy and amazement when she saw Una's baby. With masses of black hair and huge knowing eyes, she was the picture of health and showed no signs that her unorthodox delivery had affected her.

'And stop calling her "it",' laughed Una. 'Her name is,' she hesitated slightly, 'Ramona...Pawson.' In the same breath she began to cry. 'Oh Chloe, what on earth can I do? How can she possibly be christened with Cedric's surname when her own father hasn't had the chance to claim her?'

Chloe nodded with genuine sympathy. It was an awful situation. She felt sorry for Una cooped up in the bedroom in such good weather, with no company except her newborn baby to worry about all day.

Whoever would have guessed that Una would have been the first to have a child of her own?

Much to her father's annoyance, Una had refused to be transferred to the nursing home. Instead she spent her days anxiously trying to breastfeed her daughter.

'My breasts are so full of milk, Chloe, the poor little mite can't even get a grip on them. The milk runs everywhere and I'm always soaked. I'm absolutely useless at this,' she sighed and adjusted her nightdress.

'Father has not even been near me to see his first grandchild. He kicked up a real fuss when I demanded a simple little cot for her while I was here. He said it was a waste of money and to bring the one over from Grangebeck. If it hadn't been for Ella slaving away to make this one out of a clothes basket, and padding it out so prettily, there would have been even more rows.' She stared at Chloe anxiously. 'The sooner I'm allowed out of this bed and away to somewhere else with my little darling, the better.'

Chloe stiffened slightly. 'Somewhere

else? What do you mean? There is only one place for you now, Una, and that's back at Grangebeck with Cedric.'

'But Robby might be home in a few weeks.' Una gazed at her sister in despair. 'I heard Father and Cedric talking about it. I shall never forgive them for not saying anything. I don't think anyone in the village even knows.'

For the entirety of her stay Una worried. She worried over her milk supply; she worried about Ramona not gaining enough weight. She worried about the baby's appearance and whether she had slight jaundice. She worried about her mother and father and about having to go back to Cedric's.

Even so, by the end of the ten days both she and Ramona were pronounced fit and well by the doctor, and she was allowed to get up.

'There's no reason why you shouldn't get home as soon as possible,' smiled the doctor. 'Your poor old husband must have been quite lonely without you.'

On the contrary, thought Una. Cedric hadn't been in the least lonely. In fact, he'd been away all the time to various race meetings, and hadn't yet been to see Ramona.

Cedric greeted her warmly when she did arrive back. He looked at the baby and tried to show interest, but it was evident that his heart wasn't really in it.

After a couple of days in her own bedroom with the baby Una began to feel as if she were some young servant who happened to have conceived while in his employment. He was polite and friendly and asked how the baby was; sometimes he would even waggle his finger at her for half a second, but then he would disappear into his office with Miss Antrobus. Una realised it was an impossible situation.

Then, one day, when Ramona was hardly more than a month old, and just when Constance was starting to harp on about getting the baby christened, Una decided to run away.

She had thought about it for a whole day. She knew she couldn't go on this way, living like some sort of guest at Grangebeck. She also knew she could not stand the sham of having the child christened, as if everything was lovely, when plainly it wasn't. Deep down she was always aware that Robby might return at any time, especially after what she had heard Cedric and her father say.

She thought and thought about where it would be best to go and in the end decided to try getting lodgings in Altrincham again. Perhaps somewhere near the Regal Cinema, where they often needed cinema usherettes.

The Regal was a vision of modern movieland itself. It was styled with a decorative Egyptian touch, which incorporated two vast light coloured brick pillars in the external decoration above the main doors. It stood supreme on its own spacious paved plot and had only been open for a couple of years. Inside there were wide, curving carpeted stairs leading to the balcony. It was a chance for everyone to sink into heaven immediately. The air seemed scented by a thousand dolly mixtures, as soon as you strolled through the awesome threshold. A myriad glowing wall-lights teased the walls to a permanent gentle sun-set peach, as the marvellous cinema organ wafted out its sonorous tones to thousands. The cinema could seat two thousand in luxurious comfort. The Regal needed a never-ending supply of attractive torch-carrying females, wearing royal blue uniforms—who looked like Joan Bennett, Jean Harlow, or Greta Garbo—to guide cinema-goers through the darkness.

As the plan formed in Una's mind, she realised she would need help. It was too much for her now just to pick up her baby and set off into the unknown. It wasn't even as if she lived in the middle of a town with a decent transport system. She knew she would need to get settled in to somewhere very reliable with as little fuss as possible. Then her main aim would be to get a job, and at the same time set about finding out more of Robby's whereabouts.

It was at this point that she blessed her school friends. Chloe gave Una a lift to Shale Bridge to meet them, one afternoon, and she left Ramona under the watchful eye of Miss Antrobus, who adored the baby.

'Going to run away?' All three of them looked at her with a mixture of shock and admiration. Their ice cream sundaes began to melt as the long silver spoons lay idly in creamy pools.

'Surely you can't be serious?' gasped Renata.

'Of course she's serious,' muttered Delia, as she urged them into the darkened corner of the coffee house, to avoid being overheard. 'She's in a hopeless position at the moment, and the only solution is to try and get out of it completely.'

'Preferably with a load of Boy Cedric's cash sewn into your roll-ons, dear,' drawled Dolores wisely.

'What I really need,' pleaded Una, 'is good reliable lodgings, or better still a little flat. I have the money to pay for it. Cedric gives me a small allowance and puts it in the District Bank for me every month.'

'Lucky old you,' said Dolores. Then she said confidentially, 'If you're really determined, I have an ancient maiden aunt who would probably let you have her attics for a while. She's stone deaf, so the baby wouldn't be any problem, and she likes helping people.'

By the end of half an hour in the cake shop, the girls had got it all worked out for Una, even promising her a job at The Regal through cousins of the Hornbeam girls.

It was arranged that Dolores should get in touch with her aunt immediately and check up on the attics; she would telephone Una the following Tuesday. They waved each other goodbye with cheerful affection, as Chloe arrived to give Una a lift home to Grangebeck in Dudley's small van.

'So how are they all going on?' asked Chloe on the way back. 'How's life in the sixth form?'

'It must be all right because we never even mentioned it,' laughed Una.

'Never even mentioned it? What on earth did you find to talk about then?' Chloe spoke lightly, but in her bones she felt there was more going on than met the eye. She also noticed that Una was much more lively these days.

'Talk about? There's always loads to talk about when you're with friends. You know that, Chloe. And anyway, why be so nosy? If it comes to that, what has Dudley Plume been saying to you recently?'

'Don't mention it,' muttered Chloe. 'One of these days there'll be a real bust-up of gigantic proportions, when Lady Limpet's romantic bubble bursts.'

There was silence for the rest of the journey back to Grangebeck.

The following Tuesday the phone call arrived. Dolores told her the attic flat was empty and Aunty Madge Fanchurch had said Una was welcome to it. Also, the Hornbeams had got her an interview at The Regal; she was to ring Mr Obligatti and mention their name.

Cedric noticed a change in Una immediately. He took it as a sign that she was returning to normal, after a quite understandable depression following her pregnancy. He wallowed in secret, boyish delight at her cheerful young face. He watched her eyes start to sparkle again. He even began to take more notice of Ramona. It was the first time in all his adult years that he had ever been under the same roof as such a tiny one.

One day he accidentally put his hand on Una's shoulder with unthinking love, and was startled to find she didn't even shrug it off. And when he kissed her lightly on the cheek two days later and she smiled up at him, he thought his troubles were over at last.

All he needed now was for Belmane to remain buried in South America, or even some part of a big city like Manchester for ever.

Cedric's good fortune with Una continued. He even began to hope fervently that their marriage might come to something after all, and that she would at last agree to become a proper wife.

Then, one morning when he rose, he found a letter waiting for him. The envelope was written in Una's round, careful, neat hand. It was quite long, and was dated from the night before. She had placed it in one of his office envelopes.

Darling Cedric,
I know this will come as a shock to you. Specially as we are getting along so much better. But this time I have really left for good. It isn't because of you. It's because I need to be on my own with my baby until Robby Belmane gets back to claim his fatherhood.

You have behaved very kindly to me, taking me to be your wife, even though at

373

the time I hated it and despised both you and Father. But now things have changed and I can hardly stay in your house as a wife in name only.

I have arranged for a flat to go and live in, and some work, not too far away, so you have no need to worry.
Thanking you for everything.
Una

Cedric read and reread the words. At first he was dazed, then sad and then he became increasingly annoyed. The impertinent, ungrateful little madam! He'd given her everything. He'd even taken a chance on another man's child. And still, it hadn't worked. He smiled grimly.

And how would she manage to pay for a flat without her own money? He knew full well how. It would be with her monthly allowance from him, of course—the very benefactor she was happily spurning. For he knew only too well that before she married him she didn't have a penny in the world.

As soon as the bank opened Cedric was on the telephone, speaking to the manager. 'I am no longer paying into the account of my wife, Una Pawson. The payment at the end of this month is the last one. I will put it in writing.'

'Very good, sir.'

'Please would you inform Mrs Pawson of this, and refer her back to me if she's in touch with you?'

'Certainly, sir.'

Cedric replaced the receiver with a leaden heart. Now that the initial anger had worn off, he was deeply upset.

He went upstairs to Una's bedroom and looked about. Nothing appeared to have been moved except baby blankets. Una and the child must have gone with hardly any luggage. How on earth would she manage? And when did she actually go?

'I saw her on the road getting into a sportscar with the baby, just as I was getting here,' said Miss Antrobus a bit later. 'It was a four-seater, and there was a girl in school uniform in it, and a young man was driving. Una waved to me. I thought she must have been going on some sort of outing.'

Cedric shook his head dumbly.

Just before midday Cedric went round to Hubert's to show him the letter, but Hubert had toothache and wasn't at all interested. 'I just can't concentrate on it at the moment, old boy. Quite frankly I'd sooner be lying in bed away from it all. I daresay Una would have been with one of her school pals and the driver would have been the girl's brother. They're just a lot of little schemers. It's a jolly good job she left.'

'But is it?' Cedric said. 'She never really settled with me. And this time it looks as if you've lost her for good. I'm willing to bet my bottom dollar she'll be back in Altrincham again, hunting round for news of Belmane. Quite frankly, Hubert, this is the end as far as I'm concerned. No one can accuse me of not having tried. The fact is, the marriage will have to be annulled.'

'Annulled?' Hubert forgot his toothache. He looked quite startled. His eyebrows began to rise slowly. 'You mean to say you never, that *nothing...?*'

'*Nothing,*' Cedric said tonelessly. 'We slept in separate bedrooms. She's a virgin as far as I'm concerned.'

Hubert looked genuinely upset. 'But supposing she gets involved with that wretched young devil again?'

'She'll just have to then. I can't do any more. I gave my all, Hubie. I don't want to sound melodramatic, but it's true.'

They both sat listening to the grandfather clock ticking away.

Dolores Fanchurch's Aunt Madge lived in a large Victorian house with a middle-aged housekeeper and the housekeeper's husband who did gardening and odd jobs.

Mr and Mrs Parsons were in a flat on the second floor, and they all seemed to get on very well.

The attic was light and comfortable, and Una felt at home the moment she was in it.

Later that same afternoon she rang her mother and explained where she was. She did not say how she'd got there.

'All that matters now is that I take this job as an usherette and have the baby looked after while I'm working. I'm in a very good place so there's no need to worry, and they are quite prepared to look after Ramona for me while I'm at the cinema.'

'But it sounds absolutely dreadful, darling,' gasped Constance. 'You weren't brought up to be an usherette at a cinema.'

'And you weren't brought up to be Father's slave in that hotel. I shall stay here, anyway, at least until I've found out about Robby and told him about his daughter. I shall never go back to Cedric. It was never a proper marriage, and I can't possibly come back to Melmere again.'

Constance listened carefully to the young, determined voice of her daughter. At least she sounded more like her former assertive self.

'How are you managing for money, dear?'

'Oh, very well. I've got loads.'

'Well look after it carefully. You won't get enough to keep body and soul together, never mind a baby, as an usherette. What will you do about feeding her?'

There was a sudden silence on the phone. Una had hardly thought about that side of it. 'I shall just have to feed her when I'm here, and leave a bottle for her when I'm not.'

She replaced the receiver hastily, and began to feel a bit worried. She hoped they'd be able to look after Ramona properly, and feed her carefully and lovingly. She would need to go to the chemist straightaway. It would all have to be organised quickly because she started work tomorrow. She hoped they wouldn't mind if Ramona cried. She hoped they'd rock the cradle and keep her baby with them well within their sight.

She realised now how much more complicated her new life was going to be. She would have to forget about going round to Meranto's to get news of Robby for the time being.

It took her about a week to get acclimatised to everything. Madge Fanchurch and the Parsons took to the

378

baby immediately and were secretly quite shocked that such a young girl and a tiny new-born baby should be out among strangers. Una chose not to enlighten them about the real circumstances. Dolores had already painted a tale of Una, her old schoolfriend, being left in the lurch by her fiancé who had vanished abroad and left her completely homeless.

'The lodgings the poor girl was in were indescribable,' said Aunt Madge to Mr and Mrs Parsons. 'Dolores says we must help her and her child all we can.'

At first, Una's work as an usherette was relentlessly tiring. Her feet ached, her legs throbbed and she longed to sit down and relax along with all the customers as she shone her torch towards the comfortable seats. But instead she stood for hours in the dark with only the picture screen for comfort, counting the minutes until it would all be over and she could get back to Ramona.

Then, gradually, as she got to know the other women, it all improved. Some of them were old enough to be her mother, but soon she began to look forward to their company and being able to escape from the flat. Most of the films were from Hollywood, with Jean Harlow, and male stars like Gary Cooper and young

Clark Gable. Jean Harlow was all the rage in the thirties, and one of the usherettes, Joy Harley, was the image of her. She even had the same initials. She had identical platinum blonde wavy hair, her eyebrows were pencilled arches, and her face was exquisitely made up to resemble a porcelain doll. Her vivid blue eyes were lined with mascaraed eyelashes.

During the hot weather she came to work in a hand-knitted, pink frock which was as shiny as bubblegum. The cap sleeves were trimmed with fluffy white rabbit fur and she wore a small perky felt hat to match. She changed it all when she got into her uniform, but she still managed to look glamorous and Una envied her enormously. She was so independent and daring, thought Una. How wonderful to be able to stroll into The Regal dressed in such finery and with such wonderful hair, just like a genuine film star. Even Mr Obligatti seemed to be mesmerised by her, as he promoted her to supervising the ice-cream attendants.

'If you ever want to know anything about anything, love,' said Joy to Una one day, 'always come to me. I'll soon put you right.'

Some time later, Una took Joy's advice and asked her a very personal question.

CHAPTER 21

The Blonde

Robby Belmane had worked hard in Patagonia. It was a tough, isolated sort of life, primarily plant-hunting with Charlie Meranto, while they lived in tents or wooden huts.

The plants had to be catalogued and maps had to be drawn showing exactly where any species of a particular plant could be found. Meticulous drawings of the specimens were then made and coloured. They were also photographed.

Robby Belmane found that life sped by with hardly a second to call his own. He was also responsible for organising the food and clean drinking water, not to mention their methods of transportation during the working days, which sometimes entailed ponies and mules. The only thing that saddened him in this distant cut-off world was the absence of mail.

'Don't worry too much, old scout,' said Charlie Meranto, who was glad to get away from such things. 'It'll all turn up somewhere in the end.'

Meranto was right. On the very day that plans were made to return home at last, a bundle of post had been found in one of their past outposts and had been sent on to them. It was in an oilskin bag, and they spent almost a whole day going through it and sorting it out.

Robby avidly read the letters from Una. Then suddenly he stopped, not believing his eyes.

And so I am expecting our baby, but, oh, Robby, whenever will you write to me? It is so lonely bearing the thought of it without you near, and I fear that there are plans by Father to get me married off to Cedric Pawson. What on earth can I do? I haven't said a word about it being our child or there might be even more trouble.

Your ever faithful, loving and unmarried wife,

Una.

He read the words over and over again. There could be no doubt. He did some rapid calculations. Nine months or so from last August at Bylow's Tower was...good God, May. That was now! Robby began to feel quite sick with worry. Swiftly, he wrote back to her: *'Keep smiling, my love, and soon I will be by your side. Your ever adoring Robby.'*

But his letter never reached her. Along with many more it was lost in a terrific flood which swept away a whole village and disrupted roads and railway lines.

'All we can do now,' said Charlie Meranto calmly, 'is send a message home by mouth, saying we are safe and will soon be home.'

Robby Belmane's return from his travels caused quite a stir in Pover post office.

'He seems to have grown at least three inches,' twittered Miss Trill to Lady Limpet. 'He's stopped fiddling with all those little moustaches he was always trying to grow. His face is as smooth and handsome as lovely Gary Cooper.' Her eyes went all dreamy. 'They say the post never even reached them, out there in the wilderness. I expect he'll be seeing quite a lot of changes round here in Pover.'

'He certainly will,' said Lady Limpet dramatically, as she flounced away. 'He'll be seeing the finest memorial museum ever known, dedicated to Maudley Montgomery.'

'And he'll be hearing about his lady love Una Pawson running off with her baby to Altrincham,' whispered Miss Trill with relish, as she checked a large book full of ha'penny stamps.

The expedition to South America had

served Robby well, especially since he was responsible for discovering some new plant specimens.

'You can be my personal secretary from now on, old pal,' Charlie Meranto said. 'If we managed to get on well out there, we'll manage it here. And no doubt there'll be a bit more travelling to do in the future.'

Robby accepted the offer with gratitude and pride. He had enough money saved up from his months away to provide himself with a small, very old house of creamy glazed bricks. It needed a bit of work doing, for there was no indoor bathroom, but it had been offered to him cheaply by one of Charlie Meranto's friends, who wanted to keep well in with the Merantos.

'All you'll need now is a wife and some offspring to go with it,' said its former owner, Mr Lockett, smiling like a Cheshire cat. He had ten children himself, but took care to be away from home on business travels as much as possible.

Robby received a garbled version of Una's sudden disappearance from his own family, and the report was full of derisory sneers.

'Oh aye, she turned out to be a right 'un, she did,' said Robby's Mam with disgust. 'Got herself in the family way the minute she was sent back to that posh girls' school.

Nobody ever said exactly whose mistake that baby was. She was in with a very fast gang of girls there. But everybody said it couldn't have been Pawson's because folks swear he had his shot off in the war and that's why Tessa Truett turned him down. If I were you, son, I'd steer clear of that lot now you've got such good prospects with Mr Meranto. Mark my words, that cheeky young Una Lamby will come to no good, babby or no babby. She's too pretty and vain for her own good, though that'll soon vanish with a babby to feed. I 'ope she isn't lingering round Altrincham to find a mug like you. You always were too good-hearted with her when you worked for them.'

Robby listened silently, with a feeling of both anger and hopelessness. Would his mother never stop this rash, scandal-bearing gossip? She was particularly vicious about young females trying to attach themselves to her beloved sons, but she would support her own kind like a lioness, if challenged.

No one outside Una's family had any idea where Una was, except that she wasn't far away and had found a good place to live. Her own family were never ones for gossip, and Cedric Pawson was like a tomb on the subject of his runaway wife. These days it seemed he had never heard of any of the Lamby girls, even though he saw Hubert quite regularly.

Feeling strangely melancholic, Robby took a walk towards the oak trees at Swansdown before he went back to Altrincham. He no longer had any fear of Hubert Lamby. The night of the gunshots was like a dream. He walked along the drive and then branched off by the old greenhouse. He peered in at the dereliction, then seeing the old wooden chair he sat down on it, like he'd done so often in the past. After brooding for a minute or two he got up and strolled down towards the shores of Melmere, and stood, gazing at the yachts and beyond, towards Grangebeck. He walked back towards the tree where he had carved the hearts, peering between its branches to reassure himself the hearts were still there. Then he made his way back to his mother's and then to his own house in Altrincham.

It was August, a month of rain and thunderstorms. The Regal cinema was doing well, and Una had kept her promise—she hadn't been back to Melmere since she ran away.

The person she kept in contact with the most was Chloe, who was still working with Dudley Plume. One day, Chloe had brought Constance across to the flat to see her granddaughter. Ramona was just three months old, and a cheerful little bundle of love and chubbiness, with wrists that looked as if they had hidden ribbons tied round them.

It had been a tactful but rather awkward meeting. Constance had looked worried the whole time.

'Never forget, Una, that your home is always waiting for you and the baby.'

Una knew it was a kind-hearted lie. How could it ever be like that with Father there to bristle up the moment Robby's name was ever mentioned?

It wasn't mentioned now, either. Somehow Una hadn't yet had a chance to enquire about his whereabouts as the days spun along. Her main life was devoted to keeping her job as an usherette. Her rude awakening had been at the end of the first month at the flat when there was a message from the bank manager telling her that from now on her allowance from Cedric would cease. She still had a bit of money, but it would do no more than tide them over. She realised that even this was like unknown riches to most of the girls working at The Regal.

Una was one of them, good and proper now, and she blessed it. She and Joy Harley became good friends; Joy was much older and was a great comfort.

Then one day Una took her courage in both hands and asked the question she had been wanting to ask Joy from the moment they first met.

'I hope you won't be offended, but—' She paused, struggling for the right words.

'Spill it out, Una. I've got past being offended by anything. Life's too short.'

'It's your hair... Has it always been that colour?' Una felt herself blushing. 'What I mean is, it's so beautiful, but—'

'Is it out of a bottle and if so, which one?' Joy smiled.

'Well, I do realise that all fair hair can change colour a bit; my own sisters, and even my mother tints hers. But yours, yours is *exceptional*. It never changes from one moment to the next. It's such a marvellous blonde colour...' She stopped her babbling. She knew she might be getting insulting and it was the last thing she wanted.

Joy Harley narrowed her eyes. She had just put on her outside clothes. She was wearing a raincoat of shiny, imitation leopard skin and had a yellow umbrella by her side. She drew out a Craven A cigarette and smoked it slowly, blowing gentle smoke rings.

'As you say, dear,' she murmured with a cool dryness, 'it is...exceptional. Otherwise what would be the point of it? I was always

388

fair as a child but when I came to work here and kept seeing Jean Harlow on the screen I decided to help nature a bit.'

She gave Una a hard stare. 'So you like it, then?'

Una gazed at the mass of white-gold glory, 'It's truly marvellous. I wish mine was like that.'

Joy looked at her suspiciously. 'Whatever for, dear? You're beautiful enough at your age. It's only when you start to get a bit desperate and need to cheer yourself up that you get round to something as good as this. It's just a bit of fun, really. Especially for ladies over forty.'

But Una just would not be sidetracked. If she bleached her own hair like that, and Robby appeared at last—he just wouldn't be able to resist her.

'Can you buy it at the chemist then? Or do you have to go to a hairdresser?'

Joy shook her head. 'It's a friend of mine's own mixture. She does people's hair in her spare time and her daughter helps her out. I go round to their house.'

'Would she do mine?' Una asked cautiously.

'You just don't need yours done, darlin'. It's lovely as it is. And anyway if you must know, I don't need any competition around. It would kill my Jean Harlow image.'

But eventually, after persistent nagging, Joy agreed to arrange for her to meet her hairdresser friend. 'You'd never look like Jean Harlow, anyway, love. The shape and size of your face is all wrong. I'll get you an appointment, but if anything happens or you don't like the result, don't blame me...'

The following Sunday afternoon Joy took Una round to her friend Kay's house. Their front room had been converted into a small hairdressing salon, with a massive permanent wave machine with dangling attachments in the corner. There was also a big white wash-basin with a shower hose attached to one of the taps. A pink rubber cape rested on the back of a chair.

'Naturally I can't do it today,' said Kay. 'But now that I've seen what your hair's like I think my daughter could probably do it for you next Sunday morning. Would that be all right?'

Una nodded enthusiastically and was introduced to Dawn, but her excitement waned slightly at the thought of a girl younger than she was turning her platinum blonde.

Matters were made worse the following Sunday morning when Dawn admitted, by way of some rather nervous conversation, that it was her first job alone.

'This is actually my first blonding session

on my own. Usually my mother does them, but she and Joy went off for their holiday to France on Saturday with their gentlemen friends, while Aunty Flo stays here with me. They save up the whole year round for it. Mother's friend Les is an All-In wrestler who wrestles at Bellevue as The Mammoth, and Joy's friend is a very rich plumber.'

Una looked at herself in the mirror over the wash basin; she appeared decidedly peaky, and Dawn in her dark-blue overall looked even worse.

Dawn was dabbing away at the top of Una's hair.

'I don't really want to go too far down to the roots with the toothbrush in case I burn your skin, but I'll leave this lot on for a while and see what happens. I don't have the exact platinum blonde recipe, but I can remember it quite well, with Joy coming in so often to have it done.'

All Una wanted now was to call off the whole thing and escape. But she was totally trapped. Then, to her horror, as Dawn finished washing away all the froth and removed the safety pads from Una's eyes, she saw that her hair was a strange shade of greeny yellow.

'I don't think I can have put enough on,' said Dawn doubtfully. 'Would you like me to try again?'

Una was fuming. 'I certainly wouldn't like you to try again with anything, Miss Shark. All I want now is for you to cut all that green off immediately. I can't possibly have it this colour, I'd be a laughing stock!'

'I can't cut it off now,' snapped Dawn with angry petulance. 'It'll have to be dried first, and anyway I'm not good at cutting hair, my mother usually does all that. It's your own fault. It was you that wanted it dyed. My mother said you made Joy's life a misery going on about it. My mother thinks you're very spoilt and vain. I've never had a thing done to my hair and never shall.' There was an angry simmering silence as Dawn put Una under the dryer.

When Una came out from under the dryer her hair was a glowing mustard yellow.

'I think it's looking better now,' said Dawn hopefully. 'If you come back again in about a week and have it done over again it should do the trick properly. The cost for this will be two and sixpence.'

Una gave her the half a crown. She knew she shouldn't have, but all she wanted was to be away from the place. She never wanted to see Kay or Dawn again. She felt an absolute fool.

'You can borrow a scarf to put over

your head, if you want,' said Dawn, magnanimous now she had the half-crown safety tucked away. 'Just give it back to Joy when she returns from her holiday. We often lend scarves. People become shocked so easily. They're terribly fussy if it's not quite the exact shade they expected.'

When Una got back to the flat, Aunt Madge thought she was a stranger.

'Child, child,' she moaned, 'what on earth have you done to your beautiful tresses?'

Mr and Mrs Parsons were equally scandalised.

'You look like a scarlet woman,' muttered Mr Parsons.

'I can hardly be that with green hair,' said Una bitterly, as she borrowed some scissors from them and went to her flat.

Thank goodness Ramona was still asleep in the living room with Madge. Just supposing she had frightened the life out of her own child?

She took the scissors, and scowling with temper and determination she began to hack away at the disaster. But try as she might there was always a bit of ghastly greenish yellow showing through. When at last her hair was almost as short as a convict's, she gave up.

The following day she felt awful when

she got to work. She didn't seem to fit in with the rest of them any longer. She knew they were all staring at her behind her back, and she no longer sensed the wave of general friendliness. It was as if she had let them all down, even though no one said a word. There was only one girl, Doris, who was the epitome of respectability and was kind enough to refer to Una's hair as the new 'ragamuffin' look.

'It's the latest now, lovie, and the blunter the scissors the better. You're really in the fashion high spot, and no one'll see you anyway, when the lights are turned down.'

Miserably Una went about her work, tearing people's small, numbered tickets in half, and showing them to their seats with her torch. She felt that her so-called friend Joy had let her down completely, leaving her in the hands of a girl like Dawn and never even mentioning she was due to go off for some holidays. All of a sudden life seemed to be an intolerable burden.

She returned along one of the aisles between the hundreds of seats downstairs and stood behind the back rows of the stalls in the sudden blackness. She hadn't even the heart to glance at the film as the sound filled the picture house. She looked bleakly at the seats full of avid spectators, posed so comfortably.

Just as she was waiting desperately for the interval to arrive, counting the minutes towards being able to leave it all to get back to Ramona, she glimpsed the outline of a man's face in the back row as he turned slightly towards an empty seat next to him. She stared and stared with growing fascination. Was she imagining it? Surely it wasn't? Not *here*, amongst all this?

Taking her torch she slipped quietly towards him along the row, ignoring the disgruntled murmurs as she blocked the view of the screen for a few seconds. She sat down swiftly in the empty seat beside him. She could always make some excuse if she was mistaken.

'Excuse me sir,' she whispered as she leaned towards him. 'Have you by any chance mislaid your w—'

He looked towards her sharply. The lights and organ music were on, and the refreshments attendants could be seen.

Robby had no idea who she was.

'What was it you said?'

'I was saying,' she whispered the next words close to his ear, 'that you are Robby Belmane and I am Una Lamby.'

He jerked away from her with a startled look, and frowned.

'Excuse me,' he said with confusion, 'I don't quite understand all this. I do happen to know a Miss Lamby, but you certainly aren't her!'

Una didn't feel her heart flooding with angry disappointment; she felt nothing at all. She simply couldn't believe it. She knew she looked a bit different with her awful haircut, but surely he recognised her voice?

She put her hand on his, but he flinched and dragged it away.

'You're sitting in my friend's seat, too,' he said, without looking at her again.

A few moments later a young, smart-looking woman arrived back carrying two ice-cream cornets, and there was another fuss along the row of seats as Una removed herself to let the stranger sit next to Robby.

Una was close to tears. Never in her whole life could she ever have imagined their first meeting would be like this, after all his time abroad. And then, for him to be accompanied by another woman...

For the rest of the film, Una couldn't help looking at the seats where Robby was sitting. She stared especially hard at the seat next to him. She even knew exactly when they'd finished their ice creams in the darkness. She saw the woman next to him take out a hanky from her pocket and delicately wipe her fingers and dab at her mouth.

Just before the lights were due to go

on, Una took the plunge. She hurried to the staff cloakroom and changed quickly into her outdoor clothes. Then, as soon as the National Anthem had been sung, she followed Robby out.

It was quite difficult to do. There was a sudden spill of people, all crowding towards the exits and the foyer leading to the main doors of The Regal. She was terribly scared she'd lose sight of him, and she had an awful feeling that if she did, she might never see him again.

As she milled around in the stream of people hurrying outside, she lost them. *Where on earth were they?* She stopped and looked back. Surely she hadn't missed them entirely? They were there only seconds ago—Robby in his summer suit and open-neck cricket shirt, and the woman in her rather outlandish flared pyjama suit, which Una felt with secret envy should only have been worn at the seaside.

Trembling slightly with the sudden shock of seeing him there, she hesitated outside the picture house and decided to push her way back in again to have one last look round. Her heart was thumping with sudden fear. She *had* to find him again.

Then, to her joy, she saw them both still there, looking at the poster of the forthcoming film programmes. Una could see the girl in full detail now. She was very attractive, with smooth black hair and a lovely oval face. Una's heart was stung by jealousy and absolute despair. Was this the end of all these months of waiting and wanting, of worrying and praying for the return of Ramona's father, and her own real husband from that passionate vow of the past?

Suddenly she saw the girl murmur something into Robby's ear, and go and join a queue which had formed for free vouchers for boiled sweets.

Una hurried towards Robby, her face scarlet with emotion.

'Robby? It's *me!* It's Una!' She was wearing a hat now and it disguised her dreadful haircut and the dye. 'I'm working here as an usherette.'

'Una!' He bellowed her voice so loudly that people began to turn and stare.

They flew into each other's arms and hugged each other in amazed relief. Tears flooded down Una's cheeks.

'Your letters...' he said in a muffled, tear-filled voice. Quickly he explained how all the mail had been held up.

When his date came back with the vouchers, he said, 'Let's all get introduced properly.' He turned to his friend, his thin face beaming with radiance, 'Liz, this is Una Lamby, my...' he hesitated, a hardly perceivable moment. He'd heard rumours that Una was supposed to be married to Pawson. He took a chance. 'My fiancée, the person I was telling you about from Melmere.'

Then he turned to Una. 'And this is Elizabeth Fletcher, my cousin who used to live in Middleton. Her husband's in the navy. She's only just come to live in Altrincham and she's still a bit lonely.'

Both the girls smiled and shook hands. Then Robby said, 'Elizabeth only lives round the corner. My car's parked there.' He looked wonderingly at Una again; he couldn't believe his eyes. They smiled at each other. Una gazed at his face, drinking in the changes their months apart had made. His face was leaner, with stronger lines and his eyes seemed more perceptive. His hair was slightly longer and less spruce, and he had a new unassuming confidence in his manner.

She suddenly realised that she too must have changed a bit in these last two years. She was plumper, for one thing, since Ramona had been born, and she had learned to differentiate between the parts of life that mattered to her and Ramona, and the bits that were not worth worrying about.

Her face was now one of pure contentment and gratitude.

'I'll get the car and see you home, Una,' said Robby, when Elizabeth had gone.

When they were driving back she began to explain about the flat. 'I've left Cedric for good, Robby.' Then she said in a low voice, 'It was all a sham. We never even slept together. I wouldn't have been able to bear it.'

They pulled up outside the house.

'This is where my flat is. I live with a girl from school's aunty—Miss Fanchurch—and her housekeeper. They look after Ramona for me when I'm working. Our baby is adorable. She's ever so much like you, Robby. She's three months old now.'

'Look,' said Robby, as they sat in the old car Maurice had sold to him, holding hands. 'Why don't you tell them you've decided to go away next weekend? Bring Ramona to stay with me. I have my own place now. It's a bit rough, at present, but I'm gradually getting it straight, and one of these days the house'll be our home. Tell them I'm taking you back to Melmere for the weekend.'

Una hesitated. 'I'd like to, but first it would mean time off work and the cinema manager might not allow it. Secondly, I swore I would never go to Melmere again.' She looked at Robby with sheer wretchedness.

400

'You don't need to be like that anymore, Una.' His arms held her comfortingly. 'We're back together again, for good. That's all that matters.' They leaned towards each other, kissing and caressing with longing passion.

'Give it a try anyway,' said Robby, pleadingly. 'I'll meet you after work tomorrow evening.' He smiled at her happily. 'I still can't quite believe you're real. I got in touch with them at Swansdown twice to try and find out where you were. Didn't anyone ever say?'

She shook her head. She didn't want to admit that he had caught her just before breaking point, when all hope of ever seeing him again was beginning to vanish.

When she got back in the house Madge said kindly, 'Did someone give you a lift home in a car tonight?'

Una smiled. 'It was a very old friend of the family. He used to be our gardener at Swansdown. He says he'll take me and Ramona back home for the weekend next week. It should be really nice...' Her eyes sparkled with such intensity that Madge began to wonder what on earth had happened, but she was too tactful to ask.

When Una had gone upstairs to her flat with the sleeping child, Madge sat down thoughtfully. Una's life, from the snippets of conversation she'd gleaned, didn't seem a bit like the picture Dolores had painted. And that young man didn't look a bit like a gardener, though you could never tell these days, when they were all dressed up. Miss Fanchurch sighed to herself. Well at least the girl seemed happy, blissfully happy tonight.

She would never quite understand this younger generation, but what did it matter when happiness like this was in the air?

CHAPTER 22

Feelings...

When Una got to work the next day she was informed that Mr Obligatti wished to see her immediately. He was waiting in his office, and he looked at her stonily from beneath his black eyebrows. His bald head shone in the cold light.

'Miss Lamby,' he said, pointing to some small slips of paper on the desk with her name and address on them. 'These are your cards. You are sacked.'

Sacked? Her heart sank. She was still pleasantly numbed by the glorious sight of Robby. She was feeling quite grateful to Mr Obligatti for having given her a job in the first place. She wondered if meeting Robby would ever have happened if she hadn't been working here at the cinema.

Her mind was a complete blank as to why Mr Obligatti should be getting rid of her.

Mr Obligatti looked at her with blossoming hate: 'For a start your hairstyle and the colour of it is a disgrace to any decent woman, and to all the other usherettes working here.

'Secondly, you blatantly ignored your duties yesterday evening. You caused complete disruption along row A, and a great deal of fuss in seats ten and eleven.

'You tried to force yourself into a patron's seat when she had gone to collect some refreshments, and you pressed your unwelcome attentions on an innocent male customer. It was all seen and reported to me by chief usherette, Lucinda Bestwick.' He took out a large blue handkerchief and patted his brow. 'And as if that wasn't enough, you left your duties early, long before it was time to go. Ursula Merton, who was in the ladies' cloakroom putting some soap on a ladder in her stocking, saw you ready to go in your hat and coat. What more can I say?' He stared at her with raised eyebrows. 'Come in and collect your money at the end of the

403

week. Your position has been terminated from this point on and you will *not* get a reference.' He sat there with head lowered until she had left the room.

Una stood dumbly for a few seconds. Should she apologise? And anyway, how could she possibly apologise for a faulty bit of hairdressing? Or for seeing Robby? Or about little Ramona still not yet in her daddy's arms?

She glanced briefly again at the cards on the table, then turned and left without another word.

Una hurried to the cloakroom in a flush of embarrassment. She tore off her uniform, and put on her outdoor clothes. Then, because she didn't want to have to go and see Lucinda Bestwick personally, she returned with her uniform to Mr Obligatti's office.

He wasn't there, so she draped it over the back of his chair. Then she walked out for ever. No one would even know she'd ever worked there, she thought bitterly.

Little did she know that she was going to acquire a few seconds of unsought fame in the history of The Regal.

As soon as she'd gone, Ursula Merton, Mr Obligatti's girlfriend had come into his room ready for a bit of flirtation. But she had stopped in her tracks when she saw the blue uniform dress lying across Mr Obligatti's chair. With smarting passion she slipped across and saw the name Lamby written on the name tape. Immediately she went outside and spread the news that Una Lamby was at this very minute in an unnameable place with Mr Obligatti, and her clothes were spread all round his office.

Una's Lamby's name lasted two weeks in the annals of serious gossip, and was only usurped when the double horror bill of *Dracula* and *Frankenstein*, featuring Bela Lugosi as the bloodsucking vampire and Boris Karloff as Frankenstein's monster was shown again by popular demand, with an ambulance and first-aiders ready for stricken patrons.

Una and Robby lay together in the single bed at Robby's small house. Ramona was asleep in her cot beside them. It had been a tearful, passionate reunion—a true honeymoon. It was also a time of gentle madness, as they lay together more than once and made love with passionate spontaneity. They were unhampered and undisturbed in their own small paradise.

'We'll need to get a proper bed, for a start,' laughed Robby, as the wonderful weekend drew to a close. 'But first we must let Miss Fanchurch know that you won't be back.'

Una decided that the best way to do this would be for Robby to go and explain that she would no longer be needing the flat, and to settle up financially. He would also deliver a letter and a present from herself, thanking them for all their kindness and explaining that her problem had been resolved at last.

Madge Fanchurch read the letter and opened the present. It was a very pretty glass paperweight. She looked at it sadly. How could it ever compensate for the pleasure she and the Parsons had received from looking after Ramona and seeing her grow so bonny? She wiped a tear from her eye.

'Don't forget to tell her to come and see us again with the baby, will you?'

'I won't forget.' Robby nodded enthusiastically. 'She will always remember your kindness. She can't really thank you enough.'

In the middle of September, when russet leaves lay thickly on the ground and the air turned misty and cool, Constance received a letter from Altrincham. She could see it was from Una by the writing, but it was in a rather thick, good-quality envelope and seemed as if it had a card inside it.

Constance had not been in touch with her since early August, and neither had Chloe. Up to her eyes in trouble with Dudley Plume over Lady Limpet's Maudley Montgomery Memorial, Chloe had had little time for anyone in the family and Constance herself was faring no better. She was suffering more trouble with Hubert, who was going through one of his phases of wicked bad temper. There had already been some trouble because he'd shot at a neighbour's dog for trespassing on Swansdown land. Mr Carroway, the dog's owner, never spoke to him again and sent him a huge vet's bill for the repair of the dog's hind leg.

'We shall have to sell this place,' said Hubert morosely. It's been the worst August on record, with all this rain. We'll never recoup our losses.'

This happened every year. He always forgot about the good weather they had had, and how they had been blessed with a whole new batch of visitors, all of whom swore to come back again next year.

No one in the family said a word. Both Ella and Lindi wished he would sell Swansdown. Ella was deeply involved, now, with Malcolm Marqueson's son Monty, who was still trying to wrangle a divorce from his estranged wife Moira.

Ella dreamed eternally of leaving Swansdown to fend for itself. She longed for a home of her own and children with poor Monty, before it was too late.

Lindi Lamby was easing her way out of the workings of the hotel, in spite of constant nagging from Hubert. She was getting nearer to moving to Manchester for good, where she had been offered a job doing sound-effects on a children's hour radio programme.

Constance began to open Una's letter. There was a card inside. Was it a change of address?

She stared in amazement at the slightly ornate edge of the glowing white card with its silver writing. It looked almost like a wedding invitation. *'Miss Una Lamby and Mr Robert Belmane wish to invite you to their daughter's christening...'* Constance could hardly believe it. Una was still officially married to Cedric.

She began to panic and feeling quite faint she searched for her glasses to look more closely at the address. 'The Olive Branch, Sandy Way, Altrincham'. What a strange name for a house. How could anyone ever manage to grow an olive tree in Manchester?

And they were going to need much more than an olive branch to offer when Hubert heard the news. Constance tucked the card in her apron pocket and made her way upstairs to his study.

That same morning the postman delivered

an invitation to Grangebeck. It was tucked away in masses of official-looking post for Cedric, and his secretary Miss Antrobus handed it to him.

Cedric ripped open the envelope, recognising the writing immediately. What was the little devil up to now? A sudden tremor of anger ran through him as he moved away from Miss Antrobus, and gazed out from the tall sash windows. Una was still his wife, damn it.

He left the office hurriedly. As usual, Miss Antrobus was now busy leaning over a low table to attend to a potted plant. Her garters were purple today. They went well with the mauve-blue of the morning glory, as she sprayed it with tepid water. Cedric deliberately pushed into her on the way out, in silent fury.

He poured himself a stiff whisky and sat on the verandah by the terrace, next to some scented yellow tea-roses. The official white card was burnt into his mind. The Christening. An invitation from the child's mother and father. How could anything seem more natural?

Never would anyone realise what he had suffered when he became her husband and agreed to accept the baby as his own—to give it his name and a good start in life.

And then, to have her run away. It was the cruellest blow, the worst indignity in the whole of his existence. And the invitation was like a dagger in his pride. He still loved the little minx, and he despised that callow youth Belmane all the more.

But gradually in the Autumn sunshine, with bright skies above him and a drop of whisky in his veins, he began to calm down. He began to see reason...to such an extent that he wrote Una a private letter of thanks for the invitation. '...*and so I wish you all a happy christening for Ramona in my absence, and I shall endeavour to get our marriage annulled as soon as possible. Always your faithful friend, Cedric.*'

He didn't put the letter with the rest of the outgoing post in his office for Miss Antrobus to attend to; instead he decided to walk into Pover and post it himself while he called in to see Tessa Truett. What a pity he and Tessa had ever parted. She might have saved him from all this embarrassment. Was it worth trying again to capture her attentions?

He wandered into the Twinkle tearooms with a calm casual air and ordered black coffee. Tessa got one of her girls to take over while she and Cedric went into her private sitting room.

'Black coffee?' said Tessa, narrowing her observant, heavily mascaraed eyes. 'Is something rattling you?'

'It was, but it's all finished now. I've

just posted my troubles away. I've accepted the inevitability of a certain situation.' He pressed on. 'Do you fancy some time out next Friday or Saturday? We can either picnic in the grounds of Drawbridge Hall with the plebs, and see the Pover Players' performance of *Hamlet* in the afternoon? Or we can see the play at seven-thirty and have our dinner at the banqueting table in Lady Limpet's lavish mansion?'

She looked at him quizzically. 'As if I didn't already know every word of it, Cedric Pawson. Haven't I been involved for weeks arranging those very same gourmet get-togethers in aid of the Maudley Montgomery museum? I only hope it doesn't pour with rain.

'Yes, I shall go incognito to the picnic edition.' She gave Cedric a sly wink and shook her head. 'Is it all over with Una, then?'

He nodded and looked away.

Tessa sighed. 'She's a charming girl, but she's very young. I'm glad she's got the baby settled and found Robby.'

He shrugged his shoulders. It was never mentioned again.

The play was perfect. Afterwards, Cedric said, 'Have you ever thought of us getting married, Tessa?'

'Quite candidly no, Cedric.'

'Well, think about it.'

That night he shared her bed, and the following morning as he returned to Grangebeck he felt that life was looking up.

'I didn't realise you were going to be away overnight, and so suddenly,' observed Miss Antrobus on Monday morning. 'And neither did the rest of the staff.'

'Never you mind what I do, Miss Antrobus.' Cedric's face was as straight as a poker. 'Just you concentrate on the colour of your garters.'

Una had read Cedric's letter in private, sitting happily in an old armchair nursing Ramona. The crystal swan bowl which Robby had given to her was on a small chest of drawers close by, filled with bright nasturtiums. She didn't mention anything to Robby until she had replied with due formality to Cedric's peace offering. She was filled with joy when she saw she was to be released from the marriage, and she knew Cedric was efficient once he set his mind to something.

When the final official notification arrived saying that her marriage to Cedric had been abolished, she broke the glad news to Robby with triumphant relief.

'Our day is here at last, my love. We can have our own real wedding.' The simple words tumbled from her lips in a swell of emotion.

Oh, how different it was to that first macabre ceremony. She'd been nothing but a helpless puppet to the wishes of others.

Una and Robby were married in a cheerful registry office affair, on a bright and breezy October day. All the women held onto their hats and their billowing frocks and underskirts. And the wind offered no respite to the men who swept the roads, as more and more russet leaves landed silently by the hour, paving the world with vivid scarlet, pale green and golden blessings.

Robby's brother Maurice had turned up with his wife and family. The Merantos had sent apologies, but a very interesting wedding present—a synchronous electric clock.

Robby's best man was Alec Bradshaw, one of the gardeners from Meranto's, and he looked handsome in a check suit and spats.

Constance, Granny Lamby and Una's sisters were there; Tessa Truett had organised temporary staff for the few hours they were away from Swansdown, and there was an enormous sigh of relief as they mingled afterwards in the assembly rooms with relatives and Una's school friends.

Dudley Plume had arrived, looking as dishevelled as ever, but one of Una's greatest surprises was to see whom Lindi had brought with her. Lindi wore a letter-box red knitted jacket and skirt, and a small crocheted beret with a silver brooch on it. And by her side, as large as life, with a wide smile on his handsome face, was Marcus Oliphant.

Chloe, in neat navy blue with a spray of hothouse orchids, was on her own except for Beech, Una's brown and white cocker spaniel, who was allowed to stay in a small anteroom at the assembly rooms.

'He's the only creature representing Cedric,' said Chloe to Ella, with gentle irony, as she tended to Ramona.

After the speeches, and the Champagne, the wedding cake was cut and Una, Robby and Ramona set off home. The following day they travelled to Matlock spa in Derbyshire where they spent a memorable and happy week being pampered by Una's Aunty Nora and Uncle George, in their Victorian stone house.

Hubert Lamby did not attend his youngest daughter's wedding. He stayed at home and pleaded illness, with his curtains drawn in the bedroom. Miraculously, he recovered as soon as Cedric rang up with some news about the horses.

'It's no good moping, old boy,' said

414

Cedric, when he heard the latest tale of woe about all the Lamby women ganging up together.

'What about me, then, Hubert?' Cedric began to sound defensive. 'What about the way I've suffered with it all? Una may be your youngest daughter, but she was supposed to be my wife. I still love her enough to release her from our marriage and pretend it never existed. It's about time you grew up, too, Hubie.'

'That's because you've had Tessa waiting in the wings,' growled Hubert. 'Never will you know what it's like being tied to one woman for ever with four demanding, self-centred daughters. But never mind that, tell me about the horses again.'

In a calm, soothing voice Cedric told him.

Malcolm Marqueson had always carried a secret grudge against Chloe Lamby and that inefficient idiot Dudley Plume, ever since the town meeting in the village hall, months and months ago.

Rumour had it that Chloe had been sacked from the Gazette because of the scandalous report she had written about those proceedings, and that Mr Eldew the editor had burnt her report right in front of her in the office grate.

'He said,' reported Miss Trill in Pover

post office, and who wasn't even at the meeting, 'that Chloe Lamby was *lucky* to see it all going to ashes. So *there* now, Mr Marqueson, what do you think of *that?*

'Mr Eldew *said*—and these were his very words—that if her disastrous reportage had reached the columns of his noble paper, one hundred and fifty years of publishing history and local news would have been cleared away for ever—and the newspaper would have been closed down.' Miss Trill had fixed Mr Marqueson with a look fit for an ancient mariner as she took off her rimless glasses and began to clean the lenses carefully.

Malcolm Marqueson was feeling a bit put-out these days. His fame as doyen of the local history had been completely washed away by Lady Limpet's latest mad desire to put Pover on the cultural map of the world. He regarded it as far too overdone and questioned the veracity of it all. He knew for a fact that he had relatives of his own who could write poems ten times better than those accorded to Maudley Montgomery.

He noticed that a whole barn once belonging to Ely Winterbothan had been commandeered to house all the rubbish Letty Limpet had acquired, with the help of Lamby and Plume. It was behind some elms at the back of the old Pond gift shop, where Maudley Montgomery's edifice was to stand. Rumour had it that the statue of Maudley was carved in granite, and was under a sheet at the local undertakers, ready for the official opening.

The museum was built in new brick and timber, with a thatched roof, but it was still empty. It had tall, temporary wooden fences all round the site, guarding it from public gaze until it was fully furnished and ready to be opened. Meanwhile, the barn at the back was stuffed with secondhand relics of every type, from old woollen moth-eaten combinations to over-fermented bottles of Dandelion and Burdock.

Religiously, Dudley Plume entered every item into a never-ending ledger, and wrote a potted history by its side, explaining its link with the famous man.

Meanwhile, Chloe was fully occupied dealing with all correspondence and the shower of official letters he dictated to her, as his signature became more of a flourish and increasingly indecipherable.

And Malcolm Marqueson simmered away in private. He was green with envy. He longed to take part in it all, especially now that his son Monty was so obsessed with the other Lamby girl, Ella, and was showing signs of wanting to get married and leave him on his own. Malcolm still had two pairs of very good socks which Ella had knitted for him, and they were wearing very well. She was also willing to do darning, and she could cook an excellent meal. The house was quite big enough for all three of them, if his son persisted in fussing over her. It would be tragic if they left him to look after himself.

Then one day in a fit of all-round temper at his own predicament he decided to vent his spleen in the *Gazette*. He would write and describe the whole scandal of the Maudley memorial.

'*Suddenly in our midst,*' he wrote, '*We are cursed with a complete monstrosity, an insult to all the true men of letters who have graced our fair land...*' He was afire with enthusiasm as his pen scratched on and on, over fifteen pages of letter. Tucking it into an envelope and licking the flap, he strode purposefully to the letterbox and posted it.

Robby Belmane was feeling completely happy and relaxed. He had a home of his own at last, a wife he loved, and a beautiful baby daughter he adored more with every passing day.

It was October and the scattered leaves of the lime trees were parchment yellow against their bare branches. The weather was still warm, and it seemed hard to imagine that winter was close at hand.

Each day Robby went to Meranto's and worked with Charlie Meranto on his natural history records, and the specimens and photographs brought back from their journeys in South America. Then, quite out of the blue, in just the same way as he'd suggested their first trip abroad, Charlie said, 'How do you fancy setting off to New Zealand?'

Robby was stunned. Charlie Meranto had never breathed a word about going anywhere else.

'When would it be, sir?'

'The end of this month. I've got the opportunity for a return journey by aeroplane, with stopovers at various junctions. It's too good to miss.'

Robby's heart sank. He was settling down so well, and really enjoying getting the house sorted out. They spent hours poring over ideas for improvements and alterations, and they both enjoyed digging in their small garden.

'How long would it be for?'

Charlie Meranto shrugged his shoulders casually and pursed his lips. 'I reckon about three or four months.' Then he said jokingly, 'Not too long overall. We'll be back about March. I'll give you a few days to think about it and talk to your wife, but if you can't manage it, let me know straightaway because I'll have to find someone else. It'd be a damned shame, Belmane. It would mean you'd be stuck here in my office.'

Robby shivered slightly. He had to admit that the thought of being left in charge of all the office backlog was not a pleasant one. He had always hated that sort of thing, and he knew there was a mountain of paper work still to get through from the Patagonian excursion. Robby feared that one wrong move might land him in enough trouble to lose his job with Meranto's for ever.

'Naturally, I'd sooner come with you, sir,' Robby said slowly, 'but I'll have to see what Una has to say.'

Charlie Meranto patted his shoulder. 'Good lad. Try and persuade her. Tell her the journey will be of lasting value, and will give you a good chance for future promotion. Perhaps she could go and stay with her family while you're away?' Charlie smiled at him benignly.

The following day Robby felt quite ill at the thought of breaking the news to Una. When would be the best time? They were both a bit worried over Ramona at the moment; she had been restless in the night and had woken them both with her crying. She was getting her first teeth, and although they knew her discomfort was normal, it was very upsetting for both of them.

'Whatever would I do without you here to comfort me, when she cries like this,' said Una, as they took turns in nursing Ramona until she fell asleep.

Later that day when they had finished their evening meal and Ramona was safely asleep in her own small nursery, Robby took the plunge as he and Una lay in each other's arms on the large comfortable sofa.

'Mr Meranto has sprung some news on me, Una.' He moved closer to her and kissed her ear.

She drew away from him. 'Is it good or bad?'

'It's a mixture, but it could lead to good long-term prospects.'

'What is it, then?' Her face brightened in anticipation.

'He wants me to go with him to New Zealand.'

She froze with fear. 'Oh, *no*. You're hardly back from the last one! Whatever is the man thinking of? It would be cruel to take you so far away again. I don't think I could stand it.' Tears came to her eyes. Then, taking a deep breath in the heavy silence between them, she said bravely, 'Well, if it truly has to be, it has to be. It's our bread and butter, and even this roof over our head is thanks partly to Charlie Meranto.'

Robby breathed a sigh of relief at her change of heart.

'Do you think you would be able to go back home while I'm away?'

'Go back home?' Una got up from the Davenport and glared at him fiercely. 'This is our home, Robby Belmane. And here is the place I'll stay!' Then she looked away to hide her emotions. 'But it will be so lonely...'

Robby nodded bleakly, but the very next day at work, he told Charlie Meranto he was able to go.

Dudley Plume was feeling annoyed and frustrated. There had been a hell of a dust-up about the running of the Maudley Memorial project, in a seemingly never-ending tirade about it in the *Gazette*.

Lady Limpet had tried to console him. 'I have perfect faith in both you and Chloe Lamby, dear boy. There always have been and always will be troublemakers about. They are the short-sighted people of life who fail to envision where the future is leading us. But never fear, your work for Maudley Montgomery will flourish for ever.'

The pieces in the *Gazette* were written by Malcolm Marqueson, and already small flames of interest were beginning to appear in the national press. Dudley had noticed a two-line reference to it in the *Manchester Guardian,* and the *Daily Express*'s two million readers had been treated to five lines.

A week later a Sunday paper took it even further. MAUDLEY'S HOLY COMS FOUND IN BARN' read a headline.

'I'm just about fed up with the whole thing,' admitted Dudley to Chloe. 'I've slogged away at it for close on two solid years and where's it got me? I'll tell you where it's got me, Chloe. It's made me a laughing stock of the whole nation. And what sort of future is there in that?

'And Marqueson is just jealous. He wouldn't last half a second in this job.'

Chloe nodded silently. Something told her that Dudley wouldn't last half a second either, if ever he did decide to leave. She just couldn't imagine him doing anything else, but prowl about examining things and talking for hours on the finer points of some poem by Maudley Montgomery that he'd just invented.

At the end of October, exactly as planned, Robby set off for New Zealand with Charlie Meranto.

Una stood at the gate of their small garden with Ramona in her arms and waved to him. It seemed like any other day, as if he was going to work and would be back at dinnertime. Today, however, he had gone with a rucksack on his back.

When Una was inside the house again, all the energy drained from her and she put Ramona gently in her cot in the nursery with her toys. Then she lay on the sofa downstairs and sobbed and sobbed. When would she see him again? Surely the communication wouldn't be as bad as last time?

Mr Meranto had assured her that things would be different this time. He had called her a brave woman and an ideal wife. But deep down she hated him, and saw him only as a man of influence and power stealing Robby away with ruthless ease.

Una thought back to Ramona's quiet christening. Only her mother, Granny Lamby and Chloe had been there. Not a single person from Robby's side had bothered to turn up. In spite of her father her own people were the only ones she could turn to in times of trouble. Charlie Meranto's suggestion about her going back to stay with her mother while Robby was away loomed in her mind, and now, after only five minutes of Robby being out of sight, she began to consider it.

And then, something happened that completely upset her plans.

CHAPTER 23

Swapping Round

'Have you heard the latest?' said Miss Trill to anyone who would listen. 'It's not quite official yet, but all of that Belmane tribe are due to leave Pover. They're moving out, lock, stock and barrel. I can't say I'm sorry. They're a real back-biting lot. The only one who's done any good is their Robby, and he's away in the wilds again...Ma Belmane says they're all moving to Middlewich. It's all on account of Lady Limpet...' Miss Trill looked around hastily and lowered her voice. Only Miss Antrobus was there now, sticking some postage stamps on letters.

'Letty Limpet is putting up all the rents. Rumour has it she has some relatives of her own who'll soon be needing those two cottages, though I'll warrant both of 'em buildings'll need a bit of delousing and a good scrub out first.'

Miss Antrobus looked up from the letters and stared at Miss Trill in shocked silence. Then she said stiffly, 'Really, Miss Trill I do think you should keep such things to yourself. Number one, it might not be true and number two, it's both unkind and uncalled-for to spread such malicious gossip.'

'Spread such gossip? What on earth did I say that could be called gossip, Miss Antrobus? Just you tell me...'

Miss Antrobus clicked her tongue and left the shop.

Una realised that she could manage on her own with Ramona in Altrincham, after all. The neighbours were friendly and there were other families close by with young families, as well as a small private kindergarten from which children went to and fro.

A farm at the back of the garden provided fresh milk and eggs. Speckled hens ran about on the blue-black cobbles, stealing bits of food from each other, and a couple of large cocks strutted, perching occasionally on the yellow straw of the steamy manure heap to crow.

To her relief, Una received short messages back from Robby in New Zealand by cable. He'd posted her a long letter, and by enormous coincidence he'd met someone called Kendo Montgomery who had a wife and six children, and a photograph of Pover.

Una had smiled to herself. What

a difference from that last journey to Patagonia!

Then, at the end of October, her cosy new life was suddenly disrupted by a visit from Chloe.

When the car arrived, Una thought it was Cedric coming back into her life and a tremor of unease ran through her. It was his limousine, but Chloe was driving it.

'He said I could use it to help you bring your luggage back to Swansdown. A folding cot and pram will fit in easily.' Then, before Una could say a word, Chloe sat her down, and said, 'Mother isn't at all well, Una. She's suffering from pernicious anaemia, and has to go to hospital for a while. They say she will have to take injections for the rest of her life. She'll need to do far less around the hotel and try to take things easier.'

They both looked at each other with concern. It was the last thing anyone could have expected.

'What ever will Father do?' asked Una, with a heavy heart.

'He's in a serious dilemma,' said Chloe drily. 'He can't even call on Cedric to help him out because—you'll never believe this Chloe—Cedric is actually going to marry Tessa Truett at the beginning of November. He has become quite obsessed with their plans. According to Tessa, it'll

427

all be a very quiet affair, but they're going to London for a honeymoon and staying at the Waldorf Hotel.' Chloe sighed. 'Father certainly won't be able to get me back to help, because poor old Dudley is going through a bit of a crisis at the moment. It's to do with that row in the newspapers. And Ella, well, she's completely taken up with Monty Marqueson. She moved out to live with him and his father as a sort of housekeeper only two days before Mother heard the news about her condition. So there's only Lindi left at home now, and she's all set to go off to Manchester soon. She's been trying to go for ages.'

'Father will need to employ some extra staff then,' said Una smugly. 'He'll be *very* pleased about that! It'll cost him quite a packet.' She thanked her lucky stars that she hadn't gone straight back home when Robby had gone away.

'He'll have to agree.' Chloe hesitated. 'The thing is, Una. Well, to be frank, the reason I've called is to say that Mother asked me to see if you'd come back and supervise things.' Chloe couldn't meet Una's eyes. 'But hang on, Una. I know it'll be terribly difficult, but it's the least we can do to help her, and you aren't too tied at the moment, apart from Ramona.'

Apart from Ramona... Suddenly Una felt years older than Chloe. Just wait till Chloe had a baby, she thought, then maybe she wouldn't be so casual about it.

'It would only be a question of working things out with Lindi until she actually goes to Manchester,' pleaded Chloe. 'Between the two of you Swansdown could be running reasonably well again, ready for when Mother gets back. You and Lindi should be able to deal with Father...' her voice faded slightly.

'Chloe, how can you sit there and talk as if it's the easiest thing in the world after the way we've both suffered.' Una stared at her with real anger. 'And just when I'm getting settled here in my own little house. just when everything's starting to go so well for Robby and me...'

Chloe gazed at Una pleadingly from beneath her fringe of raven black hair.

'Please, please come back, Una. For Mother's sake. She would be the last one to condemn you if you didn't, but that's all the more reason why you must help.'

Una was annoyed. 'You know, Chloe, you are very good at organising the lives of others, but aren't *you* willing to leave your job and come back yourself?'

'I just can't, Una. I've had to struggle with Father all my life. He deliberately chucked me out and nearly broke my heart. No. I just can't go back there to help him out. Mother knows that only too well. I can be civil to him, but that's as far as it goes. It's different for you, though. You were always his favourite.'

'And just look what he did to me: tried to keep me a special bargain bride for Cedric.'

There was a subdued silence, then Una said, 'All right, then. I expect I'll have to agree, for Mother's sake. Call round for me and Ramona tomorrow. And tell Mother everything will be fine.'

The following day, when they arrived at Swansdown, Hubert Lamby was out, and Lindi greeted them joyfully.

'I've already found a couple of good replacements. One of them is Miss Asherton, a cordon bleu cook. The other one is Miss Greenhalgh, a very experienced hotel housekeeper. They're both willing to live in.'

'What salary did they expect?' said Una.

Lindi smiled, but there was a hard glint in her grey eyes. 'I tackled Father just before he went out. I said that if he wasn't prepared to pay them a satisfactory wage and behave reasonably, he could say goodbye to all of us. I told him Granny Lamby was willing for Mother to go and stay with her, and that you, Una, would take me on in Altrincham as your lodger. I assured him that if all that came to pass, Swansdown would be left to go to the dogs.'

'What did he say?' Una had turned pale with the thought of it. 'We could never really leave Swansdown; just leave it to rot. At least, I couldn't.'

Lindi looked a bit uncertain. 'Anyway, he just grunted and growled and said it was a criminal amount of money to pay out in wages. But he agreed! Then he stamped out in a rage.'

Una went upstairs to her old bedroom, and began to prepare Ramona's cot. It was quite strange being here as a mother. Her short stay after Ramona's birth seemed like a dream now. She hoped and prayed everything would work out, just as Lindi had made out. But most of all she hoped that she would be able to return to her own small home, even though she loved Melmere and never wanted The Swansdown to change.

When Ramona was asleep in her cot Una stood over her, admiring her baby daughter. She drank in the serene little face and the curling eyelashes. A beautiful, perfect mixture of Robby and herself.

What would happen if she was trapped here until Robby came home again? Would Father be as awful to Robby as he was before? For a few minutes she felt terribly sad. She unpacked her clothes slowly and

431

put her nightdress in an old satin pyjama-bag on the lavender counterpane. She caught sight of herself in the cheval mirror. She looked much older, with her short bobbed hair breaking back into unruly curls again.

In the past two years her face had lost its schoolgirl look. She looked more mature and alert somehow. Una could hardly believe that on her next birthday she would be eighteen. It seemed so old.

She shrugged carelessly. Life was good, and she was happy with the way things had turned out. She finished unpacking their things and hurried downstairs. She had a business to help run, and her spirits leapt at the challenge.

Although Lady Limpet had been disturbed by the coarse quips in newspapers, she put on a brave face. One always had to contend with a certain amount of envy. But she was annoyed that it had originated from Marqueson, and from home territory. The thing that worried her most was the possibility that her two untiring curators and researchers Dudley Plume and Chloe Lamby might suddenly throw in the towel and clear off.

Sometimes she had to admit that they seemed to have uncovered a mammoth amount of artefacts and literary snippets.

Rather a lot, in view of the meagre evidence of Maudley Montgomery's true worth which had so inspired her at the beginning.

And that wasn't all; she'd received a long letter from a lost branch of the Maudley Montgomery family tree in North Island, New Zealand. Somehow they had heard of all the fuss about Maudley, and they'd got in touch. There was a whole batch of them: Kendo Minstrella Montgomery, aged thirty-nine, and his wife Arcadia. Plus six children, Korin, Deena, Trudy, Bosdin, Canute and Seline. They had even sent her a photograph of eleven-year-old Canute Montgomery standing on the verandah of their small colonial style cottage. On the back of the photo was one word: 'Genius.'

Lady Limpet had placed the child's photograph in a small silver frame on her bedroom mantelpiece. Perhaps the Montgomery Museum could be expanded to include new talent. She immediately sent a letter across the seas, and the letter was an invitation to come to Pover and stay at Drawbridge Hall at her expense. They would be present for the official opening of the Maudley Montgomery memorial and museum. It would be a clear message to all the people who had ever doubted her true aesthetic intentions.

Hubert was sitting by his wife's bedside at the hospital. She was almost ready to go home, and there had been a marked improvement in her condition. Her face had natural colour in it that he hadn't seen for years and years.

'Of course it's the injections that do it, Hubert. The colour's natural, but it's thanks to a new treatment. You've no idea what a change it's been, not having to cook any meals or think about menus for other people, and the food here has been quite good.'

Hubert nodded silently. Then he said with a sort of gruff embarrassment, 'Everything seems to be going smoothly at the hotel. The two new women are quite capable. They cost a lot, but trade's been fairly brisk these past few weeks. We've had a party of power station engineers and their wives from Holland. Una and Lindi seem to think we should encourage all this specialist stuff. They say we could be full all the year round if Swansdown was publicised as the perfect base for touring round cities like Manchester and Liverpool.' He stopped, then said abruptly, 'The child's quite a little charmer...' He paused with embarrassment. 'If the hotel keeps on doing well I could probably buy that house I've had my eye on.'

When he'd gone Constance puzzled over the change in Hubert. He hadn't mentioned his ailments even once. And neither had he mentioned the fact that Tessa Truett was now living with Cedric at Grangebeck. It must have been a bit of a wrench for him, that. No longer would he and Cedric be for ever on each other's doorsteps.

She'd noticed that Hubert hadn't said much about Una, apart from mentioning her name, but at least there had been no tirades. Perhaps it was just as well that he still had his horses to dream about.

Constance began to wonder about Robby, still out in New Zealand. It was good to know there was communication this time. She prayed to be able to leave the hospital as soon as possible, so that Una could be back in her own little home again, ready for Robby's return. That way they'd avoid any confrontation with Hubert. She had no guarantee that Hubert would behave properly towards his son-in-law, in spite of his change for the better...

It was almost the end of November when Constance was finally pronounced fit enough to return home. Lindi had already been to see her in hospital. She had explained how she was fixed up in a shared, rented house in Timperley, and was going to work for the BBC at last.

Constance was quite delighted. All of her daughters had managed to escape from the tentacles of Swansdown into lives of their own. For a few seconds she wondered what would happen to the place, when she and Hubert were no longer able to look after it. Then she cast such thoughts away. No one knew what might happen, especially these days. According to the newspapers there were three million unemployed.

In some ways, thought Constance, being in Pover was like living in a completely different world. By the beginning of December she had returned to that world and was cheerfully back in the throes of things. Most of all she looked forward to a proper family Christmas.

CHAPTER 24

Proposals

'I don't suppose you'd care to marry me, would you?' Dudley and Chloe were putting the finishing touches to Christmas decorations in the new Maudley Museum. There was a silver tinselled Christmas tree, with glossy papier mâché balls, and on every ball, in tiny script, were lines from different poems by Maudley Montgomery.

Dudley had spent hours writing out the lines on the balls, which Chloe had carefully prepared in the preceding weeks.

'*Oh Christmastime is full of memories of a glorious past*'—this line went right round the largest ball—'*On frosty Melmere before it melts at last...*'

'Marry...?' Chloe peered over at Dudley. Was she hearing things?

'I just wondered, that's all. I feel I'm getting to an age when a man needs more than just a museum.'

'Mmmm...' Chloe was used to Dudley Plume suddenly spouting nonsense. She began to gather together some Christmas crackers they'd made. She couldn't really see herself marrying him, even though he obviously needed to be looked after.

'I think we could make quite a good pair,' said Dudley lazily, as he stretched up to put one of the balls near the top of the tree.

Chloe watched him working so industriously. They got on very well. She even felt a certain responsibility and affection for him, but the thought of having to look after him all her life did not appeal to her at all.

She began to rack her brains for a suitable substitute. Maybe at the small Christmas party Lady Limpet was organising she could get Dudley fixed up with someone right for him. To be candid, she felt that once the whole project was officially opened, she would be glad to see the end of it, and to try some pastures new. She knew her work here with Dudley would stand her in good stead for any other job, and that Letty Limpet would give her a glowing reference.

It was three days before Christmas when her secret prayers were answered.

She had been invited by Tessa to go round to Grangebeck for morning coffee.

'It's by way of an early Christmas present, really,' Tessa had explained, as she perched herself on a stool in the museum. 'It's Cedric's idea, but it's a secret, so do be sure to turn up.'

Chloe couldn't help but wonder what Cedric Pawson was up to. No one could ever be sure what his next move was going to be.

The following day she turned up promptly. Already the place had changed under Tessa's influence. Furniture had been moved about and one of the living rooms had been completely redecorated. The sumptuous decadence had gone, in favour of stainless steel and pale pink velvet. There was a large crystal statue-cum-lamp, and all the curtains had been changed to petroleum blue.

Cedric greeted Chloe with measured courtesy. He sipped his coffee politely, and Chloe was quite astounded.

'Tell her what your surprise present is, Ced.'

He looked at Chloe with a sightly mischievous glint in his eye, and his mouth curved into a thin line of dry humour. 'The present is, the Twinkle tearooms. We want to know if you would like them. If you don't, they'll be going up for sale immediately after Christmas...'

Chloe stared at them both in utter amazement. Had they gone mad? Never in her life had she known Cedric to give away property.

'He's doing it for me, really, Chloe. I was so attached to it. I'd hate it to go to someone strange who might change it too much. You know it so well. It's small and easy to manage, and I'm sure you'd be happy there. There's plenty of potential and I can always give you advice about the catering side. So what do you think?'

'Well, I...' Chloe flopped back in her chair. 'I don't quite know what to think. It's such a shock. Are you absolutely sure. Are you sure I'm the right person for the job?'

'We'll take a chance on it, Chloe.' They both smiled, and then Cedric said, 'We'll sort out all the legalities early in the New

Year. You don't need to say too much about it to anyone. The only thing is, I can't stand any waffling. It's either yes, or no. Make up your mind.'

Chloe took a deep breath and nodded her head. 'It's yes, then. Definitely yes.'

They both looked relieved. Then Tessa said quietly, 'Ced and I will be very busy with other things next year, I'm happy to say that I'm expecting a baby, and at my age I want to be careful. We'd thought that it couldn't possibly happen. We're both absolutely delighted.'

By the time Chloe left Grangebeck she didn't know whether she was on her head or her heels, but when she had her feet on the ground again she decided that the best plan was to forget all about it. It was just too good to be true. Perhaps in the end it would all fizzle out. What she needed to do now was to concentrate on finding Dudley Plume the love of his life. Then she'd be truly free.

'Of course, it's all a complete farce,' complained Malcolm Marqueson to his son and Ella one breakfast time in February of the New Year. 'If you ask me there never was a single blessed Montgomery linked with Letty Limpet's side, nor is there ever likely to be. She came from the Drusley-Fittcombs, and her own father was a Saddlestone. But because she's such a dominant kind of woman, and so rich, she has innumerable underlings ready to perjure themselves for her own selfish glorification.'

Ella was feeling extremely fragile. If he mentioned that wretched museum or Letty Limpet once more she'd scream blue murder. There was something else troubling her, too. Her darling Monty seemed to be cooling off. He'd started a new job working in the council offices in Shale, and was always claiming he had to work overtime. Yet, she'd heard by accident that he was visiting his estranged wife, who'd returned from Liverpool. She didn't want to chance confronting him until she knew the truth.

After breakfast, when Monty's father had gone to the library in Shale and Monty had gone to work, Ella helped the daily cleaner to dry some pots. Then she went away and sorted out some skeins of wool, rolling them carefully into balls to start on yet another Fair Isle pullover. She had reached saturation point, as far as the two Marqueson men were concerned, but she had found herself a rather poorly paid outlet for them in a wool shop in Altrincham. She liked knitting; it soothed her fears. She knew that if she didn't knit she would probably be a smoker, and

441

knitting was more pleasant and slightly more profitable.

And Ella had more fears than usual with which to cope. The doctor had warned her that she needed to relax. Anxiety was just not good for pregnant women.

Yes, she was pregnant. She had taken the news calmly, for she was the second Lamby to be expecting out of wedlock.

She knew she'd invited it, for she had treated Monty like a trusted husband after he'd promised he was divorcing his wife; he'd sworn he never wanted to see her again. But it had been difficult for all of them living in the house together. Malcolm Marqueson needed a lot of tactful management, and Monty expected as much cosseting as a newborn babe. When she had found she was expecting his child Ella had thought that this would be the perfect answer. She would be able to fuss over their child as well as him, and they would have a decent excuse to move further afield from his father. She had told neither of them the news. And now she wondered whether she ever could.

No one was ever quite certain how Kendo Montgomery managed to get himself designated to the post of supreme curator of the Maudley Montgomery Museum in time for the official opening.

Even Malcolm Marqueson couldn't resist attending the ceremony. He was sure there would be trouble and he wanted a front-seat view. He waited impatiently for the moment to arrive when someone standing at the back would denounce the whole grovelling exercise as nothing but a hypocritical sham. But nothing happened.

'I now pronounce this fine Maudley Montgomery Memorial Museum open!' roared a great one, removing a large sheet with the Limpet coat of arms to reveal the newly inscribed brass memorial plate.

There was tumultuous applause.

Neither Dudley Plume nor Chloe Lamby heard any of it. Dudley was still smarting from the gross indignity and hurt of being out in the cold, after all his hard work. He was in Knutsford with Chloe, who felt that the least she could do was to comfort him. She still hadn't found him a suitable girl; she'd been sure there'd be one at Lady Limpet's little party at Christmas, but it was choked full of men.

When Chloe had left her job to take over the Twinkle tearooms, poor old Dudley had done exactly as she feared and steadily declined. He was saved from hibernation by being allowed to become Chloe's lodger, just like she had been Tessa's.

'The only thing I can suggest you do, rather than lie in bed all day, is help me

443

to run the tearooms,' suggested Chloe one day in sheer desperation. She sensed that he might take this as the ultimate insult, but what else was there to do other than watch him become increasingly depressed?

Then, one sunny day in early spring, just when Dudley was beginning to recover, and could manage to butter scones and put portions of strawberry jam into small glass dishes, the brass bell on the tearoom door swung out with a rattling clang, and in strolled three tall, self-assured customers. They were Celia, Cadwallader Limpet and Marcus Oliphant.

Chloe and Dudley were in the kitchen behind a curtain, and Dudley was busy checking some currant teacakes, counting the currants and clicking his tongue.

'These teacakes look very good.' He held one up to the light on a plate. 'They're large and tempting, but currant teacakes, Chloe? There are only four in this one!'

Chloe left Dudley deep in thought and she peered for a few seconds through the bead screen as the three customers settled themselves down by a window. She gazed at Marcus with longing. He was even more handsome than ever. He was well on his way to becoming a veterinary student, according to Lindi.

She never saw much of him in Pover or anywhere these days. Lindi was living and working in Manchester now, and Marcus and Lindi were mostly in Manchester or in Edinburgh. He was talking in quite a serious, low voice. He seemed to be less skittish. Cadwallader hadn't changed much; he was discussing the Grand National in a loud voice.

Celia was sitting there silently, moving the salt and pepper about, and peering without interest at the menu. She was wearing a neat-fitting oatmeal tweed jacket, a rather bulky check tweed skirt, and brogues. Her long, straight hair was tied back with a black ribbon. At that moment she looked like a particular kind of Venus. Surely *this* was the answer to Chloe's prayers. Surely she was the one for Dudley.

Chloe went towards them with her pencil and notepad ready to take their orders.

'We'll have three toasted teacakes and a large pot of tea,' said Cadwallader, hardly glancing at her.

She nodded and scribbled it down.

'Chloe! I didn't know you'd moved in here!' Marcus greeted her as if he'd found his long-lost twin. 'How's life, then? How're old Una and Robby doing? And what's the old sod up to at Grangebeck? Life's pretty hectic up there in Scotland.'

'Tell you later,' Chloe said quickly, and hurried back to the kitchen. The thing now was to get Dudley to take out the teacakes,

445

and try to make him notice Celia.

'Celia Limpet's in with Cadwallader and Marcus. It seems an age since Marcus was working with me at Cedric's. Will you take the teacakes out to them? Celia seems rather lonely.'

'She's always like that,' said Dudley. 'She was just the same when she was a kid and I was polishing the shoes at Drawbridge Hall. She's supposed to be very shy, but she's a bit of an eccentric.'

'Just like you, Dudley.'

'Eh?' He looked up at her, startled. His hand was gripping the butter knife.

'When you go out with the teacakes, put them close to her and smile.'

'Whatever for?'

Chloe sighed with exasperation. 'It stands to reason that if you used to work there once, and she knows you, she'll be pleased to say hello!'

'Supposing she counts the currants?'

Chloe turned away. Ah well, at least she'd tried...

The bell clanged again as some more customers arrived in the teashop.

Two afternoons later, and when Dudley had gone to Shale, Marcus came in on his own and ordered a pot of tea.

Miriam, one of Chloe's assistants was there, so Chloe invited Marcus to come into her sitting room for a bit of privacy.

'It has come to pass,' said Marcus solemnly, 'that my rich old aunt has sadly left us. But she has, thankfully, also left yours truly a bit of her vast fortune. I am solvent at last, so my life is secure. I shall take my veterinary examinations in the Autumn, and in September Lindi and I will be following the marriage trail.'

Chloe looked at him carefully. How strange that he seemed so different now, so much more her type. All the time they'd worked together at Cedric's she'd resisted every move. Had they both matured?

She said slowly, 'I've been a bit worried about Dudley lately and I feel in my bones a bit of Celia's company might do him good. Perhaps a sort of foursome would get him off to a good start: you, me, Celia and Dudley.'

He stared at her in mock horror. 'Chloe! Am I hearing right? Are you actually proposing to go out with me? After all those rebuffs?'

'Yes, I am. Lindi will quite understand.' Then she said in a moment of sheer madness, 'And if you and Lindi ever happen to bump into Mac Haley in Manchester, send me a wire.'

'Mac Haley, eh? So he was the thorn in my flesh?'

They both laughed.

447

'Done! How about tonight, at eight-thirty sharp. I'll work it with Celia and you work it with Dudley boy.'

When he'd gone she sank back in her armchair for a few more minutes. Had she succeeded? Would Dudley fall for the right girl at last? Most important of all, would the right girl fall for him?

Chloe went back into the café again. There were quite a few people seated now, and the bell clanged again.

Who would it be this time? She smiled with sudden delight. It was Una, with Ramona.

CHAPTER 25

The Course of True Love...

Una was waiting at home for Robby to return at last. She was trembling with excitement. What would he think of Ramona now? She had grown so big, crawling about and nearly walking. She was an adventurous child and into everything, which meant watching her every second.

The post that May morning was sparse. There was just one letter.

Una stared at it, and her blood ran

cold. It had an Altrincham postmark and she recognised the writing. She knew at once it was from Charlie Meranto. But how, if he and Robby were due back in Manchester tomorrow, did this letter happen to have yesterday's local mark? She opened it gingerly. She always felt a strange sense of foreboding where the Merantos were concerned.

As she read the letter her worst fears were confirmed. The words were in Mr Meranto's personal hand on ivory-coloured, thick headed notepaper. She read and reread the lines, willing herself to take in their meaning, but staring blankly at the words... *the injury was traced back to a friendly game of rugby we had when we were in New Zealand...*

'The doctors said it could have been due to an accidental blow on the head...

'We thought it best not to worry you while you were on your own...

'Robby is now settled and quite comfortable in the Royal Eye Hospital in Manchester. He will have to be there about three weeks...

'He was admitted two days ago...

'If you need any more information or transport to visit him...'

The letter slipped from Una's fingers. She was stunned. With trembling hands she put on her linen jacket and her crocheted beret. She'd better get round to Meranto's immediately. How dare they leave it so late to inform her?

With a deep, steadying breath, she dressed Ramona in her outdoor clothes and put her in the pram. She hurried along George Street, all the way to Meranto's. She was still shocked at the way she had been treated. Why couldn't Charlie Meranto have come round in person and taken her to see Robby the moment they were back? Her heart was thumping madly and there were tears in her eyes as she pushed the pram towards Bowdon Downs.

'I have been with Robby this morning,' explained Mr Meranto, when she arrived. He fussed over her and guided her to the most comfortable chair in his study, surrounded by packing cases, valises and rucksacks.

'Now, can I get you a cup of tea or anything?' He looked at her guiltily.

Una sat silently, in an angry daze. Then she gathered her wits about her and said firmly, 'You do realise, don't you, Mr Meranto, that I am Robby Belmane's wife? I should have been notified as soon as the accident happened. It wasn't up to you to decide whether it was suitable or not for me to be told.'

'I don't think you quite understand, Mrs Belmane.' His voice hardened slightly. She could see he disliked her questioning his actions. 'Your husband had been involved in valuable scientific research and it was essential for me to find out where all his notes and diaries were, so that none of them were lost in all the uproar following his accident. I had to be at his bedside as soon as he was in a fit state to receive visitors. But I can quite understand your feelings.'

'Understand *my* feelings, Mr Meranto?' said Una coldly. 'If you can understand my feelings so well, would you please be good enough to drive me and my baby daughter to see Robby immediately!'

Una sat in silence in the back of his limousine, with Ramona on her knee. They drove along in complete silence all the way to Oxford Road, until they reached the front entrance of the eye hospital.

They made their way through the gloomy interior and up the stairs to the second floor.

'I'm afraid your baby won't be allowed into the ward,' warned the sister, 'but I'll ask one of the nurses to look after her in the dayroom while you both take it in turns to see him. Don't be too long.'

Una's heart sank when she saw the ward. It was very crowded, with black-enamelled bedsteads laid with poppy-red blankets. There were no counterpanes.

It was very quiet and there were many men lying flat on their backs with bandages across their eyes. She looked about anxiously for Robby. Suddenly she spotted him, right at the back of the ward. His hands looked thin and sunburnt as they lay across the white sheets.

'Robby?' Her voice was barely a whisper, and at first he didn't seem to hear her. 'It's me, Una.'

'Una...'

'Yes, Mr Meranto has brought me and Ramona to see you. They're both waiting in the dayroom.' She bent down and kissed him very gently on his forehead above his padded eyes.

'Oh, Robby, Robby...' She took his hand gently in her own and kissed it. Her voice broke a little. 'It was quite a shock when I got Mr Meranto's letter this morning.'

'This morning? What day is it? They do tell me, but I keep forgetting.' He put his hand over hers. 'It seems ages that I've been away from you...especially with this happening at the last minute.'

'It's Tuesday.'

'I've been in here two days then. I was expecting you straightaway. Anyway, you're here at last. Have they told you what it is?'

'Charlie Meranto said you had a knock when you were playing rugby.'

452

Robby's lip trembled slightly. 'Yes. I felt fine, really, but then my eyesight began to go all blurred. They say it may be a detached retina at the back of my eye. But there's a lot of swelling there and they're waiting to see whether it will fall back into place when that goes down. Every day I count the hours to getting back home to you and Ramona, Una.

'I pray that my sight will not be too damaged.' His voice broke and he clutched at Una's hand. 'I shall be no good to Charlie Meranto if my eyesight goes. I could be out of a job completely.'

'Don't say such things,' said Una, fiercely. 'Think of getting better and nothing else. I will come and see you again tomorrow.'

When they were back in the car again, Una said to Mr Meranto, 'I wonder if you could do me a great favour, Mr Meranto, and drive me home to Melmere so that I can let everyone know what has happened.'

'I'll find out when it can be arranged, Mrs Belmane. Which day would be the most suitable?'

'This day, Mr Meranto. Right away.'

'I don't think that's quite possible, my dear. You see, I am a very busy man. You were quite lucky to have this drive in the first place. I don't want to seem callous, but, well, there are limits. You've seen your husband now, haven't you? And he's as well as can be expected.' His voice turned fatherly and confidential.

'I suggest you trot off home to your little house. Have a nice rest and freshen up, then get through to your family by phone. How's that?'

Una ignored his words. 'I expect you've been through Pover many times. It's in the Knutsford area. It shouldn't take long, and it would be the act of a real gentleman, Mr Meranto. An act of caring and understanding, and so easy for you with this beautiful car. I should get there just in time to give Ramona a bite to eat.'

They purred along in silence; then, to her relief, and delight, Una noticed they had left Altrincham far behind and were heading straight for Melmere.

'Una! Ramona! My darlings' Constance kissed them eagerly. 'How on earth did you get here?'

'Mr Meranto brought us. But before I tell you the reason, I must get Ramona fed and put to bed in that cot. She's been very good considering what a busy day we've had.'

A frown creased Constance's face. 'Don't say something's happened?'

Una didn't answer. Instead she put Ramona in one of the hotel highchairs and fed her. When her meal was over and Ella had taken Ramona to see Hubert, Una went to sit with her mother on the sofa. Suddenly she felt indescribably tired. She rested her head on her mother's shoulder and for the first time allowed herself to show some emotion.

'It's Robby, Mother. He's in hospital.' She began to cry quietly.

Hubert was outside among the trees when Ella carried Ramona across to see him.

'I've brought her to say hello to her grandad.'

He smiled briefly and waggled his finger at Ramona. 'What's brought you here, eh?'

Ramona stared at him in silent wonderment, then she smiled broadly. Hubert was absurdly pleased. 'She's getting into quite a bonny little thing. Is Una here then?'

'She's with Mother.'

'And how are you feeling, Ella?'

'Quite well today, thank you, Father.'

'Yes, you look quite well.' There was a silence. Ella looked away towards the mere and some small yachts sailing there. Father was a bit more open these days. At one time her miscarriage would have been unmentionable.

The miscarriage had been quite un-expected. Ella had been feeling well, and had just started knitting some baby clothes. She had been secretly delighted by her pregnancy, whether it was in wedlock or not, but now that it was at an end, she almost welcomed her old position as the unmarried, oldest daughter helping her mother out at Swansdown.

That night when everyone was in bed at the Swansdown Constance moved closer to Hubert in their double bed.

'I think Una should stay with us for a while with the baby. At least until Robby is out of hospital and properly well. In fact, he could come here and convalesce...'

Hubert moved his shoulders away angrily. 'He could do no such thing!'

Constance lay in the darkness, choosing her words carefully. 'There's going to be a time when we won't be able to look after this place ourselves. We need people around us that love it and know it, like Una and Robby.'

'Sentimental nonsense' Hubert turned over. 'The young idiot wouldn't want to come here, anyway. Not even to recuperate.'

'You mean you *hope* he wouldn't. All that fuss is over now, Hubie. They're man and wife and Ramona is your grandchild. You just can't go on behaving like some

456

Victorian curmudgeon.'

He sighed and grunted. Her words had hit their mark. 'I suppose you're right. But I'll say this, Constance, no way is that young bugger going to have his handiwork marring my trees. I'm having three of those oaks felled tomorrow.' He turned over yet again and an instant later was snoring loudly.

Constance lay silently. She felt happy at last. She knew that in his own way he had relented, and a couple of hearts carved on an oak tree was but a small price to pay. She closed her eyes peacefully. She felt they were turning a corner.

A couple of days later Una took Ramona for a walk in the grounds. Out of habit she walked over to the spot where their oak tree grew. She was entirely unaware of her father's plans, and she had been busy between visits to Robby.

Una stood in amazement as she saw the hole where the oaks had stood. It certainly showed up the mere better, but what a terrible shame the trees had gone. It was a gross indignity to see them lying there, trimmed of all their branches like mutilated corpses. She walked over and sat on one of the logs. She looked down at the entwined hearts; the carving looked small and insignificant, but she was glad to see it. She fingered the grooves that Robby had carved so tenderly. She doubted whether he would ever be able to do anything like that again.

She heard the sounds of a vehicle approaching and saw Barry Marford's wagon grinding along the woodland way leading to the trees. He waved and drew up a few yards away, calling to her cheerfully.

'Nice day. Not seen you around much.' He jumped down from the truck and came over to her, glancing down at the entwined hearts.

'What's all this, then?'

'It's something Robby and I did; it's really our tree. We thought it would be here hundreds of years, with those hearts on.' She smiled wistfully.

Barry was about to make an offhand comment when he saw her expression. He softened and said kindly, 'I could saw you that piece off, take a scoop away from that patch with the carving on.'

Una looked at him with shining eyes. 'I would pay you extra,' she said joyfully.

He waved away her offer with disdain. 'I wouldn't remove it for anyone else but you, Miss Una, and that's a fact. Remember not to let it dry out too sudden or it'll warp.'

When Barry had gone Una walked back to the house with her treasure. She had wrapped it carefully in cloth with damp green moss. She would take it with her to the hospital when she went in to see Robby.

'You look very pleased with yourself,' said her father, not unkindly, as she walked past the stables. 'To be perfectly honest, when I saw you down there near those trees, I thought you'd be a bit upset.'

'Now why on earth should you think that?' she replied sarcastically.

Her father turned away. He suddenly looked very old. 'That special tree. The one you both ruined. I think we must all try and forget it. Especially now you are married with a child. These days, I have to accept that you are young Mrs Belmane. I would be more than a bit of a fool to try and deny it.'

He looked down at the ground and said hesitantly, 'If I've made any mistakes in the past you'll just have to try and forget them. I did what I did for your own good. And, as for Robby, please tell him he's quite welcome to come here to recuperate if he wishes. We'll all let bygones by bygones.'

Una's jaw dropped open. Hubert Lamby had just, for the first time in his life, apologised to one of his daughters. And for some strange reason he looked absurdly proud.

Una could tell Robby was getting better the moment she set foot in the ward. She could hear his voice calling to another man, and she noticed a new cheerfulness.

She had come to see him with Chloe, who had taken Ramona on the tram to Albert Square.

After Una had kissed Robby, he said, 'The specialist has looked at my eyes and he seems to think that now the general bruising and swelling is going down, my eyes could gradually return to normal, too. But it's a matter of time and patience. I'll need regular observation at the hospital.'

Una told him about her father, and saw a smile creep across his face.

'He's got a damned cheek,' said Robby perkily. 'Didn't he even ask for our forgiveness? It wasn't us who threatened him with a blasted gun. And we didn't have that oak tree cut down. That was deliberate malice. I expect he thinks he's got rid of the evidence that started it all.' Robby's voice was light.

'But he hasn't,' said Una, in a low triumphant voice. 'I'm going to put something in your hands. See if you can guess what it is.' She put a towel she'd brought with her across Robby's chest, then carefully she held the scoop of oak across it. The damp scent of moss and wild woodland wafted through the smell of hospital disinfectant as Robby put his hands towards it. Rather nervously he put his thin fingers towards the grooves and followed them cautiously. At first he was terribly puzzled; then he said, 'It almost seems like the hearts.'

'It is, it is,' said Una excitedly. 'Barry Marford saved them for us before he took the trees away. We'll be able to keep it for ever.' She saw him smile. She gently removed the carving and put it back in the shopping bag, reaching out to clasp his hand.

'Father says if we want to come to Swansdown while you recover, we'll both be very welcome.'

Robby's face changed.

'What about our own house in Altrincham? Recuperate there at Melmere? No thanks, Una! We'll paddle our own canoe...'

For a few seconds she was saddened. It seemed that it was Robby now who wasn't willing to forget the past. Then, after some consideration, she realised that Robby was no longer a raw innocent, untried being any more than she was. He was no longer her father's boy gardener. He was a well-travelled knowledgeable man, even though he had only just reached twenty.

'You're right,' she said quietly. 'Just

461

the three of us in our own home will be best.'

Chloe was wandering along the pavement in Cross Street at the very moment that Mac Haley walked out of the offices of the *Manchester Guardian*.

He saw her immediately and stopped in his tracks. It was almost like an electric shock, and he wondered whether to turn and hurry away.

He was leading quite a lonely life at present, trying to do up his little country home in Disley. He had never quite got over letting Myra down, and he'd kept well away from Pover and Shale Bridge ever since.

He took the plunge and walked towards her. They came face to face.

Chloe's face filled with a dazed, disbelieving joy. She almost kissed him then and there.

'Fancy meeting you,' he said, looking with raised eyebrows at Ramona.

'She isn't mine, she's my sister's,' said Chloe hastily. 'Fancy meeting you, too. Una's husband Robby is in the eye hospital. She's visiting him while I mind Ramona for her.'

There was a moment's silence. 'Look,' said Mac. 'I can't stop now, but how about meeting sometime?'

She nodded eagerly, and said quickly, 'Lindi's getting married to Marcus Oliphant. He's training as a vet at Edinburgh and she's going up there to be near him permanently.' She paused, embarrassed at her outburst. 'Yes I'd love to meet you again.' Her face shone. 'Maybe I could stay the night at Lindi's place before she gets married.'

'No,' he said quickly. 'We'll meet in Disley. I'll ring you and make some arrangements. Maybe a day out at the weekend.' He dared not see Lindi again. He dreaded being swept away by her a second time, especially now that she was committed to Marcus.

Chloe was walking on air when she arrived back at the eye hospital. She never mentioned the meeting to Una, but kept it tight against her heart, to dream about in private. Oh, the luck of it, for them to meet unexpectedly. How strange life was and, sometimes, how kind.

It was another four weeks until Robby was able to return home. He had to wear dark glasses and rest for long periods, but there was a steady improvement in his condition.

By the end of August he was back in his old job working for Mr Meranto on natural history research.

Chloe was in a state of confusion in more ways than one. She had been for a day out with Mac at Disley. He had called for her by car and taken her to his small, rather tumbledown cottage. It was high up amongst moorland views of Kinder Scout, in Higher Disley. Old stone farms were tucked away in the folds of the fells round it, and patches of the familiar industrial world of mill chimneys could be seen in the hazy distance. He had called it Brooklea, and Chloe's day spent there was one of sheer delight. She helped him to cover the nobbly, whitewashed living room walls with unpretentious pale lemon wallpaper. Shyly he asked her if she would like to come out with him again, and she agreed at once.

Chloe and Dudley were still working together at the tea-rooms, having been so unceremoniously dumped by Letty Limpet in anticipation of the arrival of her family from New Zealand.

The only trouble was, they just never arrived. The money sent for their passage was duly sent, and their picture was hung in a place of honour in the museum, but the Montgomerys themselves were never heard of again.

Lady Limpet dismissed their treachery with silent, aristocratic dignity.

464

Letty's rash sacking of Dudley was constantly criticised by her daughter Celia as pure idiocy. Chloe had done well enough by leaving to take over the tearooms, but there was no one suitable to take Dudley's place and the museum was closed through lack of staff.

Lady Limpet was forced to rethink her arrangements, and under some pressure she chose her pestering daughter, Miss Celia Limpet, to take on a new post of general administrator. And by Celia's side was the reinstated, solemn and secretly swooning with newly found passion, Dudley Plume.

Four-year-old Ramona Belmane was standing next to the Pawson triplets. They were all licking Snofruits. The triplets were only babies, at two and a half, and Ramona felt quite superior. The triplets were called Theodore, Justine and Eunice. Ramona glanced at them: they couldn't even count up to twenty or say their alphabets.

Una was taking a photograph of them with her Brownie box camera. They were in the grounds of Grangebeck and Robby was talking to Cedric Pawson. Any newcomer would never have dreamed how things had been three years ago.

'The world's in a terrible state,' Cedric reflected. 'But thank goodness for this new generation growing up, though I don't envy what they might have to face. There are rumours already that children might be issued with gas masks if things get worse with all this talk of war. There's even talk of evacuating children from all the main cities.

'We could well be sheltering some ourselves from inner Manchester, here in Melmere. Places like Grangebeck and Swansdown could be requisitioned.'

'Cedric? Coffee's ready.' Tessa came into the drawing-room, humming cheerfully. She was followed by Una and the children.

'Cedric and I will be leaving nanny to look after the triplets tonight. We're going to the cinema in Shale to see Charlie Chaplin in *Modern Times*. I wanted to see *Mr Deeds Goes to Town*, but we tossed a penny for it and Ced won, didn't you, love?'

Cedric smiled indulgently. He was like an elderly lamb these days.

A few weeks later, Una was in her own sitting room at the Olive Branch, reading to Ramona, when she received a phone call from her mother at Swansdown.

'It's nothing catastrophic, dear, it's just that Hubert and I are getting older, and with all these war threats looming on the horizon we're anxious to put our affairs in order.

'Chloe has just told me that she and Mac are getting married as soon as possible. Not that it affects us after her working in Manchester for the past two years, but all the same there's no possible hope of her ever being back in Pover. And as for Lindi—married to Marcus and him still busy with that terribly long training to be a vet in Edinburgh. Well, we'll hardly see her again for ages. And even Ella is thinking of leaving us again. She's got some mad scheme to go and lodge at Disley with Chloe and Mac and try and join the Women's Auxiliary Air Force.'

Una's heart sank, what was coming next?

Constance sighed heavily. 'The fact is, Una, your father has just informed me that poor old beautiful Swansdown is going to be let to the government as office headquarters.'

There was a silence. Una was horrified. She could hardly believe it even though familiar places like the Twinkle Tea Rooms had been put into cold storage by Tessa and Cedric.

'To cut a long story short, Una. Your father wants you and Robby to come over here to look after Swansdown for us.'

'Mother seems to think all the requisition-ing of places is something to do with the

RAF at Ringway, and parachute training,' said Una later when Robby came back from work. 'She says Father's agreed to Swansdown being taken over and kept for the duration of a war—if ever one should take place within the next few years. I just can't get over Father agreeing so easily. What about his horses?'

Robby shook his head quietly. 'People are going to have to agree to lots of strange things. Swansdown could well be full of Chiefs of Staff from all over the world, working out strategies.'

Una was surprised that Robby took the news so calmly, even the prospect of going back to Swansdown. They were so comfortable now in their own home in Altrincham. It was nicely furnished and the garden was thriving. They had a bonny little daughter, Robby had a job and they really wished for nothing more.

Una had no idea what sort of work Robby was doing now with Meranto's. She did not know they too had been enlisted to do secret work with fruit flies for a government department. Fruit flies were a group of insects which bred and multiplied so quickly that generations of them could be studied for changes in growth and behaviour patterns over a short period.

Dutifully Robby and Una visited Swansdown to find out the whole story and get things sorted out.

Ella was there to greet them. 'I may as well tell you both, first. I'm going to go and live with Chloe and Mac in Higher Disley, while I see if I'm suitable to join the Women's Auxiliary Air Force. I just can't stand it here any longer; I've just got to get out and help. I know I'm a bit of an old maid at twenty-nine, but you never know.'

In spite of seeing him quite often, Una was suddenly aware of how white her father's hair had become. He gave them both a perfunctory smile. 'I don't like asking favours, but it seems I've got to,' he spoke gruffly, and stared hard at them. 'The fact is, I want you both to come over here and look after this place.' He held up his hand. 'Don't try and talk it all away, just listen carefully to what I've got to say because there's quite a lot.'

Hubert looked straight at Robby. 'I've been speaking to Cedric Pawson and he says you'll be able to carry on with your work at Meranto's from here. He will provide you with a car because you'll be on war work.'

'But Hubert, we aren't at war yet,' said Constance, still clinging to the hope that war would not be declared.

'We soon shall be,' said Hubert grimly.

Una could see Robby's temper rising. 'With due respect, I don't really need you and Mr Pawson to organise my life.'

'With due respect, Robby, if you want to help us *and* your country, you'd better hear me out.

'From now on this will no longer be a hotel. Even if by some stroke of fate or good luck there is no war, the government will still be using it. The stipulation is that your mother and I will be allowed a self-contained retirement flat here, and that you—Una, and Robby and Ramona—will live here as the main householders. The remainder of the staff will be chosen and employed by Whitehall.'

'What about the gardens?'

'They'll see to those as well.'

'And the horses?'

'The horses are going to Cedric's.'

A wry look crossed Una's face. 'And is *his* place going to be taken over by the government?'

'Part of it may be used as a convalescent home. He and Tessa are already registered to take five evacuees.' Then Hubert added, 'There is one thing I have never told anyone all these years.' He began to pace round the room. 'I haven't even told you, Constance.'

Constance stood up and walked purposefully towards the sherry.

'This calls for a drink, Hubie.' Her face was deathly pale. 'It must be something pretty diabolical if you've never told me, in all our years of marriage.'

He took a deep breath. Una feared he was about to have a heart attack. He began to breathe very quickly now, with laboured heaviness. He gulped, as if for air. 'It's just to say that Cedric Pawson owns half this hotel.'

'What?' Una turned away in helpless amazement.

Hubert dabbed at his forehead, which was sweating profusely. He looked ghastly. His eyes glowed in their dark sockets. 'I've never managed to pay him back and reclaim it. He has always owned half, ever since the girls were very small. He helped me out when I was in trouble with gambling debts, years ago, and was going to have to sell the whole damned place. I expect it was the worry of it that's driven me to so much ill health. But he bailed me out...he saved me.'

'I always suspected something like that,' said Constance bitterly. If only Hubert confided in her more, she thought. He had always treated her like a child in anything to do with his financial matters.

Una and Robby exchanged glances, then

471

Robby said, 'We'll do as you ask, about coming here, but it'll mean having to let our own home.'

Just before they went back that evening, Una said to Ella, 'How would you feel about renting our house in Altrincham for the time being, instead of going to Disley?'

Ella's face broke into a rapturous smile.

'I'd absolutely love it!'

It was hard to imagine on such a glorious day that world peace hung by a thread.

Bumblebees and wasps still worked industriously among the plants in the Swansdown gardens as they flew backwards and forwards to their hidden homes. Orange and yellow nasturtiums crowded against paths and rambled over ageing and once white gateposts. Honeysuckle was into its second flowering and heavy with scent. A tree of golden privet spread its bushy branches and its vivid yellow-green leaves were laden with small sprays of white perfumed blossom.

The last guests had gone.

Soon, Una thought, it would be a different place. Tears came to her eyes as she took Ramona's hand and chose the path which led away from the garden down to the shores of Melmere.

The old upturned rowing boat was

still there under the trees. The ancient paddlesteamer chugged by, still full of people enjoying themselves as smaller boats and yachts sailed quietly in the distance. There were rumours that the paddlesteamer would be put away if war broke out. And there would be no more small brown yachts with deep blue sails, or scarlet-sheeted white dinghies.

Una put down a blanket on the gravel by the mere for Ramona and herself to sit on. She thought of what Father had told them all, and she felt a sudden flood of helpless anger. Surely if there was a war it would have to end sometime. Perhaps it would only last a few weeks, and when it finished, the place would belong to them properly again.

She gazed out to some distant reeds. She thought she saw the swans. It was all so still and peaceful. What could a real war possibly be like?

Suddenly she heard a familiar voice behind her. It was Cedric. These days, he hardly came near. They nodded and stared towards the water for a few moments in silence. Then he narrowed his eyes to the sun and said, 'It'll be nice to have you back. Melmere is where you belong, Una. I've always thought it and I always will.'

She turned away swiftly.

'Melmere will always be here.' His

sunburned face was smooth and calm. 'The war won't last for ever.' He moved towards her and held out his hand. Ramona pushed between them and handed him a pebble, which he tossed idly towards the water. 'I suppose it has all worked out best for both of us. I should have married Tessa years ago.

'You and I, Una, are both too much alike underneath, in spite of our ages. But we've both got what we wanted the most in the end...'

'Only by half,' she murmured to herself softly, as she walked back towards Swansdown. 'Only by half. But one day it will be all. Yes, one fine day Swansdown will be ours again.'

She drifted with Ramona amongst the flowers on the small stone path leading back to the house and watched him stroll away. A few minutes later she heard Robby's voice calling to them.

She turned to Ramona and smiled cheerfully. Ramona was growing quite tall; soon she would be a schoolgirl.

'Race you to Daddy?' said Una suddenly, with a thankful heart. Their dashing footsteps echoed in the warm afternoon and their shouts of laughter filled the whole of Swansdown.

Later, Ramona said, 'When I'm as big as you and Daddy I shall be able to win every race. Just you wait and see...'

Robby and Una looked at her and nodded hopefully. She ran off ahead to waken Beech, who lay sleeping in the dark coolness of the kitchen.

Suddenly Robby flung his arms round Una and kissed her passionately. Then they strolled off together again. It was a moment of perfect happiness, of pure contentment, as Ramona came back to greet them and pointed excitedly to an end-of-summer butterfly, fluttering industriously from flower to flower.

Who could tell, in anybody's life, what tomorrow would bring?

The publishers hope that this book has given you enjoyable reading. Large Type Books are especially designed to be as easy to see and hold as possible. If you wish a complete list of our books please ask at your local library or write direct to: Magna Large Print Books, Long Preston, North Yorkshire, BD23 4ND, England.

This Large Print Book for the Partially sighted, who cannot read normal print, is published under the auspices of

THE ULVERSCROFT FOUNDATION

THE ULVERSCROFT FOUNDATION

. . . we hope that you have enjoyed this Large Print Book. Please think for a moment about those people who have worse eyesight problems than you . . . and are unable to even read or enjoy Large Print, without great difficulty.

You can help them by sending a donation, large or small to:

**The Ulverscroft Foundation,
1, The Green, Bradgate Road,
Anstey, Leicestershire, LE7 7FU,
England.**
or request a copy of our brochure for more details.

The Foundation will use all your help to assist those people who are handicapped by various sight problems and need special attention.

Thank you very much for your help.